Grow Your Own
Fruit and Vegetables

by the same author

THE PROPAGATION OF ALPINES

DOWN TO EARTH GARDENING

GROW YOUR OWN
FRUIT AND VEGETABLES

Lawrence D. Hills

With drawings by Malcolm Hickling

FABER AND FABER LIMITED

3 Queen Square London

First published in 1971
by Faber and Faber Limited
3 Queen Square London WC1
Reprinted 1972
New edition 1973
Printed in Great Britain by
Latimer Trend & Company Ltd Plymouth
All rights reserved

ISBN 0 571 04830 7

To
MY WIFE
who also loves gardening

Contents

Contents

Illustrations

11

Illustrations

Illustrations

13

Preface

This book is written for those who wish to grow their own fruit and vegetables without chemical fertilizers, to ensure finest flavour, and without persistent pesticides to halt pollution at the garden gate. It is not concerned with argument, philosophy or generalizations but with the methods old and new that make it possible to grow better produce than could be grown in any chemicals-fed garden.

Many of these methods have been developed by members of the Henry Doubleday Research Association, of which I am director-secretary, and my first thanks must go to the president and committee for permission to use material that has appeared in Reports, and the many analysis figures from the records of the Association.

Those who want their food whole and with all its flavour and nutritional value intact are concerned with vitamins and, however valuable pills and supplements may be, healthy people find their vitamins in their food. Today our food wastes its vitamins all the way from the grower to the supermarket and later again in the kitchen and on its way to the plate. I therefore express my gratitude to my wife, Hilda Cherry Hills, for her chapter on how to cook without destroying in the kitchen the nutritional value of the food you have grown so well that it is better than anything you can buy.

This is especially important to vegetarians and vegans (vegetarians who do not eat eggs or milk products) who should always be organic gardeners because they can appreciate the finer flavour, and cannot afford to waste the vitamins in the vegetables on which they depend so greatly.

Every vegetable and fruit in this book has mention of its nutritional values, either where its growing is discussed or in one of the many tables, so that those who wish can consider vitamin values in relation

15

Preface

to what they sow and plant. In two cases it has been possible to include analysis figures for individual varieties, and I would like to acknowledge the help of the University of Bristol Long Ashton Research Station in making available the ten-year Vitamin C average for blackcurrants. The figures for apples, which for the first time make it possible to plant high-vitamin C apples that will pollinate each other, are from *Nutritional Values in Crops and Plants* by Professor Werner Schuphan (Faber and Faber, 1969).

The other figures are mainly from that standard reference work *Bridge's Food and Beverage Analyses*, by Professor Marjorie R. Mattice (Henry Kimpton), supplemented by Ministry of Agriculture publications and by Dr. A. H. Ward, analyst to the Henry Doubleday Research Association, in his reports on such tests as those for losses of vitamins in bottling tomatoes, blackcurrants and raspberries.

My thanks are due to the editor of the *Observer* for material that appeared in my 'Down to Earth' column, the editor of *Here's Health* for some from my monthly articles, and the editor of *Punch*, especially for permission to reprint the poem in the style of Thomas Tusser (1524–80) on ways of remembering the packet life of vegetable seeds.

Last but by no means least I wish to thank Mr. Malcolm Hickling for his many excellent line drawings, which have the great merit of being the work of one who is also a good organic gardener and can combine artistry with practicality and show us details which might not photograph well.

As with every book I write, I have tried to answer all the questions that the beginner can ask on the subjects covered, because when you have everything to learn you need all the detailed information which experts take for granted. If I have missed your particular problem, please write to me care of Faber and Faber, and I will do my best to help you. This is especially likely with this book because the answer may well be, 'I left it out because I did not know then, but as the research that is my life work continues, I know enough to solve your difficulty.' All good gardeners spend their whole lives learning, and organic gardeners have so much more that is of absorbing interest to learn.

LAWRENCE D. HILLS

Bocking, April 1969 to January 1970

1

Why Grow Your Own?

Perhaps the longest-lived retired couples were the gardeners and farmworkers and their wives who in the past were allowed to keep their cottages for as long as they lived on the great estates they had served throughout their working lives. Always they had long gardens and loads of manure from the home farm and grew themselves a diet with generous quantities of Vitamins A, C, E, K, and the B complex that maintained their mental and physical vigour into their late nineties and beyond; benefiting not from up-to-date scientific findings but merely from the fact that eating more of their own home-grown produce made their Old Age Pensions stretch further.

Today, though trees still grow while we are sleeping, our incomes, especially our pensions, steal silently away in the night thanks to inflation. If we buy one of these farmworkers' cottages, modernized, we pay more than the whole farm cost in the Hungry Forties, while two knocked into one are equal to the price of the farm in the early 1930's. Though its value rises year by year, we gain nothing from the increase because we should have to pay just as much for another place in which to live.

This applies still more to the suburbs of every town, where the three-bedroom semi-detached house that cost £750 new in the 1930's is now worth £12,000 and may fetch double in ten years. These houses are bargains for they are built on plots that allow back gardens a hundred and seventy-five feet long and thirty wide, which are far better value than the sawn-off slices behind the latest houses with barely room for a clothes line and a bed of camellias.

They are bargains, like the cottages with long gardens, because we do not see the value of everything we grow *going up* with every rise in wages, lighting, rates, rents and carriage costs, especially petrol, all

along the line from greengrocers through wholesalers, market sales-
men and haulage contractors to the farmers and market gardeners
who grow food with fewer men and more machines, with higher de-
preciation and interest on capital for every saving in labour.

In the 1930's it was calculated that building houses on poorish
farmland did not reduce food production, for the extra yield from
intensive garden production balanced the loss of acres under roads,
front gardens and the houses themselves. This yield does more than
provide an inflation hedge that grows higher as we grow older by
supplying vegetables to replace those we should otherwise have to
buy at prices that go with house values increased nearly sevenfold.
It has another hidden advantage as important as tax freedom for
investment in the Building Societies that once financed houses at
even 54p a week with no deposit or road charges.

There is no tax on own-grown fruit and vegetables, and though the
idea of taxing them may seem attractive to Chancellors of the Ex-
chequer in their gardenless 'tied cottage' of No. 11 Downing Street,
the money would be too difficult to collect. So the man on top-rate
supertax at 90p pays the equivalent of £1 for 7 lb. of old potatoes
when they are cheap at 2p a lb., and £3 for new ones at 4p, but if he
can find a gardener at £21 a week—thirty times what one of those
fine old farmworkers earned—he will cost him an extra £195. The
standard-rate man at 43p in the £1 on whom the Building Societies
calculate their interest rate for lenders, does not pay 10p for a pound
of sprouting broccoli in April when it is scarce, its real cost is nearer
19p. The tax-free bonus that rises invisibly with greengrocers'
prices is there for everyone who does not restrict his gardening to mowing his lawn on taxed petrol and repainting his purchase-taxed goblins.

True, the cost of everything we buy for the garden rises too, but
the more we learn the less we need to spend. Very much that is
advertised on TV or in the Press, or pushed by the fashion-conscious
gardening correspondents, is like frozen potato chips or tinned broad
beans—it may save labour but it costs more than it is worth.

We live in an age of fashion, and gardeners are just as bound by
convention as the rigidly conformist young. One of these unexamined
dogmas among gardeners is that lawns save labour, which may be true
where one gardener with a forty-two-inch Dennis can get over the
main lawn of a Stately Home on a Saturday morning before the turn-
stiles start clicking up the silver coins, but it is not for the average
suburban semi-detached.

Why Grow Your Own?

A twelve- or fourteen-inch machine takes just as long to take out, start, clean and put away as a monster that has done a day's work. It multiplies time for area by three or four—the more small beds there are to manoeuvre around, the more turning there is to do, the slower is the whole process and the greater the length that has to be edged with shears afterwards. An amateur with 680 square yards of lawn who keeps it neat expects to spend two hours a week for thirty-six weeks a year, or four hours with a full programme of spiking, moss-raking, feeding, sanding and worm-killing. He might just as well spend his time growing his own vegetables, for, as many Stately Homes found during the war, potatoes mean less labour and lower costs than lawns.

As our incomes shrink with rising prices we can increase the height of our inflation hedge by eating more of what we grow ourselves, as the old farmworkers did, with a gain in health; because, to put it non-technically and therefore not very accurately, our bodies need more vitamins as we grow older just as ageing cars need more oil. The young can get away with eating almost anything but there never was an Old People's Home where everyone did not grumble about the food, often with very good reason.

A survey in 1965 by Dr. Geoffrey Taylor (*Medical Science*, 30th July 1965) of old people in twenty-three institutions showed actual symptoms of scurvy from lack of vitamin C, just as though they were voyaging with Nelson before the days of lime-juice for supplying this vital vitamin. Even where the diet did contain green vegetables these lost up to two-thirds of their vitamin C between kitchen and patient because of the long wait in the dinner trolleys and reheating in ward kitchens. This applies of course to many hospitals and hotels.

Vitamins C and K together are important preventatives of arthritis and both can be largely lost from the green vegetables that supply them on the still longer journey from market garden to customer, but none on the shortest trip of all which is up the garden path. It is not only the aged who suffer from vitamin C shortage, for recently army recruits have shown scurvy symptoms because the only green vegetable they ate by choice was processed peas, and these are a very poor source. Though thousands of people today obtain most of their vitamin C from potatoes, eating enough to make up for the fact that they contain relatively little, even this is entirely destroyed in cooking the 'chips with everything' that these young recruits preferred.

Peas are a better source of thiamine and riboflavin, two of the vitamin B complex, especially eaten raw in salad, but our most useful provider of vitamin C is raw cabbage, which is far richer in this than lettuce and easier in winter. Though the idea of eating raw cabbage horrifies most people, they have never eaten the new 'Monarch' varieties, bred for flavour, cooked or in salad. All raw fruits and vegetables contain a substance called 'catalase' which is highly important as a defence against cancer. It is destroyed by cooking, and a campaign to 'Eat More Raw' might well reduce some kinds of cancer more effectively than one against smoking. Unfortunately prevention is less dramatic than transplantation and raw vegetables do not advertise.*

Neither do potatoes, and these are the first item to be given up by those to whom 'diet' means 'slimming'. Yet the biggest potato eaters in history were the inhabitants of Tristan da Cunha and the pre-Potato Famine Irish, who both stayed slender, because though potatoes contain starch they have the vitamins and minerals to digest it. The cakes, white bread, white sugar, sweets, chocolate and biscuits, even the special 'starch-reduced' ones (of which you have only to take three to have as much as there is in one far cheaper ordinary biscuit) are all 'dead starches' with nothing to help them break down, so they store in the body as fat. We give up not only the least advertised but the least *attractive* part of our food.

The tastelessness of modern potatoes brings us to another reason for growing our own fruit and vegetables, which is to grow better flavour than we can buy. Potatoes are the outstanding example, and every gardener knows the difference in flavour and quality as soon as he runs out of his own and has to buy. This is partly due to choice of variety, for potatoes are sold by the ton and the farmer will always plant the heaviest yielder on his soil, because housewives will not pay extra for taste. They like size for quick peeling, shallow eyes and absence of scab marks so the potatoes look nice through the polythene prepack, but flavour comes nowhere for most people, because they have forgotten that potatoes ever had a taste.

In 1960 the Henry Doubleday Research Association ran a Taste Test with twenty-eight experimenters who each had a set of four samples, distinguished only by letters to rule out personal prejudice. All were

* The *Basic Food Guide to a Green Old Age*, a diet with advice on cookery and how to avoid locking up vitamins as well as on supplying them cheaply and easily as food rather than pills, is available free from The Henry Doubleday Research Association, Bocking, Braintree, Essex. Please send a self-addressed stamped envelope.

Why Grow Your Own?

'Majestic', chosen to be as nearly alike as possible to rule out size and appearance considerations, and the 'A' samples were Comfrey group (see Chapter 2), 'B' grown with farmyard manure, 'C' grown with compost, and 'D' grown with chemical fertilizer by a local farmer on soil nearly the same as on the Trial Ground—which is thin sandy loam on the edge of a gravel pit—but deeper. None of the tasters knew what these letters meant until after the trial which was held in late spring when potatoes begin to taste their age. The tasters were divided into four groups, 'V' for vegans who are vegetarians who eat no animal product, vegetarians, who do eat milk products and eggs, and 'M.E.'s' or meat-eaters, classed as smokers and non-smokers.

FIRST PREFERENCE

	Taster	A	B	C	D	Total
V.	Non-smoker	2	–	–	–	2
Veg.	Non-smoker	5	–	–	–	5
M.E.	Smoker	4	1	2	1	8
	Non-smoker	6	6	2	–	13
	Total	16	7	4	1	28

SECOND PREFERENCE

	Taster	A	B	C	D	Total
V.	Non-smoker	–	2	–	–	2
Veg.	Non-smoker	–	–	5	–	5
M.E.	Smoker	–	5	2	1	8
	Non-smoker	–	6	4	3	13
	Total	–	13	11	4	28

THIRD PREFERENCE

	Taster	A	B	C	D	Total
V.	Non-smoker	–	–	–	–	2
Veg..	Non-smoker	–	5	–	–	5
M.E.	Smoker	2	2	4	–	8
	Non-smoker	2	1	6	6	13
	Total	4	8	10	6	28

FOURTH PREFERENCE

	Taster	A	B	C	D	Total
V.	Non-smoker	–	–	2	–	2
Veg.	Non-smoker	–	–	–	5	5
M.E.	Smoker	2	–	–	6	8
	Non-smoker	6	–	1	6	13
	Total	8	–	3	17	28

Why Grow Your Own?

This 'blindfold test' shows two extremes of flavour, with the majority putting chemical-grown potatoes last, with 1 first, 4 seconds, 10 thirds and 17 fourths; comfrey-grown scoring 16 firsts including all seven vegetarian and vegan votes for the finest flavour, 4 thirds and 8 fourths, and compost-grown and manure-grown in the middle. Vegetarians and vegans who are non-smokers have the most sensitive taste buds of all, and they should always grow their own choice of vegetable varieties, because those commercially popular will taste even worse to their unspoiled palates.

The double advantage of the gain in flavour from cutting out chemical fertilizers and choosing a good variety runs right through the garden, because the amateur and the market gardener have entirely different requirements. The commercial grower needs to clear his five acres of lettuces in a week, so he needs a variety that will be ready all at once, but even he may give them expensive dried blood to supply nitrogen for a fast finish, rather than the far cheaper nitrate of soda which means they will go flabby sooner in the shop and lose him customers. The amateur wants a kind that will *stay* ready as long as possible without bolting while he eats along his three rows, a few a day, and he will not even give them organic nitrogen because he does not want them to hurry up but to slow down.

The belief that modern tomatoes are always tasteless has come from local nurseries selling off their surplus greenhouse varieties to amateur gardeners who plant them outside. These are bred to produce the maximum weight of crop, with skins almost as tough as polythene so that they will travel safely to market by the ton. Home gardeners want kinds that will ripen fast outdoors, with a real flavour and a thin skin for that short journey up the garden path, and these special outdoor kinds can be bought as plants by those who have no greenhouses to raise their own. Those who care for flavour can rarely buy from their local nurseryman or market, garden centres or chain-stores, and this is why this book has an appendix of suppliers.

Perhaps the finest-flavoured strawberry is 'Royal Sovereign', but it is vanishing from the market because the crop is smaller than that of less tasty varieties and therefore the cost of picking is higher. One by one bush fruit will come off the market because not enough people will pay the cost of picking and a profit for the man who grows them, multiplied by wages and profits all the way to the greengrocer, so an extra 1p a pound for picking becomes 4p by the time it reaches the consumer. Our own bottled fruit and tomatoes can re-

Why Grow Your Own?

place tinned until the new crop comes and though our homemade jam may cost more and more for sugar, at least it is genuine without dyes or additives. However cheaply we buy jam fruit we cannot make jam as cheaply as we can buy it, but 'full fruit standard' does *not* mean all fruit, merely a proportion among other ingredients.

We may also lose fresh peas from the greengrocer, once again because of the picking cost. There is now a peapicking machine which gathers and shells the crop, shooting the chewed-up haulm and pods back on the field, while the peas pour into ten-ton lorryloads to the freezing or canning plant. This may well drive greengrocers' peas off the market and the only way to enjoy them fresh, or raw, when they taste almost as good as they did when we ate them illegally when we were young, will be to grow our own.

The last and most important reason for growing as much as possible of our own fruit and vegetables is to contract out of the race between resistant strains of pests and ever more deadly pesticides and to stop the build-up of these cumulative poisons in the sea, the soil and the bodies of all living creatures including Man. Our own-grown food is safest as well as cheapest.

It was *Silent Spring* by the late Rachel Carson (Hamish Hamilton, £1·25p), perhaps the most important book published in the decade between 1960 and 1970, that warned the world of this danger. It took a work of genius written by a biologist who was also a poet with a poet's gift of words, and who supported her evidence with fifty-two pages of scientific references, to sound the alarm that is still sounding.

The main danger comes from what are called the 'organo-chlorine compounds', of which D.D.T. is the best known. There are also the 'organo-phosphorus' and 'organo-mercury' compounds which were developed from nerve gases not used in World War II. The 'organo' in 'organo chlorine' does not mean that these are safe pesticides of vegetable origin like derris, but *synthetic copies* of organic molecules so made that natural agencies such as bacteria cannot take them apart. They are described as 'cumulative poisons' because they add up throughout our lives even though our yearly or daily dose is tiny.

From the mid-1940's, when D.D.T. was first used, until 1969, it has been calculated that a million tons of organo-chlorine compounds have been spread over the world as a permanent pollution. The compounds are washed from the soil, down rivers and sewers to the sea, where they are concentrated in the fat of the floating plants and tiny creatures called 'plankton'. Small fish eat quantities of these, each

23

with its tiny lifetime's accumulation, large fish eat smaller fish and so on up what is known as a 'food chain' until even Arctic seals and Antarctic penguins that may never have seen a man have D.D.T. building up in their bodies.

One of the main concentrators of D.D.T. in the garden is the common slug which is a scavenger as well as a lettuce eater, clearing up the bodies of slaughtered pests killed by many chemicals; but because they are almost immune to the poison themselves, they can go on eating till they become crawling poison pellets with up to twenty-eight parts per million of the compounds in their bodies. The birds that eat them may not be poisoned themselves but the D.D.T. can concentrate in the fat of their eggs and make these infertile, which is one of the many ways in which these pesticides are destroying our heritage of wild life.

In the autumn hedgehogs also eat quantities of slugs to help build up the fat round their shoulders under the prickles as a food store to last through hibernation. The D.D.T. from the slugs is released into the blood-stream from the fat and the result is a hedgehog that fails to wake in spring or is found dead from no apparent cause. Birds build up fat in the same way for migration and may well die over the seas as they use its energy, but we can never be sure.

Just as these substances concentrate in the fat of eggs, in mammals they collect in milk. In Australia and New Zealand, whose exported butter has been refused by the U.S.A. because of its high D.D.T. level, they are restricting its use on pastures. In Sweden a two-year ban on the whole organo-chlorine group began on 1st January 1970, not only because the level in the enclosed Baltic is ten times as high as that of the North Sea, and its salmon are now at 31 p.p.m.* which would be dangerous if Swedes could afford to eat them as freely as hedgehogs eat slugs. A long series of tests in Swedish maternity homes has shown that mothers' milk there has an average organo-chlorine content of 0·117 p.p.m. which is 70 per cent higher than the level considered safe for British babies.

The fine old farmworker and his wife with whom we began this chapter lived on into their nineties without a single cumulative poison in their bodies, and gardened very well without any. Today the average level in human body fat in Western Australia (with a world record in pesticide consumption on the land) is 0·67 p.p.m. or about three times the average British level. Those of us who are in our fifties

* p.p.m. = parts per million.

24

have had barely twenty years of adding up, but the generations that begin as breast-fed babies today may have a risk waiting for them if they lose weight suddenly after an illness when they are stout and in their sixties.

All this, in the opinion of experts (especially those employed by chemical companies), is controversial, doubtful and even 'emotional', which is not a term that can be fairly applied to the scientific articles on which it is based. The gardener, however, has no need to enter into any controversy, or to worry which of the newest pesticides will be banned as soon as he has got used to employing them. He is entitled to assume that all are as safe as thalidomide was until it was found out, and to keep them out of his garden because there are plenty of safe alternatives which are often cheaper and mean less work.

Even today there are a number of people to whom fruit and vegetables grown without pesticides are as essential for health as a controlled diet to a diabetic, and their number will rise as more people reach their personal danger level. No one who has had black-water fever, as an example, should use malathion or any of the organo-phosphorus compounds. The liver is a filter and anyone who has had hepatitis or any other serious liver complaint should avoid all modern pesticides because of their immediate as distinct from long-term dangers. Safety levels are an average, and there are unlucky people who are extra-sensitive, like the two people in every thousand who are upset by the systemic insecticides, used against aphides on straw-berries, which go right inside the plant and make its sap poisonous.

It is possible to buy Wholefood, which is the modern term for produce grown without chemical fertilizers or pesticides, at Whole-food shops, such as the large one in Baker Street,* but these are relatively few. The cost of the journey to the nearest shop or the carriage on weekly parcels, apart from the fact that Wholefood sells for more than greengrocers' prices, makes this expensive. Growing your own is far the cheapest way of obtaining it, and the exercise and interest of gardening can be of more value to health than the diet supplements, laxatives and vitamin pills of this chemical age.

* A handbook of these called 'The Wholefood Finder' is published by The Rodale Press, Berkhamsted, Herts, price 70p.

2

Muck Without Mystery

The gardens of the past had plenty of good muck even in the centres of cities, and the double primroses—once the Londoner's favourite flower—which struggle on in modern gardens, throve on dried cow-dung from the herds that were driven from door to door and milked into the customers' jugs in the eighteenth century. Then every car was a carriage and pair and every lorry a dray, so horse manure was a by-product of transport and return loads on the carts that brought fruit and vegetables to Covent Garden built up the fertility of the market gardens that ringed London and every expanding city.

The retired farmworkers of the last chapter had their free load when the dung from the well-strawed bullock yard was carted and spread, but today even the expensive trailer loads of poor-quality farmyard manure are scarce. Modern farms do not have 'yards', for their battery hens, broiler calves, 'sweat-box' pigs and zero-grazing calves are stock kept on wire or slats, and the manure is either washed out as a slurry to pollute rivers where this is allowed, or sprayed on the land which causes complications in winter.

Apart from the strong feelings many people have about factory farming (which rarely extends to boycotting its produce, so the system may replace all other methods in time), the fact that the dung contains no straw means shortage of humus. Manure contractors today will often sell battery or broiler calf manure which has been stacked with just enough straw to allow mechanized loading. This excludes air, so it cannot decay to the 'well-rotted manure' recommended by the writers of the past, but becomes a kind of 'manure silage' which is a sour-smelling mess, unpleasant to dig in, that can stay un-decayed for even a year. Many large factory farmers dry their dung with hot air and sell it under various trade names, but drying and

26

carriage are costly so the price is always higher than it is worth.

The answer is to rely on compost which is a far better-balanced source of plant food and humus than even good farmyard manure for the garden's main 'meal', with good manure to make it go further when this can be obtained, and green manure from crops grown for this purpose, with organic fertilizers as 'diet supplements' if necessary. Many thousands of successful gardeners use this system of feeding their soil, thereby improving on the productivity of the past when only farmyard manure, lime and the emptyings from primitive sanitary systems were used.

There is a clear distinction between organic and inorganic manures and fertilizers which has been established by the work of the University of Saskatchewan in Canada, reported at the 1955 Geneva Conference on the Peaceful Uses of Atomic Energy. Their researches showed that a wheat crop could take only 2 per cent of the phosphorus in theory available from a chemical fertilizer, but when the grain was fed to cattle and turned into manure together with the straw, the next crop took up almost all the radioactivity-tagged molecules. Just as water has light and heavy molecules, it seems that those of plant foods also vary and that roots pick out one sort, like a girl choosing all the hard centres from a box of chocolates. All the mineral molecules, even those of trace elements, in our compost heaps are 'hard centres', already root-selected and ready for immediate use. Humus of course has many physical properties, but you cannot gain the same flavour and crop quality by using peat to supply moisture-holding humus, and chemical fertilizers with it.

This is why compost and manures produce results out of all proportion to their chemical analysis, and we can therefore draw a distinction between a dried seaweed meal like Marinure with its 2 per cent nitrogen, 0·3 per cent phosphorus and 2·7 per cent potash all 'root-selected' from the sea, and wood ashes with vastly more potassium changed to an assorted batch of potassium carbonate molecules, of which only a few are usable. The best way to use the ashes from the very few bonfires that are necessary to burn hedge clippings, winter fruit tree prunings, rose and shrub prunings and sawn-off branches, is in the compost heap.

Many gardeners are chain bonfire smokers, burning their own money by wasting good humus and plant foods and buying peat and chemical fertilizers to replace them. Every one of these heavy smokers—the six-a-week man is quite common—is contributing a smoke containing roughly 350 times as much cancer-causing benzpyrene as that from cigarettes (70 parts per million against 0·2 p.p.m.) to air pollution.* Though we do not inhale our bonfires' smoke as we do that of cigarettes, if our neighbour is a lung-cancer case or an asthma sufferer we may be doing him active harm with our wasteful habit, for constant bonfires are habit rather than horticulture. We gain nothing from burning rubbish, for even the useful potash is quickly washed away and the salt in the ashes can replace the calcium in clays with sodium, making them permanently sticky with the same action that the sea has on flooded farmland.

Composting garden and kitchen wastes is more than a matter of rechristening the rubbish-heap, for a good compost heap is a bacterial bonfire, cooking weed seeds like grains of rice, simmering dock roots like long and narrow potatoes, and killing the spores of plant diseases with temperatures of 120° to 160° F. If your heap does not reach this heat (and at only 115° there is a risk of maggots from kitchen wastes) your methods need improvement, and the ability to make good compost is an important gardening skill, though those who have mastered the technique find it very simple. Describing it in detail makes it sound much more complex than it is.

Heaps in the open rarely decay thoroughly because the outsides do not heat and turning is necessary to bring the sides and ends to the middle. A compost box is best for small gardens as it stops the heat loss from the sides and it keeps the stack tidy. The many slatted or wiremesh containers made like incinerators have only the merit of tidiness, as they let the material dry and cool so that it never gets really hot. It is possible to make good brick-sided boxes, their open end fitted with a removable wooden front, but without cement bases, which hold moisture at the bottom. Pits are useless as they not only exclude air but hold water in winter. Corrugated iron and asbestos also offer poor heat insulation.

Wooden boxes are best and if well made they last for fifteen or twenty years. The semi-detached type with one compartment ready to use or rotting, and the other filling as rubbish accumulates, is best, but it must be built. Compost boxes are far more easily made than any shed, but those offered for sale are made with useless, open-slat sides. Making your own involves only straight sawing and driving nails

* 'Cancer and Atmospheric Pollution' by Professor F. C. Pybus, M.S., F.R.C.S., *Medical Proceedings*, Vol. 10, June 1964.

home into strong timber. The cost will be less than that of a load of inferior manure.

One with compartments 3 ft. square and high takes 200 ft. of $\frac{1}{2}$-in. × 4-in. sawn planks and six 4-ft. lengths of 2-in. × $1\frac{1}{2}$-in. timber. Saw enough planks into 3-ft. lengths for the two ends and the middle, and 6-ft. lengths for the back, then creosote the lot and leave them to dry, including the 2-in. × $1\frac{1}{2}$-in. uprights.

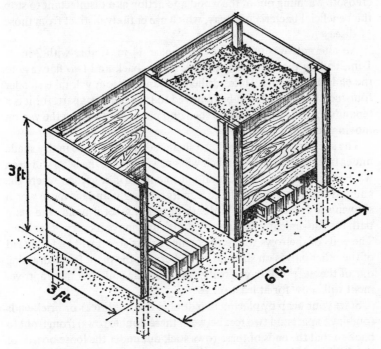

1. A two-compartment compost box: note removable board front and brick air channels for air supply from below

Lay three of these uprights a yard apart and nail the six-foot planks to their upper three feet. Then nail the three-foot planks at one end to the upper three feet of the three remaining uprights. Dig six holes at the corners of two-yard squares, fit the three uprights on the back into the first end in its hole, replace and firm the soil round it, and nail the loose ends of the three-foot planks to the corner upright, holding a brick on the inside to take the shock of hammering.

When the middle and second end are fitted in this way, you have a strong wooden letter 'E' made of two bottomless and topless boxes. Now saw some of the spare planks lengthways and nail a piece upright about three-quarters of an inch away inside the outer 2-in. × 1½-in. posts to make slots for the loose board fronts of the two compartments to slide down. Three are needed on the middle one to make slots on both sides. Creosote these and the front boards, and when all have had a week to dry, paint with black bitumen paint to prevent the creosote warming out of the wood and acting as a disinfectant to stop the beneficial bacteria of decay, which are entirely distinct from those of disease.

An alternative is to replace the 2-in. × 1½-in. timber with 2-in. × 1-in., nailing three pieces edgeways to the back and two flatways to the ends and middle. Holes drilled top and bottom will take slender four-inch bolts which can be removed to take the box apart, for it is a tenant's fixture like a portable shed and packs flat to go on the van on moving days.

The site for the heap should be sheltered, and it can be in dry shade under trees where nothing much will grow, but here the heap will need watering in dry weather. On an allotment, or in a garden where the compost heap is a garden feature in its own right and far more worth showing to friends than a birdbath or goblins, set it beside the main path for convenient wheeling of rubbish and move it every other year. The ends of the rows where the compost box stood will be far ahead of the other halves on size and yield, because the plant foods draining out of the heap will have greatly enriched the soil, and the improvement will show for at least six years.

Start your heap by placing two double rows of bricks or brick-ends (one-inch apart and two feet between these double rows) from front to back so that the ends of these rows stick out under the loose boards of the front or below the wire-netting. These provide the draught from below that keeps the 'bacterial bonfire' burning.

Cover the bricks with tough and stemmy rubbish such as privet or *Lonicera* hedge clippings or tall tough weeds to prevent finer materials from blocking the air channels. Then pile on the first eight-inch-thick layer of weeds, lawn-mowings and garden wastes with kitchen refuse in the middle. Then scatter enough dried sludge, dried blood, dried poultry manure, or fish meal to colour the surface, or a half-inch layer of rabbit, pigeon, poultry or other available manure. Add another eight-inch layer of rubbish, whiten this with slaked lime, pile on a third layer and then manure or 'activator' again, and so on until the bin is filled. This is rarely possible in a day; most heaps take weeks to build, and you add more layers as they sink and decay until the heap is cold and the worms move in. Other signs that compost is ready are a faint earthy odour (the only smell), dark brown or black colour, and a crumbly texture like that of well-rotted farmyard manure. Use it like manure; though it is richer in potash, it can be dug in before sowing root crops without making them coarse and forky, and with lime. A bucketful or two to a square yard is a fair dressing. Autumn heaps are ready to dig in by spring, spring-made before midsummer, and June-started heaps mature for autumn digging, so with material enough a bin can be filled and emptied three times a year.

Winter heaps can get too moist and rain washes out the plant foods, so a roof of some kind is necessary. Corrugated iron sheets coated with black bitumen paint supported with a frame of 2-in × 1-in. timber at the front and sloping towards the back are popular, but the wind can get under and hurl them away. In windy gardens it is better to make a permanent roof of 4-in. × ½-in. tongued and grooved prepared planks nailed to a frame of 2-in. × 2-in. timber and supported high in the front and low at the back to run off the rain, covered with roofing-felt after creosoting to prevent decay. Covering the heap with black polythene in winter is not successful because the moisture condenses on the under side and trickles back again to cool the heap and keep it too wet. Roofed heaps may dry and need hosing.

There are many proprietary activators that do not need lime layers, including Q.R. and Fertosan which are mixed and watered on, Fertosan powder in a tin with a sprinkler top, and Alginure which is a seaweed jelly. Marinure or any other dried seaweed fertilizer can be sprinkled on at the rate of 2 oz. a square yard of layer, but the quickest heating is from a mixture of 25 per cent of a seaweed meal to 75 per cent of any dried sewage sludge of 20 per cent or less moisture content, scattered at this rate. The seaweed powder becomes a jelly which has the same effect in securing a bacterial increase as the agar jelly used in hospitals for throat swab cultures, and the sludge provides ample nitrogen and phosphorus to make up their bodies as they multiply. A test in 1968 on the Henry Doubleday Research Association Trial Ground showed the difference between the mixture and sludge alone. (See table on following page.)

The cheapest activator is bedroom slops, either poured on from a jug every morning without layers of lime or diluted with three times as much plain water either regularly or as a cure for any heap that refuses

	Sludge and Marinure		Plain Sludge
7th June	120° F	7th June	100° F
8th June	145° F	8th June	110° F
9th June	155° F	9th June	120° F
10th June	145° F	10th June	125° F
11th June	150° F	11th June	120° F
12th June	155° F	12th June	120° F
13th June	147° F	13th June	126° F
14th June	140° F	14th June	120° F
15th June	137° F	15th June	117° F

to heat. Urine contains a great deal of potassium which is wasted in the effluent so that all sludges and municipal composts have only a trace, but using it as a free activator helps to restore this essential plant food to the soil, as it did in China for more than forty centuries.

Though layers of soil are sometimes recommended, where weeds are used these will always have enough bacteria on the roots among the soil that clings to them. Always shake off as much as possible, because you cannot expect the heap to have heat enough to cook weed seeds inside cold clods, and this is the commonest cause of compost producing a forest of seedling weeds. Another trick for those whose problem is heating failure is to cover the top surface with sacks to hold it in, removing these when more rubbish is added. Old carpet fragments are also useful heat holders. The bedroom slop system is the best for the lazy gardener who does not want to bother with layers.

In addition to weeds and lawn-mowings, with cut-down herbaceous plants, spent annuals and even summer tree-prunings which are soft enough to rot, many domestic wastes can go in the heap. Include tea leaves, potato and other vegetable peelings of all types, orange and fruit peelings and wastes, egg-shells, nut-shells, fish bones and wastes (not meat bones), rags, paper in small quantities well scattered through the heap, vacuum-cleaner dusts, blanket fluff, hair combings, etc.

Brussels sprout and cabbage stumps will rot if smashed with an axe back, and horrible weed roots such as couch grass, docks, convolvulus and ground elder can be spread on a wire-netting rack and laid on concrete, or the roof of a shed, to dry and die. They will then make compost rich with their pirates' hoard of robbed plant food. Seedling weeds and diseased materials are safe in the middle of the heap where they get hottest, but smash clubrooted cabbage stumps if these are used. The heat of a good heap is a safe sterilizer, though if in doubt it is best to turn it and make sure.

Muck Without Mystery

Exclude metal milk bottle tops and metal of all kinds, broken china and all really unrottable wastes, newspapers and cardboard in bulk, nylon and other man-made fibres, polythene and plastics. Exclude also tree prunings, rose prunings, pine needles, sawdust (except in small quantities), shaving wood, thick branches from hedges (though thin chippings will decay, especially if they are used several times). Leather can be composted in time, and if anything fails to rot, or a heap stays partly decayed, use it to start the next one and it usually decays. Grass mowings for composting can often be obtained from council-mown verges, parks and sports grounds, and anyone on the committee of a lawn tennis club could start a battery of compost boxes, producing fertility for the fetching by members.

Where large quantities of lawn mowings are available, or there is a bulk of soft and sappy weeds, drive upright stakes down into the brick air channels, just far enough into the ground to hold them upright, and build the heap round them. Pull them out when it is finished and there will be air channels extending down to the bottom ventilation, which can puff out steam in frosty weather that shows like a horse's breath. An alternative to brick channels is short lengths of three- to four-inch wide plank nailed into a series of 'V's' set pointed end downwards along the bottom with two-inch-wide gaps between them, but bricks are easy, cheap and lasting.

Leafmould is the most wasted humus of all, with the advantage that your council road man can often be persuaded to empty his barrows in your garden; and if you apply to your Borough Engineer's department they will often arrange a lorry load of street tree leaves. Leafmould needs no activator and no turning, merely space, time, and leaves that must be swept up anyway. If you have a dark, out-of-the-way corner where nothing will grow, it might just as well hold your leafmould heap.

Level off the site and drive in stout posts at the corners, with extra posts every four feet, and staple one-and-a-half-inch-mesh wire-netting round them, with one end free so it can be hooked shut like a gate. The object is to stop the leaves blowing round the garden, and it can be moved on to another heap each year. The leaves go in as they are gathered, with no layers of anything, but be careful to pick out any dead branches and to avoid treading the leaves too much. Pack your cube of leaves so that it is filled solid, and if it is under trees, water it occasionally in summer and Nature will do the job of making humus as efficiently as in a thick drift of leaves on the forest floor.

Muck Without Mystery

The following autumn the material will be ready for use. From five cubic yards of loose leaves as swept, making a stack nine feet long, three feet wide and three feet high, you get roughly a ton of humus, or two cubic yards. Compost shrinks much more; approximately six cubic yards of green material make one cubic yard—but a leafmould mound is not a compost heap.

Do not mix in weeds and garden rubbish or soil, for leafmould cannot heat up and kill weed seeds. Use only leaves which bind together like the pages of a book and decay by the action of fungi, not bacteria. No diseases are carried by dead leaves. Kew made the first heap in the autumn of 1760 (before it was a public garden) and if there was any disease the first century of use would have shown it! There are stories that only oak or beech leaves are good, and London plane leaves are useless, but these date from the time when head gardeners bought leafmould. They would only pay for the very best. All leaves are better on the heap than on the bonfire.

If you burn leaves all you get is the ashes (3·8 per cent), and as you see by the flat circle after the rain, this is mostly potassium carbonate which washes away quickly; and you might as well buy a bale of peat and burn it, for you have got the moisture-retaining and other qualities of peat in your leaves. The difference is that leaves are free—and Nature does not advertise.

The ideal use is as a mulch; spread on the surface between fruit bushes or even heaped round the trunks of fruit trees it gives them a larger share of the humus and plant foods which Nature intended them to use. It is low in nitrogen, 0·4 per cent against 2·1 per cent in good compost, and high in potash and phosphates, but these only in very slowly-available forms. The real value is in the lignins and hemi-celluloses which make the most lasting humus of all. Dug in to any humus-starved garden, with 4 oz. of lime to the square yard to give alkaline 'bread' for the soil bacteria to begin their meal of vegetable 'cheese', made by fungi which like acid conditions, it is good food for the soil.

Leafmould is not a manure, it is not a fertilizer, but an ideal shrub, tree and herbaceous plant food—slow, lasting and safe, and making your compost go further. The very best bargain for anyone with a heavy clay soil would be to pay the carriage cost of leaves by the lorry load from his local council's street trees, to use by the ton, when they mature; an investment like National Savings Certificates. The following table lists the mineral and moisture contents of leafmould and peat.

Muck Without Mystery

	Beech Leafmould %	Rhododendron Peat %
Ash	17·70	9·25
Nitrogen	1·80	1·20
Phosphoric Acid	0·10	0·15
Potash	0·15	0·10
Calcium (as CaO)	0·80	0·35
Moisture	12·05	13·10

The table shows the constituents but not the value as humus. There is very little difference between leafmould and peat, which is usually 'leafmould' from water plants, so far as chemicals are concerned. The question is one of cost, for a single bale of sedge peat costs about £2·50 and will cover a space fifteen feet wide and twenty feet long, two inches deep. Spread between the rows after sowing, or on top of lime, and with the cabbage tribe (especially brussels sprouts) with no digging at all, it stops winter rain from puddling the clay, and suppresses weeds; it also allows picking or cutting without trampling. Leafmould does the same job for the cost of just thinking ahead and a little trouble. It is by far the best way of lightening clay with humus because you can use enough to make a real difference.

All gardens need some manure for a change, and manures are especially useful when there has been no time for making any compost. The soil is poor, either worn out by a previous owner who has used nothing at all or chemicals, or because it is new raw subsoil. Manure contractors advertise in the local papers and the best value for money is always a full lorry load shared with a neighbour, on the basis that thirty good barrowloads, enough for 120 square yards, is roughly a ton. The essential is that it should contain plenty of straw, for this is evidence that it is the purchase of a farm that *has* a yard, not merely of an office block with a computer to work out the rations, and a few acres of factory.

When we buy manure we should get both humus and plant foods. We shall also get water, and broadly speaking it is worth looking for the manure with the lowest moisture content in order to avoid paying cartage for what the next shower will provide free. The major need is to buy the best balance of plant foods, all as hard-working, root-selected molecules, and the following table shows some typical analysis figures:

(See table on following page.)

The best buys in this table are the peat deep litter and the old mush-

35

	Water	Nitrogen	Phosphorus	Potash	Calcium
	%	%	%	%	%
Pigeon Manure, mixed-fed	31·60	5·84	2·10	1·77	—
Pigeon Manure, pellet-fed	18·50	6·51	2·49	2·32	1·80
Shavings, Deep Litter	20·40	2·25	2·50	1·50	3·70
Fresh Poultry Manure	76·00	1·66	0·91	0·48	—
Rothamsted Average F.Y.M.	76·00	0·64	0·23	0·32	—
Straw and Sludge Compost	46·50	0·80	0·55	0·15	1·50
Birmingham Dried Sludge	10·00	2·15	3·51	Trace	—
Stroud (Glos.) Dried Sludge	34·00	1·92	0·46	0·16	—
Indore Compost, Haughley	76·00	0·50	0·27	0·81	—
Comfrey Compost, H.D.R.A.	68·00	0·77	0·29	0·92	—
Old Mushroom Bed Compost	53·14	0·80	0·63	0·67	—
Peat, Deep Litter	17·70	4·40	1·90	1·90	2·20
Straw, Deep Litter	50·20	0·80	0·55	0·48	
Broiler Shavings	27·20	2·10	2·15	1·55	
Pig Manure (pure)	76·00	0·48	0·58	0·36	
Cow Manure (pure)	86·00	0·44	0·12	0·04	

room bed compost; the latter is usually sold as 'composted horse manure' if it is of the quality analysed in this table, for many modern mushrooms have to make do with straw composted with Adco M, which means far less potash for the money. Both will be weed-free, both have more humus and less water than even good farmyard manure, much less than pure pig or cow muck from factory farms, and both contain as much potash as phosphorus, or even more, which balances them for vegetable crops.

The straw deep litter is also a good buy, because it will hold plenty of humus and the birds will have eaten all the weed seeds in poor-grade straw, but neither of the shavings samples will be safe despite their attractive analysis. They will contain thick shavings and small wood ends which will take several years to decay in the soil. The bacteria that break them down will take up nitrogen to make their bodies at the expense of your crops, exactly as will stemmy garden rubbish dug in direct without composting, so the result of a 'bargain load' or free offer of this kind of manure can be a disaster of the kind that has given poultry manure a bad name.

The fresh poultry manure from a battery is even worse, for its nitrogen is in the form of ammonium carbonate, which is 'fierce' and can burn crops more harshly than nitrate of soda. In the deep litter system this is used up by a bacterium called 'Hutchinson's spirocaete' in breaking up hard cellulose wastes like straw or shavings and producing the heat to dry it. Always insist on a dry litter, peat or straw based, though shavings can be good if broken down to a dark brown powder.

Muck Without Mystery

Pig or cow manure must hold plenty of straw, and if it is fresh, stack it high and square with sheets of corrugated iron, or a covering of black polythene to keep out the rain while it rots. If these manures have no straw with them, refuse them. Horse manure is excellent if it can be obtained, and it is always a better bargain after it has grown a crop of mushrooms.

The richest of all is pigeon manure, and this has so much nitrogen that it is not safe to use it just as it comes in the garden; but is an ideal compost activator, enriching the heap with its high potash. Few pigeon fanciers are gardeners and most of them are glad to give the stuff away, to be stored in a plastic dustbin or other watertight container kept near the heap and spread at the rate of about 1 lb. a square yard of layer when enough material has accumulated. Cover your heap in winter because it will have plant foods worth protecting. Enquire at your railway station for the address of a local pigeon club, for the wicker baskets containing racing birds for release were once sent by rail.

The two dried sludges are typical of this very useful high phosphorus and nitrogen fertilizer for lawns. Spread at the rate of 1 lb. a square yard on your lawn in April this will keep it growing steadily through the season far more cheaply than any chemical lawn tonic, and growing the grass that is one of our most valuable compost and mulching materials. Those lucky enough to live near a tennis club or other sports ground can often get grass mowings free for the fetching, and these should always be accepted. The real bargain is fresh seaweed, which can even be dug in direct without composting, though it is best used to enrich the heap; and if those who drive down to the sea at weekends would spare the bluebells and primroses and instead bring back sackfuls of seaweed in the boots of their cars, they would gain lasting fertility instead of wasting wild flowers that may be as scarce as good muck in the age of factory farming towards which we 'progress'.

3

Diet Supplements for Soils

Many gardeners insist that compost cures plant diseases, when what it 'cures' are the mineral deficiencies that are so often taken for virus symptoms. Again many fungi only attack when a crop is short of an essential mineral—the chocolate spot of broad beans which follows potash starvation is an example, and, like human beings, well-fed plants have a greater resistance to many misfortunes. Some diseases, for instance clubroot and potato blight, have so far resisted dietary treatment, and many pests, including birds, appear to *prefer* compost-grown fruit and vegetables; but the healthier the diet of the soil, the healthier the crops. And of course the less work they are to grow, for even syringing with something safe and non-persistent like derris is still extra trouble we can well do without.

The most important 'diet supplement' is lime, for with too little there is a rise in clubroot risk, more moss on the lawn and between the vegetable rows, and a rapid spread of weeds such as sorrel, creeping buttercup, and mare's tail or *Equisetum*. An early warning that lime shortage is interfering with crop nutrition is a red-purple tint showing phosphorus lack in the growing tips of the weed 'fat-hen' or 'goose-foot' (*Chenopodium album*) which is phosphorus-greedy, as straw-berries are, and without lime no crop can take up this plant food.

Lime is not a fertilizer but a soil sweetener to keep the soil just slightly acid or neutral so that vegetables can use the foods that compost provides. There may be enough in the lime layers in the compost heaps to keep the right balance but the 'fat-hen's' warning is a sign that a dressing is needed. Other warnings are a great many very small potatoes, and flattened dark brown patches on the bottoms of outdoor tomato fruit. Compost gardeners need least, for every pound of sulphate of ammonia that goes on a garden can lock up a pound and a half of lime. But even compost gardeners need some lime.

Some gardeners give 4 oz. a square yard of slaked lime before sow-ing almost anything, but a heavy dressing of 1–2 lb. a square yard after potatoes every four years is best. The potato scab fungus likes lime and potatoes dislike it, so it should go on well before the potato bed returns to that part of the garden in the rotations discussed in Chapter 4. Lime should not go on with farmyard or any animal manure or it will react with the nitrogen (as it will with sulphate of ammonia and nitrate of soda) and waste what there is in a stink of ammonia. Compost and lime can go on together quite safely.

Slaked lime is easiest to buy but fine-ground limestone is more slowly released and is therefore better for sandy soils. The slowest of all is in oyster shell chicken grit, and a good double handful of this in the bottom of the hole when planting stone fruit on these soils will last a plum or cherry for years.

Another form of lime is gypsum, which is calcium sulphate, the remedy for overdosing with salt from wood ashes, and used by the hundred tons after the Essex sea floods in 1953. It costs about £2 a hundredweight, or no more than ordinary lime, and it is worth scattering 8 oz. a square yard on any horrible clay and having it rotavated in if it is not possible to dig it. If the stickiness is due to too many applications of wood ashes in the past, or of Kainite which is a dried seabed deposit from Germany containing about 60 per cent salt and 15 per cent potassium chloride, once widely boosted (and named from the Greek 'kanos' or 'new', not from a Mr. Kain), there could be a miraculous cure. Good humus and perseverance have, however, cured more clays than any soil conditioner, even this cheap gypsum made from ground alabaster rock from Derbyshire. The seaweed preparations advertised for this purpose have an effect that only lasts a year, so are not worth the money.

Over-liming is possible where a gardener has piled it on in defiance of the sixteenth-century saying 'Lime and lime without manure makes both farm and farmer poor', but it is more common in chalky gardens. Here the lime can lock up magnesium, the most important of the trace elements, which is also locked up by too much phosphorus or potash. This general lock-up, which can only be partly corrected with compost, is commonest in the one sunny bed in the average garden where out-door tomatoes grow year after year. Here it causes the familiar early yellowing of the bottom leaves with the veins staying green, and 'green-backed' fruit, and it also causes the same symptoms in raspberries, french and runner beans and cabbages. In potatoes there are also brown patches between the leaf veins, which have been taken for potato blight, though the darker brown patches from this genuine disease are larger and start at the edges of the leaf.

When apple trees shed their leaves early and keep those at the tips of the young shoots, and have large brown patches between the veins, they too are suffering from magnesium shortage which is common on chalk. Cherries show the same patches but smaller and nearer purple, blackcurrant leaves turn all purple brown with a green margin, and gooseberries red-brown to cream tints in a wide strip round the leaf edges. All these symptoms should not be confused with normal autumn tints from the natural obedience of the leaves to the signal of the shortening days that it is time to return their minerals to store in the twigs for use next spring.

Though the long-term answer is more compost, the quick and easy one is 2 oz. of Epsom salts in a 2-gallon can, watered on over two square yards, which can produce a swift return to normal if the symptoms were seen early in the season. Epsom salts are magnesium sulphate, and though the medical grade can be bought cheaply in 2-oz. containers, the industrial or cattle grade in 14 lb. bags can be ordered through good chemists. One dressing lasts many years, except on chalk, where cancelling out of the magnesium lock-up may be needed every other season.

Like lime, magnesium is not a fertilizer, but a 'soil unlocker' for use in settling the strikes and lockouts of the soil, which usually contains plenty of minerals ready to work hard at their jobs, but the shop stewards officiously added by us make them down tools. Almost every one of the symptoms of magnesium, manganese, potash, phosphorus, calcium, iron, zinc, boron and copper shortage (illustrated in colour in that excellent and out-of-print book *The Diagnosis of Mineral Deficiencies in Plants* by T. Wallace, C.B.E., M.C., D.SC., F.R.I.C., V.M.H., F.R.S., H.M. Stationery Office, 1961) can be taken for virus or other disease symptoms by anyone other than an expert, and lime, Epsom salts and compost will cure the lot.

Before any cherished shrub or fruit tree or bush is destroyed be-because it has a 'virus' try first Epsom salts, and secondly dried sewage sludge, for this is the best source of assorted trace elements we have. The important aspect of trace elements is that we only need a *trace* of them—too much can be as bad as too little. Dried sludge which contains rapidly-available nitrogen and a good set of minerals

Diet Supplements for Soils

in their efficient root-selected forms, has them spaced out in traces, with plenty of the zinc which our soils increasingly lack. Though factory farmers, who wash all their trace elements away with the dung that pollutes our rivers, and restore only calcium, nitrogen, phosphorus and potash, are the ones who suffer most, chemical fertilizers are now made so pure that gardeners who use them will miss the traces that used to be present as impurities. Sludge is cheap enough and 1 lb. a square yard in autumn or spring is worth using as a general fertilizer in its own right, though it is better mixed with equal parts of seaweed meal to balance its phosphorus with potash.

TABLE OF ORGANIC FERTILIZERS

	Water	Nitrogen	Phosphoric acid	Calcium Phosphate	Potash
	%	%	%	%	%
Bone meal (coarse)	32·94	3·35	23·19	50·62	—
Bone meal (fine, steamed)	8·00	1·34	29·02	61·72	0·20
Fish meal	—	9·29	7·70	16·79	—
Dried Blood	—	9·65	0·83	1·82	—
Meat and Bone Meal	—	4·00	16·00	—	—
Hoof and Horn Meal	—	13·00	2·00	—	—
Seaweed Meal (Marinure)	—	2·00	0·30	—	2·70
Wilted Comfrey	75·00	0·74	0·24	—	1·19
Bracken, fresh	68·00	2·00	0·20	—	2·75
Bracken, dry	13·6	1·44	0·20	—	0·11
Wheat Straw	17·80	0·38	0·19	—	0·77
Tea Leaves		4·15	0·62	—	0·40

A 'manure' contains plant foods with humus as well and usually plenty of moisture. A 'fertilizer' is concentrated, has little humus and is valued for its minerals. The problem with organic fertilizers is that most of them contain so much phosphorus that if they are used with peat to supply humus in place of compost when this is scarce they build up so much excess that they can produce potassium shortage. Fish meal is an example, and the grade sold as '10 per cent potash' has this much added as potassium chloride, but the organic gardener who wants to use a chemical on his tomatoes would be better off with straight sulphate of potash rather than adding all that phosphoric acid and the phosphorus in the calcium phosphate to his border or bed every year. Magnesium cannot be taken up without good humus to make it available, and the worst shortage ever seen by the writer was in tomato houses owned by a famous gardening authority who used peat and fish meal, and put the symptoms down to a virus.

Diet Supplements for Soils

Fish meal is a useful, though expensive, compost heap activator at the rate of 2 oz. a square yard of material, and it can be used as a general tonic for application before sowing. On sandy soils it can be balanced by adding two parts of wood ashes to one of meal, but the problem is that the potash in the wood ashes will wash away too fast to be of value for long. So if you use it, watch for yellowing leaves early in the season and be prepared to give the soil a dose of salts.

Dried blood is a quickly-available nitrogen tonic, expensive, and useful only in emergencies as when beet blister beetle compels one to strip the leaves off the crop, or a row of lettuces hold back, or where any other crop sulks with pale green leaves instead of growing away. It is a compost heap activator, but again a costly one. Nitrate of soda and sulphate of ammonia have the same effect, but will 'burn' the foliage if sprinkled too generously round lettuces, which dried blood never does. Meat and bone meal is like dried blood but adds slowly-released phosphorus as well.

Bone meal is the most important of the slow organic fertilizers that are of great value on sandy soils where compost decays fast and all plant foods wash away. The coarse grade lasts longest in the soil and 2 lb. of this, plus 2 lb. of hoof and horn meal mixed together and forked into the bottom of the hole for planting apples and pears, with the oyster shell grit to supply extra lime for cherries, plums and damsons, provide lasting food for when the trees will need it. Fine bone meal provides a store of phosphorus for lawns on sand, dug in at the rate of 1 lb. a square yard before turfing or sowing, but dried sludge is better for reclaiming subsoils, using up to 4 lb. a square yard rotavated in to start a lifeless soil growing grass.

One of the best slow-acting organic manures is shoddy, which is wool waste that can often be bought with a certain amount of sheep dung with it. This indication is more useful today as a guarantee that you have a real wool shoddy and not nylon refuse or some other man-made fibre which is useless on the land. On sandy soils this has the advantage of doling out nitrogen for as long as five years and holding on to moisture while it decays. Its value is for perennial crops that are nitrogen-greedy, like rhubarb and blackcurrants, both of which are widely grown in the north with generous dressings of shoddy from Bradford and other centres of the wool trade.

The best source for gardeners is old mattresses, for the older types still contain real wool shoddy. Test first by pulling out some of the stuffing and lighting it. If it melts and frizzles with an offensive smell,

42

exactly like burning knitting-wool, it is shoddy. If it flames it is cotton and will rob the soil of nitrogen as it decays, and there are other signs for terylene, nylon and other new textiles that will in time make even old mattresses as permanent as pyramids.

Dig in about a good bucketful to the square yard, or even more if you have it, tucking it well in the bottom of the trenches before planting bush fruit, rhubarb, or anything that will stay put for at least five years to give it time to decay. If you use it under ordinary vegetables you will bring it to the surface when next you dig.

The problem of sandy soils, and chalky ones, is crops that are potash-greedy, demanding more than one's compost can supply. Wood ashes are the traditional answer, and on these soils their salt does not build up trouble, but their potash is present as potassium carbonate, a violent alkali near to caustic soda that made the soft soap which washed Roman togas, Elizabethan ruffs and Beau Brummel's cravats. This does not stay long in sandy soils, but adding it in place of lime layers in the compost heap converts it to potassium nitrate and other rather longer-lasting forms. A roofed compost heap will hold most of it.

Few good gardeners should have more than enough wood ashes to feed their broad beans, which can take 4 oz. a square yard, more than the sulphate of potash does because wood ash is always about half lime, with from 25 per cent to 40 per cent potassium. Twigs, hedge clippings and prunings always hold most and when these are burnt the result is worth storing in an airtight tin, because the 5 per cent to 15 per cent salt takes up moisture from the air.

The best potash fertilizer that can be bought is seaweed meal, which takes about six months to have a strong effect, but it is a first-class source for all organic gardeners. Once seaweed grew all the potatoes of Scotland, including those that built the reputation of Scottish seed, and with roughly eight times as much potash as phosphorus it is a valuable balancer of plant foods, but not a source of humus.

The drawback of seaweed meal is its cost, but growers of comfrey have a cheaper supply from this perennial green-manure crop which should be as much a feature of the garden without chemicals as the compost heap. The best all-round variety for gardeners is Bocking No. 14, because it has thin stems that wilt quickly and become flat, so there is no risk of its rooting and growing where it is unwanted. It is ready early in the year, it can be eaten as a vegetable, or fed to poultry and is rich in potash for garden fertility.

Diet Supplements for Soils

Comfrey is a natural mineral mine, drawing up from the subsoil the plant foods that are beyond reach of anything else but a tree, and making them available for immediate use by our crops, instead of locking the effective root-selected molecules away in wood. It is not a legume, but a member of the order *Boraginaceae*, the Anchusa family, and therefore it needs a supply of nitrogen as manure to keep it growing fast, but it can take this in far cruder forms than most crops, so that even raw poultry and pigeon manure may be used.

Wilted comfrey has so much nitrogen in its protein that it is 'compost' before it goes in the heap, with a 9·1:1 carbon-nitrogen ratio which is almost the same as the 10:1 of good compost or the 14:1 of well-rotted manure. It has a little more nitrogen, a little less phosphorus, and over twice the potash of the best F.Y.M., slightly more potash than good Indore compost, and all three have more of this essential plant food than municipal compost. Comfrey is a balanced fertilizer for potatoes, tomatoes, gooseberries and all potash-demanding crops. In 1956 this was a theory, but since the first experiment with 1½ lb. of wilted comfrey to each foot or row, which doubled the yield of potatoes compared with the 'No Manure' halves, the trial has been repeated every year on the H.D.R.A. Trial Ground, and the various ways of using comfrey have been developed in hundreds of gardens.

POTATO TRIAL, 1961

Square 1	Square 2	Square 3
MANURE	COMPOST	COMFREY
Seed potatoes	Seed potatoes	Seed potatoes
5 lb. 7 oz.	5 lb. 7 oz.	5 lb. 7 oz.
Crop	Crop	Crop
125 lb. 2 oz.	117 lb. 7 oz.	125 lb. 15 oz.
Approximate gain:	Approximate gain:	Approximate gain:
23:1	21½:1	23:1

Square 4	Square 5	Square 6
COMPOST	COMFREY	MANURE
Seed potatoes	Seed potatoes	Seed potatoes
6 lb. 11 oz.	6 lb. 11 oz.	6 lb. 11 oz.
Crop	Crop	Crop
129 lb. 2 oz.	157 lb.	161 lb.
Approximate gain:	Approximate gain:	Approximate gain:
19¼:1	23½:1	24:1

Diet Supplements for Soils

Square 7	Square 8	Square 9
COMFREY	MANURE	COMPOST
Seed potatoes	Seed potatoes	Seed potatoes
7 lb.	7 lb.	7 lb.
Crop	Crop	Crop
100 lb.	127 lb. 5 oz.	131 lb. 14 oz.
Approximate gain:	Approximate gain:	Approximate gain:
14½:1	18:1	18½:1

In 1961 this nine-plot replicated trial of compost, comfrey and farmyard manure showed that all three were approximately equal, and on the main continuous potato plots, near the compost v. chemical trial, comfrey shows itself not only equal to an artificial potato fertilizer, in wet seasons, but ahead of this in dry.

A good compost yield for 'Majestic' is about 14 tons an acre. The above shows 16 tons an acre, for the whole plot. Our totals were: 413 lb., comfrey and compost 378 lb., so, as usual, green wilted comfrey has shown itself roughly equal to either. In terms of yield per foot of row, manure scored 2 lb. 15 oz., compost 2 lb. 11 oz., comfrey 2 lb. 12½ oz.

Unlike other green-manure crops, comfrey is a perennial and the best site for a permanent bed is in full sun and near the compost heap so that it is less far to wheel spare cuts in summer. It should stay in one place and if the wrong choice has been made, never merely dig up the plants and remove them to a new home, for every small fragment of root will grow. Therefore, chop the plants through about two inches below ground level and replant this portion, cutting it up into 'off-sets', each with a section of brown root, and a growing point, and spread sodium chlorate weedkiller on the white surface of the cut root, enough to cover this surface thinly. This will penetrate to every part of the root system and kill the plant completely, a trick that is also effective for horseradish. An alternative is ammonium sulphamate which is sulphate of ammonia 'made crooked' so that weeds choke on it, and the greedier they are the more they take. This becomes sulphate of ammonia in about three weeks, so it should be used to kill comfrey that has got into an awkward place. One pound dissolved in one gallon of water, rosed from a can over 100 square feet, will destroy comfrey growing from broken root fragments, and this is perhaps the best of the chemical weedkillers, completely harmless to soil life and birds.

The drawback of this excellent weedkiller is its high cost, but it has the great advantage that one's ground can be planted safely three to four weeks after use, and it is a complete killer for such weeds as celandine, oxalis, convolvulus, mare's tail and couch grass. It is better to spend once, or even twice in extreme cases, on something safe that will slaughter the really awful weeds, than to be perpetually trying newer and more deadly chemicals that kill only the easy ones.

It may seem strange to begin an account of growing a plant by describing how to kill it—like starting a chapter on apple trees with directions for destroying tree stumps—but more people (including most gardening writers), have heard that comfrey is hard to kill, than know how to grow it and use it well enough to value it.

Comfrey has a deformed flower structure which rarely sets seed, so there is little risk of its spreading as seedlings. The best method of garden propagation is to cut off the clumps in March or April as though they were to be killed, but miss out the sodium chlorate. The cut stump will then grow ahead and be ready to cut by June, but plants should have been established for at least a year before this is done.

Prepare the bed by digging out perennial weed roots very thoroughly, especially couch grass, and digging in manure or compost, with 1 lb. a square yard of coarse bone meal on chalky soils. Clays are ideal for comfrey, but on thin soils over chalk it will need constant manuring, because its roots must get down to plenty of minerals.

Plant the offsets two feet apart each way, at any time of the year other than December and January, with spring and autumn the usual times, and June to September excellent, if it can be watered, because it will have established itself in time for a full cutting programme beginning in April. The first summer the plants will need hoeing to keep down annual weeds, and the first flower stems to form should be removed to throw the strength into the leaves. A first cut should be possible in September from a spring planting and this will also encourage new shoots. Let the last cut die down on the plant.

The following spring manure with dried sludge, poultry manure, dried blood or any crude nitrogen-containing material, and give it 4 oz. a square yard of lime in the autumn in town gardens where the sulphur in the smoke locks up the calcium in the soil.

The better comfrey is fed the faster it grows with less weeding to do, and spreading a two-inch coat of deep-litter compost between the plants combines weed suppressing and ample feeding. As much as 2 lb. a square yard of dried sludge in the spring and again about

Diet Supplements for Soils

August is not too much. Those who are vegans, and will not buy manure for their comfrey (though they usually buy fish for the cat) can use compost or even chemicals like nitro-chalk, but they must expect a lower yield. Comfrey grows fast and demands plenty of nitrogen for its protein and calcium both as a mineral and to keep the soil neutral, neither acid nor alkaline. Compost releases plant foods slowly, which is why it produces firm and often disease-resistant foliage, and the best flavour. Comfrey grows faster than any other crop of temperate climates, and therefore must have enough materials ready within root reach.

Gardeners growing comfrey are not concerned with tons an acre but with how many pounds they get from a dozen plants. Mr. Harold Kirkman of Southport planted a dozen Bocking 14 in the spring of 1959 and harvested as follows in 1960:

		Acre Rate 2 ft. × 2 ft.		
		tons	cwt.	lb.
18th April	18½ lb.	5	16	91
5th June	88 lb.	27	3	70
24th July	52 lb.	17	5	98
18th September	63 lb.	19	11	83
	221 lb.	69	18	6

If comfrey is composted on its own it takes ten barrow loads of material to make one of finished compost. Used in layers with other material it is six to one, four or five to one if the garden rubbish is on the woody side like cut-down herbaceous plants instead of sappy weeds. Green-manure comfrey means about three barrow loads of usable material with the analysis in the table for every four cut. Apart from the saving from cutting out lime, activators, building and turning, there is no rain waste, and no nitrogen goes back in the air when some of the bacteria break down proteins too fast.

Comfrey can be cut with shears or a sickle, about two inches from the ground, and is best left overnight to wilt before direct use, which reduces the moisture by about 10 per cent, and the usual aim is for a cut in early April to go with the potatoes. Most comfrey-using gardeners hang on to their seed potatoes in chitting trays until the comfrey has grown over a foot high, and it is now that the early speed of Bocking No. 14 is an advantage. Dig out the trenches for the potatoes rather deeper than normal, spread the wilted comfrey along

47

them at the rate of 1 lb. a foot of row, scatter some soil on the comfrey and set the seed potatoes along the soil.

The cut comfrey appears to heat like a long and narrow 'compost heap'; the potatoes get away fast, using the supply of balanced plant foods directly where these are needed, and when they are dug there will be only a little powdery black humus remaining. Because comfrey is high in protein and low in fibre, which makes it an excellent pig and poultry food, one cannot expect the lasting humus that comes from composting stemmy garden wastes or straw.

Where comfrey is late in a cold season, or for early potatoes chitted and ready while the comfrey is still short of a good cut, the seed potatoes can be planted three inches deep on the flat and the cut comfrey spread on the surface as it becomes available, even as late as June. As the potatoes grow it is raked along the rows, acing as frost protection for earlies in savage springs, and then soil from the row middles is piled on it, making a smaller than normal earthing-up. Comfrey has also been spread along the sides of the potato ridges, suppressing weeds and feeding the crop below, but the gain is not as great as with comfrey in the trenches. Late autumn cuts have also been dug in ready for early potatoes the following spring, but there is a loss from the comfrey decaying in the soil during the winter and heavy rain washing potash out. The original trench method is still the best potato-growing system.

The next cut can go in the same type of trench but less deep for runner beans, french beans, or late peas. The comfrey below acts as a moisture-holder as well as a lasting potassium-rich feed for the summer. As it decays the soil will sink, allowing room for more watering round the stem.

Tomatoes need feeding when they start setting their fruit, and there are many ways of making liquid manure from comfrey. One of the best is to buy a barrel of the type used as a water butt—40 gallons is a good size. Bore a large hole in the middle of the bottom to take a 1-in. or 1½-in. pipe driven in tight, place a flower-pot over the hole, having chipped the rim a bit so that it does not fit tightly on the bottom but allows the liquid to drain under it, and pour clean gravel round the pot to keep it in place. Fill the barrel full of cut comfrey leaves, ramming them in fairly tight, put on a lid that overlaps round the edge to keep out the water, and prop it up about half an inch at one side to run off rain and let in air. In about three weeks there will be a steady drip of a black fluid from the iron pipe into a jar put to catch

Diet Supplements for Soils

it, and as the comfrey sinks, more is added. At the end of the season the solid contents can be removed and dug in as compost, which, of course, it is.

The black fluid has been analysed with the following result:

	%
Nitrogen	0·120
Potash	0·860
Phosphoric Acid	0·055
Moisture	97·300

This shows that the carbohydrates and proteins have been smashed up by decay, releasing the nitrogen, and the readily soluble potash (as potassium sulphate) probably has dissolved to come out in the fluid leaving most of the phosphorus behind in the compost. The black fluid is, therefore, a very good liquid feed for tomato plants when they are setting their first truss, and for weekly feeds through the season.

Those who have plenty of cut comfrey can pile it between the tomato rows to keep down weeds and release the high potash sap as the stems and midribs are crushed by treading for trimming and picking, but the best use for rather less material is under the gooseberry bushes or between the raspberry canes. Spread what can be spared and cover it with two inches of lawn mowings, so that instead of drying black and brittle it decays under the mulch and gives back the hard-working potassium when it is wanted. The mowings provide weed-suppressing and moisture-holding bulk here, as well as between tomato rows.

Grass mowings are as valuable as a mulch as on the compost heap but it should be remembered that they can harbour slugs which do not attack bush fruit though they will the lower trusses of tomatoes. Support these on straw or woodwool, removed before the mulch is dug in, and put comfrey between strawberry rows only after the crop has been picked.

The final cuts can be dug in as though they were manure in the autumn, but they are also of value in the compost heap, for they act as the 'paper and sticks' of the bacterial bonfire. Use them in two- to four-inch layers on top of four to six inches of woody refuse such as cut-down herbaceous plants and pea, bean and tomato haulm, and put the activator on them so that the last heaps of summer get away to a flying start with plenty of heat before they slow with the autumn rains.

Clean up the bed and dig between the plants if there are perennial

D 49

weeds beginning, and lime if necessary, which will usually be every third year. Manure always in the spring when the plants are beginning to grow, for the plant foods will wash out on a sandy soil before the comfrey is feeding again, if this goes on in autumn.

When comfrey goes dormant in winter it returns all the potash in its foliage to store in the roots, which is why it pays to let the last cut die down naturally. This gives a starting stock for the spring. So does bracken, and the difference between 2·75 per cent and 0·11 per cent shows why bracken as litter or packing is less valuable in manure or compost than wheat straw which has twice as much potash as nitrogen. Straw is an excellent mulching and compost material, provided it can be bought guaranteed free from selective weedkillers, which, as always, are most effective where they are unwanted. So few farmers today can give this guarantee that unsprayed straw can fetch as much as £9 a ton and townsmen have paid 73p a bale. At this price farmyard manure (if you can get it) is a better buy, and ready-made compost such as 'Pompost', which is the refuse from making cider vinegar, composted with deep litter poultry manure, is a bargain.

Fresh bracken cut between May and early August is wonderful compost material, but dry in the autumn it is not worth fetching. The problem is that, unlike comfrey, it will not stand repeated cutting, and three cuts a season for two successive years will kill it out completely as they will also kill perennial nettles, which are an excellent source of both calcium and potassium and heat very well while they last.

There is a thriving outdoor business waiting for anyone with the courage and capital who will start cutting bracken in Scotland or Wales, letting it dry and putting it through a shredder to sell in bags as a surface mulch for gardeners. The profit would be in the fee chargeable for every acre cleared of bracken and restored to good pasture. Until this kind of enterprise begins in Britain's great, empty North Territory, bracken harvesting is just a tantalizing possibility.

The easiest and most useful mulch for spreading on the surface under bush fruit or roses, or between pea or carrot rows, is grass mowings, and the gardener's lawn is a valuable source of humus, apart from its normal use as a green background to the brilliance of borders. Mow every three weeks, not once a fortnight, for this means more grass to the mowing even if the lawn does look a bit shaggy. Cut out selective weedkillers, and use a homemade lawn sand (see Chapter 8) to avoid any risks to crops, and feed it ideally with a dried sludge for sustained yield through the season.

Diet Supplements for Soils

Lawn mowings are 12:1 carbon-nitrogen ratio, just a bit wider than comfrey, and they can also be spread along potato trenches where they are reputed to prevent scab, but they are low in potash so do not give the same yield. They have been used in pea trenches, and in the chapter on individual vegetables their uses are given under the separate headings. Grass is a good help in heating a heap, but as it breaks down to very little it is best mixed with other material.

The last item in our table is tea leaves, which amazingly hold about half as much nitrogen as dried blood, very much more than poultry manure. This, however, is all locked up by the tannin in the tea leaves, even more than there is in the old boots which take longest to compost of anything a gardener throws away. They also contain a useful quantity of manganese and there is still more in the tea we drink, which is also rich in potash. Cold, stewed tea is an excellent high potash liquid manure and the traditional Saturday night drink not only grew the biggest aspidistras in the world in the Victorian age, but flowered them more often than any we see today. (Aspidistra flowers are stemless and rather like small purple crocuses.)

Tea leaves should always go on the compost heap to break down slowly and it is quite a good idea to dig tree holes well before planting in chalk gardens, so that the tea pot can be emptied into them to leave a lasting sponge of moisture-retaining material, plus trace elements and a kind of 'endowment policy' of nitrogen to mature when the tree begins to grow ahead fast in the future. Anyone who could obtain tea leaves in quantity could dig or rotavate them into a sandy soil at the rate of a bucketful a square yard. They have been brushed into lawns to be taken down by worms to build up humus, and emptying the teapot under a cherished shrub has long been a cottage gardener's custom.

This lock-up effect from tannin explains why the head gardeners of the past always insisted on oak leafmould, for the extra tannin in the leaves made this last longest in the soil without breaking down. It also explains why the plant foods in sedge peat stay locked up, for all peats contain humic acids of this group which preserve pollen and even human bodies in peat bogs for thousands of years by preventing bacterial attacks. Leafmould other than oak does break down faster than peat and this is why it is also useful as a 'manure'.

There is a very important difference between the plant-food-supplying materials described in this chapter, and the composts and manures mentioned in the last one. These diet supplements of the soil all serve to supply a mineral shortage that may arise, either immediately as with wood ashes or seaweed meal or wilted comfrey for broad beans, potatoes or gooseberries, or in the future, like bone meal, hoof and horn and oyster-shell grit for a peach tree or a soil that would rather grow heathers. Composts and manures have vastly fewer plant foods, but they hold *energy*.

Except for a small contribution from windmills and water turbines and a tiny one from nuclear power, all the energy in the world comes from sunlight stored by living leaves, for that in coal, petrol and fuel oil was stored by the plants of the past. Chlorophyll is the most important substance on this planet for it is responsible for this miracle of photosynthesis on which all life depends.

Plants breathe in carbon-dioxide and breathe out oxygen, combining the carbon with hydrogen from water split to provide this, and releasing more oxygen to make carbohydrates, which are the starches and sugars that are the energy food of every muscle that moves, and converts them back to carbon-dioxide, breathing in oxygen to reverse the process and use the power. Only about 5 per cent of the sunlight that falls on the leaves is trapped, but this is enough to start the complex celluloses, hemicelluloses and lignins which are the woody parts of plants and trees, apart from the proteins, the alkaloids, the oils and all the substances that plants build from soil, air and water.

When we take out the metal thermometer (the mushroom-grower's type is best for compost heaps, and it can be ordered from any good chemist) and see our heap has reached 160° F, or feel the heat of a pile of lawn mowings, we are observing the effect of the bacteria that break down dead vegetable wastes to plant foods and humus, doing the job they have done to keep the cycle of life going ever since the living soil began. They use the starches and sugars of which the energy is most easily released. Then several races of fungi, notably the *Actinomycetes* family which are responsible for the earthy smell of finished compost, take over and break down some of the woody material, and the worms move in, taking their share of energy and finishing the task of reducing material that began with about 70 parts of carbon-containing compounds to one of nitrogen, to the 10:1 of good compost.

White ants take the process further. Their digestive bacteria are the most efficient woody fibre-breakers in the world, reducing it to gases, salts and silica as effectively as a fire, and this is why countries where termites replace earthworms are the least fertile. Our compost has

52

many of its carbon compounds left, not as charcoal or coke but as high-energy foods to drive the worms, the fungi and thronging soil bacteria whose body weight adds up to half a ton in the top eight inches of an acre of fertile farmland.

Perhaps the most important of these are the nitrogen-fixing bacteria, which use the energy from this income of decayed vegetable matter to take up nitrogen from the air and release it in the soil. Sir Albert Howard recorded a 26 per cent increase in nitrogen in his famous heaps at Indore beyond that supplied in vegetable waste and activators, from the action of the commonest kinds of Azotobacter, which need oxygen in order to release the energy, and neutral or alkaline soil conditions. Unless we provide these in our gardens and compost heaps, we shall have to rely on the less efficient fungi that fix the nitrogen for the heather and cotton grass of Highland hillsides. The nitrogen-fixing bacteria in the root nodules of pea tribe plants are well known, but they are of minor importance compared with the free-living species of the soil and in lakes, rivers and the sea, responsible for the nitrogen in the proteins of fish, apart from what we now add as pollution from chemical fertilizers washed from farm lands and in sewage.

The soil in fact is rather like the Bradford wool trade. It is full of determined individualists doing unusual jobs on a basic commodity and taking a nice little profit for their trouble. Where there's muck there's money and if we give them 'nowt' for 'owt' we shall have to do their jobs ourselves, or leave the work undone, with serious consequences for our soils. Hydroponics is impossibly complex and costly in labour and materials except for certain specialized crops like carnations under glass, or vegetables for desert airports, apart altogether from the loss of vitamins, minerals and taste substances there would be if ever we have to do the whole job of growing our own food, instead of leaving the difficult jobs to our microscopic 'under-gardeners', for they do their gardening under the soil.

If we rely on chemical fertilizers alone, our soil will run out of fuel and the chemicals will lock each other up till we have a complete shut-down. If we use chemicals and peat we shall only get the mechanical qualities of humus which hold on to moisture and our soil will be underpowered because the energy foods will be locked up by humic acids, including tannins. If we rely on comfrey and green manures *alone* we can run short on energy material as well as the moisture-holding capacity of humus. A soil needs a balance and there is no substitute for good manure and good compost.

4

Gardening Round the Year

Ever since the first gardeners watched for the 'sowing stars' to swing up at dawn over the stone circle on the hill, the gardener's year has always been a wheel, and our sowings and plantings fit between the 'spokes' as it turns through months that were once 'moonths'. Miss your place on the wheel and it turns to bring only a gap. Fill it too full and time brings a struggle to give away unwanted broad beans.

Almost every gardener could grow more by sowing less and doing this more often. In the 1830's, when William Cobbett's *Rural Rides* began and ended in a greener London, his verdict from horseback over the garden walls was 'There is not a gentleman from Fleet Street to Hammersmith who has not enough cabbage running to waste to feed a cow, and enough bolted lettuce to fatten a flock of geese.'

Now, smaller gardens waste more space and time for their owners who sow and plant too much in the spring and miss the crops that fit in to grow in winter and the empty times of summer that could nearly double the garden area in some cases. For the only vegetables and fruit that count are those you eat and enjoy; the others waste room, work and what you spend unprofitably on seeds, plants or manures.

The old farmworkers who were babies when William Cobbett rode were brought up on another cycle of cropping—the Four Course Rotation which maintained fertility without fertilizers at a far higher level than medieval strip-farming. This was clover or grass, mown for hay or grazed one year, then wheat (or in Scotland oats), then turnips, swedes or mangolds to feed to yarded bullocks treading the straw from the fat, round stacks into manure to spread at twenty tons an acre, then barley with the clover and grass sown under it to start the cycle again.

The workers who will be retiring from pioneer organic farms have

54

the eight-course rotation invented by the late F. Newman Turner and described in his *Fertility Farming* (Faber & Faber, 1951), equally firmly fixed in their minds. This was kale, roots, potatoes or a silage crop in the first year, oats or wheat undersown with a herbal ley (grass with deep-rooting herbs to reach down for minerals and bring them into circulation) which stayed down four years, to be followed by wheat, and oats in the eighth season. This modern method of farming without fertilizers, with variations to suit individual soils or even fields and market needs, is still the basis of all successful organic farming, even though its inventor is as forgotten as Jethro Tull who pioneered root husbandry and the four-course rotation.

Gardeners cannot use the long slow rotations that fit farmers, for they must take vastly more food out of smaller spaces by driving the land too hard. The top nine inches of even the field at Rothamsted that has grown wheat crop after wheat crop for over 120 years, still holds 2,700 lb. of phosphorus and 6,750 lb. of potash in every acre, so there is no fear of exhausting our soil by not adding chemical fertilizers. We have to import manures and compost material to make more *available* because our crops need the plant foods faster than the carbonic acid and other exretions from the roots of our crops, and the soil bacteria and fungi, can release them. So we cannot just graze guinea-pigs on the lawn, dig it up every five years and expect a supply of vegetables from a miniature organic farm.

The first principle behind the organic gardener's rotation is to have the longest interval space allows before potatoes or cabbage tribe crops return to the same part of the garden, to reduce the risk of potato eelworm or clubroot building up in the soil; and to avoid having any crop in the same place two years running—the object is the same, but the diseases are different.

Then it is desirable to keep the lime away from the potatoes because of the scab risk, and any animal manures away from carrots or other root crops because this makes them coarse and forky. Their job is to act as the herbs in the organic farmer's leys and to bring up more minerals, but the most efficient source of all is the comfrey bed, for its roots work five or six times as deep and it grows far faster.

It is also important to keep the ground covered in winter so that the rain will not wash away plant foods, especially on sandy soils. The action of frost in breaking down clay soils is very much less important than that of lime and good humus, and on any soil other than a clay it is complete waste. A winter green manure crop such as grazing rye, or a summer one such as *Tagetes minuta*, or a compost material crop such as sunflowers, will all lead to easier digging on clays by their root action, but of course the easiest answer is to dig as little as possible.

The most important principle is left till the last. This is to organize your crops so that as soon as something comes out there is something else to plant or sow afterwards. Some gardeners insist on 'making friends with their weeds' but one year's weed is quite literally seven years' seed, because most weeds have their seeds designed so that only a fraction germinates the first year. The rest go off like time-bombs over a period that can be fourteen years, while many, such as charlock, can stay buried for a century. Green manure crops that come up all together and finish without leaving trouble in the future are a better choice of friends, though weeds should not be overlooked as a quick and useful source of compost material.

Where there is only one bed sunny enough for outdoor tomatoes, divide it in half and grow cucumbers or runner beans on one half, even making it a 'three-course rotation'. Though these will not finish till October this is not too late to sow grazing rye and have a bulk to dig in before the crops are planted again. There is time also to sow the first radishes or plant the first lettuces in the sunny bed, and clear them before the tomatoes need the room.

Asparagus, rhubarb and comfrey beds stay out of the rotation, for they are perennials, though when they wear out they should be re-planted in another part of the garden. So should bush fruit, though gooseberries will thrive as long as twenty-five years in the same place, which is about as long as apples on modern dwarfing stocks that keep them fruiting fast and well in small gardens, can be expected to live.

Everyone who comes into an established garden should, if possible, refrain from major alterations for a whole season. This gives time to see if the fruit trees are worth their space, for there are no vegetables that thrive under trees, and hundreds of gardens are now over-crowded with the results of bargain dozens that began as miserable undersized specimens and are now robbing everything of light, air and moisture. Vegetables and trees do not go together and elderly, unprunable, unsprayable, unidentifiable apples are better out, for wall fruit and new cordons or pyramids grown as a kind of 'apple fence' or hedge, are far better value.

New gardens at least should start with a plan, to be altered as the years go by and as we learn how much is enough of everything. Those with the space and money for a deep-freeze will need some crops ready at an easy time, others will find that a good frost-proof shed for stored roots and bottled fruit, especially tomatoes, will take them through the winter when prices are highest. Breaking the bonds of convention that decree salads only with cold meat makes a huge difference to the low-cost vitamin C intake, and if an apple a day, with four milligrammes (if they run four to the pound) will keep the doctor away, two ounces of raw cabbage will repel ten of them, while the crop off half a dozen blackcurrant bushes, at fifty-seven milligrammes an ounce, should cope with the Council of the British Medical Association.

Most people rely for vitamin C on potatoes, which start off with 9 milligrammes an ounce when new and provide only 2 from March onwards as old ones. This is because we eat so many more potatoes than we do green vegetables. They have the merit of being very easy to grow, easily stored, and we do not get tired of them.

The first step in planning a new vegetable garden is to work out how many potatoes we eat in a year, for we are going to need more of these than of any other vegetable. In the 1900's when a farmworker planted over half his garden with spuds, it was taken as a sign that he was seeking another job—cashing his fertility to grow sacks of good food to tide him over till his new tied cottage garden began producing. If his employer sold a load of manure off the farm, however, *he* would be rumoured to be near bankruptcy next market day.

An average married couple without children will eat roughly 3 cwt. of potatoes a year, and it is perfectly easy to grow this amount in the equally average semi-detached garden, which will have a space about ninety feet long and twenty-eight feet wide for vegetables. Take a two-foot path down the middle and this leaves beds roughly thirteen feet wide on each side. Such gardens are usually longer than this in relation to their width but Plan 1 shows only the vegetables—the compost heap, comfrey bed and bush fruit are filling in the rest.

Start the four-course rotation with the potato bed, which is the largest single crop, and by using Duke of York potatoes, which are an early variety that will grow large for keeping till March, the first 23 feet of the 45 ft. × 13 ft. area under potatoes will be clear by early September. There will be time to plant leeks after the first potatoes are lifted for scraping early, also winter lettuce, wallflowers or other biennials, or time to sow mustard or grazing rye for green manures. Maincrops are lifted later, about October for slower, long-keeping kinds like Arran Consul, and these can only be followed by early

November-sown broad beans. Potatoes, as on the farm, take the most food, with compost before the earlies and comfrey before the main-crop, and their position on the plot should be reversed when potatoes come back to it, so that each section has some in turn. After the potatoes are lifted the ground should have its heavy liming, which will be appreciated by the crops that follow them, especially sweet williams, wallflowers and forget-me-nots raised here to go out above the bulbs in the flower garden.

Potatoes are the crop that is needed most—about three to four pounds a day for some couples without children—and occupy the greatest area. So it is possible to take some of the space for two rows of remontant-type strawberries, planted in September after the earlies and to be dug under before the land is needed for potatoes again. One row can be an early variety, such as Hummi-Grundi, the large one, and the other one to start in July and finish in October. Because this is done on a rotation there are always three small beds to pick from, and this means strawberries for tea for a long period, plus a large pick for jam. This is one of the many options open, and the lists in each section are alternatives, for very few people will want to grow everything that they could grow. After a period of trials a garden settles down to growing only what the owners enjoy.

Many allotment holders follow potatoes with the cabbage tribe, but the effectiveness of liming as preventing development of clubroot is greatest roughly a year after application, so the pea tribe should follow the potatoes. These include the beans sown after the new potatoes, which, like the early peas, will leave room and firm ground for brussels sprouts and broccoli. The root bacteria of the pea tribe crops provide nitrogen for the cabbages, and the best effect is from cutting them level with the ground and using a steel-shod dibber to plant the brussels sprouts where the peas or beans grew, without digging. Compost can go in the pea trenches, or be dug in before the beans, which also appreciate comfrey.

One of the ways in which an organic gardener avoids the addition of any nitrogen fertilizer is by growing rather more than normal of the pea tribe—not only a good succession of peas, but haricot beans to dry for the winter and hardy butter beans such as 'The Czar' or 'White Wonder' grown like runners on tall canes. The last, however, are ideal in a narrow border facing south against the house, climbing up strings to hooks in the eaves on a bungalow and swapping over with outdoor tomatoes each season.

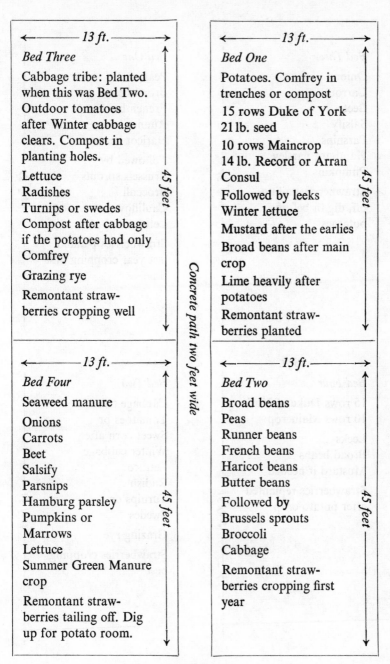

Bed Three

Cabbage tribe: planted
when this was Bed Two.
Outdoor tomatoes
after Winter cabbage
clears. Compost in
planting holes.

Lettuce
Radishes
Turnips or swedes
Compost after cabbage
if the potatoes had only
Comfrey

Grazing rye

Remontant straw-
berries cropping well

45 feet

Bed One

Potatoes. Comfrey in
trenches or compost
15 rows Duke of York
21 lb. seed
10 rows Maincrop
14 lb. Record or Arran
Consul
Followed by leeks
Winter lettuce
Mustard after the earlies
Broad beans after main
crop
Lime heavily after
potatoes
Remontant straw-
berries planted

45 feet

Concrete path two feet wide

Bed Four

Seaweed manure

Onions
Carrots
Beet
Salsify
Parsnips
Hamburg parsley
Pumpkins or
Marrows
Lettuce
Summer Green Manure
crop

Remontant straw-
berries tailing off. Dig
up for potato room.

45 feet

Bed Two

Broad beans
Peas
Runner beans
French beans
Haricot beans
Butter beans
Followed by
Brussels sprouts
Broccoli
Cabbage

Remontant straw-
berries cropping first
year

45 feet

PLAN ONE

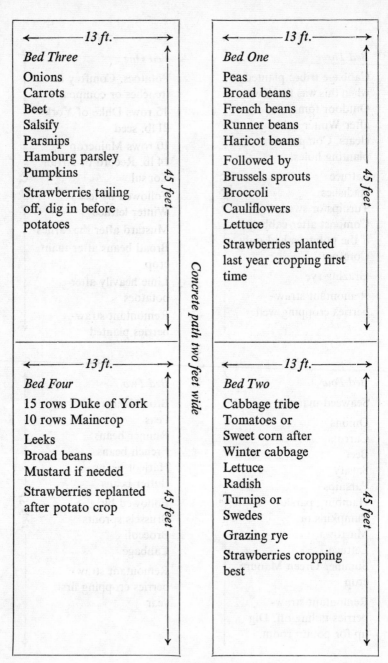

Bed Three

← 13 ft. →

Onions
Carrots
Beet
Salsify
Parsnips
Hamburg parsley
Pumpkins

Strawberries tailing
off, dig in before
potatoes

45 feet

Bed One

← 13 ft. →

Peas
Broad beans
French beans
Runner beans
Haricot beans

Followed by
Brussels sprouts
Broccoli
Cauliflowers
Lettuce

Strawberries planted
last year cropping first
time

45 feet

Concrete path two feet wide

Bed Four

← 13 ft. →

15 rows Duke of York
10 rows Maincrop

Leeks
Broad beans
Mustard if needed

Strawberries replanted
after potato crop

45 feet

Bed Two

← 13 ft. →

Cabbage tribe
Tomatoes or
Sweet corn after
Winter cabbage
Lettuce
Radish
Turnips or
Swedes

Grazing rye

Strawberries cropping
best

45 feet

PLAN TWO

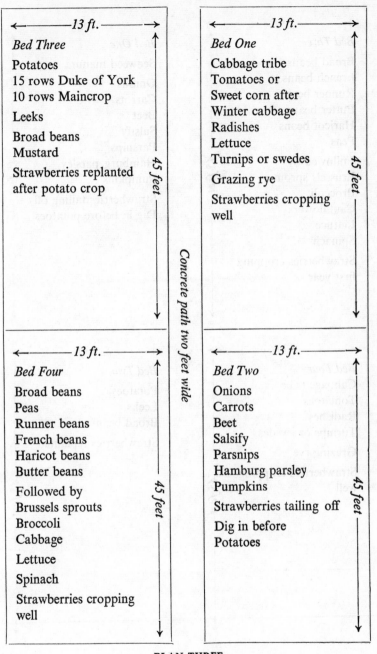

Bed Three

Potatoes
15 rows Duke of York
10 rows Maincrop

Leeks

Broad beans
Mustard

Strawberries replanted
after potato crop

← 13 ft. →

45 feet

Bed One

Cabbage tribe
Tomatoes or
Sweet corn after
Winter cabbage
Radishes
Lettuce
Turnips or swedes

Grazing rye

Strawberries cropping
well

← 13 ft. →

45 feet

Concrete path two feet wide

Bed Four

Broad beans
Peas
Runner beans
French beans
Haricot beans
Butter beans

Followed by
Brussels sprouts
Broccoli
Cabbage

Lettuce

Spinach

Strawberries cropping
well

← 13 ft. →

45 feet

Bed Two

Onions
Carrots
Beet
Salsify
Parsnips
Hamburg parsley
Pumpkins

Strawberries tailing off

Dig in before
Potatoes

← 13 ft. →

45 feet

PLAN THREE

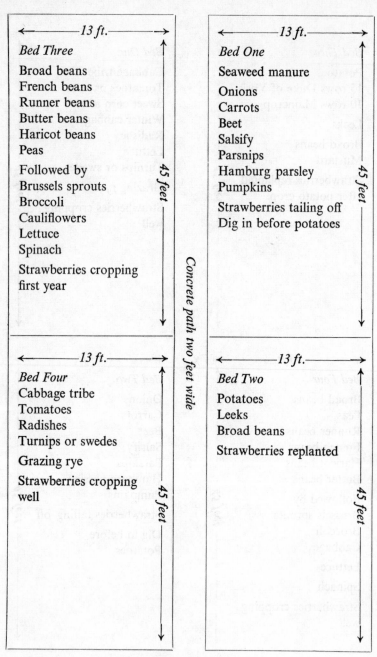

Bed Three

←——— 13 ft. ———→

Broad beans
French beans
Runner beans
Butter beans
Haricot beans
Peas

Followed by
Brussels sprouts
Broccoli
Cauliflowers
Lettuce
Spinach

Strawberries cropping
first year

45 feet

Bed One

←——— 13 ft. ———→

Seaweed manure

Onions
Carrots
Beet
Salsify
Parsnips
Hamburg parsley
Pumpkins

Strawberries tailing off
Dig in before potatoes

45 feet

Concrete path two feet wide

Bed Four

←——— 13 ft. ———→

Cabbage tribe
Tomatoes
Radishes
Turnips or swedes

Grazing rye

Strawberries cropping
well

45 feet

Bed Two

←——— 13 ft. ———→

Potatoes
Leeks
Broad beans

Strawberries replanted

45 feet

PLAN FOUR

Here also is room for spinach, picked early as a salad, or cooked for those who like it. The runner, french or haricot beans clear in time for 'January King' and spring cabbage. If the ground is going to have manure this can go on before the peas and beans, also before the potatoes, but this also increases clubroot risk; this is stressed because clubroot is the curse of all hard-cropped small gardens. Stamping it out means a nine-year rotation, and the eyes of a hawk for any shepherd's purse seedlings, for this weed (*Capsella bursa-pastoris*) belongs to the family *Cruciferae*, or the cabbage family, and also has clubroot; it is a kind of 'Typhoid Mary' of gardens and allotments that flowers and seeds almost all the year round.

When the winter and spring cabbages come off there is room to plant outdoor tomatoes with compost in the holes. It pays to grow these even though they are only ripe for salads two years out of five, because with modern easy off-the-plant ripening varieties, large quantities may be bottled for cooking in October. There is also space for lettuce (which can always be fitted in because it belongs to the beet family and does not build up diseases), radishes, which are of the cabbage tribe, and turnips or swedes. These are always tastiest when small and they fill in the fag end of the growing season, but should stay in the Brassicas (the collective word for the cabbage tribe and used hereafter) section because they are clubroot-prone. After the ground clears, grazing rye is an excellent plant-food holder, and so are winter tares, which are also Legumes (the collective word for pea and tribe plants, which will also be used in future to save space). Though these fix nitrogen they are not good weed holders and chickweed can swamp them, but this itself is also quite a good green manure to dig under in spring.

The final year is under roots and the best time to fit a seaweed manure into the rotation is in early spring before sowing. This takes some time to release its potash, and though the roots gain the benefit as they grow larger, a great deal of the effect carries over for the potatoes and the beans that follow them. Onions for all the year, with shallots if required for pickling, are the main root crop, from sets, not seed, so that there is no need to have the ground very firm and smooth, the sets just go round the rotation like the other crops. Then carrots are one of the best storable sources of vitamin A for winter, beet and parsnips for those who like them, Hamburg parsley, which has a turnip root and a parsley taste, and salsify, the deepest root of all.

Chicory can also come here for those with a suitable place to force it, and it is also a deep-rooter.

These are all selecting minerals deeply, and one of our needs is for new root vegetables for organic gardeners. Salsify is especially rich in iron and it produces a large bulk of foliage in its second year, which chickens devour. If it is grown as a biennial, with every other plant left in every other row, it should be sown in the Brassica bed and grown on into the roots.

Few people require as many assorted roots as this whole square, so there is time for lettuce to be fitted in, also pumpkins or marrows, the last two especially for those who want something to fill in and hold down weeds, also summer green manure crops. These can be the tall annual lupin with a deep root thick with nodule bacteria, or *Tagetes minuta*, as a soil-conditioner, weedkiller, compost material and, above all, an eelworm-preventing crop. For the second problem of small gardens cropped intensively is potato eelworm, which is entirely distinct from *wireworm*, the light brown larvae of the click beetle. It is a microscopic soil pest that again would need a far longer period without potatoes if it were cured by rotations (as it is on the farm) than the ordinary gardener can afford.

At least the area which had the carrots and onions on should be left dug through the winter, though grazing rye could be sown after the lupins to dig in before the potatoes. The carrot bed especially could be dug with profit again in January, to give the birds, especially the robins, an extra chance at the chrysalids of the carrot fly. Lawn mowings between the rows are a good preventative, and these too turn under, and they can also go on between other root crops excepting onions, as a weed-suppressor.

Under this rotation only a quarter of the ground is left uncropped in winter, and here it should be dug only three-quarter-fork depth, what used to be called 'bastard trenching', not the deep-spade digging of the past. The object is not only to put the green manure under to decay, but to use the birds as pest-controllers. The place where the green manure crop grew should not be dug a second time, as the decayed material must not be brought to the surface.

The onions are moved round the garden in order to avoid white rot, grey mould and onion thrip, while onion fly rarely attacks a set-raised crop. If it does, then several diggings through the winter will bare the tiny pupae that robin's eyes are specially keen at spotting. Most gardeners know their local pair of robins who always arrive

1. Compost Bin showing brick air
   channels for bottom ventilation and
   removable board front.

2. Lawrence D. Hills with a ten-foot-
   high plant of *Tagetes minuta*, the
   compost material plant that kills
   weeds.

3. Mustard sown in new gardens and dug under in September defends potatoes against wireworm.

4. Comfrey, Bocking 14 provides 4–5 cuts of 'instant compost' a season for all potash-hungry crops.

when any digging is done. There is nothing for them in subsoil, so dig shallow for bird-feeding and pest-clearing. Violet ground beetles and devil's-coach-horse beetles clear large quantities of these pupae and should never be squashed.

Rotating the strawberries is also a means of avoiding disease and pests, and for replanting after the potatoes runners from the Brassica section bed should be chosen, planted always on a different strip of it, ideally in September after the 'Duke of York' (or 'Epicure', 'Sharpe's Express', 'Stormont Dawn' or 'Pentland Beauty', any good early or second-early variety that will also keep) are lifted. Cutting out the strawberries of course gives more room for any other crop that the rotation squeezes hard, or for extra green manure.

This rotation is a specimen only to illustrate the principles, and there are other possibilities. The garden could be divided into three sections, each thirty feet long and including the beds on both sides, to allow planting half a hundredweight of early potatoes which would yield, left in to grow large, between 4 and 5 hundredweight for a larger family, and give time to plant leeks and Brassicas after them and sow broad beans on the second section. The third one would take the Legumes and the roots and outdoor tomatoes, and the ground would be left manured and dug through the winter, with compost also on the potato section, and seaweed meal before the roots.

This three-course rotation cuts out the green manures and the strawberries, probably also some of the roots to fit the needs of growing families, but the first step to a healthy diet is teaching one's children to *try* to enjoy a wide range of foods that change round the year. The mother who tells her friends in front of a three- to five-year-old that 'she doesn't like anything but fish fingers, peas and ice cream' is giving her child a serious physical handicap which is all too common in this age of parental diffidence and stupidity.

Those who have more room but also a labour problem should still 'concentrate' the cabbage tribe and insist that their paid gardener does not grow unwanted cabbages everywhere. Run the rows lengthways instead of across for easy cultivation with a Merry Tiller or other garden rotary hoe, follow the potatoes with rye and then grow onions from sets or pumpkins as crops to sell to a wholefood shop, or simply take in an extra square for a green manure or sunflowers as a compost material crop, for these take least work. Potatoes are less laborious than a lawn because their cultivation can be mechanized even on a garden scale.

Gardening Round the Year

Those who are near enough to a wholefood shop, or an organic grower selling potatoes, or can fetch hundredweight bagfuls by car, can reduce their crop to a few earlies of course, and increase their space for other vegetables or even bush fruits; but potatoes are the key item in a healthy diet, and the crop in which organic flavour shows most. A good storage shed is a real investment, of far more value than a motor mower to any young couple, because it makes possible buying cheaply in bulk; for few organic growers will bother with less than a hundredweight, and wholefood shops must put up the pound price to cover overheads.

The tightest rotation of all was used by the farmworker with a large family, or the unemployed allotment holders of Jarrow in the 1930's. This was potatoes on one side of the garden, and everything else on the other, swapping over every season. The potato was always a quick-maturing second-early to allow time for cabbage and leeks to follow through the winter, but the major part of the potato side would be followed with mustard. This was not for its green manure value, for there were still enough horses then apart from the miner's pit ponies to provide good dung for fetching, but as an eelworm preventative.

As early potatoes are cleared, knock the ground level with the fork and broadcast mustard, raking to cover it and leaving it to grow with no more trouble, for birds do not eat it. The seed is cheap and an ounce covers between four and six square yards. The sowing aims at roughly a seed to the inch, not the thickness of a salad crop. As mustard seed stays good for four years it pays to buy by the pound and use the remains next year. It can be fitted in after any vegetable crop that is going to leave even as little as four weeks' spare time, though the best season is always the eight to ten weeks between early potatoes and late-planted Brassicas. The trampling as you work across the crop is sufficient to break down the two-foot height of an eight- to ten-week crop, which should always go under when first flowers start to form. If you leave it until it is tall and stemmy or dig it in later than September, you have the troubles that make green-manuring unpopular.

The crop must be rotavated or dug in when it is green, very sappy and rich in nitrogen. It will have worked fast to gather the nitrogen harvested by the soil bacteria in summer and other plant foods, which wash from bare soil and normally feed weeds that are specialized natural fertility economizers. Because of the way in which it is sown it comes up in a solid sheet and grows taller and faster. It does a more

66

efficient job, and as it is turned under before seeding it is a 'weed' under the control of the gardener, with the superiority of cultivated vegetables over their wild parents.

If it goes under when the nitrogen is in the form of protein (mustard is a good fodder) and when the soil is warm it has time to decay like a small thin compost heap in the soil itself. Dig it in too late, or when the stems are too woody to rot easily, and it must finish decaying in the spring. This will rob the soil of nitrogen, not for so long as sawdust will, but for quite long enough, for when stemmy and seeding it will be 50:1 or more, not 28:1, with time to do this rotting job on its 'savings'. It adds very little humus compared with compost or manure, but this is well worth having, spread ready for digging, and though it has added nothing it has economized plant foods.

From the work of Dr. C. L. Duddington (author of *The Friendly Fungi*, Faber & Faber) we know that a crop of mustard after early potatoes hardens the skins of the cysts that hold between 90 to 500 potato eelworms (*Heterodera rostochiensis*) so that these hatch too late to do much harm to a second-early crop. The farmworkers and allotment holders knew that mustard helped adjust the 'Potato Sickness' which shows as small pale leaves, stunted plants with feeble root systems, and tubers small and few. Many were able to get away with that alternate-year rotation for years, but as soon as someone plants main crops there is a serious attack. Cropping only one year in four and using mustard as a green manure at least once in the rotation does keep this pest in check.

Always dig with care to remove all small potatoes or 'travellers', for these keep eelworms feeding and increasing during the rest period; and pull up the weed black nightshade (*Solanum nigrum*) for this is an alternative eelworm diet. Care in digging up these left-in little potatoes, which are awkward weeds in other crops, also helps to control potato blight (*Phytophthora infestans*) and if everyone dug up all 'ground keepers' we might well break the infection chain. The best way round this one is to plant resistant varieties, or again to use second-earlies that are finished before the worst attack.

If 'potato sickness' appears to be a serious threat in your garden, the best organic remedy (the cysts are chemical-proof and there is no really effective chemical cure) is another green manure crop, which is more expensive than mustard and occupies the ground longer so it should only be used to cure eelworm or where its weedkilling properties are required. This is Tagetes. We owe our potatoes, tomatoes, french and runner beans to the Chavins of pre-Inca Peru, and all these crops shared eelworms with local forest trees and to some extent with each other. The Chavins grew their potatoes in irrigated terraces in the Andes, among other sites, often for a hundred years without a break. They sowed the 'sacred weed' at intervals, and this was *Tagetes minuta*, one of the thirty species now in cultivation of this race that includes our French marigold (*T. patula*) and African marigold (*T. erecta*). It was most unfortunately named by Linnaeus from the small size of its *flowers* which are tiny creamy-yellow stars in heads in October; for it can grow ten feet high. It is a half-hardy annual like the bedding Tagetes and those who have a cold frame or greenhouse can sow in early March and prick out into boxes for planting in April or early May when the frost risk ends, a foot apart each way. Otherwise sow very thinly in furrows a foot apart and half an inch deep in April and thin to about four inches apart. Hoe to put the seedlings ahead of the weeds once. Then leave them to grow between four and ten feet high, cutting them down in October for compost material, leaving the stumps in. Transplanted specimens may have stems over an inch thick and these may need smashing before they will compost.

The eelworms, shut up inside their cysts, 'know' that potatoes have been planted because they have a detector mechanism that can tell the difference between the root secretions that mean food and those of unsuitable plants. Experiments at Rothamsted to wake the eelworms up only to starve by using synthetic 'false alarm' secretions failed after many years of work, because the substances were too complex. The evidence is that the Tagetes' secretions act by destroying or deadening the sensitivity of the detector mechanism, so the eelworms cannot tell potato secretions from those of parsnips, and 'oversleep'. The result of a successful sowing or planting is a good crop of potatoes, even though the eelworm count is only slightly reduced. The ordinary bedding Tagetes have an effect which varies with the variety, but only on several non-cyst-forming eelworms, notably *Pratylenchus*, which is not a problem in Britain.*

The five root secretions of *T. minuta* are all thiophenes, substances containing sulphur, which are also found in other members of the

* A full technical account of the study of Tagetes by the University of Swansea, and Wageningen in Holland (to which goes credit for the original discovery) and of the work of the Henry Doubleday Research Association in developing their garden uses would be out of place here, but full details are available, especially to those qualified to do further work in the fascinating field of plant-root secretions.

order Compositae (the daisy family) to which Tagetes belongs. They also have an effect on certain weeds, which has been observed before (see *The Biology of Weeds* by P. Martin, B. Rademacher, G. Grummer and H. Beyer, Blackwell Scientific Publications Ltd., 1960) in flax where a cruciferous plant, *Camelina sativa* which is rather like charlock, with the charming name of 'Gold of Pleasure', kills a circle of the crop round itself.

What is now known as 'The *Tagetes* Effect' is strongest against ground elder (*Aegopodium podagraria*), also called 'Goutweed' because the Romans introduced it as a cure for gout, next against bindweed, *Convolvulus sepium*, and to a lesser extent couch grass, *Agropyrum repens*. There have been cases where ground elder has been merely cut down with shears and strong plants about six inches high of Tagetes have been planted direct into the soil a foot apart each way and have produced a complete kill. The more certain procedure is to clear the surface and dig out the worst of the surface roots to give the plants a good start on the weed.

Sowing as for combating eelworm has also been successful, but strong plants put out and watered till they get away appear to be the most effective. They can be sown thinly in the open in early April and transplanted in May, like cabbage plants raised by those who have no frame. Only those who have suffered from these weeds on a considerable scale will appreciate the surprising ease with which they can get rid of these enemies of every gardener. It is also possible to sow broadcast as a very thin 'lawn', but this costs more for seed.

A break under Tagetes is valuable for destroying eelworm, but it is valuable as a weapon against these three weeds only and as a trial shot against any other perennial weed. It will not kill thistles, mare's tail, oxalis or celandine.

With time and space to spare from April onwards there is scope for a crop of lupins which are bird- and rabbit-proof; they grow more bulk to make humus than mustard does, and without its disadvantage of sharing clubroot with the cabbage family. The bacteria in the lumps on the roots gather nitrogen from the air to add to hungry soils.

The seed of *Lupinus angustifolius*, the blue field lupin with short slim spikes, or *L. albus*, the white one that makes more show, costs about 5p an ounce to sow 75 feet of rows a foot apart, but free seed for next year is easily saved. Leave a row sown before mid-May to flower and ripen, so that the fat pods can be picked as they begin to split.

Gardening Round the Year

Sow between April and July in inch-deep furrows with six inches between seeds. They quickly grow to a 'forest' three or four feet high that kills annual weeds by light starvation. Wait until the first buds show and dig them in before those open, so that the stems are soft enough to decay underground. Crush them with the roller if they grow too tall to tread down like mustard. They chop easily with the spade, for tucking into the trench bottoms. Leaving them longer in order to enjoy the flowers means that the stems get too tough for digging and a compost heap is needed to decay them, but they grow up to a hundredweight of good material from an ounce of seed, and add lasting humus to sappy weeds and lawn mowings.

Summer green manure crops all need time and take up room, for we have to forgo the crops that would have grown food in their space. The only time when most gardens are able to grow green manure without gardeners begrudging the room is in winter, and at this season the best of all is rye; not the type that makes rye crisps, but a new Hungarian variety, 'Lovazpatoni', bred to grow winter grazing for cattle in a climate colder than Britain's. Rake the dug ground smooth and sow like a thin lawn at the rate of one to two ounces a square yard between August and the end of October. The earlier it is sown the faster it is up, but even from an October sowing after main-crop potatoes, it will be two feet high by April, keeping ahead of the weeds in mild winters.

Tread it down and dig it in, gaining not only the humus from the foliage which will be at the leafy, high-protein stage, when there is nitrogen enough to decay it without trouble, but still more from the web of roots. It is an excellent nitrogen tamer and it can be sown on level ground that has merely been raked and covered with enough dried sludge to hide the seed from the birds. It is as attractive to them as grass seed and it can be swirled in paraffin like peas, or soaked with Morkit to keep them off long enough for it to get away. Those who can use a scythe or have a rough grass-cutter can cut it twice for compost during the summer and dig in only the humus from the roots in August.

Another good winter green manure is winter tares, which has the advantage of pea-tribe nitrogen fixing, but is less good as a weed smotherer. Sow this between August and October to dig under in March or April, or March or May to turn in in August or the autumn. One ounce of the large seeds sows about 80 feet of furrows six inches apart and with three inches between seeds.

70

Rabbits love them, so the plot should be wired in if there are any about. They will leave grazing rye alone till the really hard weather and then they slaughter it. With both it can pay to leave some rows for seed and save your own, for they have so little kinship with anything else in the garden that there is no crossing, and the next generation will breed true.

The cheapest and fastest crop for growing compost material on vacant land is sunflowers, the sort of seed sold cheaply by pet shops for parrot food, grown usually in southern Europe. The seed is striped, not plain like that in the 13p packets of garden varieties. Sow seeds half an inch deep and a foot apart each way in staggered rows. This is of course far too close for normal showy sunflowers, but you are growing compost material, not flowers or seeds, and packed like this they will suppress annual weeds. When the stems are an inch thick, pull them up, shake off the soil and pile them on the heap. If there is time before the next crop sow another batch, for between March and July they will grow a bulk in six weeks, but if they are left in they grow too woody to compost.

Many fortunate gardeners have weedy areas near their gardens that can be cut for compost, always before the weeds flower. Nettles are an excellent source of minerals and very good compost material, with up to 7·7 per cent carbohydrates and 5·5 per cent protein in the young growth. This is why many gardeners gather them to cook like spinach in spring when green stuff is scarce after hard winters.

Divide your nettle area into three sections and mow one with a rough grass-cutter every fortnight through the season. This type of mower keeps you entirely unstuck, but shears or a sickle will do as well with care. Rake the cut nettles, after leaving them twenty-four hours to wilt and lose some of their sting, on to a cut-open sack, fold it round them and carry the hoard to the compost heap. In two years your compost material mine will be worked out and your nettles will be dead, with their yellow roots as tough as wire ropes releasing their hoarded plant foods for your crops. This is by far the best way of killing nettles and bracken, but it is useless to allow either to seed or to build tough fibres. Cut and cut again at least three times in the growing season and you will exhaust the roots and kill off the weeds while gaining good compost material.

5

Vegetables One by One

The pests and diseases of every vegetable from Artichokes to Turnips are given under each alphabetical account, for the beginner does not start by looking up 'fleabeetle'—he looks up radishes, for something is eating holes in the radish leaves. Therefore this book has no separate 'Pests and Diseases' chapter. Some of the remedies, however, are equally useful against a number of pests and to save repeating every time, the safe pesticides are mentioned at the beginning of the chapter. Remedies that apply to one crop only will be found in the account of the crop in question.

Any good garden shop should sell derris and pyrethrum. There are many makes of both and mixtures of the two are stronger than either separately, capable of killing caterpillars and a range of pests including aphides of all types listed on the tin or bottle. They are sometimes mixed with lindane and other organo-chlorine compounds and these should be refused. Derris is available as a dust that is most effective against the fleabeetle which eats holes in the leaves of Brassica plants and radishes. As it began as a Malayan fish poison, do not let it trickle into the goldfish pond. If you keep bees and have to spray anything in flower, use pyrethrum in the evening and it will have killed your aphides and be harmless by the time your bees start work in the morning.

Quassia has the advantage of not killing ladybirds which are eating your aphides, the advantage of cheapness, and the advantage of sparing bees when it is sprayed against apple sawfly or raspberry beetle caterpillars at blossom time. It consists of chips of wood of *Picrasma quassioides* which keep dry for years in a tin, and can only be ordered through a good chemist, because although it is still used by District Nurses to get rid of lice in children's hair, it is rarely used by gardeners. Boil four ounces in a gallon of water for half an hour, pour off the yellow liquid when cool and dilute with three parts of water for an all-round garden spray against aphides and small caterpillars. Quassia tastes very bitter and should not be used on leaf crops that are going to be eaten within a fortnight.

The cheapest powerful pesticide is nicotine, which is now difficult to buy, but is easily made by boiling four ounces of non-filter-tip cigarettes (or half a pound of filter-tips) in a gallon of water for half an hour. Strain the clear brown liquid through a nylon stocking and it will keep several weeks in a stoppered bottle. Dilute with two parts of water to one of nicotine for an anti-caterpillar spray or for anything hard to kill. Water it along rows of young peas and beans when their leaves are eaten out of shape by the pea and bean weevil, a tiny beetle that is clay-coloured and hides under clods so that you rarely see it. Mix a quart of the solution with an ounce of soft soap or soapflakes and spray on spring cabbage plants, broccoli and late brussels sprouts in the autumn to kill mealy cabbage aphides, cabbage white fly and cabbage moth caterpillars before they burrow into the hearts. This strength kills celery and chrysanthemum leaf miners.

If you have a Euonymus hedge, syringe it thoroughly with nicotine in November to kill the hibernating caterpillars of the small ermine moth which are the curse of these hedges, and the winter stage of the blackfly on broad beans. These also winter on Viburnums (all species), and if everyone sprayed these we might wipe out this pest. Squirt nicotine hard into the gnarled bark at the base of old rose bushes in November because it is here that greenfly hibernate.

Non-smokers can obtain ashtray emptyings from cinemas and public houses, and the best way to keep free nicotine is as cigarette ends, for though a liquid can be drunk by mistake, no one is going to mistake a tin full of fag ends for sweets. Do not spray it on anything you are going to eat within a fortnight, but wait for the rain to wash it off, and label any ready-boiled POISON. Though nicotine costs nothing when made from boiled cigarette ends, and is powerful, keep it for weevils, large caterpillars and anything tough, wash your hands after using, and remember it is a poison. It is harmless to ladybirds and their larvae, and hoverfly larvae.

For greenfly on roses use something weaker. Cut up three pounds of rhubarb leaves, boil for half an hour in three quarts of water, and strain. When cool dissolve an ounce of soapflakes in a quart of water, mix the two and use as a general spray for any aphis. It can also be made with three pounds of elder leaves, and this mixture was used in the past as a spray against mildew on roses and lettuces.

The best slug-trap is a soup plate, dog drinking-trough or anything of china, wide and shallow, sunk level with the ground and filled with a mixture of equal parts of beer and water sweetened with a dessertspoonful of Barbados sugar to the pint. This can be cleared of dead slugs with one quick swish of a broom and the trap refilled from a can of the mixture, for one trap makes little impression—you need a dozen. Your local will provide a bucketful of beer from the contents of the drip-tray for nothing, and this is quite good enough for slugs. The object of using beer instead of the milk often recommended is to stop cats from drinking the mixture, and though hedgehogs may take it, modern beer diluted to half strength is not enough to intoxicate them. The sugar attracts to the traps codling, tortrix and yellow under-wing moths, which are responsible for the cutworm or surface cater-pillars. The dead slugs are not poisonous to birds or anything else that may eat them.

Hedgehogs are excellent garden-pest controllers, eating anything vegetarian they find creeping about at night. They eat large quantities of these cutworms, slugs and millipedes (the black creature that makes a flat coil when picked up and that eats holes in potatoes and lily bulbs). They ignore the 'ninety-nine bump' centipede (*Lithobius forficatus*) which is flattened, chestnut-brown and a good slug-egg eater and will eat carnivorous creatures if starved into it, devouring our foes and sparing our friends for the same reason that we eat buck in Africa rather than hyenas—they prefer the taste. Birds have beaks and, so far as we know, little sense of taste, while frogs and toads snap up everything that moves, ignoring flavour.*

Millipedes can be trapped by bending perforated zinc round a broom handle and sewing the edges and the bottom together with wire to make a cylinder, or by punching the sides and bottom of a tall tin full of holes. Fill either trap with potato or carrot peelings and bury upright in the border with a wire handle sticking out. Lift by this handle about once a week and dump the contents in strong nicotine or throw in the run to give the chickens a treat. This was the standard garden remedy sixty years ago, but it needs traps enough to make an impression on the pests.

This type of trap is also effective for wireworms in small quantities, but there can be too many to trap in gardens new cleared from grass-

* See *Operation Tiggywinkle*, H.D.R.A., 18p.

land, neglected allotments or any place in which ground has been left undisturbed. Their favourite food is potatoes, the usual first crop in new gardens, so the beginner should keep a lookout for the slim light brown larvae about a half to three-quarters of an inch long with a bunch of legs at each end. If many are found it means sowing peas, beans, kale and spinach in the first season, crops which they do not attack. Another remedy is to sow mustard and dig it under when it is just about to start flowering between July and October, even two crops if there is time for them. The click beetle (*Agriotes lineatus*) lays eggs in grass roots and its larvae take three to five years to become beetles, the time depending on available food. The first two years are spent as a small white creature feeding on decaying vegetation, and only the last three as the wireworms we know. Digging in the mustard feeds them so well that the majority will finish in a single season and fly off as beetles to lay eggs in grassland rather than our newly cultivated garden.

In country districts it is possible to buy linseed cake, which is rather biscuity grey flakes, and these, broken up with the flat of a spade into approximately inch squares and dug in not deeper than three inches at the rate of four to eight ounces a square yard, will do the same job. This should be carried out between early March and the end of May, or between July and October, the two feeding periods for wireworms. Timing the feed early in these seasons produces the best 'drive away'. Linseed cake can be buried in borders to 'feed them away', but here trapping is best for it reduces the local population which may be migrating from eggs laid in your lawn. Ignore suggestions in gardening books and periodicals about killing with 'whizzed naphthalene' or 'naphthalene' which is now unobtainable.

With average luck and good compost, very few pesticides will ever be needed, but because garden shops are constantly replacing old-fashioned remedies with newer and deadlier substitutes, these do-it-yourself remedies are stressed. If you can buy nicotine, by all means do; derris and pyrethrum are still on sale unadulterated at the time of writing, but there may well come a time when the only way to obtain non-cumulative poisons will be by making your own. There is, of course, a far greater profit for someone in a ready-made tin or bottle, than in a pound of quassia chips.

The vegetables are now dealt with in alphabetical order.

Artichokes, Globe

The globe artichoke is a glorified thistle with large leaves and flowers on four-foot stems that last in water for those who are willing to sacrifice some of the delicious eating buds for unusual flower arrangements.

Offsets for March, April or May planting cost about 15p each. Plant them two feet apart in deep trowel holes, with four feet between rows, and keep them well away from trees or hedges, because these rob them of the moisture they need. Dig in plenty of compost and 1 lb. a square yard of bone meal, because this is a permanent crop staying up to five years in one place. On sandy soils add 1 lb. a square yard of hoof and horn as though planting a tree. Their growing points should just peep through well-firmed soil. Water the shoots generously in a dry first summer and keep them free from weeds by hoeing.

Clean up their dead foliage every November and cover the bed with about six inches of dead leaves as protection against frost. The globe artichoke (*Cynara scolymus*) is a North African thistle and left-in root fragments from old beds die from cold, unlike missed tubers of the hardy North American 'Jerusalem' artichoke, which grow like weeds.

Dead leaves blow loose, so it is a good idea to surround the bed with 18-inch-high wire netting, folding it in half, or cutting this narrowest width down the middle. It can be stapled to short posts. This trick, incidentally, is also suitable for rhubarb beds and has a mild forcing effect in spring. Leaves raked off in April are half-made leaf-mould, ready for digging deeply into sandy soils or stacking for autumn use.

Spread manure along the artichoke rows every spring: 2 oz. of dried blood or dried poultry manure a yard is an alternative tonic. The first crop should average five 'globes' a plant, with many more as the bed matures, not counting the small side-bulbs.

Pick the latter when they are the size of pullets' eggs and fry them halved, or boil them whole with a little water. They can then be eaten like brussels sprouts. If smaller ones are preferred, take out the middle bud so that more 'globes' will grow. Italians do this and then bottle them in olive oil.

Gather both sizes before the bud scales start opening and cut the stems six inches from the ground when all the 'globes' have been picked so that the side shoots grow a second crop. If too many 'globes' are ready for picking at the same time, standing the stems in water will keep them fresh for up to a fortnight.

Start thinking of replacements in the April before the fifth cutting summer and dig up strong shoots from between the rows, slicing them off with a growing section of the parent root. Plant them like bought offsets. By then you will be acquiring a stock.

With only 6 milligrams per 100 grams of vitamin C, against 60 for strawberries, and 30 micrograms of riboflavin compared with 70, they are poor value as a substitute for the strawberry bed in the rotation, but they are easy enough for those who like them, and a good luxury vegetable for an organic gardener to grow commercially, provided that he makes sure of his market first.

Artichokes, Jerusalem

These roots, like small potatoes with knobs on, have nothing to do with Israel.

When New York was New Amsterdam, a colonist from the village of Ter Neusen sent tubers home to his gardening vicar in 1613, and Pastor Hondius raised the stock that reached London about 1617 as 'Ter Neusen artichokes', and became more popular then than the new but relatively tasteless potato. They were sold as a novelty in seventeenth-century London, and Ter Neusen became distorted to 'Jerusalem'. John Parkinson (1569–1629) named them 'Potatoes of Canada' in our first real gardening book, before Italians in 1666 began calling sunflowers 'girasole' (Girra-so-lay), which started the usual explanation of the 'Jerusalem'.

Plant them in January or February, first digging in a barrow-load of manure or compost: eighteen inches apart, in six-inch-deep trowel holes with three feet between the rows. There are about thirty plants in 7 lb. of tubers, enough to fill three 15-ft. rows to give, with good manuring, about 56 lb. for eating, which is roughly the weight of early potatoes you could grow in the same space.

Ridge them like potatoes when they are a foot high and in draughty gardens, where they make a useful summer windbreak, put a post at each end and one in the middle of each row with strings each side to hold the six-foot stems straight. In November these are cut for compost material or to store, with the leaves stripped off, to dry and harden as flower stakes. The tubers can be lifted then like potatoes, but as they are hardy they are nicer if left in and dug as they are needed until March.

Their nutritional value, including vitamins, is very much the same as that of a potato, but they have roughly seven times as much calcium. Their drawback is that we should get tired of the smoky taste if we ate them as often as we do the potato, which goes with everything and produces a heavier yield.

In March dig the ground carefully, for small ones are worse than left-in potatoes, but as American artichokes are a kind of sunflower they miss virus, blight and disease, so the stock lasts for years. Pick out the smoothest-skinned and least-knobbed tubers of pullet's egg size for replanting. If any have creatures on them looking like grey 'greenfly' this is root aphis, their one pest, and the remedy is to move the bed, replanting with creature-free tubers washed in nicotine which is powerful enough also to kill their eggs.

Those who only like artichokes occasionally can leave the bed in the most convenient place, which is less trouble but means a far lower yield, and treat it mainly as a source of compost material, digging up a few tubers when they are needed. It can be killed out by cutting it four times a year, but two cuts a season are tolerated.

Asparagus

The 'Russell' of asparagus is Kidner K.B.F., a pure strain in which every stem is a beauty, planted as a year-old crown. Allow eighteen inches between them in single rows four feet apart when deciding how many to order for March delivery. For early cutting they need soil sun-warmed; choose a sunny and sheltered place and dig it several times to remove all perennial weed roots. Then dig again to turn under a good barrowload of manure to every three square yards and leave the surface rough through the winter.

Next February scatter 4 oz. of fish meal and 8 oz. of wood ashes to the square yard, dig again to get rid of still-surviving weed roots and take out trenches six inches deep and eight inches wide for the rows. In March set out the octopus-like plants with eighteen inches between the middles and the roots spread out. Put back three inches of soil worked and firmed between the roots (with fingers, not feet) and leave the trench as a depression to hold rain or watering if summer is dry.

Keep weeds hoed, never going deeper than two inches, and use the space between rows for radish and lettuce in the first season when the plants grow only ferny foliage. Cut this down in November and clean up the weeds by forking not deeper than four inches.

When March comes again repeat the fish meal and wood ashes, for asparagus is a seashore plant and enjoys the salt, and dig a shallow 'U' four inches deep and two feet wide between the rows, to make the roots go deep in the middles instead of growing awkwardly shallow. Heap the soil by the side of and not over the plants to make another water-holding dip for a summer of fern-growing, raking it back to the middles at the November cut-down-and-clean. This time cover the plants with a two inches thick, one foot wide strip of good manure.

After fish meal again in the following March, heap the soil from between the rows four inches high in ridges over the plants. When the shoots are five to six inches above ground, cut them four inches below the surface, scraping away and replacing the ridge soil. Leave the fern to grow after five weeks' cutting this first season, and after eight weeks' cutting in others, always finishing before 21st June to allow next year's crop to grow.

Every autumn fork the ridges back to the middles to give covering soil, replacing with a coating of manure, ideally deep litter to supply the phosphorus asparagus loves, and because it will be weed-free. This can replace the fish meal which is needed as a quick feed for its early years, and can be replaced with spent mushroom compost every third season to avoid over-feeding.

Cutting the fern down in November to compost removes any eggs of the asparagus beetle, the only pest. The grubs are dirty-grey and hump-backed and will be found eating the shoots from May till the autumn, pupating in the bed, and hatching into about four generations a season. Spray with a derris-pyrethrum mixture while you are cutting the shoots for eating, and afterwards use nicotine.

Those who wish to raise their own asparagus from seed can buy 'Connover's Colossal' easily; it is a mixture widely varying in productivity like all seedling strains. Sow it thinly in furrows an inch deep and a foot apart in April, thinning the seedlings to nine inches between plants. Let them stay until the third spring after sowing and pick the shortest and most thickset plants, because these will grow the most shoots for cutting.

An asparagus bed is a permanent garden feature providing a luxury for those who like it. It is not a source of food and vitamins to compare with so many other vegetables needing less room and making less work.

Beans, Broad

The widest broad beans, for spring sowing and a fine flavour, are the 'Windsors' Green or White. The shortest is the 'Sutton', which grows foot-high bushes for windy gardens, and the hardiest and narrowest, for October and November sowing and picking before the peas, are the 'Longpod' varieties.

The beans that beanfeasters ate with the bacon and boiled beef of Old England were not the modern butter beans, which came with french and runners from Peru following the conquest of that country, but these 'Longpod' broad beans, which supplied the concentrated vegetable protein that made horses friskily 'full of beans'.

There are about 200 seeds in a pint of broad beans, enough for 150 feet of double row, so a half-pint packet is sufficient for most gardens. The seed keeps for a second season, but there is a risk of gaps in the rows if it is kept longer. Any seed that is over-age can be soaked for twenty-four hours and cooked in winter stews.

The flavour of dry broad beans is different, and once their skins have been removed by putting them in an electric liquidizer or by rubbing them through a sieve, they make excellent brown Windsor soup. The best kind to sow in extra rows for harvesting as a year's supply of Old English butter beans is 'Fenland Green Longpod' or its white-seeded companion, which combines the Windsor taste with hardiness.

Because beans are potash-greedy and the chocolate spot fungus attacks them when they are underfed, dig in a barrow-load of compost and 1 lb. of wood ashes to every four square yards before sowing. Sow in three-inch-deep trowel holes eight inches apart along the garden line. Move the line eight inches down the garden and sow a second row with the beans facing the gaps. These pairs of staggered rows support each other, and should have thirty-inch picking room between them.

When the young shoots are up three inches, heap the soil round the stems in three-inch-high ridges, so that if there is a savage spring the beans can shoot again from the base. Take out the growing points with about eight inches of stem when the plants are three feet tall and remove the side shoots for the earliest cropping. The 'Sutton' needs merely pinching in its single rows of low 'bushes' that bristle with pods.

5. Pea trenches can be dug in advance and filled with kitchen wastes to make underground compost heaps.

6. A cardboard box, painted black to trap more sun heat makes a fine cheap 'cloche' to force mustard and cress.

7. Cabbage, brussels sprouts and cauliflowers are all best sown and transplanted to waiting beds.

8. When their room is released by earlier crops, the cabbages can be moved large, and with room for lettuce between them.

Vegetables One by One

Clear whole rows for eating in May and June, cutting off the plants for good compost material. Follow up with brussels sprouts which appreciate the nitrogen from the bean roots and their undug soil. When the pods of the remaining beans turn black and split, they are ready for podding. They will keep up to five years without loss of flavour.

This autumn sowing usually misses the 'blight' or blackfly, the bean's worst enemy, because it is toughened by winter and you have removed the young growth the 'blight' needs to start on; but March sowings for July and August picking usually suffer. In the evening, when the bees are asleep, spray with liquid pyrethrum, which will have killed the blackfly and lost its poison by morning, when the bees will be on the blossom again. Broad beans picked small and eaten pods and all are delicious, and from the November sowing are ready well before the early peas.

Beans, Butter

The butter bean of grocer's shops is the lima bean of the U.S.A. which is not hardy in Britain. There are a number of crosses with the runner bean that are fast enough to ripen and dry in Britain, and the best is 'The Czar', which can be grown up a house on strings like a runner bean and is especially recommended for screw-eyes screwed in behind the eaves of a bungalow. Sow them in May as a rest for part of the tomato border, and leave them to hang and die off, cutting the strings about October. Compost the haulm, string and all, and shell the pods as if they were haricots to store in the same way.

They are smaller than bought butter beans but very much nicer and need less soaking before cooking, for our climate does not get them dead dry. Though they can be grown on bamboos like runner beans, they are best as an easy screen for a garage or shed, with white flowers in profusion and a mass of pods that can be picked to eat as runners if required early in the season. When either butter or runner beans are sown in a narrow bed against a house or fence, they are going to need watering. Water them always at the root, or with sun-warmed water, for (as we have seen) the shock of hosing them straight from the mains with cold will make them drop their blossom. Remember that all beans need potash and appreciate any comfrey that can be spared, as well as wood ashes.

Butter beans are a good source of thiamine, 525 micrograms per

F
81

100 grams, roughly the same as lentils with 500, but higher in riboflavin with 700 against 315–400 micrograms for lentils. Vegetarians and vegans rely largely on nut and bean protein, and with 18 per cent, butter beans, which can be grown easily in any garden, are a useful standby and an easy crop, since no picking is involved till the final cut down. It is possible to run two years beans and one year tomatoes in a narrow house-side border, but permanent bean beds with metal posts in concrete can run into trouble.

Though there have been many attempts to breed a soya bean that is hardy in Britain, none are much better than curiosities, with two seeds in a pod, a poor yield and no flavour to speak of. However wonderful something may be in terms of nutrition, it means a waste of space if no one likes it.

Beans, French and Haricot

French beans can be sown early in April under cloches, but it is the later sowings from the end of May until early July, fitted in after other crops clear that are the best value in small gardens. Two twelve- to thirteen-foot rows thirty inches apart take a quarter of a pint of seed sown at six-inch intervals two inches deep, and are ready to pick sooner than the fourteen weeks from sowing that brings them to full shop size.

The secret of making just two rows yield enough for a family is to keep picking, starting when the first are four inches long, for as soon as they are allowed to go yellow and large, they cease production. They need no manure if they follow potatoes on the rotation and, as Legumes, they put back more than they take out. On poor sandy soils, dig in a pound of wood ashes to four square yards and any compost available. On any soil where there may be potash shortage wilt the next cut of comfrey after the potatoes have fed and tuck it into the trench bottoms as you dig, putting it about six inches down. An easier way is to wait until the beans are up and place cut comfrey along the rows and between them if you have enough, so that it suppresses weeds as well as supplying potash, as it will if placed between tomatoes.

There are a number of varieties that are stringless, with no tough fibre along the backs to make slicing difficult, and of these 'Tendergreen' and 'The Prince' are both heavy croppers, while 'Royalty' has blue pods that turn green when cooked, and is the best for deep-freezing.

Haricot beans are rather larger and half a pint sows 100 feet of rows eighteen inches apart and a foot between seeds, sown two inches deep and staggered, so they fit together. The object is to secure complete cover to hold down weeds, and because the pods are left on to dry there is no need to leave space between the rows for picking. The best variety is 'Comtesse de Chambord', which has the thickest foliage as well as a good crop.

Soak the seeds overnight to swell for quicker germination (a trick worth using for french beans, especially in dry seasons) and sow two inches deep at the end of April or before mid-May. When they are well up draw the earth up to the stems as if earthing potatoes and repeat this if you have time, for the stems will need some support with a good crop.

Pull them whole when the pods begin to dry and wrinkle and the leaves start yellowing and falling. Tie them in bundles and hang them, roots up, under cover to dry. When the pods are dry enough to break put the bundles between sacks and beat them with a stick, which is much quicker than opening by hand. Store the dry beans in jars, for mice like them better than bought haricots and they do have more flavour.

The 'straw' is excellent compost material, and this crop is a very good one for a new garden, avoiding wireworm, holding down weeds, enriching the soil and costing far less for seed than a potato crop. The haricots keep for at least four years, though if wanted for sowing it must be in the next season; so the first year in a new house can see the incoming family with haricot beans hoarded for years ahead. The variety called 'Golden Butter' is American, and is not a drying kind, but to be eaten as a french bean when its pods are yellow. If you move in later than May it is still worth sowing until July, and so is 'The Prince', at this same spacing, to be picked green round about October for salting in jars, or deep-freezing.

The yield from a half pint varies, but 7 lb. of dried beans is a fair yield, and every ounce holds 6·1 grams of protein, 11·6 of carbohydrates, 51 milligrams of calcium, 1·9 of iron, 0·13 of vitamin B1 (the same as with lentils), 0·08 riboflavin, against 0·02 for lentils (four times as much), and 0·6 mg. of nicotinic acid (which in future will be called 'Niacin' as in America to avoid confusion with nicotine insecticide) compared with 0·9 for lentils. So a vegetarian who usually buys lentils can get just as good value and rather more riboflavin by growing his own haricot beans.

French beans, however, have only a third as much vitamin C as green peas and only slightly more vitamin A, while cabbage leaves both standing at the post.

Beans, Runner

Beans for eating and for beauty too can be grown up the side of the house as an easy annual climber. Instead of using sticks, let them grow up strings attached to screw-eyes set in a row of Rawlplugs ten to twelve feet high on the wall.

The old-fashioned 'screen bean' is 'Painted Lady', and it has long been used to hide unsightly fences or sheds with its plentiful foliage and scarlet and white blossom. Its pods are ordinary runner beans. Those of the all-scarlet-flowered 'Giraffe' are two feet long when fully grown and at a foot length are still without tough fibres down their backs.

'Blue Coco' offers purple flowers and violet French-bean-type pods that cook to normal green, and 'Du Pape', the climbing pea bean, has pale pink blossoms and fat round pods that will shell like peas or slice like beans. This has been called our most delicious bean, especially when young and topped and tailed and cooked whole like sugar peas. It often suffers from too deep sowing. Sow only half an inch deep, not two inches like the other beans, so that it has a good start in sun-warmed soil.

Beans grown up a wall need only a narrow bed. Dig compost or rotted manure deeply into it, sowing six inches apart and six inches from the wall. A quarter-pint packet does about fifty feet and seed will keep a second season. Sow in May or June: and a row of French marigolds could go along the border for a long-lasting blaze of yellow or orange to contrast with the colours above.

Metal skewers hold the lower ends of the climbing strings. These should be of tomato string to take the weight and to turn into compost with the cut-down foliage in autumn. Beds by walls are often dry, but watering with cold water straight from the mains will make beans drop blossom, so take the chill off the water.

'Hammond's Dwarf Scarlet', the new 'bush runner bean' needs tying to sturdy canes about two feet tall to keep the crop clear of soil and slugs, for, like bush tomatoes, their stems will not stand the weight. Sow them eight inches apart and two feet between rows to allow picking space.

Vegetables One by One

The best supports for ordinary runner beans since the passing of the gypsy type with a horse and van who fetched beansticks from the woods, is the six- to eight-foot bamboo cane. Tie three in a tripod at each end of the row, tie the others in 'V's' and set two, point upwards, towards the middle, and tie a couple along the top as in the diagram. Then tie in the rest and sow the seeds beside each cane. These should be two feet apart at the bottom, and if you have more than a single row have a three-foot gap between, which can be mulched with grass mowings to keep down weeds. There are a number of modern metal devices for supporting runner beans, but their problem is that they are far more expensive than bamboo, less easy to store in winter, and the stems do not get a grip on the plastic-covered wires.

The yield from runner beans depends on how often they are picked, but a fair average is 750 lb. of pods from half a pint of seeds, so very few families need more than a single row.

Beet, Seakale or Chard

'Ruby chard' is a 'rootless' beetroot that grows tall, with wide-midribbed, vivid crimson leaves for flower arrangers, and it cooks with a better flavour than ordinary seakale beet, and thrives on heavy clays as well as on lighter soils. (Swiss chard has cream instead of crimson midribs.)

August sowing brings the first leaves ready for Christmas decorations and for eating from March, when they start growing fast, until July. Rich feeding now can make them too soft for hard winters, so they go best where early potatoes had manure. Dig in compost or manure before the May sowing to grow them for late summer, autumn and winter.

Aim at two inches between the sizeable seeds in inch-deep furrows fifteen inches apart. Thin to a foot between plants in staggered rows when the seedlings have three strong leaves. When picking, always break the leaves off downwards, for cutting means bleeding, which weakens the plants.

Ruby chard is cooked in the same way as seakale beet. Cut the leaf away from the midrib, which, thickly sliced, takes about fifteen minutes' simmering. The leaf takes less, so should be put in the pan later.

Boiling, cabbage-fashion, wastes the flavour. The best method is to add only two tablespoons of water to enough shortened midribs to

85

fill a casserole, and cook slowly for half an hour with chopped onion and a lump of butter or margarine.

Though the August sowing will succeed best if some shelter is given in cold gardens, the main enemy of chard is not frost but the small slugs that spend winter safely eating inside beet and lettuce hearts, ignoring poisoned baits outside.

The green Swiss chard is nearly the same. It is similarly grown and there is a variety called 'Rainbow' or 'Rhubarb Beet' which includes purple and orange leaves, differing only in colour from 'Ruby'. 'Spinach Beet' or 'Perpetual Spinach' will be found under 'Spinach'.

The best answer to the slugs' depredations is Fertosan Slug Destroyer, a contact poison of herbal origin which should be watered on between the rows, when the seedlings are well up, about three times at fortnightly intervals and again in October, taking care to keep it off the leaves. This substance acts by upsetting the way slugs and snails take up copper, and nothing else takes it up in the same way, so it will not harm worms, hedgehogs, birds or any other creature, but slug or snail. There was a case of a doctor's spaniel that got 'hooked' on metaldehyde slug bait and died of alcoholic poisoning.

Both the Ruby and the ordinary chards are very good value in minerals, with 4·02 milligrams per 100 grams of iron, which is higher than spinach, broccoli or kale, from 2,800 to 14,000 International units of vitamin A, 130 micrograms of riboflavin, which is nearly three times cabbage quantity, and 38 Mg. of vitamin C, about five times as much as lettuce. This neglected vegetable is so easy, and has so few enemies, that it should be in every garden, especially those where clubroot is a problem and there is need for a good winter 'greenstuff' that can be red or yellow, pink or cream for floral decorations, as well as a nutritional bargain.

Beetroot

The best beetroot for modern gardens is 'Cook's Delight', so called because it needs no boiling, which is just as well because a good storing size can be two inches thick and a foot long. It is bred to grow with over three-quarters of its length out of the ground, because it has been found that sugar beet are sweetest at the tops and the taller the root the sweeter the beet.

Sow in April for the maximum crop, but these can be monsters weighing up to 3 lb., and May or June sowing, after other crops come out, is better—with the first week in July the latest date for growing them an inch and a half thick so that they are mature enough to store until the new crop are ready to lift. This is the latest for ordinary round beet which must be tennis-ball size if for keeping.

Take out inch-deep furrows eight inches apart and sow the seeds, which are like small dried raspberries in pairs, every six inches, which spreads a quarter-ounce packet along 150 feet, but as the seed lasts four years it is pointless to sow too many. Even with late sowing 1 lb. a foot of row is easy, and from April or May the roots average $1\frac{1}{4}$ lb. each, or about $3\frac{1}{2}$ cwt. from this much seed.

Pull out the weakest seedling in each pair and remove the strays from round the beet in each bunch, for beet seed is a cluster. Hoe perhaps once if the ground is very thick with weed seedlings, but otherwise their thick foliage, and tall 'trunks' (for that is what they look like once they start to move) are good suppressors of annual weeds. The early sowing in April should go nine inches apart and a foot between rows, because they grow much larger.

The main enemy of the beets is the beet fly which lays eggs on the underside of the leaves, and the larvae produce long blisters as they tunnel through them. The best remedy is to pick the blistered leaves and burn or dump them in the dustbin, then to give a tonic dressing of dried blood to start the crop growing fresh leaves fast. Watch for these blistered leaves and pick them at once, for when these hatch to flies the second generation is already on the spot and the result is a severe attack. The beet beetle is small and black like its larvae, and if this appears, water with nicotine.

In late September or October the beet will be ready to lift; this is done just by taking hold of the leaves, for they are only sitting on the surface. Wring off the tops, which are excellent 'greens' both raw and cooked if there is a shortage in summer, and they are ready to store, for they are clean, dry and with no risk of fork damage. The best storage medium, as for all roots, is baled peat, chopped down dry and spread first as a two-inch-thick layer on the bottom of a tea chest. Set out the beets in rows and not touching each other, add peat enough to level off the varied diameters and a second two-inch-layer, and carry on till the box is full. They will keep right round till the following July, for the peat holds just enough air to preserve them, and they last far better thus than in ashes, sand or sawdust. The same peat can be used over and over again, but if there is an outbreak of rotting in stored carrots, this may leave spores behind and the

Vegetables One by One

peat should be well wetted and used in potting soil or as a mulch.

There are many varieties of ordinary beet which are grown in the same way, but none produces the weight of crop, or the flavour of 'Cook's Delight' eaten raw, for most other beets taste earthy if eaten uncooked. It is a non-bleeding kind and therefore one large root can stay in the refrigerator to be shredded or grated for salads as required, until the end makes soup. Full recipes are given in Chapter 9, but the rigid convention that decrees that salads can only be eaten with cold meat on Mondays robs us of the real nutritional value of this easy vegetable.

Beetroot is an excellent source of catalase, the protective factor against cancer which is destroyed by cooking, but nothing like so good as raw apples which do not so much keep away the doctor as the cancer surgeon. Beets, cheap in terms of room and trouble, are easily stored and are available all the year round. Boiling the beet destroys it, and so does preserving it in vinegar. Beets have as much vitamin C as carrots and turnips, twice as much niacin as brussels sprouts, cabbage, lettuce or tomatoes, but their real value is in their betain. This is a member of the vitamin B complex which the body can use as a replacement for cholin, also in the complex, which is normally supplied in egg yolk, kidney, liver, brain and the other organ meats. Vegetarians have in beet an easy source of this essential substance which is important to the health of our liver and kidneys, and an important additional protection against cancer, especially of the liver. This has been established in the U.S.A. by experiments with rats, and many 'cures' and improvements in cancers have been brought about by a diet of concentrated beet juices. Beet extracts have been made and are available through health food shops, but the best way to obtain betain is to grow your own.

Borecole

Though this always comes after 'beet' in seed catalogues, it is called 'Kale' by most gardeners (including the writers of the Royal Horticultural Society's *Dictionary*) and so it will be found here on page 110.

Broccoli

There are two types of broccoli and to save confusion between them the type that is like a hardy cauliflower has been put with the cauliflowers, leaving the sprouting broccoli here because it deserves a place on its own.

Broccoli is very easy. The winter kinds are hardy, they resist club-root, and even though they can have it badly they will always grow a crop. All are available over a long period from a single planting and offer excellent value in vitamins for the least trouble and space. The following tables give their nutritional value compared with that of other members of the cabbage tribe, cooked and raw, with lettuce and spinach as standards. These are not meant to be used in working out diets to within micrograms, but purely for comparison. Varieties differ in content and vitamins go up and down with the season and soil, and though it would be possible to analyse all the current British vegetable varieties through the year for the cost of one really lavish 'Pop Star' programme on T.V., we must still depend on averages from standard reference works.

(See table on following page.)

In these tables the vitamins are given in the usual units so that those with a knowledge of nutrition can fit them on to the tables in their favourite authorities on diet. Micrograms are millionths of a gram in 100 grams (113 grams = 4 oz.), milligrams are thousandths of a gram, and 'I.U.'s' are International Units used for measuring vitamin A, which, like barley measured by the 'coombe', is odd man out.

The most striking figures in these tables are the 595 milligrams of calcium and 4·0 for iron in spinach, which led to the Popeye propaganda. It is now known, however, that spinach contains so much oxalic acid that this locks up all that it brings and even more from the body's reserves, so it operates on a nutritional overdraft—*it holds less than none at all.* It is, however, rich in vitamin A compared with cabbage, especially eaten raw.

Broccoli shows as one of the best of all the cabbage family, with Kale a runner-up, but not nearly so nice either raw or cooked; and its iron and calcium are uncomplicated, also there is a high content of pantothenic acid. This is one of the B complex, and the ingredient in the bee's 'Royal Jelly' that started the craze for this substance. A lack of pantothenic acid can cause foot troubles, or rather increase the pain from them, especially corns and bunions, and this acid also helps the adrenal glands. There is no need to go short of it when it is so easy to grow your own.

All these crops, including spinach, contain sulphur which our bodies need, but long cooking breaks down the compounds and makes

MINERALS OF NUTRITIONAL VALUE IN GREEN VEGETABLES

Milligrams per 100 grams Fresh Weight

	Raw				Cooked		
	Calcium	Phosphorus	Sulphur	Iron	Calcium	Phosphorus	Iron
Broccoli	122	59	45·00	3·30	160	54	1·52
Brussels Sprouts	27	121	77·80	2·23	27	45	0·63
Cabbage	45	26	53·00	0·50	58	16	0·47
Cauliflower	122	60	29·40	1·43	23	33	0·48
Kale	197	72		2·54			
Lettuce	43	42		0·56			
Spinach	77	40	86·50	4·00	595	93	4·00

THE MAIN VITAMINS IN GREEN VEGETABLES—RAW

	Vitamin A I.U.'s	Vitamin C Milligrams	Thiamine Micrograms	Riboflavin Micrograms	Niacin Milligrams	Pantothenic Acid Micrograms
Broccoli	9,000	70–110	130	250	0·90	1,100
Cabbages	150	60	30	50	0·50	180
Kale	7,500	155	120	350	0·80	300
Lettuce	4,000	8	60	45	0·20	110
Spinach	6,790	18				

THE MAIN VITAMINS IN GREEN VEGETABLES—COOKED

	Vitamin A I.U.'s	Vitamin C Milligrams	Thiamine Micrograms	Riboflavin Micrograms	Niacin Milligrams	Pantothenic Acid Micrograms
Broccoli	3–5,000	100	135	450		
Brussels Sprouts	400–640	65	110	60–75	0·30	
Cabbage	80–170	60	90			
Cauliflower	30–90	30				
Kale		51				
Spinach	3,445	13	50	80	0·30	6·90

a smell. The traditional cabbage-water smell of a cheap boarding-house comes from overcooked cabbage-tribe vegetables. Cook only ten minutes with little water (see the last chapter for recipes), thus banishing the smell, improving the flavour and saving the vitamins.

The most useful broccoli is 'Early White' or 'Early Purple Sprouting', because it is ready to pick at the end of February and finishes as late as May with time to clear the bed for outdoor tomatoes, or late beet or carrots. Like brussels sprouts it needs firm ground and goes best after peas or broad beans without digging. The late varieties are ready in April and can carry on until the end of June, when yellow shows in the flower sprouts and these become unattractive at last.

Sow the seed, which should produce 2,000 plants to an ounce, in April—sow very thinly, remembering that seed will keep for five years, so write the date on the packet and put it away rather than overcrowd for the sake of using it up. The seedlings will be up fast in their half-inch-deep furrow and when they are four inches high they should be transplanted to a seed bed four inches apart each way to wait until July when the earlier crops will have freed their room.

Broccoli need plenty of space, not only for growth but for picking between, eighteen inches to two feet between plants and two to three feet between rows, which are the normal spacings between pea and broad bean rows. Use a steel-shod dibber to make large holes and transplant with as much soil on the roots as possible. Water them thoroughly, ideally using an overhead irrigator to give them a thorough soaking, if they must go out in a dry spell. They will manage very nicely on the lime and compost that went in the pea trenches, which will have sunk enough to hold water round them, and if the beans are cut off level with the ground, their left-in roots will provide nitrogen for the broccoli, which is always hardy through the worst winters with this firm treatment. Hoe the weeds off the surface before planting, and because broccoli are rarely attacked by slugs in winter it is possible to cover down between plants and rows with a two-inch coat of lawn mowings to suppress weeds.

In new gardens broccoli can be planted after merely taking the turf up, without digging at all, but 1 lb. of lime a square yard should be scattered on the surface for the rain to wash in. After early potatoes they should be planted at the same spacing when the ground has been limed, as directed in Chapter 4, and trodden firm, but unlike cabbage they are better without a quantity of manure. On rich soils or those that have had plenty of compost, they may well need staking with something strong enough to come thirty inches up the stem and hold them, for they grow between three and four feet high.

The eating part is the flowering shoot that springs from where the leaves join the stem, and the central one should be cut out first with about six inches of stem. Always leave a stump of shoot to grow more, never damage the leaves, and never strip a plant completely. It is better to have a dozen plants with room to walk round and pick from them all than to waste room on twenty or more and have some get away and flower.

The 'Green Sprouting Broccoli' is also called 'Calabrese', and is sown in April to plant out in late May and be ready to pick forty days after planting, if you plant 'Green Comet', the newest variety. Space it eighteen inches apart and two feet between rows, and be ready to pick as soon as you see the small flowerheads like green cauliflower curds in small fragments in the centre. This is a very good subject for deep-freezing, but there is no point in using up this expensive space, which could be filled with strawberries that cannot be otherwise preserved, with a crop that can be grown as easily outside. Advice to freeze this crop comes from American books and the very large number of writers who merely copy them, for in the U.S.A. it is rarely possible to keep the cabbage tribe in the open through the winter as we can.

Brussels Sprouts

Wood pigeons have a 'pecking order' and brussels sprouts rate first, broccoli second, and kale right at the bottom of the list. A flock will fly over a row of gardens and peel off like dive-bombers as soon as they see the rounded leaf tips of the sprouts from an altitude of forty feet, and it may well be that the wide-spaced leaves of the sprouting broccoli are also a key sign.

Breeding brussels sprouts in kale's clothing is not a final answer, however, for one hard winter would expose the fraud to birds who learn and remember, as tits and sparrows learnt to rob milk bottles. (The answer for that problem is to put eggcups out with the empties, and tell the milkman to fit them over the tops.)

The best garden answer yet is to use the light green nylon netting that is strong and rotproof and likely to be a permanent anti-bird weapon of the future. Drive a pole in the middle of the bed and one at each corner, put an empty jam jar on top of each and cover the lot with nylon netting which will slip smoothly over the jam bottles without catching as you move about underneath to pick, or lift it at the corners.

Nylon net on short sticks, or wire pea guards along the rows, will be needed for the seeds of the first early sprouts sown in April, for these can be readily attacked by sparrows. Birds vary in fierceness with locality and availability of water in the early spring, but though it is argued that putting out water will keep them off the seedlings, there is no evidence that this will not draw still more birds to the attack. Bird lovers are rarely wholehearted gardeners.

'Early Dwarf' or 'Dwarf Gem' are the favourite varieties for October picking, but a new one, 'Peer Gynt', which is far more expensive though worth the price, gives a much bigger crop of larger buttons from October to December. 'Cambridge No. 5' is still one of the best late varieties, with 'New Year' gaining favour for the same December to February season. The brussels sprout crossed with pickling cabbage, sometimes called 'Rubine' but more usually just 'Red' has a different and attractive flavour, slightly higher vitamin C, and a crop from November to February.

All are for April sowing, though in mild districts March gives a longer start to the early ones, and all need exactly the same routine as broccoli. Unless the soil is firm their sprouts can be as large and loose as lettuces, and they need rich feeding even less than broccoli. It is not worth cherishing the stripped stumps because of any spring growth from the tips, which will always be inferior to broccoli or cabbage, because these stumps are the favourite over-wintering place for the sooty cabbage aphis. If there has been an attack of this creature, instead of attempting to smash the even woodier stems to break down in the compost heap in the depths of winter, which is the most difficult time to get up heat, stow them under a shed or somewhere to dry. Then burn them with your prunings on one of the few bonfires of the good gardener's year.

During the summer growing season both brussels sprouts and broccoli may be attacked by cabbage white caterpillars (which are green) and those of the cabbage moth (which are dirty brown). Against these and sooty aphis, spray either with a derris or pyrethrum mixture, which can be used right up to the time when they are eaten, or the cigarette-end nicotine which should not be used later than three weeks before harvest, to make sure. Its advantage is that it is cheap enough, costing only the trouble of making up for watering on with a can and soaking everything to clear an attack. Seedlings may be attacked by fleabeetle which eats holes in the leaves, and a dusting with derris powder is the answer.

Cabbages

Unlike brussels sprouts and broccoli, cabbages gain nothing by firm ground, and go out after normal digging. Sow in the same half-inch-deep furrows and transplant to a waiting bed, which should have had 2 lb. a square yard of lime dug in as an anti-clubroot precaution, if they must wait for their room.

The kings of cabbages are the 'Monarchs', summer, autumn, and winter, a new race bred not only for cooking quality but for a nutty flavour when eaten raw in salads: so good that they are worth growing instead of summer lettuces, apart from their value right through the winter. Their two- to five-pound heads have few outer leaves, minimum central core, and grow far more salad for their space, and the four to six weeks during which they will wait at readiness for eating in summer is longer than even non-bolting lettuces like 'Sutton's Nonesuch' can offer.

Sow the first 'Summer Monarch' in March, trying for an inch between seeds along a half-inch-deep furrow, for the best plants grow from uncrowded seedlings and these kingly cabbages still cost 13p a packet. When they are two inches high plant them fifteen inches apart each way in staggered rows, so that their ball shapes fit together and suppress the weeds.

They will be ready to eat ten weeks after sowing, and for a steady supply sow again in April (August holidays mean missing this one), May and June. When these come ready before a crop has cleared to release their room, transplant them four inches apart each way in a waiting bed and move them, large, to their final eighteen-inch-apart spacing, with generous watering.

'Autumn' and 'Winter Monarch' grow more slowly, so need May sowing and moving from the waiting bed in July–August for planting two feet apart each way in September, when second-early potatoes like 'Duke of York' have cleared. 'Winter Monarch' may well have finished by the end of January, however, and those who need cabbages right round the year have other varieties to choose from; the pickling cabbages are excellent for filling the gap between winter and spring.

'Red Drumhead' and 'Stockley's Giant' are large and hardy, while

'Niggerhead', if it can be found, has the best flavour. Those who want to pickle them in vinegar sow in March, plant in May two feet apart each way and harvest in autumn. For winter vitamin value sow in May, and transplant to a waiting bed to go out in July or August at the same spacing. Their flavour is greatly improved when they have felt a frost or two.

Another winter gap-filler is Savoy cabbage, which is extra hardy, with crinkly leaves. They are as rich in vitamin C as the summer crop, though this is halved when they are cooked. 'Ormskirk Late' and 'Omega' are about the best, for May sowing and July planting two feet apart each way, for eating in late March and April. An ordinary cabbage for this season is the variety called 'April' or 'Sutton's April', to sow in August, and transplant at Savoy spacing in October, like the old 'Flower of Spring': though as hardy, it is a better raw eater.

In gardens without a clubroot-free area for seed raising and a waiting bed, or where the right sowing season has been missed, plants have to be bought, but these cannot be obtained in modern varieties. In this case buy 'Greyhound' or 'Velocity' in place of 'Summer Monarch', 'Winningstadt' instead of 'Autumn Monarch' and 'Christmas Drumhead' and 'January King' to replace 'Winter Monarch', and 'Flower of Spring' or 'Ellam's Early' for April. There is no difficulty in buying the Cambridge brussels sprouts and both white and purple sprouting broccoli, but they should be bought from a local nursery good enough to have grown them in steam-sterilized soil, for the allotment-holder with plants to spare can easily pass on clubroot.

Liming twelve months before the brassica crop and rotations that concentrate this tribe and give a complete rest from it, keep this problem under control, but there are two counter-measures apart from the various mercury preparations used by inorganic gardeners, which are not a hundred per cent effective either.

The first is to smash mothballs and drop about a quarter of one down each dibber hole when planting, and the other is to use sections of rhubarb stem about three inches long, sometimes as many as three being put down the holes in the same way. Both remedies work by masking the root secretions of the Brassica plant so that the spores of clubroot do not wake to their mobile form called 'zoospores' and swim through the sea of water round every soil grain to creep in through the root hairs of the young plant. Success or failure depends on how many spores there are within five inches of the root hairs, and which strain they are.

Vegetables One by One

The clubroot fungus (*Plasmodiophore brassicae*) will develop specialized strains that prefer brussels sprouts, cabbage or any one Brassica, and these will predominate in a garden, which means that though the versatile strains are present they do not attack badly, and kale or sprouting broccoli may be missed for several seasons. The specialized strains are most easily defeated by repellents, and magnificent cauliflowers have been grown with the help of rhubarb in a garden where these had been the only Brassica for years.

Clubroot can survive on a diet of docks, couch grass, ryegrass, Yorkshire fog and creeping soft grass, the grey-leaved grasses that leave bare rooty patches in lawns. This is how the versatile strain survives in overgrown empty allotments until a new tenant enjoys a few years' freedom before the more 'adventurous' spores build up a population and attack his Brassicas. Strawberries, mignonette, nasturtiums and annual poppies are also possible carriers, though wallflowers and shepherd's purse are worst. Those who wish to learn more of the clubroot fungus, one of the worst international plant pests next to potato blight, should read *Clubroot Disease of Crucifers* by Dr. John Colhoun, M.Agr., Ph.D., D.Sc. (Commonwealth Mycological Institute, 1958).

Radishes are grown and eaten too fast for the clubroot fungus to attack, so they can be used as a catch crop on any part of the rotation, but they should never be left in to grow woody and flower. Always pull them for compost when they cease to be worth eating, and remember that kohlrabi, turnips and swedes are also Cruciferae.

A useful precaution is never to use fresh manure *before* planting any member of the tribe, for the soft root growth from plentiful nitrogen is most easily entered by the zoospores, the mobile form of the hatched spores. This is even more likely with chemical fertilizers, and only compost should be used before cabbages, though a dry sludge is safe at up to 4 lb. a square yard; but not a wet sludge, for the effect depends on how fast the nitrogen is available. Sulphate of ammonia combines with lime to produce insoluble gypsum, and the extra acidity as well as the released nitrogen makes this chemical fertilizer the worst of all for increasing clubroot attack.

Those who see their first clubroot, for many gardeners dodge it for years in new gardens with no spores on bought plants to start it, may, however, be mistaken. If the 'clubs' are round lumps, slice one open. If there is a maggot inside, gall weevil, not clubroot, is the trouble. The summer answer for cabbages wilting from this pest is dried blood sprinkled round each as a tonic. Dig, rather than pull, the stumps, so the roots with knobs on can be burnt.

The cabbage root fly (*Delia brassicae*) is perhaps the worst cabbage pest and attacks also cauliflowers but rarely brussels sprouts and broccoli. The first flies hatch in late April and May, the second generation from late June to mid-July, and there is a third one in August and September. They lay their eggs on the surface near the plants. The white, peg-shaped maggots tunnel first down and then up so that it is not possible to kill them by watering on any pesticide, and making the soil so poisonous that the small housefly-like *Delia* drops dead as soon as it alights. To do so means *more* next year because the survivors increase when the many predators that eat the chrysalids (the devil's-coach-horse beetle is one of these) are destroyed.

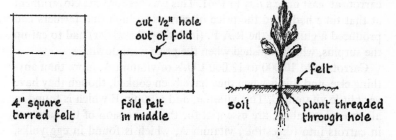

2. Roofing-felt squares are the best protection against cabbage root fly. Smear greaseband material on the square and kill your local flies which may make this precaution unnecessary in the future

The best remedy is to cut four-inch squares of tarred roofing felt and snip a small hole in the middle. Thread your plant through this and firm it in with the felt folded upwards, then spread this felt on the soil surface which needs to be level and smooth. The stem of the plant will fill the small hole as it grows and tear the felt, so it is not restricted, and if the fly arrives and lays eggs on the top, the maggots cannot get through. Cardboard has been used but felt is far the best. If there has been an attack with cabbages wilting and dying from these maggots, dig over the bed at least twice in winter to give the robins a good go at the chrysalids.

The cabbage white fly (*Aleurodes brassicae*) is a relation of the greenhouse whitefly of tomatoes, and its larvae are small, stationary, yellow or brown scales which produce plentiful droppings that feed sooty moulds. The obvious sign is hundreds of the tiny moth flies, and these can be attacked with nicotine and soft soap, while it is also effective to remove the lower leaves to compost, for this is where they always attack. Once again 'drawing stumps' instead of leaving them in to provide 'greens' of little value removes the overwintering stock. This is one of the few pests that is knocked back by hard winters, and 1962–3 produced many seasons of freedom.

Carrots

As everyone knows, the carrot is so rich in vitamin A, lack of which causes night blindness, that R.A.F. night fighter and bomber pilots were given quantities of carrots to improve their vision. This, like Russians with snow on their boots in a previous war, is a legend, and based on the regulation that all ranks, not only aircrew, were to have carrots at least once a day in 1941. This was because the Government at that time had fixed the price of carrots so high that farmers had produced a glut, and the R.A.F. (including the writer) had to eat up the surplus, which vanished when the price went down.

Carrots hold 10,000 to 12,000 I.U.'s of vitamin A, more than anything else, and this is when they have been cooked, though they have very little vitamin C. This vitamin, and vitamin E which is found in all green vegetables, are essential for the conversion of the carotene in carrots into (digestible) vitamin A, which is found in egg yolks, butter, fish oils, kidney and liver. Carrots, though nice to eat raw in salads, are not then as nutritious as they are when cooked, and they should never be one's sole winter vegetable. As is not the case with potatoes, it is very easy to get fed up with carrots, as we found in the R.A.F.

Carrots like their soil sun-warmed, so April is soon enough to sow 'Chantenay Red-Cored' for October digging to store for winter in peat, and 'Amsterdam Forcing' as the fastest variety, ready in about twelve weeks for cooking small or eating raw.

Grated raw carrot, either with lettuce or with cold potato and mayonnaise in winter, makes a good salad, but cover the scarlet pile with a fitting plate and keep refrigerated until just before serving— air spoils the flavour, and reduces vitamin C content.

Both kinds have short roots to grow well on clay, where long kinds fail, or on sand, and the best place is one that was manured last year, for fresh manure makes them coarse and forky. Compost or leafmould dug in full fork-depth now is excellent on any soil with a good scattering of wood ashes raked in as you level the bed.

Rake the bed again before sowing, half an inch deep and eight inches apart. Cover with about a quarter-inch of fine soil. Half an ounce of seed will sow 200 feet of furrows, and to get an even, thin sowing mix the seed with eight times as much bone meal—it mixes better with seed than sand does and shows up well along the furrows.

Without rain the bed needs soaking when the seeds are well up in three weeks, and hoeing if the surface cakes. When the ferny leaves are a good inch long, pull out all but the largest carrot in each cluster, thinning furrows first to three inches apart and to the full six- or nine-inch spacing a fortnight later. After thinning, give 1 oz. of dried blood a square yard as a tonic and water again, unless it is good showery carrot-thinning weather.

It is the scent of the crushed foliage from the thinnings that draws the carrot fly (*Psila rosea*), a relation of the cabbage fly, to lay its eggs in the disturbed soil. They develop into maggots that work upwards into the root in the same way. The fly attacks in late May and early June, but some of the maggots finish growing, become pupae for only a few days, and lay a second batch in August and September.

The normal March or April sowings come ready for sowing just when the fly attack is at its worst, so one way round is to sow at the end of May so that the crop is thinned when the flies have finished. This needs a fast carrot that will reach the one-and-a-half inches or more across the top that is the minimum keeping size when sown as late as this, and 'Grenadier', bred for the prepacking and quickfreezing trade, will grow this size in the time. Another way round is to buy pelleted seed, which is carrot seeds set singly inside small pellets of clay, which should be sown four inches apart with no need to thin at all. This limits one to the varieties available, but is perhaps the best way so far discovered for getting round the problem.

The traditional answer is to sow onions next to the carrots so that the foliage scent baffles the pest, but this is effective only for the distant flies. Incredible as it may seem, these greenish-black flies, less than a quarter of an inch long, will travel up to seven miles in quest of carrots, and though the onion scent will mask the foliage, it is not effective at a point-blank range of a mile; or if there are pupae in the soil of the garden next door, the creatures have only to use their eyes.

Lawn mowings spread between the rows and renewed after every mowing provide a cheap and constant scent barrage, and pine sawdust and paraffin-soaked sand have all been used with success; but it is difficult to be certain which is the most effective, because the fly hatch varies with the season. Digging over the carrot bed in winter or three times to feed the robins and wagtails is also useful after an attack to get rid of the local pupae.

The naphthalene flake often recommended as a scent repellent and even as a maggot poisoner in old gardening books and the books of those who copy them, cannot now be bought, for North Sea Gas 'whizzes' no naphthalene.

Dig carrots for keeping in October, cutting the foliage off an inch from the roots and leaving them in the sun to dry sufficiently for the soil to flake off without washing. Throw out for immediate use any which have been damaged in digging. Wrapped in greaseproof paper they will stay fresh for a fortnight (polythene quickly turns any carrot soft and mouldy).

Store the rest in boxes in non-touching layers with peat between. Keep these away from damp or frost and the carrots will keep through hard winters until the new ones come round again.

Cauliflowers

Cauliflower and heading broccoli plants are better sown than bought, for the cost of postage now makes it impossible for any nursery to specialize in vegetable plants, and local nurseries have always a very poor selection.

Though seed is relatively expensive, it will keep for four years, so it pays to buy a set of varieties and date the packets, sowing a little from each, for even a quarter of an ounce grows 250 plants. April is time enough to sow the cauliflower kinds, and May, the hardy broccoli types to come through the winter and head up in spring, but those who want really early cauliflowers can sow 'Early Snowball' in a frame in January, plant out in April, and eat them in July.

Normally 'Early Snowball' is ready in August and September, with 'Veitch's Self-Protecting' for November and December. Then 'Snow's Winter White' (broccoli) takes over till February, 'Dobie's Purity' for March and April, and 'Late Queen' for May and June. There is of course no need to have the whole range—this is for the gardener who enjoys cauliflower and broccoli curds and is prepared to take the trouble.

Sow thinly in the usual half-inch-deep furrows, firming each after covering with the rake head, six inches between rows and with better labels than packets on sticks. When the seedlings have three cabbage-shaped leaves, transfer them to the waiting bed four inches apart each way, just like brussels sprouts and broccoli. This transplanting breaks the tap roots so they make plenty of fine ones that take hold of new soil better, and in hot weather it pays to shorten the leaves by half, which seems cruel but saves flagging.

Plant with a steel-shod dibber, ideally in July where the peas were hoed off, eighteen inches apart and with thirty inches between rows, on firm soil. If there is no undug room clear, firm it by treading or with a roller, for cauliflowers and broccoli need to be as firm as brussels sprouts for the best results. If they are not growing away well after three weeks, scatter 2 oz. a square yard of dried blood as a tonic, and keep them hoed and watered, for they need to get a good deal of growing done before winter.

Bend a leaf or two over the heads to shade them and hold the curds in flower longer. 'Veitch's Self-Protecting' has foliage that is some defence against frosts, but it is worth bending some over against early snow. Cauliflowers and heading broccoli are less easy than most vegetables, and suffer badly from clubroot if there is any about. A common cause of failure is loose soil, and this is why it is never advisable to plant these slow cabbage tribe crops between potato rows to be freed when these are lifted. Not only does this mean leaving many odd potatoes in the ground, but it disturbs the roots of the broccoli and sprouts. The waiting bed system is very much better.

Celeriac

This is also called 'Turnip-Rooted Celery' which describes it rather better, a root vegetable with a celery flavour, but of little more nutritional value in return for the considerable trouble of growing it.

Vegetables One by One

The roots are not easy to prepare and rather resemble a Thing from Outer Space. Again, however, many people find them delicious.

Celery plants are easily bought, but celeriac must be raised at home. Nurseries could grow and post plants anywhere, but until more people try it and like it there is 'not enough demand'.

The modern electric seed-raisers which save heating whole greenhouses are ideal for early March sowings, though windowsill raisers should wait until March ends. Sow thinly in pots of John Innes seed soil, half-filled with small coke or cinders for drainage, and flatten the soil with the bottom of a bottle. Cover with just a sprinkling of soil and stand the pots in water until the surface shows wet, leaving them outside to drain off the surplus. Boxes suit greenhouses better, and the same routine can be used for the seeds.

Kitchen windowsills are best because the steam from cooking provides moister air. All seeds need sunny sills. Each pot should stand in a saucer, to be filled for a soak only if the surface really dries. The seedlings take fifteen to twenty-five days to appear, and when they have two celery-shaped leaves they are ready to be transplanted two inches apart each way in boxes, or closer in other pots. These should be moved to a cold frame or a cooler but still sunny windowsill, and given ordinary watering. By mid-May or June each strong seedling should have a slight swelling at the base and be ready for planting.

Make their bed where manure or compost was dug, but not lime, which they dislike; plant them a foot apart with eighteen inches between rows, with the swellings just on the surface. Give them some water to start off with. The bulges become swollen stems sitting on the surface, so that they look like turnips with celery tops.

These tops can be eaten as a mild celery-flavour spinach, but taking too many from one spoils the 'roots', which can weigh 4 lb., though the one- to two-inch-diameter sizes from late starters are better than monsters. They need no earthing, but the roots should be covered with soil in August.

Lift and store in sand in October, or leave them with bracken or leafmould over the rows for protection in districts where the weather is mild, and dig them up when wanted.

Celery

Celery is valuable because it is one of the few vegetables ordinary people will eat raw in winter with cheese, thus gaining some catalase,

102

though it is far inferior to raw cabbage in every vitamin and mineral. It has been regarded as a good source of calcium (68 mg.) and iron (0·60 mg.) but the first is half that of broccoli and the second a fifth as much, and because you eat only the bleached stems it contains no vitamin A or vitamin C. Many people, however, like the flavour and decide that this is worth the trouble of growing celery.

The simplest celery is 'Golden Self-Blanching', grown on the flat without trenches or trouble and, from mid-May or June planting, ready to eat in late August till the first hard frost.

Plants cost about 10p a dozen. Plant with a trowel a foot apart with eighteen inches between rows, digging in 1 lb. of dried sludge or a bucketful of manure to a square yard. Water for the first fortnight if the weather is dry; all that is needed afterwards is hoeing against weeds.

Ordinary celery lasts till January. It can be planted as late as July after early potatoes, saving room and growing smaller sticks that are just as lasting and hardy.

Manure as for self-blanching celery, but take out wide 'V's' with the hoe, four inches across and three inches deep, two feet apart, and put in the plants at foot intervals along the bottoms. Water weekly, adding liquid manure to the water on poor soils. By mid-August—or September for July plantings—the plants should be about a foot high and ready for any side-shoots to be broken off before their first earthing.

It takes two people to earth a row of celery—one to hold the stems of each plant bunched and the other to heap soil shovelled from between the rows to fill the furrow and go three inches up the stems. The final earthing three weeks later, right up to the leaves to ensure freedom from frost, is best done with peat or leafmould. Break up the peat bale with a spade, and water to swell it, or chop down the leafmould heap made last autumn and sift before heaping either into tall ridges. Whack down firmly.

Both peat and leafmould need protection from wind and rain. Black polythene strip, slit in the middle to let the leaves through and weighted with stones each side of the ridges, has been used, but it can tear off in gales and makes harvesting awkward, apart from harbouring slugs.

The best protection consists of fifteen-inch squares of flat asbestos leant on the ridges. They store flat in the shed and last for years. Lift off the asbestos sheets to dig the celery as required, and spread the peat or leafmould to dig in next spring.

Vegetables One by One

Moving this trenchless bed to a new place each year adds to a crop of simplified celery the gain of a generous dressing of the good and lasting humus that town gardens need.

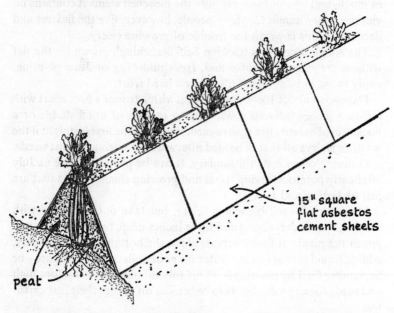

15" square flat asbestos cement sheets

peat

3. Tie paper (not shown) round your celery, heap peat round them, then protect from rain with asbestos square that last years. This saves digging trenches, means an easy winter harvest and weathers peat for garden humus

The chief garden pest is celery leaf miner with grubs that make winding tunnels in the leaves. Pick these attacked leaves off in July and August and destroy them, which prevents a second-generation attack in October. If there is a great deal to pick off, give a tonic of dried blood, about 2 oz. to ten feet of row, and the same if the plants appear strangely stunted, for this will be Leaf Spot or Celery Blight, which is rare in gardens and highly unlikely from bought plants, for it is carried on seed, and today this is sterilized with formaldehyde before sowing.

Chicory

This is an easy root with no pests or diseases, grown for forcing to eat the blanched shoots either in salads or cooked in winter, but again

104

they are a flavour and a luxury of low nutritional value, though they do help with making salads more attractive to the conventional-minded.

Whitloof chicory for cooking and salads is not the powerful root grown in the Fens to make coffee essences; it is much smaller and a quarter of an ounce sows fifty feet of rows a foot apart. They keep about seven years in the packet, so there is no need to use them up. Sow thinly in May or June and thin them to nine inches between plants when they are three inches high.

They need hoeing to keep the weeds down and will be ready to lift in batches from early November onwards, and packed in boxes with soil in dark cellars or sheds at about 50° F to grow crisp white leaves for salads, which will of course be without the vitamin C or vitamin A which cabbage will supply in the salad mixture. They should produce two if not three crops of leaves which should be gathered by breaking, not cutting, and the spent roots should be dumped on the compost heap to rot down and release their hoard of root-selected minerals which are not in the foliage that is eaten.

Another way is to sow them two feet apart in May, either with lettuce or radishes between the rows, or between early potato ridges—parting the potato foliage to see when the seedlings are ready for thinning. Dig the potatoes with care and the chicory will be left well spaced to grow two inches across.

Cut off the leaves (too bitter for raw salads) in late September and heap soil from between the rows over the root tops as if you were earthing potatoes or celery, whacking it firm with the spade so that the ridges stay high through winter rain.

Dig away the soil after January to gather the cream-yellow leaves by breaking, not cutting; they will have a finer flavour than if you had forced them. Replace the soil for a second batch and dig the spent roots for compost when this is finished.

Chinese Cabbage

The Chinese Cabbage or 'Pei Tsai' (pronounced 'peasay') came by tea clipper in the 1840's, with its companion the Chinese radish, but generations of gardeners have had it bolting to tall cowslip flowers from sowing it in spring. Now we know that, unlike our lettuce, it hearts in the shortening days of autumn, finishing in December.

Dig over and rake after early potatoes or anything cleared between mid-July and mid-August, with half a pound of dried sludge a square yard if the crop before had nothing. Aim at sowing the large round seeds at four-inch intervals along half-inch-deep furrows a foot apart. A shilling packet will do six twelve-foot rows, not necessarily in one year for the seeds will easily keep for three. They will be up fast and need thinning to eight inches apart when their crinkled-edged leaves start touching in the rows.

Pei Tsai is like a giant cos lettuce, twelve to fifteen inches high and up to four inches wide, folding itself without tying. The hearts have very wide midribs and stay good to the last, even with rain-rotten or frozen outer leaves. One too large for a small salad should be stood in water, for they wilt instead of crisping in refrigerators.

Though Chinese cabbage is usually an autumn salad, it is cooked in the U.S.A. by slicing lengthways and dropping in very little boiling water, for three minutes, like an egg. The original Chinese street pedlar's recipe modified for modern kitchens is far nicer. Put a small lump of butter or a tablespoonful of oil in the bottom of a saucepan, cut up about a quarter of the available cabbage leaves and drop them in, light a low flame under the saucepan and wash and cut up the remaining leaves. Then drop these in the saucepan where the first leaves will have exuded enough juice to make water unnecessary. Add salt and simmer gently for about eight minutes and serve like spinach. The Chinese pedlars used oil in place of butter and had a charcoal stove for cooking by this traditional method that cut out the weight of any water when everything was carried slung on poles over his shoulders. The result was sold in small bowls with mysterious delicacies and sauces, and the tea clipper captain evidently liked his so much that he tracked down seed and brought it home.

Because it is a separate species (*Brassica pekinensis*) it takes a versatile clubroot spore to wake up to it, so it may be safe for several years, but it does best on the Brassica part of the rotation. It is attacked by other cabbage pests, especially the white fly. Unlike the other brassicas it is low in sulphur and has no cooking smell, but no analysis is so far available, though it should have rather better vitamin C than a cabbage heart because it is more open and green.

Cresses

American cress is as easy as the kind that goes with mustard, but whole plants pulled like lettuce to add larger cress-flavoured leaves to salads means less sowing, stooping and snipping. 'Land Cress' is another name, *Barbarea praecox* the botanical one, and seed keeps three years with a quarter-ounce packet sowing fifty feet of rows for 5p.

Sow in April, May, June and July, each for a month of salads; the cress takes seven weeks from sowing to grow to eating size—four inches across. Choose a shady place, preferably not too dry, and dig in compost on poor soils, especially in the sunless town gardens where it thrives.

For summer salads sow half an inch deep and thin to six inches between plants in rows nine inches apart. Space the rows a foot apart and thin to eight-inch spacing for August and September sowing, choosing a sheltered sunny place. The cress makes a change from chopped savoy hearts and costly lettuce through mild winters. Set wider, so that plants never touch, and with slug bait defence, American cress is hardier than winter lettuce.

Ordinary cress of the kind that goes with mustard can be forced easily in the open under foot-square cardboard boxes three to four inches deep with the flaps cut off for all but windy gardens. They last longer with a coat of cheap black paint which waterproofs them and absorbs more sun heat in the early spring. Rake the ground level on a strip as wide as the box but more than four times as long, water well, and when the water has soaked in, sow the seed thickly but evenly on the surface of the first square.

Cover the seed with the box, leaving no air gaps at the edges (leaving the flaps on and weighting them with stones in windy gardens) and in five to seven days the seedlings will be up, each wearing its seed-coat like a hat. Then transfer the box to another sown square, sowing the third when the first is ready to harvest with scissors. Each square foot yields about four good mustard and cress teas for two, and by the time the first patch is finished, it can be redug with a hand fork for another cycle of sowing and covering with the box.

Several boxes each on its own strip are better than a single large one for those who need a larger harvest, and a polythene bag stretched over bent wires can serve as a tiny 'greenhouse' to cover the growing-on cress after the box has moved to the next sequence. Real salad mustard and cress has far more flavour than the rape which is now sold forced in plastic punnets.

Vegetables One by One

Cucumbers

Ridge cucumbers are almost as easy as marrows, but they contain 95–7 per cent water, more than any other vegetable we grow. They contain very little vitamin C and the 200 I.U.'s to 100 grams they have is in the peel which is thrown away. There is, however, a new hardy outdoor cucumber, rather inelegantly called 'Burpless', which has edible skin and is far more digestible than the ordinary kinds. Of these the Japanese varieties are nearer to frame varieties than the old 'Bedfordshire Prize', and 'Kaga' and 'Kariha' are rather odd looking, with stripes, but worth eating for those who like cucumbers.

Dig holes fifteen inches square and a foot deep about two feet from side to side each way. Half fill them with compost and then top soil well firmed. In the centre of each hole sow your cucumber seed edgeways and an inch deep in the first week in May. Then bend two eighteen-inch lengths of 20-gauge galvanized iron wire into staples about four inches wide and thrust the points into the ground so that they leave a loop like a croquet hoop over your seed. Put the other one the other way and fit a small polythene bag over them, with a rubber band round the mouth at ground level to prevent any risk of blowing off.

Water well in the hole, and leave them to grow, removing the bag when the two rounded seed leaves can be seen open, or for weeding if the weed seeds have forced faster than the cucumber. When the young plant has seven real cucumber-type leaves, pinch the tip out to produce more side shoots, otherwise just let them run. Keep the cucumbers picked, for a single large specimen will take all the strength of the plant, when a dozen could have been enjoyed off it by a more attentive gardener.

The Japanese climbing cucumber can also be grown in the open but, like 'Burpless', it appreciates a tripod of canes over it and some strings to climb. This produces plentiful small cucumbers, and is best as the only variety that will share a greenhouse with tomatoes without sulking for more heat. Sow it in pots under glass in late April, or early in the month with heat, to plant in an unheated greenhouse in May with the tomatoes, and train them up strings like the frame varieties.

Gherkins for pickling are grown in exactly the same way as ridge cucumbers, and when there is a threatened frost in October at the end of the season, all the small cucumbers on the ridge plants as well can be picked and pickled.

Vegetables One by One

Herbs

Thyme flies, for most bushes are woody beyond recall after four summers, but, as is the case with lemon balm, marjoram and sage, 4p thyme packets sow easy replacements in March or April. These herbs need sun, but mint must be planted as roots, with shade, moisture and better feeding.

Lemon balm (*Melissa officinalis*), delicious cooked with peas or potatoes or in salad, is fully hardy though often raised in greenhouses. It merely comes up slowest in the half-inch-deep furrows six inches apart that suit all four, and 'pot' marjoram (*Origanum onites*) for stews is as hardy as sage or thyme, but the 'sweet' kind is not.

Thin these herbs six inches apart when the best are an inch high, to move as replacements in September, or transplant at this size to a foot apart each way to give enough for drying this summer, and plants to give away in spring, when fewer but larger specimens yield the same quantity from less room.

Cut the foliage for drying when the first flowers are opening, tie it in bunches with a paper bag fitted over each, and hang these indoors to dry slowly. When all are crisp, put the herbs through the mincing machine and store in screw-top jars, some mixed, but with thyme and sage separately for stuffing.

Mint likes a thin coat of rotted manure for the winter, and a spring one is better late than never. Old plants may have the orange patches of mint rust on the leaves, and this can be cured by digging up and washing the strongest roots. Then warm some water to 110° F and leave the roots in it for ten minutes before replanting. Heat over 115° F kills the roots, and less than 105° F will not kill the fungus, so use a household thermometer and replant the treated roots in another part of the garden.

Good mint is worth curing, and the best is *Mentha rotundifolia*, with hairy leaves and the rounded tips that go with good taste, but the pointed type with wavy edges is *M. spicata crispa*, which has the 'mintiest' flavour and is worth buying from a firm that knows these names.

Well-fed mint rarely rusts, so new beds or old that are dug, split and remade every fourth spring, need compost, manure or 4 oz. a square yard of fish meal under peat dug in before planting. Make the trenches two inches deep and eight inches apart with six inches between plants, though the long roots can overlap. Tread the rows firm after covering, and water in dry springs.

In August—or when more has been grown than is to be used—cut, wash and chop enough to fill a screw-top bottle. Pour in sufficient cold, boiled malt vinegar to soak in and leave the jar brim full, then screw on the lid. When mint-sauce is wanted, spoon about two-thirds of the needed amount into the sauceboat, add sugar, more vinegar and a little boiling water, but never pour any back in the jar, for the sugar ferments and spoils the rest.

All herbs are hardy, but their savouriness depends on sunshine. At a pinch they can be grown in a pot placed on an outside window-sill. A window-box is preferable and a tiny plot of cat-haunted, soot-black soil is better still.

The best soil for pots and window-boxes is John Innes Seed Mixture, which is sandier and more suitable for herbs than the Potting Mixture, and is now sold in small polythene bags by garden shops and chain stores. The mixture is dust-dry, so water it well and shovel it about to spread the moisture evenly. For drainage, put a two-inch layer of small coke, cinders or even broken glass or crockery on the bottom of the window-box. If you have the large 32-size (6-in.) flowerpots— they are better and roomier than the ordinary $3\frac{1}{2}$-in. pot-plant type— cover their drainage holes with the same materials.

Lemon balm, marjoram, sage, thyme all spread to six- to eight-inch-wide clumps, so each plant needs a pot to itself, or a six-inch square of window-box space. Chives and mint are more powerful and deserve half a window-box each at the same spacing.

Make the soil in the box or pot firm and, to allow plenty of room for a good watering (never a dribble), leave a clear half inch between the surface and the top of the container.

Kale

There are two kinds of kale and both are perhaps the best bargains of all of any leafy vegetable for growing the most winter vitamins on the smallest space for the least trouble. They are hardy through the toughest winters, clubroot-resistant, unattractive to pigeons and easy for everyone. If only they were just a bit more palatable they would be the perfect vegetable, but so far no one has devoted his life to breeding a 'Russell Lupin' kale, which could make his name as famous as that of Mr. Cox of Slough (who sowed a pip and grew his Pippin) in the hungrier world of the future.

110

Vegetables One by One

The Rape Kales are descended from the wild *Brassica campestris*, the ancestor of our turnips and swedes, and these must never be transplanted. Sow them in July or early August in pinches of four to five half an inch deep, two feet apart in staggered rows with thirty inches between them. Thin the clusters to the best in each and hoe between the plants if they get too weedy, otherwise they make no more work till picking time from January to even May in hard winters when everything else fails.

In November it is worth syringeing with nicotine if there are any signs of grey aphides on the leaves, because there is plenty of time for this to wash off and kale is a favourite overwintering crop for mealy cabbage aphis and cabbage white fly, while any caterpillars can be caught earlier with the same spray.

The nicest of this type is 'Asparagus Kale' and this should be gathered by breaking the shoots out sideways from between the big leaves, for these are a protection even when tattered by icy winds. The curled, dark green leaves of 'Hungry Gap', the next nicest, should never be stripped from a single plant, but gathered from along the row so that the plants keep on growing. These two are ideal winter green food for chickens, which never 'free range' far in winter, but delight in uprooted kale plants to peck at for exercise, interest, and the vitamin A that means deep orange far-from-battery yolks through the hardest weather.

Rape kales hate rich feeding as much as they do transplanting, for this makes them too tall and soft to stand up to wind and frost, so they should follow crops that had manure, though they appreciate generous liming. The pinch-sowing system makes a packet of seed last for ages, and the date should always be written on the packet, for seed keeps up to six years, which is just as well for many of these varieties are dropping out of cultivation.

Apart from the two most popular kinds there are 'Buda-Pest' or 'Hungarian', 'Delaware', 'Favourite', 'Labrador', 'Lapland', 'Ragged Jack', 'Russian', 'Shepherd's' and 'Siberian'. 'Russian' is reputed to be nice enough to eat raw, but it is the rarest, and those who find a kale they like should save their own seed. Leave a plant with its best side shoots unpicked so that these grow super mustard flower spikes in spring followed by long fat pods that should be gathered when they are light brown and starting to split at the tips. Hang them in a large paper (not polythene) bag head downwards to dry, and store in a cool dry drawer with other vegetable seeds.

111

Vegetables One by One

The other group of kales is often catalogued as 'Borecole', and is nearest to the original wild cabbage to the mutations of which through the ages we owe brussels sprouts, broccoli and cauliflowers as well. This is *Brassica olearacea* and the original species still survives on the Muldornich, a rocky islet off Barra in the Outer Hebrides, which has never been colonized by rabbits, and the sheep cannot reach it on the cliff ledges.

These are grown in exactly the same way and are just as hardy, but should be sown in April or May for transplanting in June or July at the same spacing, or to a waiting bed like brussels sprouts, for a move to their final homes before August ends. This is a great advantage when they must follow early potatoes, and makes this type more popular.

Leading kinds are 'Hearting Kale', 'Thousand-Headed Kale', 'Scotch', 'Dwarf Curled', 'Tall Curled' and 'Cottagers' ', and all are gathered on the 'cut and come again' principle of breaking away the shoots or leaves, but never all off one plant, so that all keep growing through the winter. The 'Flower Kale' with red or pink leaves for decoration is entirely tasteless and hardly worth growing except by those desperate for coloured foliage in winter.

The kale that shares with whisky the right to be called 'Scotch' by Scotsmen has a vitamin A content that can be equal to that of a carrot, and apart from the vitamins in the table under Broccoli (Sprouting Broccoli is a cross between the two races in the past) both types have more vitamin E than any other vegetable. Kale has 8 mg. per 100 grams compared with 1·5 for carrots, 2·6 for celery, 1·9 for leeks and 6 for fresh peas. Wheat germ (with 27) and the grain oils hold more, but kale is the only form in which we can grow our own share of this very important anti-arthritic vitamin that is essential to the health of our muscles.

The kales are among the leafy vegetables that contain vitamin K and are a better vegetable source than cabbage, cauliflower or tomatoes and rather better than spinach, rating higher than soya bean oil, egg-yolk and liver. Vitamin K is extremely valuable in helping the blood to clot, and those whose livers are defective need more of it. Little is known of it, and it is a 'trace vitamin' needed in small quantities, but kale is the best source so far identified and this could well be important in the future.

In the nineteenth century there were a group of Scottish novelists, including S. R. Crockett and Ian Maclaren, known as 'The Kailyard

112

School' because they wrote of humble crofters, for kale, which won for Scots gardens the name of 'kailyards' was all-important to them. The original 'Scotch Kale' may well have been developed from the wild cabbage of the Hebrides by the clansmen of the past, or more likely by their gardening, hen-tending, spinning and tartan-weaving wives.

It stood the climate, grew with little trouble, and would thrive for years without clubroot in the isolation of the 'in-by', a tiny field enclosed by stone walling to keep out the sheep. Kale provided the vitamin C to ward off scurvy through long Highland winters, and the vitamin A missing from a diet of oatmeal porridge (oats have only 2 mg. per 100 grams of vitamin E); 'brose', which was mutton broth with the oats that provided the main filling for haggis; salt herrings and fresh fish. It was cooked in a kind of thick soup, and because it is so rich in these vitamins, enough were left after even long simmering over the peat fires. Those who have seen the crowding ruined homes among the lofty bracken in the empty islands will give the kale due credit for balancing the diet that has made Scotsmen Scotland's finest export all through her history.

Kohlrabi

This is *Brassica olearacea caulorapa*, a wild variety from Israel that was brought back to Europe by returning Crusaders. It looks like a small, grey-green, leafy turnip sitting on top of the soil, and the important word is 'small', for the eating portion is not root but swollen stem, and this can very easily grow to a football-sized monster that is not even good compost material.

Sow them between April and June in inch-deep furrows a foot apart, and thin to nine inches between plants, using the thinnings in salads, for they have the typical nutty flavour that made the Crusaders gather seed to take home. Pull them for eating at cricket ball size, and if there are too many, take them up, pull off the leaves and store them in peat as recommended for beetroot. The best summer system is to sow a few at a time, and transplant some of the thinnings to the same spacing, for this delays them to come on later. Kohlrabi take from ten to twelve weeks to be ready for eating, but the last sowing in June is slower, and though they can be left in the open to eat as required, they are better dug in October for storing.

Cut off the top and root before cooking and cut (do not pull off)

H 113

the leaves before boiling the globes like turnips, but without peeling, or they will lose the nutty flavour which made the Crusader treasure his bag of seed on his long journey home. Eat them like turnips; slice after boiling and fry with egg and breadcrumbs as fritters: cut them in slices to serve cold with mayonnaise sauce like potato salad; or grate them to eat raw like young carrots.

Kohlrabi is very much lower in vitamin C than the other members of the cabbage tribe, because it is not leafy but stemmy. It has 37 mg. per 100 grams compared with 155 for kale, and this is reduced to 8 mg. if it is boiled for forty minutes. Cooked quickly as recommended in Chapter 9 they still have 35 mg. The control over temperature with the instant switch on and off instead of the slow build-up of heat on an old-fashioned range, has given the modern housewife assets in vegetable cookery that she far too often wastes. Kohlrabi's main value is in its vitamin A with 2,500 I.U.'s per 100 grams, about sixteen times as much as cabbage and twenty-five times as much as cauliflower, though it is not in the carrot or kale class.

Leeks

Leeks as big as bolsters and nearly as tasteless have graced flower shows for the past century, and there are still Leek Societies, like those specializing in giant gooseberries, in the North, where members bring their cherished monsters to their local for hotly-contested cups, and many liquid bets are placed on potential winners judged on past form before the great unveiling and weighing ceremony.

The best leek size for the modern gardener is about as fat as a candle, but because the leek is the easiest of the onion tribe, and the finest rest from clubroot-conscious crops a garden can have in winter, it is easy to grow more and smaller leeks from your own seedlings, planted when the ground is cleared and giving value from otherwise wasted space.

'Musselburgh' is the most usual variety, with 'The Lyon' a favourite with those who are trying for size. Sow thinly in April in a half-inch-deep furrow, bearing in mind that there are about a thousand seeds in a quarter ounce and that they will keep for four years, so it is better to sow for the few you need and have all strong plants than to crowd them in the row.

Dig over the ground after July or August early potatoes, both to level it and to remove any left-in little ones, and make dibber holes eight to nine inches deep and nine inches apart, with a foot between the staggered rows. Then drop a leek plant down each hole, and fill with water from a spouted can to settle it in. Apart from hoeing or weeding between the rows if there is a thick growth of chickweed in a wet autumn, this is all the care they need. If the plants are very tall, cut back the leaves with a knife before planting, and if the soil is poor, scatter a pound of fish meal to four square yards, but with normal compost rotations they manage on what the potatoes have left.

Dig them for eating between November and May, and do not cut back too much of the foliage, as market growers do. Their main value is in their 1,000 I.U.'s per 100 grams of vitamin A, better than cabbage but nowhere near kale, and most of this is in the leaves. They are extremely tasty both on their own and in soups and stews, and the Durham miners and Staffordshire potters made some very savoury hot-pots with those they grew for eating rather than show.

Leeks share diseases with onions, and these are avoided by rotating them round the garden, for the passing of the fixed onion bed has reduced the risk of soft rot, white rot, smut and smudge that they caught in the past. The leek moth (*Acrolepia assectella*) is a brown moth, half an inch across the wings, that lays eggs near ground level in April and early May on leek plants, onions, shallots and garlic. The caterpillars, eventually yellow-green and half an inch long, bore long tunnels in the leek leaves that show as white streaks until these join and leave the plants tattered and robbed of strength. The moths emerge in July and produce a second generation that over-winters as chrysalids in the ground or under rubbish, to attack next year.

The best remedy is the nicotine wash described earlier in the chapter, watered on the young plants in the seedbed and on the crop in late July and August. The tunnel surface is thin enough for the nicotine to kill the caterpillars inside as it does celery leaf miner maggots. Digging over the cleared portion of the bed gives the robins a chance at the chrysalids.

Lettuce

The first and most welcome lettuce in May begin best if bought as plants from a local market or nursery. They will have been raised under glass and hardened for the outdoor market garden crop that can earn more than 5p when warm weather stirs salad longings, while our first sowings wait for June. 'Lobjoit's Green' (cos) and

'Cheshunt Early Ball' (cabbage) are favourites, but the local nursery's choice of a fast one is better than plants that have been dried by posting. They will be ready still faster for those who can dig a greenhouse bed and plant them now six inches apart each way in double rows, between where the tomatoes go later.

Dig a bucket of compost or well-rotted manure into each square yard of an outdoor bed: 4 oz. of fish meal, dried sludge or poultry guano are alternatives. Then rake level and plant with eight inches between the plants (six for cos) in rows eight inches apart.

Lettuces look small and frail when dug (carefully) from their boxes, but are tough for their size if planted without squeezing the stems or burying where the leaves join. Water well with a rosed can to start them and generously in the showerless Aprils that harm them more than frost does.

Wire-netting pea-guards in short sections, with legs to thrust in the ground, solve the sparrow problem. When the plants reach the tops of these birdproof tunnels the lettuce are safe from pecking and you can move the guards to the next sowing. They fold flat for winter storage and last for years.

Sown lettuce need the same kind of bed, and half-inch-deep furrows eight inches apart. Aim at an inch between the seeds. Unlike the plants chosen for speed, they must be slow to bolt in hot summers. 'Nonesuch' or 'Little Gem' (cos) or 'Webb's Wonderful' (cabbage) will wait four weeks in the rows for cutting without running to seed.

Sow in May for June salads, then every three to four weeks until the end of July with the last 'Nonesuch' sowing to eat far into autumn. Thin to plant spacing when they are about two inches high. Though both cos are 'self-folding' they heart quicker and faster if tied half-way down with bast or wool as soon as their leaf tips point inwards.

The leafier the lettuce the higher its vitamin A, up to 4–5,000 I.U.'s per 100 grams, down to a mere 100 for the white bleached leaves in the centre of one very well hearted. This is true also for their very low vitamin C, with 8 mg. for hearts, 18 for fresh green leaves.

Sutton's 'Windermere' is the best of the new frilled leaf edge varieties which are highest in vitamins and slowest of all to bolt. They are best nine inches apart with a foot between rows, because they are always rather larger than the usual kinds. Like all summer lettuce, these kinds transplant well, and putting out the best of the thinnings at the same spacing on any vacant ground will bring on a between-sowings batch that can be very useful.

Vegetables One by One

The best all-round winter lettuce is 'Arctic King', an old variety that reddens at the leaf tips with frost but has a sporting chance of coming through the winter alive. 'Winter Density' is the hardiest cos variety, but except in the extreme south it is usually finished by hard weather after Christmas. Sow either or both in August thinly in a sunny place, remembering that the seed lasts at least three seasons.

Dig up the seedlings when they are an inch high, about early October, and plant them eight inches apart and eight inches between their staggered rows, ideally on a border sloping south. With care in the final picking and pulling it is possible to fit in winter lettuce after the outdoor tomatoes which are usually occupying the sunniest place. Keep them as weed-free as possible, and free from dead leaves because these hide the slugs that are the lettuce's worst enemies.

In most gardens it pays to water the bed a fortnight before planting with a solution of Fertosan Slug Destroyer, which is most effective against the small ones, but less so against the tough monsters. It should not be watered on seedlings but can safely be rosed on between the tomatoes before these are pulled up. In many gardens, especially on clays in wet summers, Fertosan between the rows or before planting makes a real impression, though the soup plate trapping system reinforces the effect.

The other major pest is the lettuce root aphis (*Pemphigus bursarius*) which spends most of the year on poplar trees. In July the winged creature flies off and spends a summer holiday on the roots of sow thistles, fat-hen and lettuces. The sign of their arrival is when large healthy lettuces suddenly flop in the sun, and when their roots are examined they will be found to be covered with yellow aphides hiding under wool. The remedy is to water the neighbours of the slaughtered plants with liquid derris. You are eating the lettuce, so never use nicotine. Keeping the garden free from sow thistles is also helpful.

Lettuce beds are also attacked by grey mould fungus (*Botrytis cinerea*) and the best answer is rotation. Abandon the bed, compost the crop and grow something else, planting or sowing more lettuce elsewhere. If the trouble persists, sterilize the soil with Jeyes' Fluid, which is mostly phenols, and there are bacteria specialized to break these down. A less drastic remedy for between the rows or where there is no more room for lettuce except the afflicted bed, is 1 oz. of potassium permanganate in two gallons of cold water, watered on freshly mixed. This is mainly used where the seedlings vanish from damping-off fungus, and it can only leave behind a little useful potassium.

Vegetables One by One

Marrows

The traditional monster marrow is very poor value for space in the modern garden, for at normal eating ripeness it is between 95 and 99 per cent water, rather less food value than cucumbers which are 95 to 97 per cent. Its vitamin A is about 30 I.U.'s against up to 1,610 for cooked pumpkin, while its vitamin C at 11 mg. and its 30 thiamine is one third of that in lettuce. The dry matter rises at Harvest Festival sizes, but mostly in the skin which needs a saw to get through so that the flesh can be used in marrow jam, which is mainly ginger and sugar. Those who need jam would do far better to take some vitamin C with all that expensive and weight-making sugar and make black-currant instead.

There are smaller marrows, the French courgettes, and the Italian cocozelles, also the 'Vegetable Spaghetti', but these are eaten small and immature, often cooked by recipes of the 'wrap in bacon, place a clove of garlic in the middle, soak in wine overnight then fry in butter and season with red peppers before serving with brandy sauce' type. Some simpler ones are included in Chapter 9.

These can all be grown by the methods used for pumpkins, and rather than repeat them, I ask the reader who has an affection for marrows and is determined to grow them, to refer to the pumpkin pages. The small European marrows can be grown in the same way, but should be picked small, no larger than six inches long, and kept picked to keep up the succession from the plant, as with a bush marrow. Ornamental gourds can also be grown on the pumpkin routine, but if you are saving seed of one of the new high-dry-matter pumpkins, grow only this because the whole family crosses recklessly.

Onions

Modern onions are mild, but those that sailed with Drake and kept scurvy at bay as long as they lasted were strong enough to send a pirate's parrot squawking into the rigging. There were acres and acres of long-forgotten varieties grown in the West, mainly round Bristol, for customers who bought them for strength, to mask the taste of salt beef and pork, and for the acids that softened meat so tough that the ready-use container was called 'the harness cask' because its contents were so often like leather.

Vegetables One by One

The 'gentlemen adventurers of England' did not know that they were also buying the best storable source of vitamin C, or ascorbic acid, available at the time, with 9–15 mg. per 100 grams, against 6–10 for carrots. Turnips with 30 mg. would have been better eaten raw, as they were in the fields in the Hungry Forties, but they do not soften tough meat, and lemons with 45 mg. or the lime juice of Surgeon Lind of the Royal Navy, at 37 mg., are far superior. It took five centuries of failures to defeat scurvy at sea, but it still survives in Old People's Homes where they do often not prepare or cook their vegetables properly or serve enough of them.

Only one onion remains in cultivation from the past that demanded a *real* taste, and this is 'Up-to-Date', which was new in the 1890's when it was bred to go with bread, cheese and beer for the countryman's lunch. The farmworker by tradition had free manure at muckspreading time and his fertile garden would have grown onions with rather more than the 50·7 mg. per 100 grams of sulphur which is the modern average (about twice as much as cabbage) and therefore his would have been stronger, especially when eaten raw. We say that onions 'demand' potash, but though they grow more weight with this added as a chemical, they also take up less sulphur and so are 'milder'.

Some onion addicts insist that 'Giant Zittau' is a larger and more powerful variety still, reputed in the North to be capable of opening the garden gate with a single breath from the proud grower, but it is a question of soil, skill and taste. It is certain that those who took a 'snap' to work, tied up in a red-and-white spotted handkerchief, and grew most of it themselves, had a finer appreciation of flavour than the modern who fills up on fish-paste sandwiches.

Those who want to grow old-fashioned onions fit for the farmworkers of even fifty years ago, must raise them from seed. Start by digging in 1 lb. of lime to four square yards in February or March a fortnight before sowing, and then scatter eight ounces to a square yard of a mixture of equal parts of salt and soot, plus four ounces of fish meal. The salt is rather a cunning trick in this traditional recipe, for wild onions were seashore plants, like beet which also appreciates salt, and this acts as a substitute for potash.

If you have good weather and a nice fine surface on the bed by mid-March, sow then. Otherwise, wait till mid-April before treading and rolling the bed, then raking it, till it is 'as firm and level as a billiard table' yet fine on the surface. Sow your 'Up-to-Date' thinly in rows eight inches apart, covering the half-inch-deep furrows carefully with fine soil after scattering an ounce of flowers of sulphur to every three yards of furrow to prevent onion fly.

Thin the seedlings in May or early June to three inches apart for small bulbs, or six for large, if the ground is rich, otherwise leave unthinned (which defeats the onion fly completely) for pickling size. Many countrymen still sow very thinly, to avoid trouble and fly risk, and enjoy onions two inches across of a strength ideal for raw eating and for offering to appreciative friends over a lunch-time pint. 'Up-to-Date' is quite something as a pickling onion compared with 'Paris Silver-skinned' which has merely white colour and mildness to recommend it.

After thinning, scatter two ounces to a square yard of fish meal between the rows and hoe the weeds away in June and again in July, the fish meal giving nitrogen and phosphorus, not potash, to bring both size *and* flavour. In August when the leaves begin to yellow at the tips, bend the foliage over at the necks, loosen the roots with a fork, and lift them finally after about a fortnight of this treatment.

All this sounds (and is) a great deal of trouble, especially the achieving of the billiard table effect in the early spring, and this is why gardeners kept their best-draining, sunniest and richest strip for the onion bed, which built up a population of diseases and onion fly chrysalids. It was possible to grow hefty onions this way, with an even heftier flavour, but there is no need to bother. Every year fewer onions are grown from seed, and at last the more conservative Flower Show Committees are being driven to have classes for onions raised from sets, which have been disqualified as 'unsporting' until now, because they take no skill to grow.

In the past onion sets were chancy, small bulbs raised by peasants in Cyprus, Greece and Turkey. Now the Dutch have taken over the trade with Stuttgarter Riesen, 200 to the pound, grown for minimum bolting and a level crop of large flat onions as reliable as any other Dutch bulbs. There is now a British variety, 'Marshall's Giant Fen', a round one bred for size which will grow to four or five pounds with rich treatment, and even with little care yields far more than the ten-ounce average of the ordinary kind.

If you want large onions, start in March; for smaller sizes, wait till April. The only essential is that the soil should be firm, for all onions like something firm to push against when they heave themselves out on their roots and sit in the sun. Those who have soot and are on a sandy soil can rake in that salt and soot mixture if desired, but on the rotations recommended in Chapter 4 the soil will have lime enough to supply their needs. Stand the pea-sized bulblets at six-inch intervals along inch-deep furrows a foot apart, first twisting off the dry tops so that nothing shows when the soil is firmed back over them with the rake head. Let the tops protrude, and modern birds will peck up every one.

Hoe them to keep down weeds, and if you are growing 'Giant Fen' the two feeds of fish meal recommended for seed crops will increase the crop weight while improving the flavour. Bend them over as soon as the tips yellow, loosen the roots, leave for ten days to dry, then lift and spread on sacks in the sun to go on drying, three to four weeks sooner than any variety raised from seed. The flying start from the small bulbs means an easier, hardier crop that is less fussy about its soil, a faster finish giving a better chance of drying the bulbs in a wet season, and a greater variety of possible plantings afterwards. Above all there is hardly any risk of onion fly and it is likely, as the seed-raised onion becomes a crop of the past, that the onion fly will again become only a rare controller of the wild onion weed.

There are several methods of storing the onion crop which can easily weigh a hundredweight from a single pound of sets. The simplest is to pack the bulbs into laddered nylon stockings or tights, and hang them in a dry shed after most of the foliage has been removed. Some ladders in the nylons are essential to provide ventilation, as onions must breathe and be kept dry (unlike beet and carrots, which store best in peat). Another easy method is to nail inch-mesh wire-netting on a frame of 2-in. × 1-in. timber and hoist it to the roof of the garage to be lowered for inspection and selection at intervals. This device is also excellent for keeping gladioli bulbs.

The professional way is to make ropes, which are easily enough made to non-Breton standards once you have been shown how. This is the problem, and it is hoped that the diagrams will make it clear. Start with a three-foot length of fine strong string, tie the ends together and loop it over a nail or hook. Secure one large onion at the bottom, as in Fig. 2, then twist the dried stem of the second onion round the double string and flop it over, followed by the third and so on until the string is finished. Ten pounds is a good weight for an onion string and they hang well from the rafters in ventilated roof spaces, taking up to 45° F comfortably.

Those who have a mighty store of golden onions, compost grown and full of flavour and vitamins, should beware of eating too many.

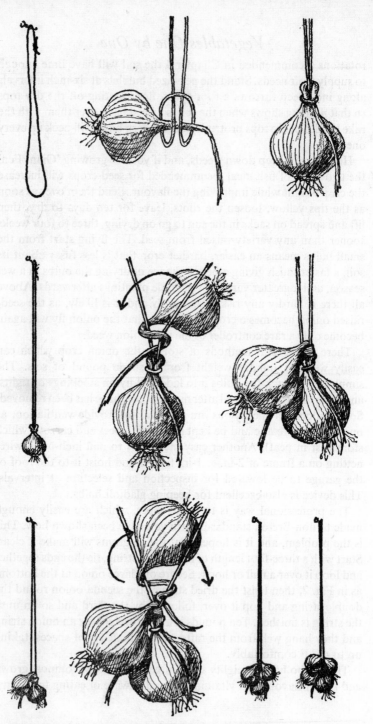

4. Making an onion-rope is easier shown than described, but start at the top left hand corner and work down. It is easier than it looks

Vegetables One by One

According to Dr. Magnus Pyke, onions contain a small quantity of an alkaloid that can be harmful if more than 1 lb. a day are eaten regularly. This consumption is very rare, for even those who indulge in orgies with large baked onions do not have them every day, and few addicts enjoying them fried or in stews get through more than eight ounces in twenty-four hours.

Stored onions rarely last beyond May without growing, but spring onions can bridge the gap. Buy salad bunches in April, when they will be far cheaper than the greenhouse-grown 'Ailsa Craig' sometimes offered for planting at the same time and spacing as onion sets. Choose the smaller plants from the bunch and plant four inches apart and eight inches between rows, without any need for special soil preparation. As they grow it is possible to snip the tips from the leaves to add an onion flavour to salads, which does not seem to interfere with their progress. Dig up the swelling bulbs as required for soups and stews, aiming to finish them by the time the set crop are ready to lift, for they will be 'White Lisbon', a non-keeping variety, which is a very useful stopgap.

This is the best of the salad onions to sow thinly at the end of August or in early September in half-inch-deep furrows, nine inches apart; hoe or weed them clean before November, when they should be well up. Dig them unthinned through the spring as a useful winter crop for a sunny place. Another way to enjoy spring onions and to evade the problem of getting that billiard table bed in March on a clay soil, is to sow ordinary varieties at the same spacing in the autumn and thin them to four inches apart, eating the thinnings and leaving the best to grow on. The winter rains and the settling of the ground will have provided all the firmness they need. Varieties for this purpose are 'Rousham Park Hero', a monster that will achieve two-pounders from seed, with a powerful taste; 'Reliance', 'Autumn Triumph' and 'Solidarity', the first being resistant to white rot. Though 'Up-to-Date' is not suitable for autumn sowing it is also resistant to mildew, while 'Giant Zittau' can catch both, if grown too long in the same bed or where others have over-onioned the environment, as on old allotments.

Pickling onions are sown unthinned, ideally on poor soil in a dry place about April, so that they should 'run out of steam' about July and ripen off for early August pickling. Though 'Silver Skinned' in one or other of its forms, or the newer 'Cocktail' (which will grow inch-diameter bulbs for pickling or parties in twelve weeks) are bred for this fast finish, any other variety can be tried by the pickler, especially the old flavour kinds, for very few pickled onions are eaten at a time.

There are many recipes for pickling but the following is relatively simple. Wash the onions and place without skinning in a brine made from 1 lb. salt (sea salt, not table with additives) in a gallon of cold water. Leave them for twelve hours, then peel and leave in fresh brine of the same strength for thirty-six hours. Remove and allow to drain, pack into jars and fill up with cold spiced vinegar, making sure always that all the onions are covered.

The mildest onion of all, if it can be found still, is the 'Potato Onion', which grows from offsets like shallots. Plant single offsets, about the size and shape of just flowering grade tulips, in January six inches apart and a foot between rows. Keep them hoed and they will die down about July ready to dig with large clusters of offsets at the base, for storing like tulips, and for replanting to keep the stock going. These are so mild that they are literally 'without tears' at peeling time, and resist all the pests and diseases that are baffled by the lack of scent, though they still have enough to be useful in cookery. A stock may survive somewhere in a cottage garden, probably in Somerset where it was common in the 1940's.

A mild garlic to grow at the same spacing, but on a smaller scale, is *Allium moly*, which at 10p a dozen as a hardy small bulb is cheaper than cloves of real garlic in a greengrocer's. It grows six to twelve inches high with bright yellow flowers in large heads in July. The real garlic is *Allium sativum*, and the cheapest way to buy a small quantity of cloves for a start is at a greengrocer's, for they cost about 60p for a pound from seedsmen, and a pound is far more than most people need. Plant the bulblets in March nine inches apart and a foot between rows with the tips just under the surface. Keep them clean through the summer when they will probably have white or pink or pale purple flower heads on plants up to two feet high; lift them when they die down in August, and dry them thoroughly in the sun for storage and replanting.

Anyone who wishes to sell a surplus from the garden would do well to start with garlic, which has a ready sale to Wholefood shops, as have all the onion tribe. They are not only easily grown, but easily stored, and instead of struggling to sell broad and runner beans and about-to-bolt lettuces when trade is at its lowest, with summer holidays, garlic and onions can be started with trial consignments and follow-up orders can be spread through the winter. Garlic and Allium, best sold as 'Mellow Garlic' because few people know it is one, are the crops which earn the highest price in relation to weight, though the market soon saturates.

Parsley

Though parsley is as rich in vitamin A as kale, and second to it in vitamin C, 5·5 mg. against 8 mg. to the 100 grams, it contains an alkaloid, Apiol, which prevents our using it as a main vegetable. It is, however, a very useful addition to soups and sauces and may be chopped raw over boiled or new potatoes. We like the curled types, but on the Continent the large-leafed French variety is preferred for eating as a salad item rather than as a garnish.

Both are grown in the same way, and both are slow to germinate, taking four to six weeks to come up. This period can be shortened by soaking the seed overnight in urine, but it is always as well to sow radishes along the inch-deep parsley furrow a foot apart in March and July. These will be up quickly and will mark the rows; they can be hoed and pulled for eating when the parsley is thinned to three inches between plants. The second sowing is the most likely to last the winter and produce foliage for picking right the way round till spring.

Parsley is a biennial and it is usually only necessary to sow it every other year, though those who like it can sow some every spring to make sure of plenty of what is a herb rather than a vegetable. It is possible to dig plants up and pot them to keep on an inside windowsill for use through the winter in cold districts, but be sure you dig up *all* the slender tap root, or they will not thrive.

Parsnips

The parsnip contains no fat-soluble vitamins—A, D, E and K are all missing from its makeup entirely, but 100 grams holds 80–120 micrograms of thiamine, about 20 per cent more than in carrots or turnips, 90 of riboflavin, a third higher than carrots but under a quarter of the turnip quantity, 0·2 of niacin against 0·5 for carrots and 1·2 for potatoes, but 18–30 of vitamin C, which is higher than in any other root though under half the average of cabbage. Because parsnips are deep rooted they are well off for minerals, especially calcium and phosphorus, but are beaten on iron by both beet and salsify, as the following table shows:

MINERALS IN ROOT VEGETABLES

	Calcium	*Mg. per 100 grams* Phosphorus	iron
Parsnips	56	76	1·07
Beet	24	37	2·36
Carrots	46	38	0·43
Potatoes	14	58	0·85
Salsify	60	53	1·23
Turnips	64	46	0·70

Another 'distinction' parsnips have is that the seed is not only slow to germinate, it is also rarely usable for the following season, so always throw the half-empty packet away. The longest parsnip, and of the finest flavour, with an absence of hard core when it has grown slowly in a dry season, is 'Tender and True', which has gone two feet deep on rich soils, and will go down deep enough to gather moisture on sands. The shortest is 'Offenham', fat and stumpy for thin soils over chalk or heavy clays, and 'The Student' is an intermediate type.

Their major complaint (not disease) is canker, caused by assorted fungi rotting down from the cracks in the root tops, which they cannot heal naturally as carrots do when they split from dry weather. Therefore sow them as late as the second week in April, or even the first week in May, for smaller and better-keeping parsnips. Those who like to leave theirs in the open to lift as required, instead of lifting in November and storing in peat, can lose their whole crop with canker in winter.

Sowing as late as this means that a quarter-ounce packet grows between 80 lb. and 1 cwt. of parsnips, and fills about 100 feet of rows fifteen inches apart. Begin by spreading 1 lb. lime and 8 oz. fish meal to four square yards before digging and raking level. Then make an inch-deep furrow with the hoe corner along the garden line for the first row, and set out clusters of four seeds at nine-inch intervals along it. These are going to take between twenty and thirty days to appear, which is long enough for weeds to swamp them in the high tide of spring, so sow radishes in the intervals between the clusters. These will be up fast to mark the rows, as for parsley, and by the time the radishes are pulled for eating the parsnips will be up far enough for the best in each cluster to show, and the other three can be removed.

Except for benefiting from hoeing when necessary the parsnips need little more attention, but if they have celery leaf miner tunnels in the leaves, these leaves should be removed; or they are stunted with mildew, scatter a teaspoonful of dried blood round the affected plants. They grow slowly, and this tonic has all the effect of brandy in an emergency on a non-drinker.

Peas

The best peas of our lives were those we ate raw from illegal pickings when we were young, for they held more than three times as much vitamin C and four times the B_1 and B_2 as garden peas from the giant 'gardens' attached to every canning factory. They are perhaps our nicest vegetable, leaving more nitrogen in the soil than they take out, and giving their haulm as compost material, apart from the crop. Eat them raw in salads and cooked with almost everything. If you use the quick cookery methods described in Chapter 9, very little of their value is wasted and many more can be eaten; and they can also be dried for winter pea soups (summer ones can be made from the pods).

There are a great many varieties of pea, from very short early ones to lofty maincrops, but perhaps the best all-rounder is 'Kelvedon Wonder', sown every three weeks from the first week in March to the last week in July for a constant succession from May till November. Though there are faster earlier peas than 'Kelvedon Wonder', with about sixty days between sowing and picking, this one has considerable resistance to mildew, and this ensures later pickings in dry summers. 'Laxton's Superb' is not quite so fast, but a heavier cropper, and this is the best one for leaving till the pods wrinkle and go brown, and the haulm is hung up to wither till the round firm seeds are ready to store dry.

Both grow two feet high, which is short enough to provide the modern answer to the peastick shortage and delinquent birds. Mice can be defeated either by buying seed ready treated with a herbal mouse repellent (from Messrs. Chase) or by emptying the packet in a basin and swirling the peas with paraffin till all are wet with a taste that will not reach the crop but which makes nasty nibbling. There is no reliable bird repellent and the best protection for the early sowings will be wire pea guards arched over the rows.

Peas that are to stand persistent picking for eating raw before the pods pack tight, and for cooking afterwards, need trenches six to eight inches wide and deep, two feet apart and half filled with trodden lawn mowings and even sink-basket refuse, with the unrotted top of the compost heap useful for the earliest rows before the first mowing. Whiten this layer with lime and add two inches of soil before sowing the 240 odd seeds in half a pint two inches apart in two rows with three inches between them down the middle of each trench, which makes this many fill twenty feet of trenches. Then cover them with another two inches of soil and leave them safely growing under their pea guards.

Before these are outgrown buy 1½-inch mesh wire netting thirty inches or three feet wide. At each row end drive in a length of creosoted 2-inch × 1-inch timber a foot taller than the width of the wire to allow enough in the ground to hold it. Then cut a length of netting twice as long as the row, plus a foot for the ends, and wrap it round the outside of the posts joining it by hooking the ends together. Canes, thrust through the meshes and into the soil in inverted 'V's' at two- to three-foot intervals hold the wire apart at the bottom and prevent flopping. The pea tendrils can grip the wire and climb, the middle pods can be picked by reaching down inside, but even those that hang outside are usually safe from birds which dislike flying between high netted rows. Two short ones are therefore safer than a single long one.

The distance between the rows can be varied to suit the brassica crop that follows, so that the brussels sprout plants are dibbed in where the peas are cut short. Through the summer the long, narrow 'compost heaps' of the buried material will sink, leaving hollows to hold waterings or hosings in drought, and using the nitrogen gathered by root bacteria to help rot the rubbish into plant foods and humus. If sink-basket refuse is used, especially early in the year, avoid including many potato peelings, because the eyes on these, or any cut-off green portions, will grow easily where they are unwanted and crowd the peas. On chalky or very sandy soil, dig the trenches down a bit deeper and line with four thicknesses of newspaper to retain more moisture.

On good soils, or even on others, where one is pressed for time, it is possible to get good crops by scattering 1 lb. of lime to four square yards and digging it in with any available compost in early March, then taking out spade-wide trenches two inches deep and setting out the peas in the same double rows before replacing the soil and covering with peaguards. This is often done for the first sowing, and if soot is available it pays to scatter enough to blacken the surface of each row to trap rather more sun heat and bring the peas along earlier. Those who want a very fast early pea that needs no support should choose 'Meteor' which can usually provide four good pickings from its foot-long stems.

'Alderman' and 'Admiral Beatty' are both heavy-cropping, six-feet-high late varieties which are still in the catalogues on merit, but their rows should go four feet apart and they need tall supports well spread so that you gain by making rather fewer sowings, but lose on space which is usually the scarcest commodity in a small garden. 'Dobie's Everbearing', with pairs of pods growing three feet high, will reduce the number of sowings by keeping in production longer, but how long depends on soil and season.

The French Sugar Pea, 'Petit Pois', and its dwarf variety, are grown in exactly the same way as 'Kelvedon Wonder', but the first is a three-foot kind so needs four-foot-width netting. These have smaller pods, but the raw peas are rather sweeter, and they are cooked pods and all at first, slicing as for French beans, but later podding in the ordinary way.

The main enemy of peas, apart from birds and mice, is the pea weevil (*Sitona lineata*) which can build up a huge population in 'no digging' gardens. For these offer plenty of surface litter for the beetles to hide under, and no chance for birds to eat them; they hibernate in winter and are nocturnal, so this quarter-inch-long beetle, brown with yellow stripes, is rarely seen. It eats the young leaves into scalloped edges and a bad attack can cripple a sowing. Water the young plants and the surrounding area with the nicotine was recommended earlier, to catch the creatures in hiding and to leave enough on the leaves to kill the night-nibbling beetles. There is of course no risk of poisoning with the nicotine, for it has long been spent by picking time.

Pea thrips (*Kakothrips pisivorus*) are small black creatures that lay eggs on the flowers and foliage in May and June. The orange nymphs (not larvae) are like aphides and swarm on the flowers and young pods until they descend to the soil to hibernate till next year. Spraying with nicotine wash is the answer, for though the attack is soon over, it will be worse next year when the sleepers awake. Do not use the sprayed pea pods for soup; or if the creatures attack when the peas are pickable, use a derris and pyrethrum mixture, as they are too

I

tough to be affected by either alone. The pea moth (*Cydia nigricana*) lays its eggs between June and August and is responsible for the maggots inside the pod, where the moth cannot be reached by spraying. The caterpillars drop to the ground and hibernate four inches deep in white cocoons, and the best procedure after an attack is to dig over the ground shallowly in winter to give the birds a chance to eat the chrysalids. If the attack is a bad one, grow only March-sown peas and use French or runner beans to fill the gap later. This will starve them out in time.

Though peas have a number of fungus problems these are all curable by using rotations and keeping up both the lime and the humus. If the foliage has pale yellow markings between the leaf veins, water with Epsom salts, for the pea mosaic virus is rare and magnesium deficiency very common. Dusting with flowers of sulphur is a means of checking mildew where a non-resistant variety is grown.

Peas are one of the nicest sources of the green vegetable vitamins, and the one whose value is most reduced by canning, though deep-freezing retains the vitamins very well. Tinned peas are common in canteens and restaurants today, and where they are the sole source of vitamin C, health can suffer. Those who garden enjoy their peas as one of the delights of summer, but work them in with other crops as well. The table that follows shows their strength and weakness.

	Vit. A	Vit. C I.U.'s	Vit. E	Niacin	Thiamine Micro- grams	Riboflavin Micro- grams
Mg. per 100 grams, unless otherwise stated						
Peas Raw		25·00		2·10	400	200
Peas Cooked	680	6–8	6·00	—	—	—
Peas Canned	—	8	—	0·90	110	60
Peas Dried	530	2	—	3·00	870	290

Drying one's own peas concentrates their vitamins B_1 (thiamine) and B_2 (riboflavin), and keeps a useful supply of vitamin A and niacin, although one cannot expect to keep the vitamin C, and there is plenty in the cabbage tribe. Even with only a few stored, this means pea soup free from dyes and additives, and you have only the trouble of drying and pouring into screw-top jars where they will keep as easily as home-grown butterbeans.

Vegetables One by One

Potatoes

The potato is the pivot of every garden rotation, and our most important vegetable, one that we never tire of, one which can be cooked in a wide variety of ways and, next to the onion, the most useful addition to made-up dishes. It can be used with advantage as a substitute for white flour in every slimming diet. Cut out the white sugar, the biscuits and the cakes that you buy, and eat the potatoes that you can grow of better quality and of a finer flavour than any that the greengrocer sells.

Only two out of about fifty varieties are known to greengrocers' girls—'King Edwards' and 'whites' which are usually the tasteless and heavy-yielding 'Majestic', because farmers are paid by the ton and nothing extra for taste. Apart altogether from the flavour advantage from compost or comfrey, those who grow their own can choose the varieties to suit their individual preferences, and though a few are given here as a starting choice, it always pays to try seven pounds of something new each year to see if it is any better. On your soil it may outyield any of the varieties mentioned, its cooking quality may be better and its flavour finer. Very many old varieties remain in cultivation because of conservatism, but some have survived on their merits, and the new may be no better than, or even worse than, the old. New qualities, such as blight resistance, can, of course, put the latest triumphs of plant breeding far ahead.

There are two types of potato eater—'waxy people' who like theirs firm and yellow, the kind of spud that stays whole in a salad and fries well, and 'floury people'. The latter are in the majority and responsible for the extra price that 'King Edwards' still earn after all these years. It is not a good garden potato, because it likes a deeply cultivated soil, which is cheap and easy on the farm with tractor cultivation, but impossible for any normal gardener to achieve. Try it if you like, but the yield will be a disappointment.

My wife and I are 'waxy people' and therefore we consider that 'Duke of York' is the potato for every garden, to lift and scrape, and also to leave in to grow large and keep till at least March. It is an excellent 'new potato', though not so fast as some, a good frier, firm in potato salad, slow to cook to smash, and a really first-class baker in its jacket. Save even the smallest, because their skins are tender and they are good when liquidized in soups. The only snag is that it

131

is attacked by potato blight, like most of the familiar varieties still grown out of sentiment and conservatism, but it finishes fast and so has usually grown its crop before blight strikes. An additional asset is that it needs no 'settling down period', for most main crops need a month or more to mature after lifting, just as celery needs a frost on it for the best taste, and Cox's are better after Christmas.

The best maincrop to follow 'Duke of York' is 'Record', raised as 'Bintje' in Holland, which is now our most widely grown potato next to 'King Edward'. The potato-crisp makers have discovered that it is not only the finest frier of all, but it has the least dry matter of any variety, which saves tons of fuel and produces the crinkliest crisp, even with great blisters on some, and this means that however full the packet may look it contains far fewer than with 'Conference', that was merely the roundest for rolling down the chutes of mechanical peelers. 'Record' is only grown by farmers with contracts for crisping, because the yield is lower than 'Majestics' and the public will not pay extra for flavour.

'Record' has been described as 'the Cox of the kitchen garden' and its yield is far higher than that of 'Golden Wonder', the famous floury-flavour variety, or 'Pink Fir Apple', the best-known of the Continental frying kinds. The higher dry matter shows in the fact that it does not splutter when cooked in oil, and of course the gardener is still growing as much food, merely carrying less water up the garden path. Another good keeper and a splendid cooker is 'Desirée', pink skinned, yellow fleshed, a good salad and frying variety, and the best flavoured of all the blight-resistant kinds.

The finest keeping potato of all is 'Arran Consul', 'the potato that grows old gracefully', which is white, but firm and a good cooker as well. The gardener who wants the best-quality eating potatoes for longest should buy all three, reversing the usual procedure by buying most earlies, and just a few, 7 lb. or 14 lb., of 'Arran Consul' to eat when his 'Records' are showing their age.

There are many floury potatoes to replace 'Duke of York', and perhaps the best is 'Pentland Beauty', which has pink patches on the skin and is immune to the common strains of potato blight. Another one, but rather later—a second-early rather than an early—is 'Maris Peer', which is also blight-resistant. 'Pentland' means a variety raised at the Plant Breeding Station at Edinburgh, while 'Maris' is the Cambridge prefix.

'Epicure' is a famous early, but it has deep eyes that make it awkward to scrape and it will not keep well if left in to grow large. 'Ulster Chieftain' grows coarse as it matures and the popular 'Arran Pilot' and 'Home Guard' are not good in this dual-purpose role.

The sign that all these early or 'second-early' varieties have enough tubers ready to be worth digging is fully open flowers, but always lift only as many as you need for immediate use, because even an extra three days in the ground means more weight to the foot of row. Potatoes for lifting and storing stay in till the foliage dies down. Leave early varieties twenty-four hours before cooking to lose the earthy flavour.

There are many floury maincrops, and 'Maris Page' is a variety high in dry matter that is a good keeper and blight-resister, but without the flavour of 'Record', for so far none of these new blight-resisting kinds has a really outstanding taste. 'Pentland Dell' is like a blight-resistant 'Majestic', a heavy yielder but rather tasteless, while 'Pentland Crown' resists scab, slugs and drought, but not blight, and is best eaten after January. The best maincrop for a new garden is 'Kerr's Pink', because it has the thickest haulm for weed-suppressing and it is a good cooker and keeper in the white and floury class. It is the fish and chip shop favourite because chips prepared in advance will stay out of water longest without going black.

Those who want an extra-dry and floury potato should try 'Golden Wonder', especially in Scotland and the North, for it could crop well for them, though it is almost always a disappointment in Southern counties. 'Sharpe's Express' is also a quality potato for the North, while 'Orion', a rather yellow-fleshed maincrop, is the ideal creaming potato, making the smoothest mash of any. Almost every variety will taste far better if compost- or comfrey-grown than if grown with chemicals, partly because most modern potato fertilizers contain potassium chloride (muriate of potash) which gives them the 'soapy' taste organic gardeners recognize when they finish their own and have to buy from the greengrocer. This also makes farm crops thirstier, taking up to 5 per cent more moisture or a hundredweight bag of water in every ton.

Early or second-early potatoes need a foot between seed tubers, which should average the size of a 'small' grade egg, and 14 lb. of seed fills 120 feet of rows, eighteen inches apart. Maincrops go fifteen inches apart but the seed is larger, so 14 lb. is also enough for 120 feet, but with twenty-seven inches between rows. This is the optimum distance apart worked out by the Royal Horticultural Society for victory diggers in the 1914–18 War, and if they go closer, yield is lost by overcrowding.

Easter is our traditional potato-planting time, because this was the farmworkers' holiday that gave them a chance to do the heaviest planting work in their own gardens, leaving lighter sowings to their wives. This can fall early or late, and at any season the weather can be horrid, so the best insurance against nasty springs is chitting trays, in which seed potatoes can wait without losing growing time long past the mid-March for earlies and mid-April for main crops, which are the ideal planting times.

Farmers' chitting trays are strongly and specially made, but the best for gardeners are the Dutch grape or tomato trays with corners raised so that they stand on top of each other and allow light and air to circulate between. There are other types of these non-returnable crates, all cheaply bought, and it is worth deciding on a size and buying up well in advance of the arrival of the seed potatoes in January or February, ideally ordered before Christmas.

The newly arrived potatoes will be seen to have all the eyes at one end—known as the 'rose end'—and they should be packed into the trays with this end upwards. At this stage potatoes need light and air so that their first shoots grow short, dark and firm, not as thin white tentacles which result from struggling to grow in the dark. So take down the cover from the windows of the shed where eating potatoes were stored in the *dark*, or stack the trays in a potting-shed, greenhouse or even an unheated spare room. The one misfortune they can suffer is aphides on the shoots, and dusting with derris will deal with this.

The lazy way of potato-planting is to dig or rotovate the compost in first and then make seven-inch-deep holes with a large dibber and drop a potato down each, firming the soil to fill the hole. The disadvantage on clay soils is that the dibber packs and puddles so that the hole holds water, and this may rot the tubers, bringing a loss of perhaps a third of the crop, though this procedure is safe on sandy soils.

The best way is to take out furrows to a full fork's depth, put three inches of compost, or 1 lb. to the foot of row of wilted comfrey, as described in Chapter 3, and spread about an inch of soil on top. Then set out the tubers, 'rose end' up on this layer, fill in from the next trench and repeat the process all down the bed. Heaping the soil should leave a ridge that marks the row and gives about six inches of soil over each tuber in the trench made shallower by compost and soil.

This digging over makes it possible to turn in compost or manure spread on the surface, also seaweed meal on soils short of potash, and 1 lb. a square yard of dried sludge in addition on poor soils. In this case the trenches need not be so deep—about six inches is enough—which also gives a chance for removing perennial weed roots. Any minimum digging system means taking every chance to get these out.

On sandy soils where there is compost or comfrey to spare, dig out the trenches to even a foot deep, with flat bottoms so that a thicker layer can be added. If spent hops, leafmould, or even raw dead leaves are available in quantity, tread these into the bottom of the trench, add the compost or comfrey on top, and plant as before. This is of course a modern version of the old-fashioned double-trenching, and putting a moisture-holding layer of potential humus well down will make a permanent difference to fertility. On sandy soils this is less hard work, and plenty of air can get down to help decay.

There is no need to be especially careful not to break off the shoots on the sprouted seed potatoes, for there are usually plenty. If extra-large potatoes are needed for baking or showing, disbud the seed by removing all but two or three of the best, and plant these with care. It pays to halve large seed potatoes before planting, slicing from the rose end downwards, and they can even be quartered if poor-quality seed contains too many big ones and not enough in-dividuals to fill the calculated row length.

When the young shoots show through in frosty weather, the easiest protection is newspapers held down with canes, taken off in the day time, or sacks, for the tubers have spent a great deal of their 'capital' in growing so far, and they will be handicapped greatly by having to start again. This extra work is worth doing, for the earliest at least, for perhaps a week.

When the shoots are six inches high and the weeds are starting to grow on the ridge sides, draw the soil up towards them with the hoe in the operation known as 'earthing-up', so that the ridges are about two inches higher, and give another earthing if the weeds are very fierce. Otherwise just leave them, for the smother of the foliage or haulm will kill out the annual weeds.

When the haulm dies down at lifting time, thrust the fork in from the sides of the ridges and lever the tubers out. Most jobbing gardeners dig along the ridges, which means far more good large potatoes speared so that they will not keep. What is the good of growing the best if it is to be spoilt in the lifting?

Spread the tubers on sacks in the sun to dry, merely rubbing off any lumps of mud in a wet season, sort out the forked ones, and store in ordinary jute sacks in the dark. Neither paper nor polythene is safe, for potatoes breathe out moisture which condenses on the insides of the bag and causes rotting. About a month after putting them away, sort them over in case of soft rot, dry rot or even tuber blight which can infect the whole sackful. Store them under the conditions described in Chapter 8, remembering that they are the most important bulk food grown in your garden.

The main danger to potatoes is blight caused by the fungus *Phytophthora infestans*, which killed more people by starvation and disease in the Irish Potato Famine of the 1840's than nuclear weapons have killed so far. The first sign of this disease, that was once responsible for a million deaths, is dark brown patches at the tips and edges of the leaves. These spread rapidly, especially in moist weather, and can blacken the whole haulm including the stems. The potatoes stop growing, and when the tubers are lifted they rot in store. Organic gardeners who doubt the existence of disease are referred to *The Great Hunger* by C. C. Woodham-Smith (Hamish Hamilton, 1962) and reminded that all the potatoes concerned were organically grown, for chemical fertilizers had not yet left Rothamsted which was started in 1841.

There is still no cure for the disease, and the standard preventive treatment is still Bordeaux Mixture, made of copper sulphate and lime sprayed on every fortnight in the dull, wet weather that favours the spread of the fungus. Because almost all farmers in potato-growing areas spray, the disease is nothing like so serious as it was, and it is possible that the new systemic fungicides may break the infection chain which will lower the risk for gardeners still further. It is also possible that these very new fungicides will produce 'Silent Spring' or thalidomide side effects, but the gardener has no need to use them.

There are a number of strains of fungus, and though the new resistant varieties are proof against some, none will resist them all. 'Pentland Dell', the first on the market, was badly attacked in 1968 in Cornwall, and if farmers rely entirely on these, only the versatile strains will survive, but these will increase, as happens with clubroot.

Vegetables One by One

Most gardeners take a chance, for their plots are scattered and there are fewer spores about than when the crops of all England lay waste, except for a field near a copper refinery at Swansea where the fumes left enough residue on the foliage to prevent disaster. That rare but excellent book *The Advance of the Fungi*, by E. C. Large (Jonathan Cape, 1940), gives the best detailed account of this, and all the other plant diseases that swept the world when steam transport began to carry spores swiftly between continents, before fungicides or quarantine regulations.

Bordeaux Mixture is best bought ready made as the lime and copper are finely ground and dissolve better than any home-made mixture. Those who wish to take the precaution, which is far more worth while on tomatoes which belong to the potato family and are even more readily infected, should make up the mixture according to the directions and spray first in early July in the south, late July in the north, spraying again if, as often in a blight year, the rain washes the spray off again. If blight appears in the district, spray again.

Just one infected plant on two hundred acres is enough to start an outbreak, and in potato fields centres of infection spread from a single left-in tuber. The most important control on a garden scale is never to have potatoes two years running on the same ground, and to take very great care to dig out all the tinies, because it is on these that the blight over-winters.

Blight has two harmful actions. The attack on the foliage reduces the crop, by stopping the food supply of synthesized starches from the leaves, and the spores wash down and infect the tubers which go rotten in store. One of the ways in which blight danger can be reduced in wet years is by giving the potatoes a second earthing-up to make sure there is plenty of soil above them. 'No digging' potatoes have this risk as well as that of being exposed to light and turning green. Green potatoes contain the poisonous alkaloid Solanine which is present also in the potato berries, and neither should be eaten.

When the first tips or side blotches of blight attack are seen, it is possible to spray with Burgundy Mixture and prevent the spores from spreading. This is used mainly for fruit trees and the recipe will be found in Chapter 8, but it is more powerful than Bordeaux, and though it may damage the leaves, they are lost anyway if the blight spreads. If it continues to increase, cut down the haulm and compost it (this should be safe as 120° F kills them, and the spores do not live long on foliage) or spray with double-strength Burgundy Mixture, which is cheaper and safer on a garden scale than the sulphuric acid used by farmers as a potato-haulm killer. This destroys both haulm and spores and is recommended for allotments where one man carrying his cut haulm to the compost heap risks spreading the disease to his neighbours.

Then wait a fortnight before lifting so that any scattered spores die on the surface before the potatoes are in contact with them. It is important to look through the crop later because though blight itself does not spread, the soft rots that attack afterwards go from tuber to tuber, and picking over is all-important. Sometimes blight strikes very late, just a few tips or side patches on the leaves, and though the crop is not reduced, a great many tubers are infected and rot in store. In this case a Burgundy Mixture haulm kill, or a cut-down, is very good value.

Wart disease, caused by the fungus *Synchytrium endobioticum*, which produces brown, warty or cauliflower-curd-like masses round the eyes, was formerly a very serious potato problem, but the invention of immune varieties broke the infection chain and it is rarely seen. It is notifiable, and any outbreak should be reported to the Ministry of Agriculture. If you have it, the spores stay dormant in the soil for up to twelve years, but there is no need to give up potatoes. Both 'Arran Consul' and 'Kerr's Pink' are immune, so are 'Craig's Alliance', 'Di Vernon' and 'Ulster Premier' among the better earlies, and 'Arran Banner' and 'Great Scot' among second-earlies.

Corky Scab (*Spongospora subterranea*) is also rare, producing round pimples on the skin that burst and release a brown powder with mild attacks, but canker-like masses in bad ones. This fungus likes poorly drained soil, so better drainage is the best answer, using the methods described in Chapter 8. The fungus will still last for five years in the soil, causing milder attacks, so digging in 3 oz. a square yard of flowers of sulphur (which is quite cheap) is advised before the next potato crop. This is useless unless the drainage is corrected first.

Common scab, which looks like tiny brown moon craters on the skin, is caused by *Actinomyces scabies*, a related fungus; it likes lime, so liming *after* the potatoes as directed in Chapter 4 gives the longest gap before they are planted again and plenty of humus also helps. Few gardeners worry about it, as the scabby skin is removed when peeling, and the scab-resistant kinds so far have less flavour.

There are a number of other diseases, all of which are best controlled by good humus and crop rotations, apart from making good mineral deficiencies described earlier. Virus diseases are carried by seed tubers and the best answer is to buy Scottish-grown seed, for the winds of Scotland prevent the aphides from carrying these viruses from plant to plant, though there are fewer of these than we think, for most are 'cured' by better feeding.

The potato is the gardener's best bargain in giving most food from least space, for an acre under potatoes will feed twice as many people as an acre under wheat. As William Cobbett, who called it 'Ireland's Lazy Root' insisted, it is the crop which grows with the least trouble. Every civilization has been based on a storable source of good food, including the rice civilizations of the East, the wheat ones of the West, and those based on maize from South and Central America. Pre-Inca Peru and Ecuador were potato based. Blight was unknown, as it came from North America, probably a disease of a weed like our black nightshade (*Solanum nigrum*). So was Ireland before 1845, and Tristan da Cunha still is. The potato compares as follows with other roots and foods:

	Moisture %	Carbohydrate %	Protein %
Biscuits (average)	10·00	66·10	variable but small or non-existent
Bread (white)	33·80	55·50	variable but small
Potatoes (boiled)	76·40	19·70	2·10
Artichokes	79·60	16·90	1·50
Carrots	87·00	9·30	1·20
Parsnips	85·00	11·30	1·30
Turnips	91·50	5·70	1·00

The slimming wife and the weight-worried husband should look first at the top of the table. Very roughly every pound of biscuits adds three and a quarter times as much fattening carbohydrate as a pound of potatoes, while a pound of bread is equivalent to 2½ lb. of the despised spud. If you spent about four times as much for half a pound of 'slimming' biscuits with their starch reduced by half than for the ordinary kind, they are still more fattening than half a pound of potatoes grown in your own garden.

Forget about slimming and look at the rest of the table. This shows that the potato has the highest dry matter, carbohydrate and protein of any of the root vegetables, and the yield with good compost can be higher.

On minerals, however, the picture alters:

| | Milligrams per 100 grams | | | |
	Calcium	Phosphorus	Iron	Copper
Potatoes (boiled)	4	33	0·46	0·15
Artichokes (boiled)	30	33	0·41	0·12
Beet (boiled)	30	36	0·70	0·14
Carrots (boiled)	46	38	0·60	0·11
Parsnips (boiled)	59	76	0·45	0·10
Radish (raw)	30	31	1·36	0·16
Salsify (boiled)	60	53	1·23	0·12
Turnips (boiled)	55	19	0·35	0·04

Here the shallow-rooting potato is beaten on calcium by all the other roots, while the deepest of the lot, salsify, is near the top for iron. Unlike white sugar which has no minerals and vitamins, the potato has quite a reasonable supply of both copper and phosphorus. The vitamins are as follows:

| | Mg. per 100 grams | | | |
	C	E	Niacin	A (I.U.'s)
Potatoes (boiled)	10–14	0·10	1·20	20–40
Beet (boiled)	5	0·20	0·20	0–20
Carrots (boiled)	6	0·00	0·50	10,000
Parsnips (boiled)	18	0·00	0·20	0
Turnips (boiled)	18	0·20	0·50	0
Radish (raw)	25		0·10	30

| | Micrograms per 100 grams | | | |
	Thiamine	Riboflavin	Pyridoxine	Pantothenic Acid
Potatoes (boiled)	100	40	320–650	220–320
Beet (boiled)	10	30	120	120
Carrots (boiled)	60	60	200	120
Parsnips (boiled)	80	90	0	0
Turnips (boiled)	60	60	110	37
Radish (raw)	40	60		

Potatoes are quite a good source of niacin, though not to be compared with meat or fish, and of pyridoxine and pantothenic acid, about half as good as wholemeal bread, though far inferior to yeast. These are minor water-soluble vitamins, but are connected with the digestion of proteins and the symptoms of senility. Their presence explains how the ancient and modern potato-based civilizations got away without the grain vitamins.

Because such relatively large quantities of potatoes are eaten they can add up to useful vitamin sources, though it is far better for example to eat leafy vegetables for one's vitamin C than to expect 10–14 milligrams in potatoes to supply it, while a few carrots supply all the vitamin A one needs without bothering about a mere 20–40. There is no need for us to live in our own potato-based civilization, though it may well be more pleasant, and even cheaper (allowing for future inflation) than a synthetic food-based one.

Pumpkins

Pumpkins have been garden Cinderellas, fit only for fairy coach-builders or weight-guessing in aid of Oxfam, but the new Japanese hybrid, bred for hungrier countries than ours, is also a good winter vegetable for England.

It has about five times the dry matter of a marrow or a homesick American pie pumpkin, with rather more protein and less carbohydrate than carrots and ten times a cabbage's vitamin A. This is roughly a third less than the record quantity carrots hold, but more easily stored, for pumpkins need no sand, ashes or peat, only hanging in a cool loft or shed from October harvest until May.

The pumpkin programme begins in April with digging holes about biscuit-tin size, four to five feet apart each way, which is close enough for their foliage to suppress annual weeds. Half fill the holes with compost for plant foods and moisture-holding and fill up with top soil before sowing one large seed edgeways and two inches deep in each.

Then make giant 'staples' with two-foot lengths of stout galvanized iron wire and thrust two of these over each seed to hold an eight-inch by six-inch polythene bag stretched over them to make a cheap and unbreakable 'cloche', secured against wind with a rubber band round the bottom. Water them to start the seed and until the cloches come off in May, then only when they flag in drought.

When each shoot has grown one plain-stemmed male flower, cut it short after the next female one which will have a round miniature pumpkin behind it, to give the best chance of ripening more and smaller pumpkins rather than single monsters. Colour is no guide to ripeness and it is best to leave them on till frost bites the leaves, like jam marrows.

This particular variety, known as 'Japanese', is a cross between a Japanese and a Belgian variety, and though it varies, with the most desirable type the football-shaped orange kind that can weigh up to 25 lb., its analysis is much the same.

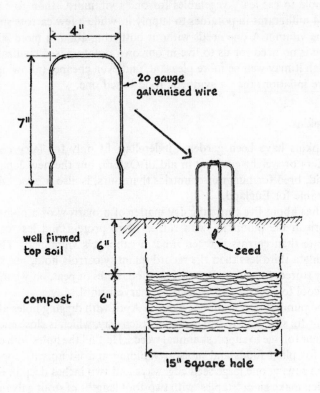

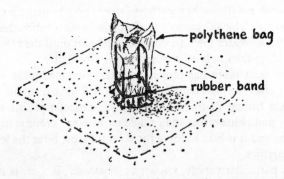

5. This polythene-bag cloche serves for cucumbers, marrows and pumpkins in the open better than any more expensive kind

Vegetables One by One

	Japanese Pumpkin %	American Pumpkin %	Marrow %
Moisture	86·90	97·2	97·8
Carbohydrate	8·10	1·40	1·40
Protein	1·80	0·50	0·40
Calcium	0·04	0·03	
Phosphorus	0·04	0·01	
Carotene m.g. per kilogram	27·00	5·90	

These figures are for pumpkins grown in England, and with more sun in America the average pumpkin is 90·5 per cent water, which is near the South African level, but this new hybrid is a pumpkin for a temperate climate, with a better performance than that of the many American squashes now in British seed catalogues.

This system of cultivation can be used for all the marrow family, but those who have a warm greenhouse can start their seeds in peat pots early in March and plant out when the risk of frost is over. In wet years there is a risk of rotting where the pumpkins lie on the ground, so some gardeners hang theirs over wire-netting racks, or place upturned saucers under them to keep them clear of the damp.

Never break off the stalk when gathering pumpkins, for this makes a wound which is certain to let in decay. Always break or cut where the stalk begins to fatten, about two inches up the stem from the fruit, and never use this as a handle to hang the pumpkin from, for it will break as it dries, and nothing is more alarming than to wake up in bed with the thump of a 25 lb. pumpkin falling in the attic overhead. Collect the small nylon net bags in which nuts, brussels sprouts and many other things are delivered to greengrocers today. These provide the same all-round support, hanging from nails in the rafters, that special melon nets gave to the hothouse crops of these low-food-value luxuries in the England of a hundred years ago.

Radishes

The radish is our fastest-growing vegetable, with twenty to thirty days from sowing to salad, and though it belongs to the *Cruciferae* or cabbage family, it grows too fast for clubroot to attack, so that a row can be cleared completely with none left to grow bitter and woody.

The fastest are 'Sparkler' and 'Scarlet Globe', but, like the old 'French Breakfast', they need sowing at ten- to fourteen-day intervals because they finish so fast. The best radish for the modern gardener

143

is 'Cherry Belle', because it will last up to four weeks from a single sowing, staying crisp and tasty longer than any other variety.

Sow the first in early March in a sunny place, thinly in half-inch-deep furrows in pairs two inches apart, then a gap of nine inches and another pair, always remembering that you will have to tread between the rows to pull them. Keep on sowing, using single rows for the later ones, which can go between larger members of the cabbage tribe,

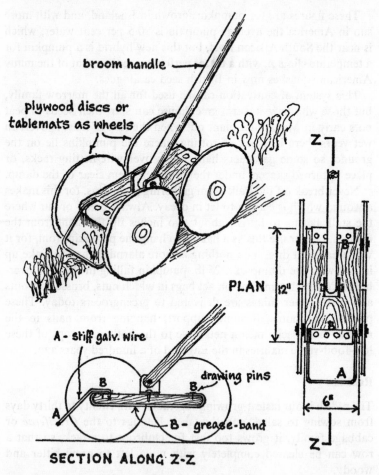

6. A fleabeetle trolley could be made by anyone handy with tools, and, lent up and down a road, could clear a neighbourhood. The wire in front disturbs the beetles which jump up and stick to the greaseband. The large wheels prevent sideways jumping

right on until early September. There is no need to dig. Hoeing off the weeds and scraping the furrow with the hoe corner is quite enough, and they can manage well on the leavings from other crops. Dried blood can be used as a tonic if any have been attacked by their only pest—this is the fleabeetle (*Psylliodes affinis*) which eats their leaves to lace, and attacks seedling Brassica, turnips and swedes in the same way. The answer is to dust along the rows with derris or to make a trap. This can be contrived by using toy wheels and a board to the underside of which is fastened some paper smeared with sticky band mixture either bought or made to the recipe in Chapter 8. The diagram shows the idea, which is to disturb the hiding beetles so that they leap up and stick to the sticky paper which can then be detached and dumped in the dustbin. Derris is easy, but if the attack is a bad one, wheeling the trap up and down the rows is more effective.

There are three other radishes and perhaps the most useful is 'Japanese All Seasons', to sow between mid-March and the end of July. It is like a white and less tapered parsnip about nine inches long and two across the top, maturing in from eight to ten weeks. The second sowing grows roots to lift as October ends, to store in peat and cook as parsnips with a radish flavour.

Sow the sizable seeds six inches apart and nine between rows, in half-inch-deep dibber holes and they will be up fast. Do not leave the first sowing in too long, for they grow past their best. It is the second one that is of value, sliced or grated raw in winter salads as well as cooked. As the root analysis tables under potatoes shows, the radish is even richer in iron than salsify, and has more vitamin C than any of the other roots. All four races have much the same composition, but their nutritional value is not to be despised.

The two others are 'Black Spanish' and 'Chinese Rose', which should be sown only between mid-July and the end of August, because earlier sowings are inclined to run to seed. These are sown in the same way but need nine inches between plants; the first looks like a black-skinned turnip three inches thick and the second a huge red and white radish. Both are quick roots to dig in October or November to store in peat for the winter. 'Black Spanish' has the disadvantage of needing peeling before either cooking or raw eating, and 'Chinese Rose' can go rather hard if sown too early, but all are useful root vegetables, with, of course, the disadvantage of clubroot risk, though in most gardens they can evade it for some years. They make a pleasant but pungent pickle in vinegar.

Vegetables One by One

Rhubarb

This is treated here as it is not a 'soft' or 'tree' fruit. It comes before the gooseberry dares, as the first 'fruit' of every spring. Bird-proof, frost-proof, town-proof, it is nutritionally superior to plums and green-gages and for the least trouble of almost anything that grows in a garden. A modern substitute for the bottomless buckets that coaxed crop after crop of welcome pink sticks from the black and nameless shapes beside the rubbish heap in the preplastic age is the five-gallon oil drum. Have holes about six inches across cut in the bottoms by the garage, clean them with detergent and thrust them well down over the clumps, with bricks on top to prevent their blowing noisily round the garden in the small hours of a wet and windy morning. Cover them inside and out with cheap bitumen paint, not only to prevent rust but to provide a black surface that absorbs sun-heat and increases the forcing effect, making the drums far more effective than flowerpots or up-ended earthenware drainpipes.

When the fruits of summer take over, the rhubarb should rest un-picked after a final June or July jam harvest, while the leaves grow to feed the clumps for next year's forcing. By November they will have died down. The remains should then be cleared away, and a winter feed of half a pound of fine bone meal should be applied to each square yard, with some compost or manure on top. Connoisseurs who serve their rhubarb with Barbados sugar to bring out the taste, not with chemical custard to hide it, heap dead leaves a foot deep over the clumps in autumn, and surround the bed with inch-mesh wire-netting to prevent their blowing away. This provides slow forcing for the best flavour and makes leafmould for spring digging. Their choice among the twenty or more varieties still in cultivation from the early-nineteenth-century rhubarb boom is usually 'Hawkes' Champagne', or 'Timperley Early', which is the best jam and bottling variety, holding its flavour and colour longer than the rest. The analysis of rhubarb will be found in the next chapter in the table for bush fruits.

A rhubarb bed is past its best after fifteen years, and rotten hollows in the black surface roots are signs of wear. A crown costing from 18p to 33p will be a root section six to nine inches long with a fat bud at one end. These can be cut from the youngest and strongest roots of ageing clumps from January to March. Scatter 2 lb. of coarse bone meal to the square yard, and tuck half a barrowload of manure

146

or compost well down in the trench bottoms over the same area of new bed. If possible, dig in a barrowload of feathers from poultry plucking or an old pillow or wool shoddy from an abandoned mattress, for these provide slowly-released nitrogen to go with the delayed-action phosphates of the bone meal. Plant the crowns upright, with the bud just peeping through the surface, at two-foot intervals in rows three feet apart. Pick nothing the first year, when lettuce or radishes can be sown between the rows. In the following spring the roots will be ready for gentle forcing under leaves but oil drums should not go on until the third spring.

Most rhubarb is bitter in summer from the oxalic acid which is always present in the leaves. It makes them dangerous for eating as spinach, and the top inch of stalk should not be cooked. But 'Glaskin's Perpetual' is a rhubarb that never grows bitter as it grows old; it can be picked and eaten right on to November, provided that the clumps are rested in alternate years to recover.

This rare variety is best raised from seed, which should be sown very thinly in furrows half an inch deep and three feet apart, on ground that has been prepared as for planting. Lettuce, radish or even carrots can be sown between these wide rows so long as these are marked to avoid stepping on the tiny seedlings. Thin them to about a foot apart when it is clear which are the best, and cover them down with leaves along the rows. Cabbages can go between them through this first winter, and lettuces and radishes up the row middles through the summer when the young rhubarb will start to move.

Every other plant can be removed to provide more space, and these will be about the size of bought crowns, while those left in will be ready to pick in their third spring. The disadvantage of this cheap and easy method of growing replacements for an ageing bed, is that some of the clumps will flower. A stout shoot will thrust up like a fist and if left alone will produce a six-foot-high plume of creamy flowers which are often a delight to flower arrangers, but they weaken the clumps. These should be cut out at ground level both on the seedlings and ageing clumps that feel life is passing them by while they lie like stranded crocodiles at the bottom of every garden.

Salsify

This has grey-green leaves like those of a 'Red Hot Poker' (*Tritoma*) and long white roots which should not be confused with Scorzonera which has black ones that are brutes to peel. It is an easy root vegetable with remarkably deep roots that belong to the Compositae (the Daisy family) so misses all the pests and diseases that attack other vegetables. Its analysis will be found in the table of roots compared with potatoes, which it beats on iron, calcium and phosphorus (page 140).

Sow salsify in April in furrows an inch deep and nine inches apart, thinning to nine inches between plants. The seeds are large and long so there is no difficulty in making a quarter ounce do six twelve-foot-long rows. Beyond hoeing they need no attention, but should always be sown after compost, never fresh manure because they go very coarse and forky, and are then most awkward to dig.

Lift some in October for storing, or leave them in to dig as required, for salsify came from Russia in the reign of Henry VIII and is used to a colder climate than ours. Estimate how many you will eat as roots, and cover the rest down with dead leaves, a trick that is often used for rhubarb. These leaves can blow round the garden, so buy brickwork reinforcement netting, which is a kind of tough but cheap wire-netting $4\frac{1}{2}$ inches wide, and nail it to short posts round the bed. Two strips, one above the other, will keep a generous leaf coat tidy over forcing rhubarb or salsify.

Early in March scrape aside the leaves and pick the young leaves that look like wide, thick, folded grass blades at four to six inches long for salads or cooking as a spinach with an asparagus flavour. The roots have a taste of oysters, hence the popular name of 'Oyster Plant', but these young leaves, especially when they are clear of the leafmould coat, and thrusting strong and dark green, deserve the title of 'No-trouble Asparagus'.

The analysis in the table is for the roots, but the leaves are still richer in iron, and though the sap stains the fingers red with this, it washes off easily in *cold* water. The leaves can be used as an 'asparagus spinach', or even salad, if they are picked hard enough, until June, when the plants run up and flower like a Sweet Sultan with red-purple blooms two inches across.

They can be cleared as soon as they start growing flower stems in the centres instead of new leaves. but if room can be spared they will become a three-foot-high mass of foliage, which is good compost material and chickens' delight: for poultry evidently know good minerals when they taste them. In the second summer the roots go deeper still, but die off and decay after flowering and seeding as all root vegetables would if left in. A large salsify bed rotated round the garden for salad and compost material would be a most useful rest for a tired soil, apart from the mineral-gathering effect. Seed is easily saved and the plant is a species (*Tragopogon porrifolius*), so there is no fear of its crossing with anything and growing inferior variations.

Shallots

This small onion increased only by offsets is also a species, *Allium ascalonicum*, from Israel and another of the useful introductions by returning Crusaders. It needs exactly the same soil conditions as onion sets—ground that has had compost for the previous crop and does not lack lime, and 8 oz. a square yard dug in the previous autumn is a good beginning, for shallots do best planted in February, so the bed is best left ready for them.

Tread the ground and rake it level, then thrust the large offsets into the soil so that they are firmly planted to half their depth. They should go four to six inches apart in rows nine inches apart. After this they may need hoeing once or twice to keep down weeds before the leaves turn yellow in June or July.

Dig them then, leave in the sun for a few days to dry, and store in a dry and frostproof but cool shed after the dead foliage has been removed. Each seed bulb will have grown six to eight offsets, and though the increase is usually pickled, shallots have roughly the same analysis as onions, and a milder flavour, apart from being easier. Though the first cost of the offsets is higher, they keep well and one's own stock can be planted next February.

Store them in laddered nylon stockings, or non-returnable net bags from a greengrocer or a garden shop, for today bulbs are often received in these useful, free and well-ventilated containers. The advantages of shallots rather than onions are that they are always smaller; for one only, or just one or two, may be needed for a stew, and they give less pungent peeling. From the gardener's viewpoint they gain a faster finish, freeing the ground in June rather than the end of July or early August for onion sets, but they do not produce quite the same yield from the area. The decision should be made in the kitchen on family needs, for monster onions of full-strength flavour may be better to boast about than to cook.

Vegetables One by One

Spinach

It would be possible for a spinach addict to eat his favourite green food every day, by growing enough of the prickly-*seeded* winter variety and the round-seeded summer kind to last the year, but it would be far more work than the cabbage tribe, because of the constant sowings as each batch runs to seed and needs replacing, and the quantity of leaves that have to be picked to make a cooking. This is particularly important in winter when one dash down the frosty garden to pull up two savoys means several days' green food, while picking winter spinach leaves in the cold is a long, slow job.

In addition it could produce deficiency symptoms of calcium and iron, for the oxalic acid in spinach locks up all that it contains of both, and more beside, so that it holds less than none of these minerals even though its analysis shows how rich it is in them. Though spinach is very high in vitamin A, and quite a good source of C, the oxalic acid problem makes it clear that the child who will not eat up his nice spinach is wiser than his parents. If a child is to be coaxed into eating a green food, make it kale, which is far better value in minerals and vitamins, and a great deal less work to grow.

The most useful sowing of summer spinach is in January or February, on ground that was manured for a previous crop, making inch-deep furrows nine inches apart and sowing the seeds either very thinly along them to thin to six-inch spacing, or in clusters at six-inch intervals to thin to the best when this can be seen. Cover the furrows and firm with the rake head, and in April they will be well up.

First use the thinnings for salad, and then the leaves, taking a few from each plant until they begin to taste bitter. Early in the year they are low in oxalic acid, just as rhubarb is, but their vitamin A content is high, while C is about 78 mg. per 100 grams, but drops to 29·7 after cooking, so they are better value raw. At this young stage their midribs are not stringy and they are a change from the cabbage tribe at a season when lettuce are barely ready without glass.

The best variety is 'Nobel', a commercial favourite because the leaves are larger, meaning fewer picks to the pound, with 'Monstrous Viroflay' second best. When the leaves begin to coarsen and taste bitter, let them bolt, running up to flowering spires and foliage up to three feet high. Tread these down and dig them in to provide a lasting store of slowly-released oxalic acid in the ground. Before planting the cabbage family after spinach scatter 8 oz. to a square

Vegetables One by One

yard of dried sludge, poultry manure or fish meal, or wait till the young plants have taken hold and give them a teaspoonful of dried blood each, for there is a risk that the spinach will have grown too stemmy and rob nitrogen as stemmy mustard does.

Each sowing of summer spinach takes about five weeks to grow and provides three weeks' picking, so the next should be in March for May eating and every three weeks until mid-July. Then in August sow the first 'prickly', which is usually called 'Long Standing Winter' or variations on this name for the same plant, at the same spacing to last through the autumn.

Winter spinach is best sown along furrows on the tops of three-inch-high mounds spaded from between the rows that should be eighteen inches apart. These provide good surface drainage and a picking path, but on clay soils they need a trench along the ends to run the water away, for the object of the raised sowing is to keep the plants dry in winter. Sow the winter crop in early September thinly so that the plants can be thinned to six inches apart and have time to make strong growth before they slow down for the winter. An ounce of the quite large seed should sow about a hundred and twenty feet of row.

Pick only the outside leaves, and from plenty of plants, so that none are overworked. The secret of winter spinach is to sow enough on vacant ground so that it will last through the hard weather. It is not suitable for winter salads as it soon goes stringy.

Spinach beet, or perpetual spinach, is much easier, and one sowing in April and another in August will give a year-round supply of leaves from what is in fact a rootless beetroot, which is rather lower in oxalic acid than ordinary spinach. Sow this one on manured or composted soil, for there is no need to worry about the uneaten roots forking, in inch-deep furrows fifteen inches apart, spacing the large seeds at inch intervals. When it is clear which are the best, thin to six-inch spacing. The September sowing is exactly the same but there is no gain from ridging; the plant is very hardy, though watering between the rows with Fertosan slug destroyer in October helps winter slug problem.

Pick by bending the leaves down, and use only the young ones, taking off the largest and toughest for compost in summer, because if these stay on there will be fewer young ones; and remove any flower stems that start to run up.

New Zealand spinach (*Tetragonia expansa*) is not a member of the

151

beet tribe, but belongs to the *Aizoaceae*, a race mainly found in Australia, but it still has quite a high quota of oxalic acid. It is half hardy, and the seed is best sown in March under glass in peat pots and planted two feet apart each way at the end of May. It can also be sown under polythene cloches like pumpkins in early April, or in the open in May.

The seed is slow to germinate so it is a good idea to soak it over night in cold water before sowing in threes and thinning to the best when all are up and growing well. Hoe between while it is getting ahead of the weeds, and start to pick when the sprawling fleshy shoots with thick, arrowhead-shaped leaves are eight inches long. Pick off two to three inches, not more, of these shoots, which are not in any way stringy for cooking, and keep on picking from about June or July (according to when the seeds were started) until the frosts kill it. These shoot tips are low in oxalic acid and very nice, especially in soups made with a liquidizer, and there are plenty of them so there is no need to bother with the older leaves.

New Zealand spinach never bolts, the flowers are along the stems, yellow and insignificant, and with compost dug in well before sowing and enough watering to get it moving, it will produce a great bulk of green food from a small area. The constant tip-removal produces a solid mass under which few weeds can grow. As always, however, beware of excess oxalic acid, for it is this that gives the taste that makes a spinach.

The following table shows oxalic acid and calcium in common vegetables. Many have very little and their small quantity of either can be cancelled out. The normal man who drinks plenty of milk will have calcium enough to balance New Zealand spinach soup twice a week and serving it as a green vegetable three times, but vegans who refuse all animal products should take note of this table, as part of the very great care they should give to their diet.

	Calcium %	Oxalic Acid %
Chenopodium album		
(the weed Fat-hen)	0·0990	1·1100
Spinach, ordinary	0·1330	0·8920
Beet leaves	0·1200	0·9160
New Zealand Spinach (leaves)	0·1100	0·8900
Seakale Beet (Chard)	0·1100	0·6600
New Zealand Spinach (stems)	0·0830	0·6500

Vegetables One by One

	Calcium %	Oxalic Acid %
Rhubarb (cooked stems)	0·0440	0·5000
New Zealand Spinach (tips)		0·3400
Parsley	0·2900	0·1900
Beetroot (unpeeled)	0·0180	0·1380
Broccoli	0·2100	0·0054
Kale	0·3100	0·0130
Cabbage	0·1890	0·0077
Carrots	0·0440	0·0330

It is the oxalic acid that handicaps the order *Chenopodiaceae* as good vegetables, and it will be seen that though they are high in calcium they take it all away again and more. The highest level of oxalic acid is in the weed we call Fat-hen, and Americans call 'Lamb's Quarter', which was formerly a vegetable, known as 'Melde' to the Anglo-Saxons, naming both the Melbournes in Cambridgeshire and Derbyshire which were originally spelt 'Meldebourne' after the crop that grew there. When young this can hold as little as 0·012 per cent oxalic acid and compares very favourably with spinach on its other nutritional contents, as will be seen in this table:

	A I.U.'s	Mg. per 100 grams C	E	Niacin	Microgram per 100 g. Thiamine	Riboflavin
Ordinary Spinach	8,400–25,000	59–75	1·70	0·70 0·20	50, 120	240–300
New Zealand Spinach	1,400	62·50	0·20			
Chenopodium	19,000	85	1·80	1·00	59	690
Beet leaves	21,000	34–50		0·30	50	170–300
Carrots	10,000	6–10		1·50	60–70	60
Kale	7,000–20,000	100	8·00	0·80	120	350–500

As the successive analyses for the New Zealand spinach show, where you pick matters almost as much as the growth stage, and only rhubarb stems are safe. The leaves are highly poisonous because of their excess of oxalic acid, which has caused a number of deaths, especially on the Continent. Every now and again a women's page writer will copy a famous French cookery book and recommend the leaves for flavouring or 'as spinach', followed this up by a swift warning the next day before many readers are poisoned. Rhubarb leaves

153

can be dug in where cabbage tribe seedlings are to be sown as a possible check on clubroot, or boiled in a furred saucepan or kettle to clean them, but NEVER eaten, for they are our only poisonous vegetable.

There have been cases of Melde poisoning in Germany (see *British Poisonous Plants*, Bulletin No. 161, H.M.S.O., 55p) where a Dr. Scheuer Karpin reported in 1948 that many refugees were receiving hospital treatment in Dresden, Berlin and Leipzig after eating the foliage two or three times a day for several weeks. They were gathering the plants that grew among the rubble of bombed buildings and cooking them with whatever else they could find. All recovered after treatment, but the symptoms were mainly caused by the excess beta carotene putting too great a strain on the liver, called upon to break it down to vitamin A. They would have been even more swiftly poisoned on spinach, and had they tried to live on nothing but kale or carrots the effect could have been the same. Enough is as good as a feast, and a feast of spinach could be dangerous.

Sweet Corn

What we call 'maize' the Americans call 'corn', the collective word we use for wheat, oats and barley as in the name of 'corn-chandler', a man who today sells mostly bird seed and tinned pet foods. Our 'sweet corn' is the American 'corn on the cob', which is maize grown to the stage when it cooks soft and delicious, for our climate will not ripen it to a hard and storable grain.

We can only grow the hardiest and fastest varieties, like 'Canada Cross', 'Golden Bantam' and John Innes Hybrid, which are going to grow up to four feet high, so should go at the bottom of the garden or where they cannot shade other crops. In any event the thick stems and broad, grasslike leaves make splendid compost material. Because the crop must grow a bulk of foliage fast, the ground should have had manure the previous autumn, or compost before sowing.

The best site is the kind of sunny border that grows tomatoes well and these crops can alternate from one end to the other of the bed, but in southern counties they can follow spring cabbage, so long as they are reasonably sheltered from strong winds. Sow the seed in threes, an inch deep, and fifteen inches apart in staggered rows with thirty inches between them. Maize is wind-pollinated and it is best to have a block of four short rows than one long one. Four good rows across a garden will grow plenty of both cobs and compost.

Vegetables One by One

They can be sown in early April under polythene bag cloches like pumpkins, or in peat pots in a cold frame, because they dislike root disturbance. Otherwise wait till May and sow without protection, thinning the plants to the best when they are well away. At first they will need hoeing to keep them ahead of the weeds, and a teaspoonful of dried blood to each plant is a cure for 'sulking' which might occur round about July on a poor soil.

The test for ripeness is when the cobs feel plump and firm and the 'silk' or tassel beyond the green sheath that covers them begins to wither and turn brown. Though it is possible to turn back the sheath, remove a grain and press it hard with a thumb nail, when the milky inside should come out, this wastes the cob if you are wrong. When the silk withers, try one, and remember that if they get too yellow and ripe they are only a rather expensive poultry food in terms of time and space.

Always gather corn immediately before cooking, ideally about half an hour from plant to pan, and then you will know why cobs bought from greengrocers are tasteless. Hold the solid stem of the plant upright and break the cob off with a sharp, downward jerk. They can be kept in a refrigerator for a week without losing taste, but it pays to pick as they are required.

Corn on the cob, as cooked in the U.S.A., holds roughly 300 I.U.'s of vitamin A, 1·4 milligrams of niacin, 12 of vitamin C, 150 micrograms of thiamine and 60–140 riboflavin per 100 grams. Ours may be less rich, with less sunshine, but we are not trying to start a maize civilization in Britain. We merely want to grow something very nice to eat that makes a change and is quite easy once we have learnt to cook it well and appreciate its quality.

Tomatoes

In Britain we average two good ripening years for outdoor tomatoes in every five and therefore it is important to take every advantage of the skill of the plant breeder to help us beat the weather. Our problem is that very few nurseries will take a chance on growing the best modern varieties for their retail customers, and most of them sell their surplus greenhouse varieties which ripen slowly and are responsible for the legend that tomatoes have lost their taste.

Commercial growers need a thick skin to their tomato if it is to travel safely to market, and the maximum weight of crop, for housewives will no more pay extra for flavour here than they will with potatoes. The worst variety is 'Moneymaker', and though 'Ware Cross' and a few others are supposed to have a taste, none can compare with home grown. This is partly due to using compost instead of chemicals, because the potato family shows this most clearly, but mainly because the gardener can grow the kinds that suit his needs.

The most famous variety is 'Harbinger', which has a skin too thin for long journeys but perfect for a trip up the garden path, a fine flavour, and a genius for ripening off the plant so that it can be kept as a storing fruit as late as Christmas. It held the record in the Trials at the John Innes Horticultural Institution in the 1940's for the most fruit ripe on the plant before 10th September, and was a favourite Somerset greenhouse kind then, because it cropped most heavily without heat when the controlled price was highest.

The other one was new in 1961, 'Outdoor Girl', and is about a fortnight faster still, with the same thin skins and a real tomato taste. But they ripen all together after picking, so that they are better for bottling. Outdoor tomatoes bottled in quantity are better value in terms of food, to last the year round, than a small greenhouse full, because they grow the bulk for a low cash investment. Those who have a greenhouse find it easy to sell their summer surplus, but it is the bottled store that gives value in vitamins for just the cost of the heat and the rubber bands.

The problem is to buy these varieties, which are both ordinary upright types; for the bush kinds, such as 'The Amateur', are bred to grow under cloches and lie ripening on straw, which means a feast for the slugs in wet summers. The bush varieties are flavourless compared with these outdoor ones. Grow 'Plumpton King' or 'Market King' for flavour in the greenhouse where 'Outdoor Girl' is unsuitable, but 'Harbinger' also is excellent.

If the few firms in the suppliers' list at the end of this book are out of stock or out of business (carriage and mounting costs have led many firms to give up supplying plants, as too much trouble) 'Outdoor Girl' and 'Harbinger' are tough enough to raise in an unheated greenhouse or cold frame, though they do far better with even an oil heater to warm them along.

Sow thinly in a box of John Innes Seed Compost (which can be bought at most garden shops) in the last week in March or the first in April and keep the lights or ventilators closed to build up heat during the day, and put newspapers over the seedlings at night when frost threatens. They will be slow, but should be ready to pot in size 72's in plastic or peat, using the same John Innes compost (which is sterilized to kill all weed seeds) when their first tomato-type leaves are half an inch long. Prop the frame open on sunny days, or open the greenhouse as the spring gathers speed, and they are ready to plant between mid-May and early June.

Outdoor tomatoes need all the growing time they can get, and if plants can be delivered early or brought ahead in a warmed greenhouse, get them out in mid-May, but put a cardboard carton over each at night. The flaps can be spread to take half bricks if a windy night threatens, and this system is quicker and easier than paper cones, or large polythene bag cloches, which force the plants too much. Though it means lifting on and off each day, this is only for a short period.

The best tomato bed should face south, ideally with a wall behind it, but even a bed of bush fruit will help to keep off some of the wind. Dig in two buckets of compost, or roughly this much wilted comfrey, to the square yard, tucking either well down in the fork trench bottoms, if you are planting on good soil. Another way is to make a hole a foot square and deep for every plant and half fill it with trodden compost, putting back the top soil to fill the rest. If you use the first method sink a size 48 pot by each to take waterings, but the hole method means that the compost will sink enough to make a depression for water, and the compost below will hold enough to keep the roots down. Do not fill the hole with comfrey leaves because these will sink so fast and far as they decay that the disturbance checks the plant more than the extra potash encourages it.

Drive dahlia stakes, five feet long, to go a foot or a bit over into the ground beside each, well clear of the soil ball, and tie the first string tightly round the stake and again round the plant so that this is firmly held in a loop two inches in diameter, because the stem is going to grow to at least an inch thick. Take out the side shoots, especially those that spring from the base, by pinching them if possible so that the plants do not waste strength on unwanted growth; or cutting with a knife will do. Do not shorten the leaves or remove any unless they are dead or broken, because it is the outside temperature that ripens tomatoes, not direct sunlight, and the leaves should carry on with their job of gathering food for the fruit as long as possible.

As the summer wears on, and the first fruits begin to form, it is advisable to spread comfrey between the rows, with lawn mowings, and to water with comfrey liquid manure as described in Chapter 3. Those who have no comfrey, or who see signs of magnesium shortage, can also spray with one of the seaweed foliar feeds, reputed to improve the flavour. 'Outdoor Girl' is very short-jointed and it is worth putting straw or pieces of wood under the bottom trusses, which will ripen first, to keep them off the ground.

Keep the plants trimmed and tied, especially as the crop grows, for the string (waterproof garden string is best) may have to support ten pounds or more of foliage and fruit; and never tie the string so that it can tighten round the stem. At this season when the plants are glossy-leaved and thriving, the blight may strike and leave nothing but blackened and rotting fruit for all your trouble.

Unless the weather is clear and sunny spray with Bordeaux Mixture as directed on the tin, in mid-July and again in August, which is usually enough unless it has rained immediately afterwards, when an extra spraying is advisable. The other diseases of tomatoes in the open are mainly curable by good nutrition, adequate watering and rotation, but blight needs Bordeaux and this spray is worth the trouble.

Start picking as soon as the fruit is a real red, for the finest flavour for raw eating is from on-the-plant ripening; but if there is a risk of blight or frost, pick at pink stage and ripen indoors. It is very rare for tomatoes in South Africa or Spain to have any flavour, as all are picked unripe for with so much sun they would be soft and over-ripe by the time they reached the customer, who has never learnt to appreciate quality in this fruit, just as we never learn to be proud of what we grow best.

When October comes and frost threatens, get ready to clear the bed. Pick with care to avoid damaging the skins which are a shield against decay, leaving the stalks on as their removal makes a wound. Then spread draper's wadding, as used for lining dressing-gowns, on the bottom of a drawer and set out the tomatoes on it with stalks up and not touching. Another wadding layer provides room for more tomatoes, and so on till the drawer is full. A normal unheated bedroom will hold the 54–6° F drawer temperature at which tomatoes ripen to full flavour without haste.

The easiest method of bottling is to slice the fruit into halves and quarters and stuff the 2 lb. Kilner jars full. Then fill up with plain cold water, screw the lids tight and then give a quarter-turn back to avoid bursting. Pad each one with a tie of thin foam plastic or old blanket so that they do not bounce about when they boil, and pack them into a container deep enough for water to cover them.

Set the gas or electricity very low so that it takes ninety minutes to bring them up to 190° F, and leave them at this for a final twenty-minute boil. Stand them on a wooden or formica surface, not cold metal like the stainless-steel draining-board of a sink unit, which may crack the jars, and give a final tightening before storing in a dark cupboard or behind a dark curtain to preserve their vitamin C, and to keep through even three years of soaking summers.

Though there is a loss of vitamins from bottling, a great many remain, together with the meat-tenderizing acids, and the flavour which keen gardeners will recognize still as due to their own growing.

	Vitamins		Thiamine	Riboflavin
	A I.U.'s	C Mg.	Micrograms	per 100 grams
Ripe tomatoes	1,000	13–20	75	60
Canned tomatoes		7·29	50–80	40–45
Bottled tomatoes (six months stored)	2,400	3·67	27	206

The higher vitamin A and riboflavin for the bottled was because these began as fresh 'Harbingers' from an English garden. Varieties vary and British can be the best.

Turnips and Swedes

Greengrocers' turnips are poor bargains, because though they sound cheap they are over 90 per cent water and thud into the scales like cannon balls. They contain a little sugar, but no starch, its place being taken by pectase, which is a jelly substance resembling the pectin that sets fruit. The jam that is 'full fruit standard' contains an agreed proportion of treated turnips. Their vitamin C is rather easily dissolved and during the 1939–45 War it was suggested that an anti-scurvy drink for infants could be extracted by grating the root, boiling the flakes in water for fifteen minutes and then squeezing through muslin. (See *The British Medical Journal*, 1941, No. 4206, p. 226). This drink needs to be flavoured with honey before any child will take it, and was little used because rose-hip syrup or blackcurrant purée or juice was so much nicer. There is of course no advantage for the amateur gardener to add turnip and marrow to make his fruit go further, for the heat and the sugar and the trouble are just the same for real fruit jam as for imitating the imitation.

Vegetables One by One

Their analysis is as follows, with potatoes for comparison.

| | *Milligrams* | | | | *Micrograms per 100 g.* | |
| | A | E | C | Niacin | Thiamine | Riboflavin |
	I.U.'s					
Turnips, raw	20	0·20	38	0·50	60	60
Turnip greens	10,000		100	0·80	100	350
Swedes	25		36	0·50	60	60
Potatoes	20–40	0·10	15	1·20	100	40

MINERALS

| | *Milligrams per 100 grams* | | | |
| | Calcium | Phosphorus | Iron | Copper |
	%	%	%	%
Turnips	55	19	0·35	0·04
Turnip greens	98	45	3·08	0·09
Swedes	74	56	1·07	0·15
Potatoes	4	33	0·48	0·11

NUTRITIONAL VALUES

| | Water | Protein | Carbohydrate | Fibre |
	%	%	%	%
Turnips	91·50	1·00	5·70	0·90
Turnip greens	88·40	2·20	5·30	1·50
Swedes	88·50	1·30	8·10	1·20
Potatoes	76·40	2·10	19·70	0·90

These tables explain the reply of the Scottish Lowland farmer who was told by a Ministry adviser that feeding turnips to his cows was an expensive way of giving them a drink—'Och, but it's damn guid watter'. Practical experience shows the value of vitamins and minerals in balancing a high carbohydrate diet digested by the bacteria in the stomachs of cattle and sheep from hay and barley straw, by giving them both turnip roots and tops. Folding sheep and cattle on late-sown turnips will get the best value from the foliage, even though half the root may stay in the ground.

The gardener is growing for the kitchen rather than the cow shed, and his concern is to grow enough for the golf-ball to large-Jaffa-orange sizes that have the best flavour by successional sowings, which take from six to eight weeks from sowing to maturity. Sow 'Sutton's Early Snowball' in late April and it will give tender roots like small white apples by mid-June, to last and grow larger until August, with a second sowing in early June to eat on into the autumn.

9. Salsify is a useful root and leaf vegetable, that chickens love. This plot is netted against pheasants.

10. Wire 'peaguards' are also excellent for protecting lettuces and all other seedlings against birds.

11. Kholrabi are strange vegetables, not roots but swollen stems, with a nutty flavour, cooked or raw.

12. Onions from sets defeat carrot fly and finish faster when bent over to dry and lift in early August.

Winter turnips need hardiness rather than speed, and the 'Green Top' varieties which have their top quarter dull green are the hardiest and the best at keeping their foliage through arid winters. Sow them between mid-July and mid-August, with September not too late if leaves are the main need. Some can be lifted in November and stored in peat, but they are best value if dug as required. If you like turnip greens, it is quicker to pick along the rows than along those of winter spinach, and you gain a genuine 3·08 milligrams of iron per 100 grams, compared with 4·0 for the spinach, where it is all locked up by the oxalic acid.

Scatter a pound of lime to four square yards before digging, raking fine and sowing thinly in inch-deep furrows a foot apart, filling and firming these with the rakehead, for like all the cabbage tribe, turnips appreciate a firm start. They should follow a crop that had manure, or have a pound of fish meal or two of dried sludge to four square yards, as they are fond of both nitrogen and phosphorus. Thin them first to two inches apart, and then to six, spreading this process over several weeks to use the thinnings as 'greens' which are more palatable than the spring tops and just as nutritious. Hoe between the plants once or twice to keep ahead of the weeds, and dust with derris or use the trap if fleabeetle attacks the seedlings.

The July sowing for winter can easily miss clubroot if your local strain is an early one, but this is the major turnip problem, to be fought with lime, rotations and dug-in rhubarb leaves. Cut these, let them wilt and tuck them along the bottoms of the trenches as you dig across the plot. Turnips, especially late-sown, have a better chance of profiting than other cabbage-tribe vegetables or early sown turnips.

There are a number of fungi that cause soft rot, dry rot and other conditions, but these only attack underfed turnips without enough humus to hold moisture. If turnips look perfectly healthy, but the flesh contains (towards the lower part of the root) grey or brown areas that later decay, this is from boron deficiency, which is usually caused by excessive liming. This can also cause browning of cauliflower curds and round the edges of the leaves, in a wide solid band, and corky soft growth up the stems. The cure is to dissolve 1 oz. of borax in a two-gallon can of water and apply this with a fine rose over fifteen square yards, or an area nine feet wide and fifteen long. One treatment should cure the condition which is quite distinct and not very common, except on chalky soils. Anyone with persistent troubles

L

with a member of the cabbage family that are not clubroot, could try boron to cure them. Boron is, however, a *trace* element and more than a trace can produce toxicity symptoms from excess. Turnips are extra-sensitive and show it first, so if they have no symptoms and cauliflowers have no wide brown scorched leaf margins, the soil does not lack boron.

Swedes are grown in exactly the same way as turnips, and as these have their carbohydrates mainly as sugars, they are rather nicer grated raw or cooked, according to the same recipes. Their leaves have roughly the same composition and are as good value as spring greens.

Both turnips and kale await the skill of the plant breeder to produce leaves that are more attractive to more people; or maybe we must hope for a change in British tastes. The tables in this chapter have shown how rich they are in vitamins and minerals; but breeding for flavour, rather than hardiness, earliness or weight of crop, is an unexplored field.

6

Soft Fruit Without Spraying

$\mathbf{B}$oth soft fruit and tree fruit differ from vegetables in having to stay still as a target for the pests, for not even the mobile strawberry can move far to leave its troubles behind. No plant that dies down in winter, however, can offer a permanent home for either its pests or the useful creatures that prey on them, that are called 'predators', so that our bushes and trees hold not only foes but far more friends.

The object of the gardener should be to spray only when he must, and to spare as many as possible of these friendly predators. Only with luck will he avoid spraying entirely, and it is just as much hard work to spray with something safe for birds and without risk to human beings, like derris, which is just as deadly to the larvae of the ladybird that are eating the aphides as to the aphides themselves. Nicotine spares these, adult ladybirds and hoverfly larvae. Its replacement by deadlier remedies is partly responsible for present pest increases. A recipe for making it from cigarette ends will be found in Chapter 8.

The ideal answer to any pest problem is one that involves a trick of cultivation or pruning that evades the pest, but we have not nearly enough of these. Work continues in this field and later editions of this book may well contain new answers.

Our most useful predator on both tree and soft fruit in Britain is *Anthocoris nemorum*, a creature which has unfortunately no popular name. It is one of the bugs, a relation of the water boatman beetle of ponds, not an insect, so its young hatch looking like miniature adults, black and brown in colour and only about a sixth of an inch long. It eats aphides, scale insects, apple suckers, midges, capsid bugs, small caterpillars and mites, including the 'big bud' one on blackcurrants. Unlike the more famous introductions from one country to another, such as the Capsid wasps that parasitized the larvae of the greenhouse

163

white fly, it does not 'eat itself out of a job' and then vanish, leaving the gardener defenceless. It is sufficiently versatile to make a living even on such creatures as Springtails (*Collembola*), tiny primitive insects that live on decayed vegetable matter between pest feasts.

There are hundreds of organic gardeners who give credit to their freedom from pests to everything from compost to cosmic rays and 'Devas', when what they have really done is build up a good population of *Anthocoris*, plus a few other useful predators such as ground beetles, rove beetles, hoverflies and ladybirds. The less you spray the more help you will gain from these often very inconspicuous friends.

So follow the two basic principles of pest control. Never spray as a preventive measure, for you may well never have the pest whose picture is on the label. Never spray unless a pest is really bad, because the price of one hundred per cent freedom from pests is constant spending on chemicals and constant trouble. It is much easier to settle for 98–9 per cent and tolerate a reasonable number of pests whose quantity will diminish as your *Anthocoris* increase.

Anti-pest and disease measures will be found mentioned under each fruit separately and though recipes are given in these accounts, they will be repeated in Chapter 8 for quick reference. So far as diseases are concerned, the main one with all fruit is due to mineral deficiencies caused by underfeeding, and good compost in quantity is the best answer.

The Analysis of Soft Fruits

Soft fruits are largely a source of vitamins and minerals, and they are also extremely good to eat. All contain sugars, but these are non-fattening, and though their vitamin C falls when they are bottled, a useful quantity still remains. When we eat root vegetables, we are 'stealing' the stored power of starches and sugars that the plant had hoarded to send a mighty seed head towering high next spring. Fruit, however, is *designed* to be eaten, it is the bush's bribe to the birds to swallow the fruit and spread the seeds in their droppings, and it was also a similar bribe to us, for stewed fruit and sanitation are quite late inventions in the history of Man as a species.

Today we spend more on sweets than on meat, and this demand reaches back to the rare treats of finding blackberries and wild raspberries and strawberries ripe and delicious in a Britain where apples were still crabs, and plums only the bitter bullaces and sloes. Our synthetic foods of the future will be flavoured with the tastes that encouraged the meat-eating Mesolithic men, women and especially children, to vary their diet to include the vitamins and minerals in soft fruit.

All soft fruit are mostly water, but not more than there is in the leafy vegetables, and all contain sugars and starches, though the taste of the latter is masked by the sugar. The following table shows the water content and the available carbohydrate, roughly what we digest out of the mixture.

	Water %	Carbohydrate %
Blackberries	85·30	6·10
Currants, black	77·40	6·60
Currants, red	82·80	4·40
Currants, white	83·30	5·60
Gooseberries, green	89·30	3·40
Gooseberries, ripe	83·70	9·20
Loganberries	85·00	3·40
Raspberries	83·20	5·60
Rhubarb	83·20	2·40
Strawberries	88·90	6·20
Oranges	80·90	14·70

Oranges are included for comparison in all these tables, and they serve incidentally to show why there has never been a fruitarian race living in England—our native fruits lack the carbohydrate to keep us warm in our climate. Leaving some gooseberries on to ripen and eat raw is evidently worth while, and the British blackcurrant has qualities that make it our best soft fruit, which shows even more in the following table:

THE VITAMINS IN SOFT FRUIT

	Milligrams			Micrograms		
	A I.U.'s	C Raw	C Cooked	Niacin	Thiamine	Riboflavin
Blackberries	75–100	10	—	—	30–35	60
Currants, black	400	150		—	30	140
Currants, red	120	45		—	45	
Currants, black bottled	380	27	17·80	—		144
Gooseberries	380	27	17·80	—	150	
Loganberries	—	38·80	21·10	—	33	
Raspberries	130	30	8·00	0·30	20–30	70
Raspberries, bottled		21·2				154
Rhubarb	64	15–25	3·20	0·10	10–25	30
Strawberries	60	71·40	37·50	0·30	30	70
Oranges	190	49		0·20	80	30–60

Soft Fruit Without Spraying

In terms of vitamin C, blackcurrants hold three times as much as oranges which are also beaten by the strawberry, which can be enjoyed from June to October. They may be largely water, but they beat raw cabbage and even broccoli in vitamin C, and who would eat any cooked green vegetable if they could have strawberries instead? Rhubarb makes rather a poor showing in the table, but it is very easy and welcome as a change from bottled fruit in the spring.

THE MINERALS IN SOFT FRUIT

	Calcium	Milligrams for 100 grams Phosphorus	Iron	Copper
Blackberries	17	34	1·00	0·16
Currants, black	60	43	1·27	0·14
Currants, red	36	30	1·22	0·12
Currants, white	22	28	0·93	0·14
Gooseberries, green	28	34	0·32	0·13
Gooseberries, ripe	19	19	0·58	0·15
Loganberries	35	24	0·44	0·73
Raspberries	49	52	0·99	0·13
Rhubarb	44	18	0·83	0·05
Strawberries	41	28	0·66	0·02

All are quite good as mineral sources, and in available form, for the copper in egg yolk as an example is locked up by sulphur, and none, except the rhubarb, have enough oxalic acid to lock up their own calcium and iron.

The Fruit Cage

Gardeners have what is called, in this age of ready-made phrases or clichés, a 'love-hate relationship' with birds, for all of them are of value as insect-eaters for part of the year, usually in the spring when they are foraging for high-quality protein for their nestlings. Then they turn on our fruit and there is only one way to beat really determined birds, and that is a fruit cage.

The old type had wire-netting sides, and this has to be smaller than two-inch mesh, for the modern bird simply flies straight at large-mesh netting, declutches, folds wings, coasts through, engages third and accelerates away on the other side. Birds have learnt to deal with wire-netting of wider than body size as easily as with milk bottles. Wire-netting rusts with time and is relatively costly, but today it is being rapidly replaced with nylon netting, of which 'Netlon' is the best known make.

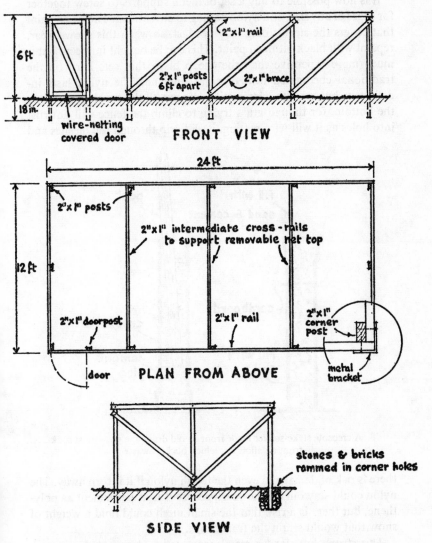

7. A fruit cage is the best answer for birds, and can now be covered with nylon
   netting that lasts longer than chickenwire if taken in for the winter

167

It is now possible to buy a set of metal supports to screw together for cages of any size, and nylon netting to cover them. The green paint that covers the steel tubing may not last, so when this shows wear, repaint with black bitumen paint. This can be bought in green, but is much more expensive than the cheap black that sets hard on the traditional corrugated iron of rural England. The nylon lasts indefinitely, but, as with wire-netting, dig out all the couch grass along the bottom, for though grass trying to climb the fence will not rust into holes as it will wire-netting, it will grip through the meshes and

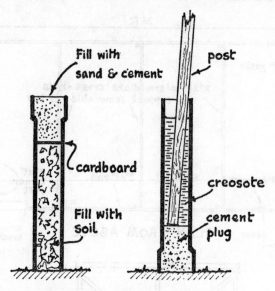

8. A creosote stake-soaker made from an old drainpipe gives most soak from a gallon tin, which buckets waste

there is risk of damage to even the tough nylon if it is torn away. The nylon could stay out all the year because it is as permanent as polythene, but there is a risk that the small mesh could hold a weight of snow that would strain the framework.

This strong but slender metal construction does not dominate a small garden as badly as the older wooden type, but anything is better than being dominated by birds. These wooden ones are easily made by anyone who has a saw (and can saw straight), a hammer, a screwdriver and a gimlet for putting in the screws for the iron-strengthening brackets at the corners and the latch and hinges for the door, and a good creosote brush, for plenty of creosote must go on or the timber will rot before it has earned its keep.

A cage 12 ft. wide and 24 ft. long needs uprights 7 ft. 6 in. long, of 2-in. × 1-in. timber, for each must go eighteen inches in the ground with soil and brick-ends rammed firmly round. One for each corner, one in the middle of each end and three along each side with an extra door for a door post makes 75 feet of this timber, in fact rather more, but if the merchant is told you want it to cut 'seven-foot-sixes' there will not be more than 5 ft. of short ends left over. Then you will need five 12 ft. lengths of 2-in. × 1-in. timber, one along the top of each end and three across from side to side, two 24-foot lengths, or another two 12-foots for the sides and six diagonal braces between the side posts, plus enough for the door frame which also needs a diagonal brace like one on a chicken run. All this will take a bit over 200 feet of this very useful garden timber, which should be bought 'prepared' or ready-planed.

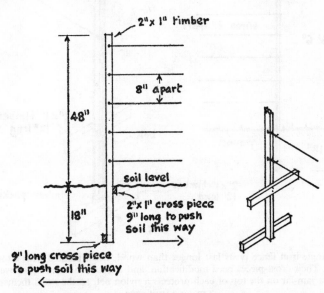

9. Blackberries and loganberries lie on their wires and raspberries need stout support. Note the underground crosspieces to take the pull of the posts and transfer it to pushing the soil

Building needs two stout chairs and two pairs of hands, one to hold a brick endways against each post to take the shock of hammering the top members in place while the other drives the nails. The black-painted iron corner brackets are standard from any ironmonger and should be fixed with woodscrews *after* the creosoting. Those who have skill and an electric drill will, of course, drill the diagonals and uprights to take long quarter-inch bolts, but these directions and the drawing are only a guide for the less carpentry-minded.

It is best to cut the wood to size and then give everything two coats of creosote, leaving it to dry before putting it up, as it is the ends and joints that rot, and these do not get creosoted if the cage is put up and painted afterwards. The buried parts of all the posts want the most, because these always rot through at ground level.

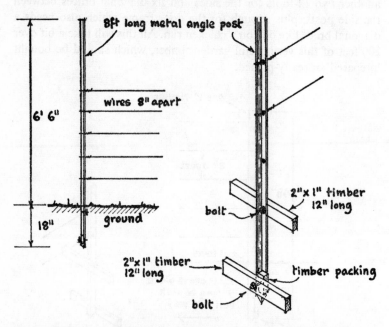

10. Angle-iron fence posts last longer than wood, when painted with bitumen paint. Their cross-pieces need modification, and if they are taken up above the fruit, a jam-jar on the top of each protects a nylon net, so the posts themselves make a fruit cage

As this applies to posts for all the bush fruit that need support, a 'creosote-soaker' is useful. A length of old drainpipe filled with soil all but six inches, with a cardboard disc cut to fit on top and allow a cement plug to be cast in, makes a 'creosote-soaker' which lasts for

170

years. A packet of ready-mixed sand and cement as sold in Wool-worths is plenty, and when it has set the soil can be emptied out and the pipe turned over so that the weight in the bottom holds it upright like an old-fashioned umbrella stand. How many posts this will do at once depends on the diameter of the pipe, but four is a minimum, and when you pour from a gallon tin of creosote, only a little of it fills the 'soaker' to the full eighteen inches, when two-gallon bucket-fuls would merely soak them for a foot. Leave them in for twelve hours if possible, so that all the buried parts are soaked rather than painted and almost decay-proof. The drawing shows the prin-ciple (page 168).

The cage can be covered with one-and-a-quarter-inch wire-netting, six-foot width, if this can be bought by the yard, for it needs forty yards. If not, buy three-foot width, and have two fifty-five-yard rolls, so the surplus will come in for pea-supporting. Otherwise cover with 'Netlon', hooking it to the large-headed galvanized iron nails used for holding roofing-felt, and tying it to the posts. After the fruit season the nylon can be rolled up and put away for next year, so the birds can have a chance at the pests between times.

The Strawberry Cover

Bush fruit stays in one place, but the strawberry bed moves round the garden, so it cannot stay under the fruit cage, though birds more determinedly slaughter strawberries than almost any other fruit. Drive twenty-inch lengths of well-creosoted 2-in. × 1-in. timber, eight inches into the ground at each corner of the bed, and at two-foot intervals all round it, with their inch sides facing the plants. Place a one-pound jam-jar over each to save wear on the netting and cover with six-foot-wide 'Netlon'. Make four-inch-long 'hairpins' of stout wire and pin down all along one side of the net, and staple the other side and the ends to odd lengths of 2-in. × 1-in. creosoted timber. These hold the net tight across the top with their weight and make it easy to lift up and fold back for picking and weeding. The net rolls round them for winter storage and the pegs pull out and bundle up with them. Larger cages can be made, with jam-jar-crowned poles in the middle, so it is possible to creep inside, but those who are rotating their strawberries will be picking some from each of all four at times, and they need something they can fold back and replace quickly.

Soft Fruit Without Spraying

Soft Fruit Support Posts

Currants and gooseberries stand up by themselves, but blackberries, loganberries and raspberries need strong posts and wire support. One way to do this is with metal angle-iron fence posts eight feet high, which can be bought with holes drilled right down to the points and all the way up, for holes are free, though the posts are relatively expensive but more lasting than wood.

Begin by painting them thoroughly with black or green bitumen paint, taking care to get it well inside the holes for it is here that they rust. Then drill holes in the middles of the two-inch sides of foot-long pieces of creosoted 2-in. × 1-in. timber, two for each post, and bolt one through the bottom-most hole near the point of the post and one about a foot higher. Set these stakes in eighteen-inch-deep holes and fill them with rammed soil.

Stretch the wires eight inches apart, tying at each end as in the diagram. If these narrow metal stakes are used without the wooden cross pieces, the weight on the wires (especially from blackberries) will draw the stakes together, cutting through the soil like knives through butter. The cross pieces push against it in two directions and hold it firmly upright. The advantage of having stakes so much taller than the normal four feet for raspberries is that a jam-jar can go on the top of each, and nylon netting can cover the lot (seamed together where a twelve-foot-width piece for the top joins a six-foot one round sides and ends), with just a flap at the sides to get in by. Weigh it down at the bottom, for the risk without the netting stretched over a cage is that birds will get in and entangle themselves.

Posts of 2-in. × 2-in. timber of this length, of 5 ft. 6 in. to allow eighteen inches underground if no netting support is required, can be used in the same way, but these need creosoting, ideally with the buried ends soaked, and the cross pieces must be nailed on opposite sides, for if they go on the same one as on the metal posts (which are bolted) the nails will draw from the lower one as the leverage of the weight on the top wires starts to push. This should be clear from the diagram.

The ordinary plastic-covered 'garden wire' is so thin that it can rub through the bark of raspberry canes fretting at their ties through a long and windy winter. The best is the 'faulty telephone wire' often advertised in the gardening papers as 'cheaper than string—stronger than rope', which it is, and a reel of this is a good investment in any garden, for the heavy insulation cushions anything tied to it, while the wire inside takes the pull, and it will last almost indefinitely.

Blackberries

The commercial blackberry is 'Himalayan Giant', which is used for a windbreak in Norfolk, and this is a genuine giant with twelve-foot-long shoots grown in a single season. It has vicious thorns and large but tasteless fruit. A better blackberry for those who want one sufficiently strong and spiny to make a hedge on a metal post and wire support fence, is 'Bedford Giant', which runs to eight- to ten-foot shoots, and has large fruit with a real taste that begin in July, rather clashing with the raspberries.

The blackberries with pleasure in their pruning are the new thornless kinds: not the old 'John Innes' which fruited late, but 'Thornless Giant', a form of 'Bedford Giant', which also crops in July, and 'Oregon Cutleaf Thornless', which is a sport from the old 'Parsley-Leafed' variety, with a real blackberry flavour and sizeable berries ready in August. Its leaves hang on like those of a beech, so it too can

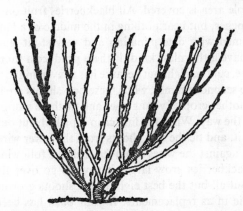

11. Pruning blackberries involves opening up the middles and removing the oldest branches and the weakest each autumn. The all-black shoots on this bush would be removed

make a hedge for fruit without ferocity. If this is a boundary one, agree with your neighbour about going round to pick and prune, or have it six feet away from the bottom of your garden so that you can get round behind it.

Blackberries need six feet between rows, and even 'Oregon Thornless' goes six feet between plants, while 'Thornless' or 'Bedford' Giants want eight, for the problem of blackberries in small gardens is one of size. It is therefore important to feed them adequately but not generously.

Start by digging in two pounds of a mixture of equal parts of coarse bone meal and hoof and horn to every six feet of a two-foot-wide strip along where they will be planted. As with all bush fruit, take great care to remove the roots of perennial weeds such as couch grass and convolvulus, because these are hard to fork out later.

Put in the posts, with an intermediate one every six feet, stretch the wires, and plant your Oregon blackberry in the middle between each pair. If your garden is twelve feet wide you can get two in a row of this one, but only one of the others. November is perhaps the best planting time, but they can go in at any time between then and mid-March. Shorten all the long shoots on the new plant to fifteen inches and tie them to the bottom wires in a fan, so that they can do their job, which is to grow the leaves that will feed the shoots that will grow through the summer and fruit the following year.

As these grow, tie them in to the wires, spreading them widely so that the whole area is covered. All blackberries fruit on both young and old branches, but bear nothing in the middle of a tangle, so they are best pruned with determination and very stout leather gloves, unless you have a thornless kind. If these produce a thorned branch from the base, cut this right out because it is a reversion to the original. Through the second summer, while these new shoots are blossoming, watch for another crop of young ones and tie these along the bottom wires out of the way. When the first crop is picked, cut out the shoots that carried it, and tie the new shoots from the lower wires and train them up flat against the wires again for fruit the following season.

As the blackberries grow larger it pays to go over them in July and to cut out all but the best eight to ten shoots growing from the bottom to tie in as replacements. If your bush has been neglected until November, locate the best shoots, take hold of each one a foot from the tip and push it down, back and clear, never bending it sharply, and cut out the old growth in sections. Do not remove any young shoots till you have them clear, because you may have some breakages. Take them off by scraping the soil away so that you can snip them through with the secateurs two inches below ground. This is useful if you have a thorned kind, because it provides a smooth 'handle' to pull it out by.

174

Wild blackberries are never fed, and in the garden these cultivated kinds have roots that go just as far and deep. So except for comfrey on the surface to provide potash, covered down with mowings every three years, there is no need to worry about feeding them. Wear gauntlet gloves because the cut-off branches can slash your wrists even when you are dragging them to the bonfire. Bush fruit prunings are among the few items of rubbish that should never be composted, not only because of the difficulty of decay but because of the fact that they can often hold the stray eggs of pests.

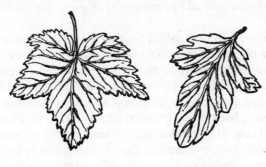

**Healthy
black currant leaf**   **Leaf
with Reversion**

12. The big bud mite of blackcurrants carries the reversion virus which brings brighter flowers, dwindling crops and leaves distorted until they can look almost like oak leaves

Blackberry pests are few, and mostly shared with raspberries, and this cutting out and burning of the old wood stops their only exclusive pest, the blackberry mite (*Phytoptus essigi*). There are reputed to be some stray fungi or virus diseases and the remedy is first to spray with a seaweed foliar feed in June or July to see if the condition clears up, and then to spray with Bordeaux Mixture at the same strength as recommended for potato blight when the leaves have fallen. Do both and you hit the pest either way.

Currants, Black

Blackcurrants are the best value, for space occupied, in vitamins, but they should go four feet apart and with four feet between rows. This means that if your garden beds are twelve feet across you will just get in three to the row. There is no gain in cramming more into your fruit

175

cage and having them produce a smaller crop than if they were less crowded.

The finest early variety is 'Laxton's Giant', ready in July, with the largest fruit of any, often as large as cherries, but with the same quantity of seeds, so they are splendid for bottling or jam, and so sweet that they can be eaten raw without sugar like dessert gooseberries. Their drawbacks are that they make a large bush so are better five feet apart each way, and because they are early, late frosts can catch the blossom. With some shelter such as a wall, or a blackberry windbreak as used by commercial growers, they are an excellent kind.

Blackcurrants usually spread their crop over three weeks, and this provides a big batch for bottling as well as for eating raw or stewed. Those who like them fresh, rather than harvested all together for bottling, can plant several kinds. The best mid-season kind for flavour and cropping quality is 'Wellington XXX', to be followed by 'Westwick Choice', both strong growers, and with fruit that spreads over a period. Those who find that one catches the frost, or even that they like one best of all, can increase their bushes so easily from cuttings that they can grow on replacements and have only one kind. For very small gardens where only three feet can be scraped up between plants and rows, grow 'Amos Black', the smallest and most upright of all, fruiting late and cropping well, but with more acid fruit than 'Laxton's Giant' or the other two which are famous for size and flavour. 'Baldwin' is also a late one and compact, with berries recommended as the highest in vitamin C of all, which give it a sharp flavour, and both can be relied on to miss frosts in the most northern and exposed gardens.

The lead that 'Baldwin' has in vitamin C was established by the National Fruit and Cider Institute at Long Ashton, by analysing the fruit from every picking on a range of varieties from 1944 to 1953, which produced the averages over the ten-year trial:

	Vitamin C *Mg. per 100 grams*
Baldwin	242
Seabrook's Black	205
Wellington's XXX	204
Davidson's Eight	203
Westwick Choice	235
Boskoop Giant	198
Mendip Cross	196

176

13. The small heaps are of potatoes grown on soil that had only artificials for four years, the large had compost, which gave humus as well as chemicals.

14. An orchard of dwarf pyramid apples showing the 'safety-valve shoots'.

15. The side branches of dwarf pyramids can be grafted together so they 'join hands' and save staking.

16. Bush Cox, dwarfed by summer pruning, showing grease band on trunk to beat many pests without spraying.

Soft Fruit Without Spraying

The figure of 150 given in the earlier table is for blackcurrants bought in an American greengrocery, and though it may have started as low as the second picking on the 'Seabrook's' in 1950 of 155 mg., it is more likely to have been as good as the British samples when it left the grower. This trial was done with fresh fruit grown at Long Ashton, and nearest the quality that a gardener would pick from his own bushes.

Blackcurrants are nitrogen-ready and they need a starting stock dug in, ideally shoddy as recommended in Chapter 3, but if none is available, use 2 lb. a square yard of hoof and horn. This is to be used slowly over the next ten years, after which they are past their best. They need manure rather than compost; perhaps a good barrowload to two square yards gives them the garden equivalent to the commercial grower's 20–30 tons an acre, for immediate use.

They are also shallow-rooting, so make wide, six-inch-deep holes, spread the roots and firm the soil well round them. They should be planted as deep as the soil mark on the stem shows that they grew in the nursery. Then cut back their long new shoots with yellow-brown bark to three or four buds, whichever one is on the outside and pointing away from the middle of the bush. There will be no fruit the first season after planting, which will be spent growing strong young shoots from these buds. The following summer sees a full crop, with fruit all the way up these strong young branches.

Blackcurrants fruit best on this young wood, which should never be shortened, but also on spurs from two-year-old branches. Every October go over the bushes and take out a third of the older branches to leave room for the new recruits. Those with reddish-black bark and light markings grew the previous summer and will fruit another season, but take out the black ones down to the lowest light-brown-barked side shoots they have. If the oldest branches have no low shoots, take them right out, leaving only an inch to grow new buds. Always take out the oldest and weakest, and shoots that have not fruited well, really low, because the lower on the bush you cut, the longer will be the fruiting length of the new shoots.

These prunings will have to include some young wood which has grown high up on the old. Select six- to eight-inch lengths, cut them off cleanly and set them thickest end down six inches apart along a spade-cut in part of the garden where they can stay undisturbed, so that only two inches of the tips is above ground. Tread the soil firmly back round them, and keep them hoed free from weeds during their

M   177

first summer. The following November dig them up, cut back the strong shoots that will have grown to three or four buds, and replant at one foot apart and two feet between rows, ready for a move to their permanent homes the following November, which is the best planting month.

After the first picking and pruning in the late autumn, spread manure between the rows, so that it washes down and decays and the roots can take the nitrogen they need in spring. Pig manure is best because it has rather more potash, but deep-litter poultry compost based on straw or peat is odourless, easier to spread and richer in nitrogen. In April or May cover down with lawn mowings, which are cheaper and tidier than the straw mulch used by commercial growers. Manure in the autumn and mulch in the spring, forking the mulch in shallowly after pruning, keeps blackcurrants cropping at full speed, and cuts out the need for weeding.

This autumn 'fork-under' buries the fallen leaves, but if it does not, collect the rest and dump them on the leafmould heap, because this controls leaf spot fungus (*Septoria ribis*) which shows as small irregular brown spots on the leaves. In wet seasons this can result in the leaves falling completely in June and July and the fruit withering on the branches. In this case clear up the leaves and burn them (one of the few cases where burning leaves is justified) and spray the bare branches with Burgundy Mixture. As a further precaution stop using manure under the bushes in autumn, spread compost or comfrey in spring instead, because both this fungus and blackcurrant rust attack only where there is excess nitrogen.

Both European and American gooseberry mildew can sometimes attack blackcurrants and this needs the treatment to be found under 'Gooseberries'; here too the attack occurs after too much nitrogen, especially sulphate of ammonia given in spring. The really serious disease of blackcurrants is 'reversion', which is a genuine virus, with symptoms of leaves longer and narrower than normal, and the shape altering till they look almost like oak leaves. They flower earlier and more brightly than normal, but crop poorly and finally die.

It is useless merely cutting out attacked shoots. Once a bush has reversion there is nothing to do but dig it up and burn it. It is safe to plant a new bush in the same hole, for this virus is spread not by contact or 'spores' in the soil, but by the big bud mite (*Phytoptus ribis*), and though you remove the branch that shows the symptoms, the virus is in all the sap of that bush and it will be transferred from bush to bush by the migrating mites.

The big bud mite, also called the currant gall mite, is microscopic and also attacks red and white currants and more rarely gooseberries. The bugs work their way into the buds of the new season's shoots in June and begin egg laying. The young mites feed inside the buds which start to swell in July, and continue breeding and feeding inside them until spring, when up to five hundred may migrate from a single bud. The migration takes place between late March and the middle of April, and the mites are carried long distances by the wind, and short ones by the feet of birds (they are too small to be eaten even by tits) and on pollinating insects, including bees. They can also be carried by clothing if you walk between the rows during the migration period.

Though they can be controlled by lime-sulphur or a derris and pyrethrum mixture as a routine spray at the correct time, this has the disadvantage of killing off their natural enemy which is *Anthocoris nemorum*. Wait till the leaves are the size of a shilling (5p) and the flowers are at the 'grape bud stage'—just about to open—and spray with 1 pint of lime sulphur to $2\frac{1}{2}$ gallons of water, or use the mixture at the strength recommended for mites, if your currants are sulphur shy. Very few people who inherit gardens know their fruit varieties, and 'Blacksmith', 'Davison's Eight', 'Goliath' and 'Wellington XXX' are all likely to have their leaves damaged by lime sulphur. Though a weaker strength can be used, derris and pyrethrum together are safer.

The gardener who wishes to keep his predators controlling his pests as far as possible, should look for oversized leaf buds at pruning time, pick them off and burn them. There will always be a chance of stray mites blowing in on the wind, and picking and burning before they spread is the best control. Even though it may be tedious, it is possible to clear a dozen bushes in a few hours. Waiting and spraying during the short period when they are vulnerable, may mean missing some and having to spray year after year to keep them in check.

The alternative is to plant 'Seabrook's Black', a mid-season kind that makes a compact bush, with a heavy crop of rather acid fruit with a good vitamin C content. This is resistant to both the mite and the virus. At the other end of the scale comes 'Goliath', which catches big bud as easily as some people catch colds.

Currants have three aphides, two shared with lettuces and one private one, the currant aphis (*Capitophorus ribis*) which curls the leaves at the tips so that they are very awkward to spray. They stunt new growth and cover the fruit with honeydew which can then be attacked by sooty moulds. All three migrate to lettuces, sow-thistles and nettles after they have done the damage, and return to lay eggs behind the buds and among the bark of the older wood of the currants in the autumn.

With careful timing it is possible to kill these eggs and miss the *Anthocoris*, which is a late hibernator. In mild winters these are moving about hunting for eggs and small creatures like mites in the crannies of the bark right up until January, when they hide under leaves and in hedges, returning usually in April. Delay winter washing, therefore, until late January or early February, and then squirt it hard into the crevices and catch the eggs before they hatch. Where bullfinches are common, put up the Netlon on the cage in February and March to protect the fruit buds.

The really spectacular pest is the magpie or currant moth (*Abraxas grossulariata*) caterpillar, which is a looper, with black and white markings and yellow stripes down the sides. These go for all the currants and gooseberries, and can attack apricots, plums, laurels and Euonymus hedges. The eggs are laid in July and August, the caterpillars hatch and feed for a time and then hibernate under dead leaves and rubbish, in cracks and crannies in walls, and even under sheds, where a great many are eaten by assorted predators. If they can be found when they are small at this stage, spray with the nicotine was recommended earlier, for this is a sure killer for caterpillars, and there is plenty of time for it to be washed off. When they wake up they return to the currants with such vigour that bushes can be completely stripped by May or mid-June. Spray with a derris and pyrethrum mixture, ideally before they have done too much damage. This will kill *Anthocoris*, but the caterpillars will kill the bushes, so spray with the least dangerous substance to birds and bees, apart from the long-term risk to humanity.

Two other pests, the currant clearwing moth (*Aegeria tipuliformis*) and the currant shoot borer (*Lampronia capitella*) work inside the shoots and their attacks show when foliage wilts in hot weather on single branches. Cut these off and burn them, snipping till you find the grub tunnel and going down past it. The shoot borer can be serious and then it is worth winter-washing in January to catch the small white cocoons hidden in the bark cracks.

Soft Fruit Without Spraying

Currants, Red and White

White currants are as white as a 'white' wine so do not complain if they are not candle-coloured. The best is 'Versailles', which is a light yellow with large and long bunches and a fine sweet flavour, excellent eaten raw with brown sugar. Fruit sugars are not fattening and those who can learn to enjoy them unsweetened, which is after all the natural way to eat fruit, learn new tastes, instead of just the blanket of sweetness. I personally find that the top of Channel Island milk poured over raw fruit takes off just enough of the sharpness.

Red currants are mainly required for jelly, though they are also suitable for stewing and raw eating. The two best varieties are the old 'Laxton's No. 1' which is an early with a fine flavour, and 'Red Lake' to follow it. Both are vigorous and heavy-cropping varieties for those who like red currants enough to spare the room in which they are far less value than blackcurrants.

These two can be grown as cordons against a wall or fence, which saves a great deal of room in a small garden. They are more expensive than ordinary bushes but are worth the money, for they allow a wall of any aspect, even facing north, with a bed as narrow as nine inches, to grow enough for most family needs, without taking up room in the fruit cage. Large metal shelf brackets screwed to the wall or fence above them can take an expanding curtain rod over which a nylon netting curtain can be draped to defend the buds and fruit against even the fiercest bullfinches.

Dig plenty of compost into the bed, plus 2 lb. of coarse bone meal to a square yard and either 4 oz. of wood ashes or 4 of seaweed meal as well, to enrich what is usually a narrow bed full of builders' rubble; but treat fertile soil beside a garden fence less generously. The cordons come ready-pruned, and all they need is planting fifteen inches apart along the wall, straight upright, and tying in to wall nails.

In July or August pinch out the tips of the new side shoots that will have grown to strengthen the fruiting buds round their bases. After the leaves have fallen, shorten these shoots to an inch and the new growth on the main leader reaching up the wall by a third. Red and white currants fruit like apples, on wood two years old and older, so are pruned like tiny apple trees, and can be cordons and even espaliers with tiers of horizontal branches trained against a wall, and

181

while these are more expensive compared with three-year-old bushes, they save space. Cordons cost roughly a third more than bushes, and it is possible to grow low bedding plants or even vegetables in the bed below them, but nothing tall between their stems and the sun, or their wood will fail to ripen and bear a crop. It is possible to grow cordon currants with wire supports like raspberries, and eighteen-inch-long cross-pieces nailed to the tops of the supports, with wires connecting their ends, to hold the nylon net apart so that birds cannot perch and peck through at them.

13. Redcurrants fruit like tiny apple trees and need snipping back to leave 'spurs'. The lines show where to snip on this branch

Bush red and white currants should go in the fruit cage, because the birds go for them more than any other fruit. Plant four feet apart each way, then cut back all the side shoots to inch length, and shorten the leaders, which are the smooth-barked shoots at the branch ends, by a third, if they do not arrive ready-pruned. This is one of the few advantages of modern transport costs—fruit bushes and trees often arrive well pruned by an expert, just to save the weight of the branches that gardeners may not be ruthless enough to cut away.

In later years cut back the side shoots to two or three buds in November, and the leaders to the strongest upward-pointing bud, which is very rarely the one at the tip. These currants are slower growing and less greedy than blackcurrants, they can be slowed down by tip-pinching like their cordons, and always remove any weakly branches, especially to keep the middle open.

They can be mulched with mowings like blackcurrants to keep down weeds, but there is no need to manure under these, though in spring they appreciate seaweed meal or wood ashes at the rate of 4–8 oz. a square yard, the higher figure on sandy soils. Cut comfrey under the mowings mulch, which should go on in May, also supplies the potash they need.

Their pests are the same as those of blackcurrants and a sharp lookout should be kept for the sudden wilting in hot weather that shows one or other of the borer caterpillars to be at work inside a branch. Diseases too are much the same, but both red and white currants can suffer from coral spot fungus (*Nectria cinnabarina*) and dieback (*Botrytis cinerea*). Both cause sudden wilting of whole branches, when they are in full fruit, and these should be removed with the secateurs and burnt. Cut again and again till the wood shows white and clean, not only when there is a disaster, but when any branch dies back at the tip. The best prevention is not to give these currants manure, only compost and low-nitrogen organics, and not to try to keep them longer than twelve years—they are easy enough to increase and grow as replacements.

Take these in the autumn just like blackcurrants, removing whole young shoots from the ends of discarded branches. Insert them like blackcurrants, but with only three inches in the ground, and they will root just as easily. If you want a cordon, cut back to one or two strong buds about eight inches above ground on the best shoot and snip all the others back to a single bud. Do this for three years and you will have as good a cordon as you can buy, and if you have left two buds, a double cordon, which would be much more expensive if you had bought it, but even better value for space.

Gooseberries

'Careless', the commonest gooseberry, sprawls wide and low, filling itself with strangling couch grass that has to be dragged from under the prickles every autumn. It is a strong-growing commercial variety, with large fruit for eating green, but it loses its flavour as it ripens. The best varieties for gardeners are those that are good for jam, bottling, stewing and eating raw, as well as upright by breeding, so that summer mulching with lawn mowings will keep them weedfree.

The two best all-round varieties are 'Langley Gage', with rather smaller berries than 'Careless', but first class for stewing and with the finest flavour of all when ripe to a transparent pearly green-white colour, and 'Whitesmith', which fruits earlier, is amber-yellow when ripe, but equally good green. Both are of upright habit and resistant to American gooseberry mildew (*Sphaerotheca mors-uvae*). 'Lancashire Lad' is also resistant, and a good variety, but not up to the other two for ripe flavour, so search for 'Bedford Red', which has the same upright habit, and a better flavour, though not such a heavy crop.

All these upright kinds make good cordons, for gooseberries fruit like red and white currants, on the previous year's and even older wood. Plant these in exactly the same way as currants, fifteen inches apart, and tying them straight up the wall to stout galvanized iron nails, for they will come ready-pruned. These have the great advantage that they can be kept under control by pruning, so the fruit can be picked without stooping and searching among the prickles. They are also easily protected with a nylon curtain from birds, and though they cost about twice as much as bushes, gooseberries live up to twenty years and one kept under control on a wall is more likely to live this long than a large and sprawling bush that may get broken by the weight of snow in a hard winter as a teenager. Apart from saving space they have the advantage of fruiting early on a south wall and late on a north-facing one, so a single kind serves for both seasons.

It is worth offering to pay extra for longer 'legs' when ordering bush gooseberries. A gooseberry's leg is the length of bare stem between the soil mark that shows how deeply they were planted on the nursery, and where the branches fork first. A good length of leg means that it is easy to reach under for weeding and picking, as often some of the finest fruit hangs awkwardly and low, and with plenty of room it is possible to bring the mulch of mowings right up to the stem. Some may well have been planted too deep in this age of mechanization, so it pays to pick over the plants offered in a Garden Centre and measure three inches from the flat spreading roots, which is as deep as they need be planted, then the rest above ground is leg. Six inches means a good one, but more is desirable if it can be found.

Dig new beds thoroughly to remove all perennial weed roots, because the accumulation of these through the long life of the bushes is their worst problem, and though there are surface weedkillers they do not kill the worst weeds. These are *Convolvulus sepium*, the one with the big white flowers and wicked white roots, couch grass, also called twitch, *Agropyron repens*, false oat, *Arrhenatherum elatius*, also called 'running couch' or 'oat grass' which can climb up and *fill* a gooseberry bush, creeping buttercup, *Ranunculus repens*, and ground elder, *Aegopodium podagraria*.

With time to plan a bush-fruit planting, it pays to attack the weeds in the spring, either with *Tagetes minuta* sown in April and cleared for November planting, or with ammonium sulphamate when the weeds are growing well in late April, which allows sowing four weeks later with french beans or lettuce to clear before planting time, and a chance to dig out any stragglers.

This need for weed clearance applies just as strongly to the narrow beds beside walls, and here it pays to dig right down to see if any convolvulus roots are hiding in the brickwork, for once the cordons are planted they will be devils to get out. After the clearance, dig in compost, not manure, and 2 lb. of coarse bone meal plus 2 lb. of seaweed meal to four square yards, to supply food for the future.

Plant bushes four feet apart each way, three inches deep and with the roots spread. Firm them well and cut back the light-brown-baked branches to between three and five buds to give a choice of one that points upwards and outwards away from the centre. The first year it is possible to grow radishes or even carrots up the row middles while there still seems plenty of room, but in that autumn shorten the new shoots that grew that summer to eight inches long and take out any that are growing towards the middle completely. The ideal shape for a gooseberry bush is that of an empty ice-cream cone, with the main branches pruned round a hollow centre to let in the sun for ripening and the hands for picking without prickles. Normal pruning time can be February, shortening the shoots that grew the previous summer to three inches, removing any weak or elderly branches that have ceased to fruit, and clearing the middle. The object is to keep the bullfinches off the buds which are exposed by orthodox autumn pruning.

Cordons can have their buds protected by the rot-proof nylon net so can be pruned in November by removing completely any shoots at or near the base, digging away the soil and taking off suckers below ground, then shortening all side shoots to two inches and the leader to eight. About July pinch back the side shoots by an inch to strengthen the fruit buds (like summer pruning of apples).

About March, scatter 4 oz. a square yard of wood ashes or seaweed meal under the bushes or along the cordon border, before spreading a mowings mulch in April or May. This is before grass is seeding, so there is no risk of the weeds from this, that are so often mentioned by those who sell peat. A better way of providing the potash is by spreading cut comfrey between the bushes or along the border before the mulch goes on, for it rots slowly and releases the potash gooseberries need.

The signs of potash shortage are a light brown band round the leaf edges, that look as if they had been scorched, while the middles stay a normal green. The equally distinct sign of *too much*, usually where sulphate of potash every year has locked up the magnesium, is broad red bands fading to yellow and cream right across the leaves, and the 'cure' is Epsom salts plus comfrey and good compost to keep the plant foods balanced.

The coral spot and leaf spot of currants can attack and need the same treatments, but the serious disease of gooseberries is the American mildew which is a white fungus on leaves, stems and berries that later turns brown. Cut off the shoot tips with about three inches of stem in August and burn them, because this is where the fruiting spores form and spread the fungus. Then spray with $\frac{1}{2}$ lb. of soft soap (which can still be bought from ironmongers, as it is used for cleaning paint) and 1 lb. of washing soda in 5 gallons of water. Spray again in the spring when the bushes come into flower, and again when the fruit is well set. Though lime-sulphur wash is recommended, this kills *Anthocoris*, and strips the leaves off some varieties, known as 'sulphur-shy', of which 'Bedford Red' is the only one mentioned.

European gooseberry mildew (*Microsphaera grossulariae*) is a white delicate mould on the leaves rather like rose mildew, and the same mixture will cure it. The pest cure for both is prevention, by not giving gooseberries manure or any nitrogen-rich fertilizer, only compost, because both fungi only attack bushes overfed with nitrogen; planting resistant varieties is, of course, another method.

The gooseberry sawfly (*Pteronidea ribesii*) is the worst pest, with three generations a season of caterpillars with black heads, green-and-black-spotted bodies and three orange-yellow areas near their tail ends. These can strip all the leaves off a bush in a few weeks, leaving only the veins, and the best control is a derris and pyrethrum mixture of derris alone, sprayed upwards to catch the small caterpillars under the leaves. Look for them gathered there in colonies just after flowering in April and in June and September and spray at once. Do not wait till they are slaughtering the whole bush. In an emergency boil up cigarette ends and use nicotine, but as these are sawfly caterpillars it is also possible to kill them with strong quassia, which has the advantage of sparing *Anthocoris*.

This creature is desirable as the best controller of the gooseberry red spider mite (*Bryobia praetiosa*) which attacks in April and May, especially in hot, dry weather, making the leaves turn grey or silvery with loss of sap and fall early, starving the fruit and weakening the bushes. These mites hibernate among ivy, under the eaves of sheds, under bark on posts and in crevices in old walls. One of the reasons why I insist so much on creosoting posts for fruit support and everywhere in the garden, especially at the joints, is to make the hiding places they offer unattractive to mites and other pests.

The mites are rusty red or grey and just visible to the naked eye on the undersides of the leaves. Any spray, such as the lime-sulphur usually recommended, will kill the *Anthocoris* on the job, but hosing the bushes with a forceful jet, or syringeing with force, as for carnation red spider in greenhouses, will knock off a great many mites which will have insufficient 'fuel in their tanks' to get back. *Anthocoris* are better clingers and capable of climbing back if knocked off. Three hard squirtings at week-apart intervals can lower the numbers till *Anthocoris* can cope, and as red spider is worst in dry years, the extra watering will do the bushes good. After June the damage ends, because the surviving mites have laid eggs and died, but the eggs will hatch in the autumn, the young mites will feed for a short period and migrate in search of winter quarters. An extra squirt in September will catch these and lower the numbers facing the hazards of hibernation.

Red spider travels like big bud mite, on the wind, and even hitch-hikes on bullfinches and bees, and it can turn up anywhere; a neglected outbreak can build up a local population that will have only a short journey to your gooseberries. So winter-wash the fence or wall, or anywhere near the bed that offers hibernation room in November, and the bushes themselves only as a last resort. Try the 'water cure' and wait till the next summer. If there is again an attack, then winter-wash the gooseberries in January or February, before the leaves as for currants, with a chance of missing the *Anthocoris*, if the attack has got beyond them.

The gooseberry aphis (*Aphis grossularia*) attacks the tips of the young shoots only, twisting the leaves so that it is very difficult to get a spray inside. The best answer is to snip off about an inch of stem with these tips, drop them in a basket and dump in the dustbin or burn. This treatment improves the crop next year, as a version of the summer pruning given to cordons, and though it sounds time-consuming, it is probably quicker to go over even a dozen bushes than to get the car out, drive to a garden shop, buy something deadly and then spray it on several times. The new shoots are soft in early summer and this pruning is the least prickly. Winter washing as for the mite will also destroy aphides (the currant ones join in too) when these return from their summer holidays and are wintering as eggs, ready to hatch and attack in spring.

Gooseberries are increased from cuttings of the young shoots, and those who wish to increase a bush that is failing can deliberately give it dried blood or fish meal after picking to get more shoots between ten inches and a foot long. Remove these in October, slicing them off the branch with some of the old wood to form a 'heel'. Then take off all but the top four side buds (see diagram) and insert the cuttings six inches apart along a trench with only the tips protruding, and tread the soil firmly back round them. A quantity of cuttings should have two feet between rows to allow for hoeing and weeding between them.

The following autumn dig up the rooted cuttings and trim off any roots that may have formed up the stem, to prevent suckering, then replant a foot apart and two feet between rows, with the spread of the roots from the bottom of the cutting three inches below the surface, so that the young bushes 'show their legs'. Usually there is one terminal shoot and three or four side ones. Cut the terminal one out, leaving only an inch of it, and cut the side ones back to three inches, so that they finish with an out-pointing bud. If you are growing cordons, cut these side shoots right off and train the terminal one up a cane. The third autumn the two-year-old bushes will be ready to plant permanently. Snip back the side shoots on the cordons to two buds each, which is how bought ones will be found pruned on arrival.

From about 1860 onwards there were Gooseberry Clubs in Cheshire and Lancashire, like the Leek Clubs of Staffordshire, whose members strove to grow the largest specimens for contests held in local inns. These giant gooseberries were only for show. Most were tasteless, but some weighed as much as an ounce, and today a mere sixteen dives among the prickles to get the pound would be commercially desirable if the weight per bush were economic; and if it had a good flavour and was value in food for space, every gardener would want it.

Today we are becoming a nation of a hundred house plants and one gooseberry—'Careless'—and not more than ten varieties are listed in catalogues when there were hundreds in the 1890's and over sixty in the 1930's. Many died out after American gooseberry mildew crossed to Ireland in 1900 and reached England in 1908, because many varieties had no resistance at all, and others were so 'sulphur-shy' that lime-sulphur as a precaution killed more than the fungus.

Some of these Gooseberry Clubs have survived into the TV age, and their favourite varieties still live on in isolated gardens in the North. The 'London', the biggest of all, was tasteless and is not worth finding, but 'Green Overall', with a really delicious flavour, 'Match-less', and 'Thumper', the sweetest ripe of any, all had their partisans in the hard-fought contests. 'Lord Derby', 'Rifleman' and 'Echo' were large and well-flavoured reds, far better than 'Lancashire Lad', the only red one now sold by greengrocers, and 'Bedford Yellow', 'Catherina' and 'Lady Houghton' were the best yellows.

All are worth gathering and increasing from cuttings, but there are variations of these raised from seed and kept jealously in families like lost Rembrandts. Gooseberries are quite easy from seed, and slicing open berries from one of these large varieties when fully ripe will produce plenty of seed to sow in a half-inch-deep furrow to be marked and kept free from weeds. The seedlings should be two inches high by the autumn, but it is best to wait until they are in bud in the spring before transplanting them six inches apart and a foot between rows. They will not fruit till their third season above ground, and their problem is that they will have no 'legs', but if the seedlings, when they finally are planted two feet apart each way, produce something special, this can be raised from cuttings.

The seedlings will produce variations on the ancestors of the parent mainly, and the raiser should discard ruthlessly all but the best, which should be upright, compact, and with large well-flavoured fruit. If any seedling, or just one branch on *any* variety, produces a prickleless 'sport' like those which have given us the thornless black-berries, peg the tip of that shoot to the ground and let it root itself, then when it is growing well past the peg, cut it off and grow it on, taking the main shoot as a cutting in the autumn.

This 'layering' by pegging down the tip is also easy with black-berries, but it brings a host of suckers, which mean plenty of cuttings, and this is why good seedlings are increased in this way. A thornless gooseberry is what every temperate climate gardener is waiting for, and now that Plant Patents are internationally recognized it could mean a small fortune for the raiser.

189

Soft Fruit Without Spraying

Loganberries

Loganberries are probably not a cross between a raspberry and a blackberry, but they need the same strong supporting posts and wires, and like blackberries they have now a 'thornless' variety that is sweeter than the older kinds, and delightfully gentle to prune. The only thorned variety worth growing is the new 'Malling Hybrid L.Y. 59', which has much larger berries and a heavier crop than the original discovery in 1881 by Judge James H. Logan of California, who sowed American blackberry seed and got a chance mutation.

They fruit between mid-July and the end of August, with dull maroon-red berries like blackberries but up to two inches long, and their drawback is they do not come off the 'plug'—the white core behind the blossom stalk—easily, and if they are not just ripe they squash and smear in the fingers. Loganberries make a very fine sharp jelly, and add a sharpness to raspberry jam, while the 'thornless' one is suitable for raw eating as well as stewing. Because they blossom late they miss the frosts, and crop easily and well on almost any soil.

Start them like blackberries, with compost and coarse bone meal rather than manure dug in, and plant them no closer than two on a twelve-foot-long row across the bed, with four feet between rows. Cut back the newly planted clumps to a foot high and during the first summer tie the strong shoots that grow from the base in a fan on the wires. They fruit the next summer, and as soon as they have finished the crop, cut them down to inch length, and tie in to the wires the new shoots that grow afterwards to fruit the following season. Unlike blackberries, they fruit only on this young wood, and if the old is cut out at once this is awkward for the pests that are shared with raspberries.

In the spring, about April, scatter 1 lb. of wood ashes to four square yards, if you have no comfrey to go under the mulch of mowings between the rows that keeps the roots cool, and should be dug under in October or November. The berries are rather less attractive to birds than raspberries and it is often possible to get away without nets. Though loganberries have the same trailing habit, they cannot be used as a windbreak like blackberries, because they come through each winter as bare young canes and do not thicken up enough to be useful until too late.

There are a number of other hybrid berries, all reputed to be blackberry and loganberry or raspberry crosses, including the Low-

190

berry, Veitchberry, Boysenberry and Phenomenal Berry, all introduced with a blaze of publicity in the past, and now almost out of
cultivation. All have vicious thorns and other drawbacks, so gardeners
are advised never to buy any 'new' berry advertised in the national
Press, for it is probably an old one discarded as not worth growing.

Raspberries

Next to the strawberry, the raspberry is our nicest fruit, to eat raw
over a long season and to bottle for the rest of the year, apart from
jam-making. The problem for those with dentures is the pips which
can rush under our plates with almost indecent haste, by what an old
gardener once described as 'caterpillary attraction'.

The nearest yet to a pipless raspberry has been bred at East Malling
research station, by the late Mr. Norman Grubb, who raised the
famous 'Malling' raspberries that are now almost the only varieties
in modern catalogues. It is 'Malling Hybrid 53–16', much darker than
an ordinary raspberry, but cooking and bottling and jamming to the
normal colour, and with the fewest pips of any variety. It crops well
in August on tall strong canes and bridges the gap before the autumn-
fruiting kinds, for those who have room can grow delicious desserts
and raspberry teas from June until November.

The earliest variety in cultivation today is 'Malling Promise', which
can be ready in mid-June, but it is not a good-flavour kind and there
is a risk of frost damage to its young canes and its blossom, by trying
to start just too early. 'Malling Exploit' is the best to begin the season,
ready at the end of June, with very large berries of delicious flavour
and strong and hardy canes that will bear an autumn crop as well on
the new growth. This is the variety that shows why the 'Mallings'
have beaten all the older kinds off the market.

Next comes 'Lloyd George', which is not quite so delicious, but
still well ahead so that this kind alone has kept going in competition
with the 'Mallings'. It is a heavy cropper with smaller berries and the
ability to be either an early July fruiter or an autumn one, according
to how it is pruned. Follow this with 'Malling Enterprise', which is
also a fine-flavour variety that comes off the plug easily; this is important, because the amateur who picks the first fruits ripe at the
tip of a blossom truss can easily break the stem and waste the rest
of the bunch. It is a heavy cropper and fills in before the 'Hybrid
53–16'.

Soft Fruit Without Spraying

'Lloyd George' is one of the best autumn-fruiting kinds, but the variety 'September', which carries on until October, has larger fruit but not so fine a flavour, and once again has driven the older varieties like 'Hailsham', 'Lord Lambourne' and 'November Abundance' out of the catalogues. Some people are fond of the old yellow raspberries, and 'Antwerp Yellow' can still be obtained, as it is the heaviest cropper in its class, but it needs a search to find it, for there is a constant drive to reduce the number of varieties of almost everything in cultivation, and few firms want to do more than grow just the best sellers, with a commercial demand to provide bulk orders.

Begin with strong measures against perennial weeds, for a raspberry bed should stay down for ten to twelve years, and dig in as much as a barrowload of compost on two square yards. With it turn under 1 lb. of coarse bone meal and hoof and horn mixture and 1 lb. of seaweed meal to a square yard as lasting foods, rather than the quantities of manure used commercially.

Raspberry canes may look lonely planted a foot apart in the rows with four to five feet between them, but this is the space they need to fruit all the way up the canes. Cut down the room to a yard and you will break the trusses as you pick, and above all the canes will only fruit at the tops for lack of light.

Put in the support posts and wires first if possible, so that the canes can be tied in at once after planting. Canes from good firms will be shortened to two feet long to save carriage, and the root will be like the lower arm of a capital 'L'. Have this not more than three inches below the surface and firm the soil round it, at any time between the end of October and even early April, but avoid planting in wet weather on heavy clays if possible, because the firming puddles the clay and makes it hold water, which means a harder start.

Tie the canes to the wires, not to fruit but to produce leaf to support the plants while they grow the strong new shoots that will fruit the following season, and these should be cut out when these new shoots are well up; in any event before they start trying to blossom and fruit, which will be too big a strain on the young roots—like students demonstrating in their first week at college.

In November, after they have been tied in so that they do not damage themselves by swaying in gales, or when you are hoeing between the rows, they will be ready for their normal autumn pruning. Cut only the tips from the tallest and strongest, shorten the next grade by a third and halve the next quality. Then remove any smaller still, having kept the best, not more than six on each cane, and tie in the pruned canes. As they fruit most towards the tips, the three lengths of cane will ensure three 'storeys' of blossom.

Autumn-fruiting varieties newly planted will fruit on the tips of the new canes the first year, and because they have had a summer to take hold in, they can be allowed to do this. Then in February, cut them right down to ground level, and tie in the new shoots that grow afterwards ready to fruit that autumn. After the ordinary raspberry crop has been picked, cut out the canes that have fruited and burn them, for burning bush fruit prunings can save many pest problems. Then tie up the new shoots ready for their November pruning.

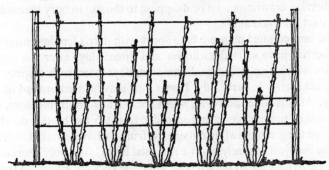

14. Raspberry canes blossom most near the tips, so shorten the strongest to come above the top wire, the next strongest to the next lowest and the third grade lower still, to give three 'storeys' of fruit

All raspberries appreciate 4 oz. a square yard of wood ashes or seaweed meal each spring, or cut comfrey under a two-inch-thick lawn mowings mulch, put on first in April or May, so that the ground has time to warm up, but not in the first year because it cools the soil too much for the young canes. A second coat can be added in June, and through the years these weed-suppressing mulches serve to build up the humus. It is possible to put manure under the mulch to feed the canes on poor soils, but not more often than every other year, for only blackcurrants are heavy nitrogen takers.

After pruning in November, dig the mulch under and remove any suckers, or small shoots wandering from the roots, from between the rows. With time and open weather dig again in January, and turn the soil over a second time in February: not to put any untidy pieces of decayed grass mowings on the surface, but to give the birds, especially robins and pied wagtails, three goes at the chrysalids of the raspberry beetle (*Byturus tomentosus*). These will be sleeping four to six inches down between the rows, so there is no need to do more than light forking, but the robin has sharp eyes that can tell the difference between chrysalids and small stones, and his natural diet is better for him than any bread or 'wild bird food'.

This winter exercise obviates quite an awkward problem later on. The beetles hatch in May and have a month's holiday and honeymoon feeding on the stamens and pistils of a number of flowering trees and shrubs, before the females return to the raspberries and lay eggs in the fertilized blossom. The tiny grubs, when they hatch, crawl into the developing fruit and become the familiar grubs in the raspberries, crawling down or dropping to the soil to bury themselves and start the cycle again.

The best counter-measure is to spray with derris ten days after the raspberries have started to flower and fifteen days after the loganberries which also suffer, and again ten days later, with a spray for the blackberries in early July. Derris dust may be used instead of the spray. At this time, however, when these fruits are in blossom, the bees are at their busiest: and in order to catch the beetles on their visits, or the grubs crawling outside the fruit, we have to risk slaughtering the bees just as surely as if we had used B.H.C. The only alternative is to use pyrethrum in the evening when the bees are asleep, so that it will have spent most of its force by the morning when they are about again; but this will not kill the beetles, only the smaller grubs. Rather than spray in summer and risk one's own or one's neighbour's bees, it is possible to control the pest by a little extra digging, and the choice is ours.

The raspberry moth (*Lampronia rubiella*) is a tiny creature only a quarter-inch across the wings, that lays eggs in the opening blossoms in May and June, like the raspberry beetle, but rather too early for the same derris spray to catch it. The caterpillars soon leave the fruit they have spoilt, crawl down the canes and hibernate round the base of the canes where the digging may well expose them to the robin's beady eyes. They wake in April and burrow into the young shoots, eating out the pith until these shoots wither and die. The best control measure is to watch for withering shoots in dry springs to cut out and burn.

It is also possible to catch the hibernating caterpillars by spraying along and round the cane bases with a winter tar oil wash in January, which also catches any stray aphides and their eggs. Several aphides

194

Soft Fruit Without Spraying

and a thrip can migrate from wild blackberries in summer, and spraying with nicotine is the best answer, getting it well under the leaves.

Rapsberries have a number of diseases, but these are relatively rare, though the mosaic virus is serious. Our original stock of 'Lloyd George' was so badly infected that it went out of cultivation, until we were able to import a stock from New Zealand that had missed the virus. The symptoms are deformed yellow patches near the midribs, sharply-defined yellow spots and crumpling and twisting of the leaves. The only action one can take is to dig up and burn the plants and start again with clean stock in another part of the garden.

These symptoms are uncommon, but poor growth, purple tints and early leaf fall mean a shortage of phosphorus, best cured by 4 oz. a square yard of fish meal. Older leaves with yellow or red margins, or yellow all over but with the leaf veins still green, show magnesium lack which can be cured by Epsom salts; and leaves curling backwards from light brown scorching round the edges show potash shortage. All these are curable with compost.

The fungus diseases are mainly favoured by poor drainage and lack of lime, and on soils where this is likely add 2 lb. of lime to a square yard when starting the bed. Cane spot is the commonest of these, caused by the fungus *Elsinoe veneta* which makes purple spots on the young canes, that can also appear on leaves and fruits in May and June. Cut out badly-attacked canes and spray the rest with Bordeaux Mixture just when the buds start opening, and again ten days later. This is also the treatment for spur blight, caused by *Didymella applanata*, which produces darker blotches on the canes at the joints. In the event of any other symptoms, cut out the attacked canes and burn them, give a compost dressing under the mulch next spring, and if this has no effect, dig up and destroy the bed. There are no other *orthodox* remedies for these raspberry diseases.

Strawberries

Strawberries are the nicest source of vitamin C we can grow and though they cannot be bottled, blackcurrants which have far more vitamin C, can. We can enjoy our strawberries raw from June to November, and as jam round the rest of the year, by choosing our varieties for succession and sustained yield.

They need good humus and a slightly acid soil, so each new bed should have a barrowload of good manure (pig is perfect) or compost

195

to three square yards plus 3 lb. of coarse bone meal to this area. If possible dig in old mattress shoddy as for rhubarb, tucking it well down in the trench bottoms. As strawberries travel round the garden on a four-year rotation, this is long enough for the shoddy to have rotted but also to have left some value for the next crop. Though in the rotation plans in Chapter 4 the strawberries are all shown at the same end of the plots, on the next time round they should move to the other end, and the third even into the middle, though they could go back to the original positions. Disease- and trouble-free strawberries, like onions, depend on moving round the garden instead of of in a permanent bed.

The best time for planting the ordinary varieties is August, for this gives them time to take hold and fruit the year after they go in. Just as with raspberries, the choice of varieties is getting ever narrower, but it is still possible to buy flavour and disease resistance. For the earliest crop choose 'Cambridge Rival', with large fruit on erect foliage so that it is clear of the ground in wet seasons, and with resistance to red core disease. Follow it with either 'Royal Sovereign', the famous old kind still unbeaten for flavour, or a new one, 'Templar', with a heavier crop, a good flavour and disease resistance. For a late one to crop well into August have 'Cambridge Late Pine', with a delicious pineapple flavour and resistance to both mildew and frost. For a fourth row, to take the season right up to November, plant one of the Remontant varieties, such as 'Red Rich' or 'Hampshire Maid', which will need to have its early flower trusses snipped out if it is to put its strength into the autumn crop.

As anyone who has seen a strawberry field knows, 'early mid-season' or 'late' mean the times when varieties have their main crop, but there are always stragglers that it does not pay to pick commercially. This four-row strawberry bed will at times have something to pick on every row, and if all four on the rotation are in full production at once, there may well be too many, so watch how the yield builds up and miss one, or even two if season, soil and luck are likely to put you in the rare position of having more strawberries than you can eat.

There is no need to have the same four kinds on each square, and at least the first two should be different, so that you can decide which have done best before you plant up the beds with their runners for the next time round. Begin with 'Cambridge Vigour', another well-flavoured red core resister, which is earlier than 'Rival', followed by

'Gorella' which is large and vigorous, with big fruit of quite a good flavour, followed by 'Talisman', which is rather nicer, very upright and cropping over a long period, and with whichever of the two Remontants you did not plant in the other bed.

These Remontants, also called 'Perpetuals' or 'Ever-bearers' are widely grown on the Continent, but have never become commercially popular because the town public seem to feel that June and July are the strawberry months, and will not buy the later crops, though the gardener can always enjoy his own, and even sell to his neighbours. They have the advantage of making fewer runners, and of resisting many diseases of the ordinary kinds, though they have the disadvantage of cropping best in their first year and then tailing off. They were formerly grown as annuals, but the second-year crop is always worth having before they are divided.

As a trial, start the third bed with an early one, 'Hummi-Grundi', which is advertised as growing three-ounce berries and will certainly do between one and two ounces for anyone. These are not tasteless like the old 'Huxley Giant', but excellent for eating and jam, while the advantage of fewer stoopings to the pound applies to gardeners as much as it does to commercial growers. This is a June-July fruiter, and there is a later one that takes the season up to August, 'Hummi-Gento'. Both are expensive but the price will come down as they become popular. Follow these either with ordinary Remontants or the one that is called a 'Rollerberry'.

It is an odds-on chance that any 'new' berry advertised in the Press will be a remontant strawberry (if it is an 'Eveberry' it may well be an apple tree at four times the price you would pay to any good fruit nursery) and the 'Climbing Strawberries' are simply remontants that make runners on which they flower and fruit. If you tie them up to a fence or trellis, you spend a great deal of time on growing much smaller fruit than they would produce if trailing on the ground, because the strawberry is not a climber and is not specialized to pump the 88·9 per cent of water in its fruit up its runners. The 'Tumbleberry' is an Alpine strawberry, a seedling of a slightly larger version of our wild strawberries, and neither is worth a place in the garden. They are 'gimmicks' and will be forgotten like this craze word.

The 'Rollerberry' does not 'suppress all weeds' as its advertisers claim, but it is a low-runnering kind that will crop right on from July to November, with very well-flavoured berries that are on the small side after the first two years. It is useless commercially because it never has a 'flush', which is a quantity of berries ripe together to pick in bulk for market, but it does offer strawberries for tea every day for the least trouble of any. With this one it is possible to have a full season's fruit with one early variety, 'Hummi-Grundi' or 'Cambridge Rival' or 'Cambridge Vigour', and three rows of 'Rollerberries' propagated from your own plants, which saves the high price that pays for the advertising.

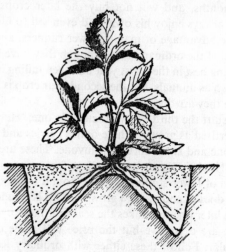

15. Strawberries should be planted in wide, shallow holes with their roots spread down the sides of a mount in the middle, so their growing-points are well above soil level

All strawberries are best planted in August, though the Remontants can be put in as late as October and still fruit the next autumn, because they have more time in which to grow. The rows can be fifteen to eighteen inches apart with a foot between each plant and a foot from the plants to the posts that support the nylon net all round. On clay soils it is worth making a trench down the middle, heaping the soil into flat-topped ridges two inches high to plant on, which is an old-fashioned method that gives better drainage.

Take out trowel holes, about four inches round and two inches deep, but shallower in the middle. Spread the roots of each plant and sit it on top of this small mound, so that when the soil is firmed back it has its growing point well clear of the surface, and plenty of soil on its roots to prevent frost heaving it out of the ground in winter (see diagram). Strawberries are shallow-rooting, they need to start with their roots wide, and planting these bunched together in a dibber hole is a handicap.

Hoe between the rows if the weeds grow fast in a mild winter, and again in April, before spreading a two-inch-thick mulch of peat between plants and rows to hold down all annual weeds, and there should be no perennial ones in a bed for bush fruit. This peat can well be 'secondhand', having served to store vegetables in, and when the bed is dug up its humus is added to the soil. Those who have made leafmould in quantity could use this, but never mulch strawberries with lawn mowings because these attract slugs.

The peat acts as a substitute for straw and has a slug-repellent effect, but it means that there may be fine dry peat on the berries. Straw is less good as a weed suppressor, or as humus to build up in the soil through the life of the bed (it needs renewing each spring, because worms take it down), but it is much cheaper, and when the crop was over it used to be burnt to kill the spores and pest eggs that wintered in the older leaves. With Remontants and a late finish, this means waiting for a dry day in late November to set it alight, for it is not easy to burn only part of the bed.

Those who use straw could well remove it to the compost heap, partly rotted and ready to break down, together with the weeds and surplus runners from cleaning up the bed in the autumn. Cutting out unwanted runners was one of the ways in which the strength of straw-berry plants was conserved for fruiting, but it does not make as much difference to the crop as we once thought, and it is all extra work. So clean up each bed in the autumn, mainly to make room for next year's straw and to get rid of dead leaves, with the weeds that will have seeded themselves or got through the mulch.

'Rollerberries' and Remontants need least weeding, and, unless you fall for the 'climbing varieties', least runner removal. Each spring, about April, feed the bed with 4 oz. of fine bone meal and 4 oz. of bonfire ash (not more) to the square yard, because strawberries need both potash and phosphorus, but do best without too much nitrogen, and their starting stock will last them. When you finally dig up a bed, beat as much soil as possible off the plants and burn them if you cannot put them on a really hot compost heap, for some of their accumulated troubles will be tough ones.

Their common pest is aphides, and a nicotine and soap spray in April is the remedy. Squirt it hard into the plant centres where the brutes then are, for later they spread out under the leaves and are

Soft Fruit Without Spaying

less easy to kill. One good April spray, using the cheap cigarette-end preparation very generously before the aphides multiply, saves many later sprayings. Use liquid derris then for anything eating the foliage, even when the fruit is being eaten; never nicotine in these circumstances, which must have time to break down before picking.

Mildew and grey mould (*Botrytis cinerea*) are the main diseases, and the most effective counter-measure is to dust with flowers of sulphur, but where the last is a problem year after year in a damp part of the country, the remedy is to grow 'Red Gauntlet', which is proof against the disease. It is a mid-season kind with large fruit but only a fair flavour, though it is hardy and vigorous and holds its fruit well off the ground. If you fail with the others, even the Remontants, grow this one, for even a 'fair' flavour is better than no strawberries.

7

Tree Fruit Without Troubles

Little that we buy for our new houses will last as long as the fruit trees in the garden, for cars, cookers, cleaners, spin-driers, TVs and radios will be obsolete by the time our trees are in full bearing, forgotten in the forty or fifty years' life of a plum, and history in the hundred and twenty that are a walnut's usual span. Our problem with trees is always that our mistakes live as long as our successes, and when at last we realize that our bad bargain is not worth its space, we have wasted the years in which a first-class tree from a good firm would be preparing to fruit.

No one with a garden of under an acre can afford to buy a bargain dozen with two of everything. Because these are cheap they will be grafted on strong-growing seedling stocks, and will usually be kinds that are unpopular, often with good reason. Only the best from the very best firms are good enough for a beginner, who may have to pay £3 for a standard tree, but it will pay back its cost in fruit over the next three years.

Bush fruits are grown on their own roots, but tree fruit has the complication of being grafted on to a 'stock', which used to be a seedling crab for apples; but now a number of special kinds are available, and only the good firms will have a full range of varieties on each. If a nursery does not know what you are talking about when you mention the stocks in this book, they are not good enough for a beginner to buy from.

Small gardens need dwarfing stocks, the ones that are used for cordon and other trained apples, and 'Malling IX' are about the best for keeping their size down as well as hastening their fruiting until they give a worthwhile picking in the second summer after planting. On poor soils and in chalky gardens, where apples do not grow large

201

anyway, they need a faster stock or they will be *too* slow. Here choose 'Malling VII' or 'Malling Merton 106' which last has the great advantage of giving immunity to the lower part of the tree from woolly aphis, and it is a sound gardening principle to grab any immunity that is going if it is not secured at the expense of flavour. Apples taste the same whatever their stock. For standard trees choose M.M. 104, which is moderately vigorous, and has the same woolly aphis resistance, or M. III.

Pears should be grafted on 'Malling Quince A', not a seedling quince, and plums on 'Brompton' or 'St. Julien A', never on 'Mussel' which is the one that produces suckers all over the lawn and round the base of the tree. No good firm uses it now, but it may be offered by a cheap one. Peaches are also grafted on 'Brompton' and 'St. Julien', but with them the bad buy is 'Mariana' stock, which makes a large bush quickly that fruits badly. The best stock for peaches, apricots or nectarines is, however, a seedling peach or an almond, and these live longest of any, and fruit best. Cherries and damsons have no special stocks, and those recommended for stone fruit are not dwarfing—the object in insisting on good stocks here is to avoid suckers and gain a rather better crop.

The Analysis of Tree Fruit

Every gardener always wants to grow more than his garden can hold, and in considering tree fruit it should be remembered that there are no vegetables that thrive under trees. You will manage some for the first few years, but after that there is nothing for it but to grow grass under your trees. Of course you can grow cordons and trained trees on support wires or against walls.

The decision on what to grow should take into consideration the best value in vitamins:

	All per 100 grams fresh weight					
	Milligrams			Microgram		
	A I.U.'s	C	Niacin	Thiamine	Riboflavin	Water %
Apples	5–10	5–30		45	10–50	84·50
Apples in pie		2·20				
Apricots	2,790–4,000	10·00		30–45	40–75	86·60
Cherries	150	10·00	0·20	50	40	81·50
Cherries, stewed		2·10		30	20	
Nectarines	2,800	25·00		72		82·90
Peaches	880–2,000	8–10	0·90	20–40	50–60	86·70
Pears	10–30	4–7	0·10	20–45	20	83·00
Plums	350	5–7	0·60	50–150	30–45	85·10

Tree Fruit Without Troubles

The striking fact about this list is that the peach tribe are right up on vitamin A, with roughly between half and a third as much as kale or broccoli, but with the very great disadvantage that usually they are only eaten fresh. It is, however, possible to bottle them (see Bulletin No. 21, 'Domestic Preservation of Fruit and Vegetables', H.M.S.O., 48p for directions). This booklet is perhaps the best bargain one can get from *any* Government department, but bottling loses most of the vitamin A.

By far the best value on this list is the apple, because it is storable for eating over a long time. Pears have such a knife edge between exquisite ripeness and 'sleepiness' that they are a long way less useful than the easily-bottled cherries and plums. Tree fruit is mostly a luxury, and a delicious one to enjoy fresh in summer and bottled in winter, but apples are a necessity. They could be described as 'the potatoes of the air', just as the French for potato is the 'apple of the earth', for they can be enjoyed for at least eight months of the year, from the first Worcesters to the last stored Cox's, and are a fruit one never gets tired of, as one will tire of peaches, even with new cider. Too many plums can be dangerous, but one cannot have too many apples as a source of catalase and stored vitamin C.

We have always considered that fine frothy cooker 'Bramley Seedling' to be our apples highest in vitamin C, and many have tried to enjoy its sharp taste when eaten raw, but from the work of Professor Werner Schuphan of the University of Mainz, we know that there are far nicer eating apples that score higher. The following table is based on Professor Schuphan's *Nutritional Values in Crops and Plants* (Faber & Faber, 1965).

C = Cooker
E = Eater

	Mg. per 100 grams Vitamin C
Ribston Pippin E	30·60
Sturmer Pippin E	29·00
Golden Noble C	25·10
Orleans Reinette E	22·40
Ontario C	20·60
King of the Pippins E	18·10
Reinette du Canada C or E	17·20
Northern Spy E	16·70
Belle Boskoop C or E	16·40
Adams Pearmain E	16·30
Baumanns Reinette E	16·20
Bramley Seedling C or E	16·00

Tree Fruit Without Troubles

C = Cooker
E = Eater

		Mg. per 100 grams Vitamin C
White Transparent	C or E	15·30
Beauty of Bath	E	14·00
Peasgood's Nonsuch	C or E	13·20
Blenheim Orange	C or E	13·20
Winter Banana	E	12·90
Lane's Prince Albert	C	12·70
Cox's Orange Pippin	E	10·50
Gascoyne's Scarlet	C or E	8·90
Worcester Pearmain	E	8·20
Golden Delicious	E	8·20
Bismark	C	7·90
Gravenstein	E	7·80
Court Pendu Plat	E	7·50
Allington Pippin	E	7·30
James Grieve	E	6·80
Edward VII	C	6·30
Laxton's Superb	E	5·10
Early Victoria	C	4·80
Rome Beauty	E	3·80

The original list was mainly of German and other Continental varieties, with 'Calville Blanche d'Hiver' topping the list at 31·8, and 'Ohringer Blutstreifling' bottom out of 134 with 2·3. The many American and Commonwealth varieties we import are missing, but there are enough 'foreigners', including the French 'Golden Delicious' and the Italian 'Rome Beauty', and the many low-scoring but brightly-coloured German kinds, to confirm the general picture. Though sharp apples have plenty of vitamin C, this can be also high in aromatic-flavoured apples such as 'Ribston Pippin' and 'Orleans Reinette', what we call the 'Cox type'. It is low in the very sweet ones with thick skins such as 'Golden Delicious', and Professor Schuphan calculates that while one 'Ontario' would hold 62 milligrams of vitamin C, to meet our minimum daily need of 50 mg. for an adult, six 'Golden Delicious' would hold only 53 mg. This means that it would take ten 'James Grieves' a day (allowing for the extra waste on more cores) to 'keep the doctor away', to only two-thirds of a 'Ribston Pippin'. The table is intended to help shopping housewives as well as gardeners, for if there is a choice between 'Northern Spy' from the U.S.A. and 'Rome Beauty' from France or Italy, she can buy the one giving most vitamin C for the money.

This is a book on gardening, not nutrition, but it should be said that though the raw material of our diets may be high in vitamin C,

204

this can not only be wasted by overcooking, by a long wait between cooking and serving, and by combining with sugar as in stewed fruits, but can also be nullified by smoking, taking aspirins, saccharine, cyclamates, antihistamines, antacids (indigestion powders), baking soda (sometimes added to cooked fruit to 'take off the sharpness') and some chemicals used in processing other foods. A number of conditions increase the body's need for vitamin C, including stress of illness, injury or emotion, exposure to extreme cold or toxic substances, the effects of benzedrene and barbiturates, arteriosclerosis, spinal disc lesions, all forms of 'rheumatic' disability, low blood pressure, diabetes, ulcers, anaemia and excessive oil in the diet.

It is the effect of vitamin C on some of these conditions, many of which are most frequent among the elderly, that gave rise to the old saying about 'an apple a day'; and medical references can be supplied to support every statement in the last paragraph. In *theory* a good mixed diet contains all the vitamins we need, but in practice that 50 mg. is far too little for most people because of the quantities they waste and the quantities they need because of breakdowns in health and because of their habits. One can take over ten times this much with nothing but gain to one's health, and though it is possible to take vitamin C tablets, it is cheaper and better to grow your own vitamins.

Planting Tree Fruit

There are a number of principles that apply to all fruit trees, and they are gathered here because there is very little difference in the routine of planting a plum or an apple, and one account can serve for all. The first and most important principle is never to plant any tree closer than twenty feet from the house, because however small it looks when it goes in, it will tower up in time and block the windows. The nearest trees, even twenty feet from the house, should never be cherries, damsons or plums, because these cannot be bought on a dwarfing stock, and are pruned very little, so they will grow far bigger than any apple and there is no way to slow them down.

The place for tree fruit should be at the bottom of the garden because there is less need to visit them so often as vegetables, where there is something to pick or dig up almost every day of the year, and the shorter the journeys that you take most often, the more time you save. There is also the very much better view of the blossoms from the windows, especially in the case of a garden sloping either up or down from the back, when the best display is seen from the bedrooms, looking down.

Apples in particular can be chosen for a succession of blossom, and many fruit trees are beautiful in their own right, while many flowering trees take up a great deal of room for a very short season and could well be replaced with fruit. It is only convention that bars the Morello cherry from the north wall of the front garden, or standard apples from the front lawn, where they are far more attractive and easier to cultivate than cabbages among the roses. Most gardens in cities suffer not from soot, fumes, or poor soil but from too many trees, and before we decide that we just have not room for any more tree fruit, we should consider what can come out.

The gain in fertility from the lack of robbing roots, and in light and air from getting rid of shading branches by taking out any large tree, can make an immense difference to any garden. Really large ones need the help of a tree surgeon, and though this may be expensive, speed and skill come cheaper than having a jobbing gardener do it badly and perhaps inflicting damage on sheds and fences.

If you are buying standard trees of any type to plant in a lawn, order them early, even well back in the summer, and buy them extra tall, because you need seven feet between the soil mark that shows how deep they should be planted, and the lowest boughs. If they are too low you will have to duck every time you run the motor mower under them, and though the action becomes automatic there is no need to thrust it on others who may later occupy your house.

The best place for the lawn is under the trees, with room for tea, sun bathing and cricket in school holidays. Standard apples, pears, plums and cherries, all take the same spacing of sixteen feet apart each way and ten from each row end. The average semi-detached garden will therefore take two rows of six on its lower fifty-two feet. Bush trees on dwarfing stock go ten feet apart each way, which means three rows of four, allowing six feet at each end, putting a dozen in the same space but without the clearance underneath. These should go in round beds, a yard in diameter to start with, but increasing to five feet as they grow, if they need it. Nothing much can grow in these beds but daffodils, though the grass between is a useful source of mulching and compost material.

Those who wish to pack the maximum number of apples into their gardens formerly grew cordons, single stems pruned hard like those of red currants or gooseberries, trained slanting along a support fence like those for raspberries. Today dwarf pyramids as used commercially produce a greater weight of crop from the space, need no support fence, and cost less to start. They grow a kind of hedge of apples, planted four feet apart and nine feet between rows, which packs six across the standard semi-detached garden, three across each bed, and allows four feet picking room top and bottom, packing twenty-four trees in the space of ten bush ones. As these are grassed between, and without beds round them, it is better to have the rows running lengthways, and a slightly wider garden will have room for one each side of the path and one five feet from the boundary on each side.

Dwarf pyramid trees are unsuitable to run chickens under, because they bud, blossom and fruit low, but poultry are an alternative to grass provided that care is taken to prevent their eating windfall apples, which cause digestive disorders. They reduce the number of pests considerably, and this was why they were so popular in orchards in the past. Those who have blackcurrants can run the chickens on these also in the winter, to supply plenty of nitrogen from their droppings and peck up any pests, without touching the buds, though they will eat the fruit. The best apples to have chickens under are half-standards (which are useless for beds in lawns) which keep the crop out of beak reach, and if they are grafted on 'Malling VII' or 'M.M. 106', they will take the ten-foot-apart bush spacing.

If your birds are officially 'free range' or 200 an acre, the 25-ft. × 26-ft. space for that dozen trees will hold six, and with five in your family this should mean all the eggs one can eat. The essential is to divide the plot in two up the middle and have two doors on the poultry house, so that the chickens can be released on alternate sides, one in use and one resting. Even better is a chicken house on wheels, for otherwise the birds will trample the end near the house into mud and ignore the other. If chickens are given a choice they keep to an area little larger than a poultry run, and never 'free range' at all. Six birds on this space will not mean too much nitrogen for the trees, which is reputed to mean poor-keeping apples. It would be safe to have twelve, if they were taken off in winter and run between the same area of blackcurrants.

Fruit trees usually spend a considerable and variable time on road or rail and good nurseries pack them with care to arrive between October and early March. If they come at an awkward time, say with heavy snow, it is better to leave them wrapped than to expose the roots to drying hot air in the garage as heaters struggle to keep the car radiator unfrozen and get too warm at mid-day. Otherwise, dig a foot-deep trench, open the bundle and spread the trees along it, heaping back the soil over the roots to 'heel them in', as in the diagram.

When the positions have been decided in the autumn, the holes can be dug in advance two feet square and eighteen inches deep, forking up the bottoms if hard. Then drive the stake, which is best well creosoted (ideally in a soaker) $1\frac{1}{2}$ in. $\times$ $1\frac{1}{2}$ in. if this size can be bought, if not 2 in. $\times$ 2 in., into the bottom, for if you drive it in after the tree is planted it may damage a root as it goes down. As described in Chapter 3, scatter 2 lb. of coarse bone meal and 1 lb. of hoof and horn on the bottom of the hole, with 3 lb. of oyster shell chicken grit for any stone fruit, except on a chalky soil where they have plenty.

Before planting, wheel away the subsoil that has come from the bottoms of the holes, and use it, if your garden is new, to fill in under paths or in odd corners, taking the good top soil that was dug out. On poor soils or chalk, you might even buy enough good top spit loam to fill your holes. Measure how far it is from the soil mark on the stem of the tree to the root bottom, and see how much you have to fill in of top soil; spade this in with compost if you have it, to about a quarter of its bulk; or use well-rotted manure and firm it by treading, which also helps to hold the stake.

Planting a tree takes two people, one to hold and one to shovel and tread, but this is a job that should never be hurried, because no one has anything more important to do with the ten or twenty minutes saved by scamping. No TV programme or personality will last as long as a Cox on a good stock.

First examine the roots, and if any are broken snip these off cleanly with secateurs. Then stand the tree in the hole, fitting the roots round the stake and standing back to make sure you have it upright. Now spade the soil in carefully, working the tree up and down a little to make sure all the cracks are filled, and pushing some down with your fingers to be certain there are no hollows. Fill in for three inches more and start treading in the hole, because if you tread too soon you may scrape the bark on the roots. Go on filling and treading till you finish with the soil mark level with the surface, and the bulge on the stem that shows where the stock ends and the tree begins well above it, for if this is buried the tree can make its own roots and 'un-dwarf itself'.

Tree Fruit Without Troubles

There are many patent tree ties, but the best of all are laddered nylon stockings. Tie the first one about a foot from the ground, on a standard tree, round the stake three or four times to allow a good cushion of knot, then tie it round the stem of the tree, with a reef knot as shown in the picture. Repeat the tie at the middle of the stake and at the top, while a bush only needs one on its short stake. It is the

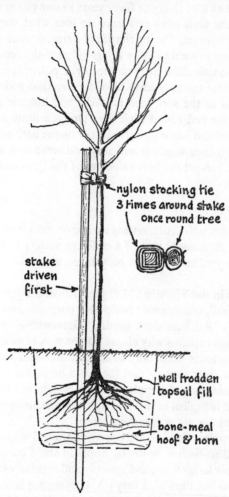

nylon stocking tie
3 times around stake
once round tree

stake
driven
first →

well trodden
topsoil fill

bone-meal
hoof & horn

16. Fruit trees should be planted with care and deliberation, for they will be at their best when your new car is an old crock. The same principles apply to all fruiting and ornamental trees

wind swaying newly planted trees to and fro until they have made a hollow each side of their stems, leading cold rain and frost and air down to the roots, that kills them young and damages some so that they take years to recover. A good stake, good tying and careful planting make all the difference to any tree.

Because a tree is more permanent than our tenure of our houses, for very few of us stay thirty or forty years in one place, most people inherit their first fruit trees and have no idea what they are, while even owners can forget. During the life of a tree, or even a fruit bush, someone is going to want to know if it is 'sulphur-shy', or a tip bearer, because that means different pruning: or a pollinator for another tree, which if removed may leave the Cox a fruitless widow. So order lead-cast labels of the sort used in parks and botanic gardens and thrust one in the bed round each tree. Or even draw a map of the garden on a card and nail it up in the loft or on the back of the potting-shed door, anywhere where it will stay and serve as a reminder, so that the future can get the best value out of the trees you planted.

Apple Varieties

All bush fruit are self-fertile, setting their crop with their own pollen, but most tree fruit needs that of a different variety to fertilize their blossom—the gardener has not only to consider the birds but the bees as well.

The winner in the Vitamin C League, 'Ribston Pippin', is what is called a 'triploid', which needs *two* pollen partners, and so do 'Blenheim Orange', 'Reinette du Canada', 'Gravenstein' and 'Bramley Seedling', which explains why all are uncommon in modern gardens. Most other varieties need only one, for instance a Cox, but must blossom at the right time so that there will be pollen for the bees to carry from tree to tree. So apples must be bought in matching threes or pairs, and it is neglect of this principle that means so many gardens where the trees are not worth their room.

An eating apple chosen for maximum vitamin C would be 'Ribston Pippin', a yellow-fleshed aromatic apple in the Cox class, keeping from November to January, and a sturdy and regularly-cropping tree, with 30·6; 'Sturmer Pippin', a very late-keeping apple, crisp, firm and juicy, with rather the same flavour, lasting from March to May, which should be left late on the tree to finish, picked in November, with 29·0; and 'Adams (not '*Worcester*') Pearmain', with 16·4, to eat from December to February, again a yellow and spicy apple, so it is possible to eat Cox-type apples from November to May, with over twice the vitamins. Those who want a cooker should plant 'Belle de Boskoop', to make a fourth (16·4), for a triploid with two pollinators is likely to fruit even better, and enjoy them from December to April with very much the same spicy taste if eaten raw, but cooking well too. The fourth tree could be another Ribston, planted diagonally across at the other corner of the plot, and those who have pyramids can grow three Ribstons with a Sturmer at one end and an Adams Pearmain the other, because the bees work up and down these hedges of blossom and spread the pollen farthest, and this is why the system is a favourite with commercial growers who know everyone clamours for Cox's at Christmas.

This set has the disadvantage of blossoming early, earlier than a Cox, so if you plant a Cox in the collection it will stay a spinster; and they blossom too early for cold, northern gardens. For these, and for frost pockets where the promise of the blossom is broken again and again, there is another high vitamin C set. Base this on 'Orleans Reinette', 22·4, a good spicy eater to keep from December to February; 'Reinette du Canada', which is again a triploid, and is a good aromatic eater as well as a cooker, and an excellent keeper, from November to April; and 'Worcester Pearmain' from August to November, for it is possible with a cool storage shed to keep Worcesters for quite a while.

'Worcester Pearmain' is, however, a 'tip bearer', bearing its best fruiting buds at the tips of the new shoots, so if it is pruned in the normal way, you cut away the best of the crop. Therefore, it is not possible to grow it as a dwarf pyramid, a cordon or any other intensively pruned tree. 'Court Pendu Plat', keeping from December to May, low in vitamin C, but a delicious apple making a small tree and doing especially well on clay, is a good substitute, and is a good single pollinator for 'Orleans Reinette', if you only want two trees. 'Gascoyne's Scarlet', a cooker or eater, ready from September to January, is another apple of taste, with higher vitamin C, and rather easier to buy. It is a stronger tree and does very well on chalk as well as on clay.

'Cox's Orange Pippin' does not do well north of a line from Birmingham to the Wash. This is not because it blossoms mid-season, in between the early and late groups, because many varieties that also blossom then thrive in northern gardens—it is a native of Slough, and it is not hardy enough. It is possible, however, to grow a mid-season set of near-Coxes that will act as its pollinators, and if the Cox does not crop well it can be replaced with something tougher.

The most popular pair of apples in southern gardens is a Cox, to eat from November to January, with a 'James Grieve', a tasty early eater from September to October, and these two won a flavour contest organized by the *Observer* many years ago. With 10·5 and 6·8 this is not maximum vitamin C, but here are two kinds that fit together like fish and chips. 'King of the Pippins' (October to December) with 18·1 is better, but of a sharper taste, and inclined to crop very well one year and miss the next, while 'Allington Pippin' is slightly higher in vitamin C and a regular cropper with a fine aromatic flavour, and one of the only self-fertile eating apples. If there is room for only one tree, plant an Allington to enjoy eating from October to December, while if your need is for a single cooker, have 'Crawley Beauty', which blossoms very late to miss all frosts, and may be cooked from December to February.

Northern gardeners who want to try Cox should plant it with 'Sunset', for November to December eating, 'Tydeman's Late Orange', for March to May, and 'Laxton's Superb' to fit in between. All three have 'Coxy' flavour and if the Cox fails, replace it with a 'James Grieve' as the most flavoursome early apple.

The best cooking apple to go with a Cox is 'Golden Noble', in season from September to January, a good regular cropper and a strong tree, recommended as a first-rate tree for amateurs by the Royal Horticultural Society, and with the highest vitamin C of any cooker, though cooking more than halves this, so you would get just as much by eating a Cox raw as from an apple pie made from 'Golden Noble'. On the other hand 'Edward VII', a cooker that keeps from December till April and blossoms late to miss frosts, but is a martyr to mildew, is only about 2·2—it was probably the one that made the pie in our first table.

The nicest cooker is Bramley Seedling, which is a deliciously frothy baker with high vitamin C, but it is a triploid, and such a strong grower that it will not fit on a dwarfing stock, so it cannot be a pyramid or do well in a small garden. Those who like cookers and have the room could choose 'Blenheim Orange', November to January, another large and awkward apple that takes some time to come into bearing, but then crops massively with big eating or cooking apples of a delicious nutty flavour; and it is mildew resistant. 'Peasgood's Nonsuch', for October and November, is also a fine frothy cooker, not as tasty as a Blenheim when eaten, but a useful third man for a Bramley.

Though the selections here are carefully chosen for all-round garden merit as well as vitamin content in relation to space occupied, there is the problem of making up sets with what can be bought, for many of these apples are rare, because the idea of growing for maximum vitamin C is new. So the list has been sorted into pollen periods, with the time of eating by each, which is when they should be at their best if kept under the conditions given in the next chapter. A 'T' against a kind means a triploid, which needs any other two from the same group to pollinate it; the others need only one companion. 'T.B.' means a tip bearer which needs no pruning (merely sawing out of dead or crowding branches) and § is an extra variety not in the Vitamin C League table, but introduced for garden merit or as an extra pollinator in special circumstances.

EARLY BLOSSOMING APPLES

E Adams Pearmain   December to February
E Baumann's Reinette   December to February
E Beauty of Bath   T.B.   July to August
C Belle of Boskoop   T.   January to March
C Bismark   T.B.   November to February
E Egremont Russet   §   October to December
E Gravenstein   T.   September to October
E Ribston Pippin   T.   November to January
E Sturmer Pippin   March to May
C White Transparent   August

MID-SEASON BLOSSOMING APPLES

E Allington Pippin   October to December
E Blenheim Orange   T.   T.B.   November to January
C Bramley Seedling   T.   November to March
E Cox's Orange Pippin   November to January
C Early Victoria   July to August
C Golden Noble   September to January
E James Grieve   September to October
C Lane's Prince Albert   November to March
E Laxton's Fortune   §   September to October
E Laxton's Superb   November to February
C Ontario   December to May
E Rosemary Russet   §   December to February
C Sunset   §   November to December
E Tydeman's Late Orange   §   March to May
C Upton Pyne   §   January to March

Tree Fruit Without Troubles

E Court Pendu Plat   December to May
C Cox's Pomona   §   October to December
C Crawley Beauty   §   December to February
C Edward VII   December to April
C Gascoyne's Scarlet   September to January
E Heusgen's Golden Reinette   §   February to April
E Orleans Reinette   December to February
E Reinette du Canada   T.   November to April
E Worcester Pearmain   T.B.   August to September

The extra apples added are 'Egremont Russet', a very good cropper and a favourite as a dwarf pyramid for commercial growers, of excellent aromatic flavour, probably quite high in vitamin C, with the powdery brown russet skin so many people like. 'Rosemary Russet' is very like it but keeps later and fits the mid-season pollen group, so it can be grown with a Cox if required. 'Laxton's Fortune' is the best of the early apples, with a Cox flavour if eaten straight off the tree, and better in every way than 'Beauty of Bath' or a 'Worcester Pearmain', keeping longer than either. 'Upton Pyne' is a cooker and eater, included because of the beauty of its large pink blossom, a flowering tree in its own right for the front garden, and should pair with the paler pink 'Sunset'. 'Cox's Pomona' is another cooker or eater, rather acid in flavour, but a good large apple for awkward and frosty gardens.

Apples—Pruning

Many nurseries send out apple trees ready pruned to save carriage, and it is worth asking for this when ordering, so the trees start with expert pruning. If this has not been done, shorten the longest shoots on bushes and standards by a fifth and the lesser ones by half, always to a bud pointing away from the middle. Prune no more than this in their second winter too, because modern stocks can give too slow an increase of leaf area if trees are cut back hard when they start. If apples on any type of stock make fruitlets during their first two summers, pinch these off early, as they are a strain on young trees building up to a fruitful future that starts in the third summer after planting.

If we grew apples only for blossom we would leave them to nature, but as we need fruit of a totally unnatural size in far greater quantities than crab apple trees could ever provide, we must prune these arboreal pekes and pugs that we have bred for our enjoyment in the past two thousand years. Pruning is our way of controlling our trees, and the old system of snipping off everything every winter merely makes them grow more shoots for snipping next year, and far less fruit than we gain by pruning also in summer on the system that keeps commercial orchards cropping well, and low enough to pick without ladders. Trees grown out of control are danger traps for the elderly, and had the late George Bernard Shaw not fallen from one like this, but picked his apples from a twice-pruned pyramid on a dwarfing stock, he might well have lived to attend the first night of one of his own plays on his hundredth birthday, which was his last ambition.

Pruning is also an important part of the pest and disease control and merely delaying the traditional Boxing Day attack with the new secateurs from Christmas until February or even early March, avoids the risk of brown storage rot. The fungus responsible, *Gloeosprium* spp. (there are several), against which orthodox commercial growers spray once a fortnight from July till picking time, is blowing round the orchard ready to get into pruning cuts. Wait till January ends, and the spores have finished, and your apples will keep better, with no extra work and no chemicals to buy.

By sweeping dead apple and pear leaves off the lawns under our trees, or picking them off the soil to tuck harmlessly into the middle of the leafmould heap by Christmas, before the spores of common scab (*Venturia inaequalis*) start blowing, we can get rid of 85 per cent of the scab in our gardens. The other 15 per cent is on the trees, so after you have pruned your apples and pears look carefully over what you have left on of the young wood and the smoother bark of the fruiting spurs for blisters that run together and make small cracked areas. Cut the spurs or shoots right out before the second spore spreading season, at its height in May, can bring the familiar black or brown blotches on fruit and leaves.

Look also for small depressions in the bark with roughness round the edges and dead centres. These are cankers, starting from damage, often from hail but most commonly from scab fungus or insect bites, which let in the spores of the fungus *Nectaria galligena*. Good drainage and ample humus in the soil lower the risk of scab, which can be very bad in old orchards. Saw out large branches affected by it, removing all diseased wood, even using a sharp chisel to clear a cavity, and paint the cut surface with a white lead paint. Canker fungus is also responsible for apples rotting round the stem and falling early, so it is a problem to prune away before it gets too bad. Winter prunings should always be burnt to make sure of getting rid of the spores of these two diseases and those of apple mildew.

Winter pruning ordinary bush apples is quite a simple routine. Shorten what is called the 'leader', the longest and strongest of the new shoots that grew last summer, at the end of every branch to a third of its length. Then snip off its lesser contemporaries after the third or fourth bud, whichever points away from the centre of the tree, not counting those close together where the shoot joins the branch. If there are any branches rubbing together, saw out the weakest one and cover the cut with Sellotape, to keep out the wet till the tide of spring begins to flow and the tree can heal itself.

Tip bearers, like 'Worcester Pearmain', 'Blenheim Orange', 'Lord Lambourne', 'St. Edmund's Russet', 'Mr. Gladstone', 'Cornish Gilliflower', 'Beauty of Bath' and 'Irish Peach' often have all their best fruiting buds cut away year after year. They cannot be pruned normally in winter or summer, so it is not possible to keep them under control, or to grow them as pyramids or cordons. All they need is sawing out of the weakest branch or two every year, together with any that are crossing, crowding the middles or having dead wood on them. This is also the policy for old trees too large to prune in the ordinary way. Always saw off some of the branch separately, to reduce the weight, then take most of it off about a foot from the tree, after sawing upwards for about an inch from the underside of the branch. Finally cut off the stump close to the branch. This is so that a large branch cannot break and tear off a great strip of bark down the trunk. Small ones can, of course, be sawn off in one cut. Prune and saw *first*, then take your time, and use a pocket lens to search the remaining shoots and branches for scab and canker to prune away—this is far quicker than spraying four times with lime-sulphur, Captan, or even deadlier compounds in May.

Hard pruning in winter makes trees grow more wood, because the roots have less growth to support, and this leaves more sap for the rest. Sawing branches out of an elderly tree, especially if some were cankered (for these are a drag on the whole system like a decayed tooth in a human being), may well give it a new lease of life, but pruning in summer slows them down so well that the strongest-growing apple of all—'Bramley Seedling'—should only be summer pruned.

Trees feed not only with their roots but through their leaves, for it is the sunlight on every leaf that builds into the wood the heat that

216

we feel when we make a bonfire of hissing and singing sawn-out branches. When we summer prune we can reduce the leaf area by more than two-thirds, which slows down the photosynthesis that gathers the starches and sugars that put on wood as we put on weight, and we push the strength of the tree into making more fruit buds.

There are many systems of summer pruning, but the simplest one for amateurs is to shorten the leaders by a quarter of their length in July and the side shoots to about two-thirds. Then at winter pruning time you take off about one bud of the old growth and all that has grown since, so the trees look the same, but have had many fewer leaves working through the summer. The advantage of this method is that all the apple aphides can only start multiplying on the soft young shoot tips, and if these are all removed there is nothing for them to start on, no aphides and no need to spray even with derris or pyrethrum. The prunings are soft enough to compost, aphides and all, though bad infestations can be dumped in the dustbin.

The other, more orthodox method is to shorten the leaders in May by a quarter of their length to make them grow better side shoots. Then in June for pears, and July for apples, snip off the side shoots that are as thick as pencils at the base, after the second leaf, not counting those round the base. Leave those that are not pencil thick or that bend like plant stems, not breaking like wood at the base, until August and September, three prunings in all, taking them all off after the second leaf as they graduate. Then in winter prune back to two leaves on the new growth, and shorten the leader by two buds on the old wood. This means that the tree starts the new year with some old and some late-grown wood on each fruiting spur, and though the side shoots have been cut harder, they have not been all done at once. They can get aphides while they are waiting, and it is the simplicity and the ease of controlling those aphides on the same principle as on broad beans or gooseberry tips, that makes the first way the most popular.

A two-year-old dwarf pyramid tree should have eight or nine good branches arranged spirally round a central leader. It will be cheaper than a four-year-old bush or standard, but they are not often catalogued, so write to a large firm and ask for a price, because this is the type of tree most often sold for planting commercial orchards. It should have been pruned when it arrives, but if it has not, shorten the side shoots to half length and the leader to nine inches. This should have a cane or slender stake to support it because this will not be needed for long. Its job is to support the leader which should be shortened to nine inches each winter for the first three years, always to a bud opposite last year's one, to keep it straight. Halve the new growth on the side shoots each winter too, while the tree is building strength, for it will be on a dwarfing stock.

In the third summer after planting snip back all the side shoots to three leaves beyond the little ones at the base in July, also doing in September any that have grown since. Leave the leader unpruned in summer, and its first winter and second summer, and take it out completely in the second winter, but leave the strongest shoot growing near its base un-summer-pruned to replace it. The object of these lofty leaders is to act as 'safety valves', preventing the problem that can arise with hard-pruned trees as they grow old, of strong shoots thrusting out in all directions.

The lesser branches are cut back to a single bud beyond the summer-shortened shoot in winter. If any of the lower branches cease to bear, cut these out completely in winter, leaving about a three-inch stump to grow new shoots that are summer and winter pruned in the same way as the rest of the pyramid, which should fruit all the way up. Good pyramids should be producing 20 lb. a tree by their fourth year.

Dwarf pyramids need no stakes after the third year, for by then it is possible for them to hold each other up. Bend a side branch from each of two adjoining trees so that their second-year wood comes together, and tie these firmly together with a plastic-covered rose tie, which has a wire in the middle. During the summer the two will grow together and the tie can be removed at next winter-pruning time, so it cannot constrict the joined branches as they grow. If they will not meet, it is possible to cut away the bark on each and fit the bared parts together, so that they 'graft'. This system of joining trees as though they were holding hands for 'Auld Lang Syne' saves the cost of stakes, though it is only suitable for strong, low, dwarf trees on this system, not bushes or standards with more sail area. During the summer it is possible to tie in awkwardly out-growing branches to make them 'shake hands', a process that shows in the photographs.

Cordon apples and pears need supports like those of blackberries or raspberries, and they are planted two feet apart, at an angle of 45°, if possible pointing towards the south. Tie them to a long cane and tie this to the wires, because if these rub away the bark this will let in canker spores. Be sure that the bulge above the stock does not touch the ground on the underside nearest the soil, or it will make its

own roots and defeat the dwarfing. They should come pruned, but
their main winter pruning consists of shortening their leader to a third
of its length in February each year, cutting it back to buds on alternate
sides to keep it straight. When this eventually reaches the top wire
which should be six feet above the ground, untie the tree and bend the
whole tree a bit lower, slanting it down till it is nearer 75°, which
must be done with the whole row. This slanting system restricts
the flow of sap, and was very useful before the new dwarfing stocks
were bred, but now dwarf pyramids are replacing them because of
the awkwardness of the angles and the cost of supports.

Their summer pruning consists of cutting any young shoots newly
sprung from the main stem to three leaves in July, and any from the
existing shoots to a single leaf. When their side branches reach a foot,
saw them back to six inches in winter, and saw back the leader when
this reaches seven feet.

Horizontal-trained trees are the most expensive, because they take
years to train, but they take less room than cordons because they go
upright, and in many old gardens they edge every path. Pears do
extra well as horizontals, and three-tiered specimens cost between
two and three times as much as bush. They can be grown on walls
but this is rather a waste when these could grow peaches, and they
are best on strong, well-creosoted posts and wires, though they have
been rather inelegantly grown on old gas piping. Their branches
should be tied to canes and these to the wires to avoid the canker
risk. Prune them in summer by shortening all side shoots to three
buds in June or July and in winter snipping off completely what has
grown since, shortening the leader at the end of each branch to a
quarter of its length. They should go twelve to fifteen feet apart, and
no closer than ten feet between rows, but they are usually grown as
edgings.

The advantage that they share to some extent with cordons (which
are more awkward), is that their support posts can have 2-in. × 1-in.
timber bolted to them to make wooden 'Y's', to take wires and hold
nylon netting to protect the fruit from birds; this can be stored away
after picking, with the gain over old-fashioned fruit netting that it
will be found unrotten and ready for use when it is needed next season.

Apples—Management

Few amateurs think of feeding their trees, but as the years go by they

219

will need plant foods to supplement their starting stock and above all they need humus to hold the moisture in the soil, and to feed the many friends that help to control pests and diseases. The first essential for any large area of apples, not the few at the bottom of the garden but a garden pretty well given over to dwarf pyramids, is a rough grass cutter of the 'Rotoscythe' or 'Flymo' types. This serves to mow the grass and weeds between the trees and it is left to lie for the worms to take down.

It is worth while borrowing one of these machines for its most labour-saving job. Organic fruit farmers who use no sprays do not spend their time sweeping up dead leaves; they run one of these machines over the fallen leaves, and this chews them up so small that the worms take them under as easily as they do the grass, taking the scab spores with them. If you think of it, the main humus supply of any tree is dead leaves, and the best way to build up humus under an orchard is to write to your Council and see if they will deliver you several loads in the autumn, not only for leafmould making but also for spreading and chewing for worms. These are most active in the autumn (you often find when leaf-sweeping that some of the leaves are stuck in the worm holes) but you can add half-made leafmould in the spring. They do not have to be apple leaves, for even those of plane trees rot in time, and you are not aiming for lasting humus but at feeding your 'vegetarians' under the soil.

If you build up the humus in the surface layers a great many creatures apart from worms will gather to feed on it, and these will support a population of carnivorae, notably the ground beetles, of which the large violet one is best known, and rove beetles, of which you will know the devil's-coach-horse beetle, but there are about seven hundred species of each. When codling moth or apple sawfly larvae drop full fed and pupate, the more hungry mouths there are waiting for them the better.

Ideally dwarf pyramid trees, which work hardest of any, should have compost spread along the rows every year, but few gardens can make enough. Municipal compost is too rich in nitrogen, and about the best bought substitute is spent mushroom compost, and a three-inch layer in the bed round any fruit tree in a lawn, given every other year, is a help to them. A sickly tree, or one that seems to be hanging about, can nearly always be improved by a couple of forkfuls of manure.

If yields of fruit are low, the apples brightly coloured and small, the leaves pale green when they first develop and tending to turn yellow and fall early, the problem is nitrogen shortage, which is common in old orchards. Deep-litter poultry compost on the surface round the tree will correct the problem. Excess is much less common; it shows when there are few but large fruit that are poor-flavoured, in very dark green leaves and in a great deal of wood. Apart from summer pruning to slow them, let the grass grow long and take only two or three cuts a season, carting it away for compost.

Keeping the grass mown reduces its root action and slows down its demand for nitrogen, so the grass under the trees acts as a kind of 'throttle control' for nitrogen. Because the trees spread their roots wide they can also compete with the grass, and if this appears to be doing poorly, scatter 1 lb. a square yard of a dried sewage sludge in spring, to keep it moving. It is possible to buy a 'shade mixture' from a good seedsman to keep the grass going well as the trees grow larger, and there are cheaper 'orchard mixtures' specially made for this job.

A neglected orchard with long grass can be greatly improved merely by regular mowing, and it is important to keep land free from docks which can be killed, like nettles, by continual mowing, because these are an alternative host of the apple sawfly. There is no gain in having deep-rooted weeds in the sward, because the trees themselves root more deeply than any weed.

If trees become short of potassium, the leaves will be scorched light brown round the margins, and the best answer is up to 2 lb. a tree of dried seaweed meal or 1 lb. of wood ashes. The quickest way to cure any odd symptoms that could be a deficiency or a 'disease' is to spray with a seaweed foliar feed. Trees can feed through their leaves as well as their roots and will take what they are short of, so if symptoms are observed one year, later than September, spray in the spring or during the summer, even when in fruit, because the spray is utterly non-poisonous.

Magnesium shortage, as mentioned in Chapter 3, shows as brown blotching between the veins, usually beginning near the midribs, and there may also be a purple tint on the leaves. Scatter 2 oz. a square yard of Epsom salts (cattle grade) and the trouble will be cured for years. It is most common on chalky soils or where chemical fertilizers have been used in quantity, and it shows up most after wet winters, and first on the cooker 'Edward VII' which is extra-sensitive.

Careful picking is all-important, because fruit punctured by long fingernails lets in the spores of the fungi of decay. The skin of an apple is Nature's substitute for polythene, a 'gift wrapping' like the shell of an egg designed to preserve the fruit as long as possible. Apples must never be picked without stalks, and the test for ripeness is to lift the fruit and twist it very gently. If it is ready it will part from the spur easily; if it does not part easily, leave it for a few days more. Support the fruit with the palm of the hand, do not squeeze between the fingers and thumb, and, above all, never tip a basket of apples into another container with tumbling and thumping. Ideally pick into a box or basket lined temporarily with old blanket, then set the apples out in the storage boxes, which can double as potato chitting trays at least for the earlier varieties, as the trays are not wanted until January when the seed potatoes arrive.

Pick *all* the apples, for the small shrivelled ones that hang on are always harbouring pests, and the destruction of these and of windfalls is an important part of pest control. Though chickens should not eat windfalls, pigs can devour them with pleasure. It is better to bottle them like tomatoes, or make large batches of apple jelly, rather than leave them lying in the orchard for the codling moth caterpillars to finish their meal and escape to hibernate in comfort. The better your balance of predators the fewer the windfalls.

The 'June drop', when millions of small apples rain down, saves thinning, but if there is a long dry spell in late July and apples start falling, run the hose on the beds round the trees to strengthen the stems. This is not, of course, possible commercially, but it prevents the tree economizing in water at the expense of the crop.

Ample humus will, however, make this unnecessary by holding on to more moisture, so import extra dead leaves if you can, and cherish your worms for the good work that they do.

Apples—Diseases and Pests

Common scab and canker are the two most common apple diseases, and both can largely be controlled by pruning with observation, for the most important part of the pruning operation, so far as disease control is concerned, is to use sharp eyes and a good lens. The runner-up is apple powdery mildew, caused by the fungus *Podosphaera leucotricha* which produces a white, powdery appearance on leaves and shoots which are checked and stunted. It appears with the unfolding of the buds in spring and often injures the blossom, so no fruit is set. The answer is to remove any infected shoots as soon as they are seen, at blossom time. The fungus hibernates in the tips of the young shoots, even those which have grown since summer pruning, so winter pruning means an extra bonus in mildew control. 'Bramley Seedling' apples should have about three inches taken off the tips of each new-grown shoot, if mildew has been seen in the orchard, an exception to the rule of pruning it only in summer.

The fourth disease is blossom wilt, from the fungus *Sclerotinia laxa forma mali*, which attacks the young flowers. The first sign is that the small leaves round the blossom are wilting and dying, followed by the trusses themselves. The fungus works down the flower stems into the spurs and down into the branches. The remedy is to cut off the attacked spurs and burn them. Infected spurs can be seen with grey cushions of fungus on them, and in this case cut off the spur till the wood shows white and clean; if it fails to show white, cut off the branch, for there is no known spray that will stop this luckily rare fungus.

With good drainage, good compost and plenty of humus, there should be no trouble with apple diseases, for most garden trees are widely separated so that there are few spores blowing about, compared with those in fruit-growing districts. Common scab can be almost completely controlled by pruning and leaf collecting or 'chewing' for the worms, but if it does get out of hand, spray in January with Burgundy mixture as for gooseberry and rose mildew. Mix it over-night and use it fresh, for it does not keep, and if possible use it in frosty weather when there will be no risk of washing any *Anthocoris* off the trees, and the buds will have shrunk so that there is a chance of destroying some mildew too. Lime sulphur, sprayed at green-bud, pink-bud, and open-blossom stages is the orthodox remedy, but this slaughters *Anthocoris*, so Burgundy Mixture is the best answer, as a harmless spray killing only fungi, and especially valuable in old orchards full of scab, mildew and canker.

The worst destroyer of *Anthocoris* is winter tar oil wash, and when this was invented after the 1914–18 War, it solved many pest problems, but cleared all the algae and lichens off the trees. The red spider mite (*Metatetranychus ulmi*) fed peacefully on these all through this long history of British apple growing that started with the Romans. The loss of its food supply drove it to eating apple leaves and because the tar oil killed its worst enemy, the *Anthocoris*, it increased so fast it is now a major pest—one of the first to be *caused* by chemicals.

The second-best controller is the black-kneed capsid (*Blepharidop-*

terus angulatus), about a quarter of an inch long, pale green and yellow with black backs to its knees, which lays eggs in slits in the bark at the base of the young shoots which stay safe inside till the winter-wash danger is over, but unfortunately they catch the lime-sulphur and B.H.C. or light oil washes in May. The old-fashioned 'hedgehog with crew-cut' pruning throws away a great many black-kneed capsid eggs, which the less drastic method described earlier spares to survive and eat up to 4,230 red spider mites each in the course of their lives. Capsid eggs show as smooth bulges one over the other, and the shoot should be snipped off above them.

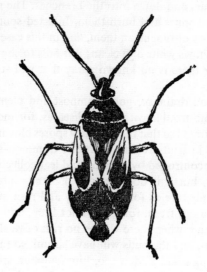

17. The fruit-grower's best friend is *Anthocoris nemorum*, a relation of the water boatman beetle, shown natural size in the lower drawing. It eats red spiders and their eggs and many other pests, so spraying should be limited to seasons and sprays that spare it

The black-kneed capsid has only one generation a year, *Anthocoris* has two, and averages fifty mites a day, but these mites have *five* generations a season, so one surviving winter egg can lead to 160,000 mites by the autumn, if it were not for the predators, which can give complete control. This can also be secured by a number of chemicals, but so far no resistant strain of red spider, immune to D.D.T. and the other organo-chlorine compounds, has developed.

Anthocoris is a versatile predator, a 'broad spectrum' one, as modern jargon has it, and before the winter washes every apple tree had a very large population of springtails, feeding on the algae with the red spider, rather like herds of zebra and wildebeest grazing in Africa, which the *Anthocoris* preyed on like lions. Without winter washes there are always enough ranging up and down a tree looking for a change from this rather monotonous diet. A high population in a mild autumn and winter keeps on working, and hunting for the eggs of the last red spider generation, also those of the apple sucker (*Psylla mali*) and the apple capsid (*Pleisiocoris rugicollis*) a vegetarian species that attacks both fruit and blossom.

If we have to winter wash, we destroy our built-up population and its stand-by food supply, but we keep our black-kneed capsids, and we shall get some *Anthocoris* moving in from the rest of the garden, ready to start egg-eating and build up again. If we have to spray with something savage late in the summer we have nothing left to start building up again in spring.

An amateur gardener does not risk his living if a pest gets out of hand, so he has no *need* to winter wash or use any sprays. There are also, however, commercial growers who have waiting lists for their apples at premium prices, who have let their pests and predators balance out with just the kind of simple controls that are described in this chapter. There is scope for a great deal of research to find better methods, and any good ones will be included in later editions of this book.

The red spider mite is not common in gardens, but the apple sawfly (*Hoplocampa testudinea*) is one of the commonest causes of 'maggoty' apples. The grubs can cause ribbon-like scars on the outside of the fruit and when they bore into the fruit they leave a fuzz of black droppings at the entrance to the burrows. These signs one year show that it is possible to take counter-measures the next by waiting till six or seven days after the petals have fallen and spraying with quassia, which is too weak to kill *Anthocoris* but will hit young sawfly larvae just hatching where the eggs have been laid in the blossom. The quassia recipe is in Chapter 8, on page 274.

This has no effect on the codling moth caterpillar (*Cydia pomonella*) which lays eggs from mid-June to early August, and the best control is to tie bands of sacking round the bottoms of the trees in early

P

July and take them off and burn them in October. The full-fed caterpillars drop to the ground, or fall in fruit after four weeks, and a number of them try to climb the tree to pupate in the bark cracks. They unwisely end their journey in the sacking. The sawfly pupates in the soil and cannot be trapped in this way, but collecting fallen apples at least once a week, so that the larvae cannot finish off and escape, and picking any left shrivelled on the tree, are quite effective controls for both. If any apple appears to be ripening faster than the others, pick it. There is probably a maggot from one or other of these common pests inside, and if you cut it up for cooking that means one less pest, and you have saved more apple than if you had left it on. These two pests are also man-made, for once they had to creep from crab to crab to find enough food to mature on, which gave a great many predators and parasites, including birds, a chance to catch them. Ever since the Romans brought us large apples they have stayed safely inside for long enough to become common.

The apple blossom weevil (*Anthonomus pomorum*) lays eggs in the blossom causing the petals to turn brown and die, becoming 'capped' or looking like small leather buttons. The grub pupates and becomes an adult which feeds a little on the foliage before crawling down the tree to hibernate. If the codling moth sacking is put on in June, instead of July, it will catch the weevils walking down, and the caterpillars crawling up, and both can be burnt together in October.

Grease bands to stop upward traffic are extremely useful pest controllers, harmless to birds, bees and predators, for nothing useful has a regular seasonal migration up or down the trunks. Ready-spread bands which need only to have paper torn off are (or should be) available at garden shops, and these should be tied a foot from ground level round the trunks of standards, or a number of them round the limbs of bush or pyramid trees. The object is to prevent the rain splashing soil on to the band and providing a bridge across, and it is worth inspecting them to be sure that no blown straw or leaf has provided a gangway for ants carrying aphides aloft, or for any of the creatures for which these bands are the best control.

The bands should go on when the sacking comes off, in October, and stay till early June. They stop the winter moth (*Cheimatobis brumata*), whose wingless females crawl up the trees from early October to January, laying light green eggs which become green creatures with a white stripe that feed on buds, foliage and fruit. Also they stop the March moth (*Erannis ascularia*) which climbs in

February and March, with 'looper' caterpillars, and the mottled umber moth (*Hybernia defoliaria*) with chestnut brown loopers.

The apple capsid and the apple sucker are both active on the trees in April and May, the first feeding by inserting their 'beaks' into the young fruitlets and causing brown marks that develop into corky patches, while the latter suck the blossom and leaves. Spraying the foliage with a hose after petal fall will bring down thousands, together with the apple fruit weevil (*Rhynchites aequatus*) which lays eggs in the developing fruits in July. The object of leaving the grease bands on is to catch them trying to crawl back, and cashes in on the fact that *Anthocoris* is a very good clinger, and the adults can return by flying. In any event, less damage is done by plain water than by any other spray.

A recipe for making the sticky material for grease bands is included in Chapter 8, because these may be off the market by the time this book is in print since manufacturers find it more profitable to sell deadlier remedies. Readers should insist, complain, order specially, and if they fail, write to the author care of the publishers, for the address of any firm that has kept an old remedy that is safe, even though it may not be one hundred per cent effective.

There are several ways of controlling the woolly aphis or American blight (*Eriosoma lanigerum*) which is a pest that makes cotton-wool-like masses on apples and can cripple whole branches with its sucking, which can leave wounds where canker spores can get in. The easiest method is to paint the patch with methylated spirits, and those with sharp eyes can find this creature starting at February pruning time or in April, when they are looking over their blossom to see if there is any sign of blossom wilt; at these times there will be only small patches as it has not had time to do much damage. The old idea that growing nasturtiums up the trees would repel the creatures rests on the foundation that between July and October the aphis migrates as a winged form in search of fresh trees to attack, and the nasturtium gets the credit. It is easy enough to sow climbing varieties of *Tropaeolum majus* in March and tie them up the trunks, where their flowers are quite attractive.

A biological control method is to sow buckwheat (*Fagophyrum esculentum*) in March or April in half-inch-deep furrows eight inches apart in the orchard, or round the beds in which the trees are growing. It can be sown as late as May, but the earlier the better. It will flower right on till frost, ripening its broad flint-shaped brown seeds, which

227

are normally grown for feeding pheasants and adding whiteness to the flesh of broiler poultry, in succession.

Its white flowers (which are good bee fodder) are an excellent source of nectar for hoverflies, especially *Syrphus balteatus*. The slug-like larvae of this creature, and that of other hoverflies including the large grey and cream one *Scavea pyrastri*, will creep in under the wool and eat the woolly aphides, where *Anthocoris* will not go. Hoverflies take a great deal of trouble to find colonies of aphides among which to lay their eggs, unlike ladybirds which appear to lay at random. Though mustard in flower attracts more of these flies, it has only a short season and must be resown repeatedly, unlike buckwheat, which lasts the summer on a single sowing.

Hoverflies normally visit orchards at blossom time and are minor pollinators, but attracting them with buckwheat, which starts flowering when the last blossom is going over, should mean more late larvae to control woolly aphis and other creatures. The larvae eat between 800 and 900 aphides in the course of their lives, and will eat red spider and even young lackey moth caterpillars. This creature lays eggs in broad bracelets round the young shoots, which should be smashed with the secateurs if they are too low to be pruned away. The lackey moth (*Clisiocampa neustria*) is about an inch and a half across the wings, brown, and lays eggs in August to hatch in April and May. The caterpillars are blue-grey with brown hairs and make silken 'tents' among the foliage, which they can strip completely. They are a pest of the south, and as their egg bands are immune to winter tar oil washes they are on the increase. Pruning and watching for the egg bands are the best answers, but spraying with nicotine, even at the expense of predators, may be needed to clear a bad attack.

Cherries

If we have room we can enjoy the cherry, hung with snow from every bough, but today it is only rarely that we can enjoy the fruit. Modern birds are so much more intelligent and destructive than those of the past that the gardener's few trees are stripped every year, though commercial orchards protected by automatic acetylene guns, reinforced by shooting so that the noise is associated with danger, can still grow them.

The answer is to keep them as wall fruit, so that they can be protected by nylon net curtains like cordon red currants, for a fruit cage large enough to hold standard or even bush cherries would be too costly and awkward for most gardens. Only those who have grown wall cherries protected in this way realize how many the birds take without a really serious attack, when they see their first full crop.

The best cherry of all for amateurs is 'Morello', the cooking and bottling one, because it is self-fertile so fruits alone, and on a north- or east-facing wall, for it is tough enough to take cold winds and lack of sun. The sweet cherries must face south, and here the peach family are better value, but those who are fond of cherries, or who live in the north where peaches fail from the cold, can grow 'Late Duke', which is the only self-fertile dessert variety, ready in August, a bright red that hangs for quite a time on the tree. Like all the 'Duke' cherries it will cook and bottle as well.

The problem of the other varieties is that they need pollen partners, and with twelve feet between the trunks, this means over twenty feet of south wall to take a 'married couple'. Very few people today can afford the seven- to eight-feet-high walls that ran round the kitchen gardens of the past, but those who inherit one that is covered with ailing pears can replace with cherries under netting.

The fruit farmer can aim at having all his cherries ripe within three weeks, so one gang of pickers can get the lot away to market. The gardener who has decided to devote his walls to this non-keeping fruit wants to spread his picking over as long a period as possible, and yet have his cherries blossoming together with matching pollen. Cherries are far more awkward than apples, and many that blossom together may finish with a splendid crop on one and nothing on the other, because of incompatible pollen. So the following sets are chosen from good pollen pairs, that do well on walls and do not fruit at the same time.

'Bigarreau de Schrecken' has large black cherries in mid-June, of really fine flavour; it has large flowers and grows strong and well on a wall. Its best companion is 'Merton Heart', to fruit in late June, with dark crimson cherries again of first-class flavour, and a good cropper; and a third is 'Merton Bigarreau', for late July, which is again black, juicy, and just as vigorous. All three are among the nicest cherries, but as always they will need quite a bit of finding, for the commercial demand is for weight of crop rather than flavour, and the amateur must hunt for his needs among the few firms who still grow a real collection. Luckily they are all grafted on the wild cherry or gean (*Prunus avium*) so there are no stock complications.

229

Tree Fruit Without Troubles

Of this collection, 'Merton Bigarreau' will fit 'Merton Heart', and *vice versa*, but 'Merton Heart' will have nothing to do with 'Bigarreau du Schrecken'. 'Early Rivers' is one of the best known of all cherries, large, black and ready in mid-June, which fits 'Merton Glory', a yellow one with a red flush, ready in late June and early July, which pollinates 'Merton Reward', bright red, of rich flavour and eaten in August. The 'Merton' varieties were bred at The John Innes Horticultural Institution, and like the Malling raspberries they are outstanding introductions. Two old favourites for walls that are still unbeaten are 'Bigarreau Napoleon', pale yellow with red mottling for late July, and 'Frogmore Early', also yellow and red, for June and early July. Both have large blossom which makes a fine show against red brick, and both crop heavily which explains why they are commercial favourites, though sweet and tasty, and they are easy to buy.

It is easiest to fit the supporting wires before the planting holes are dug, so make holes to take vine eyes, which are long screw eyes, strong and heavily galvanized, to hold wires at eight-inch intervals up the wall, with a masonry drill or a Rawlplug tool, and fix these in with Rawlplastic. If the wire must stretch for more than eight feet, you need another eye in the middle. Then thread the wires through, which can be 13-gauge galvanized or the 'faulty telephone wire' recommended for raspberries, tying it firmly at the ends, or twisting it over and over with the pliers if it is galvanized.

Soil by walls is often poor, for builders usually dispose of a great deal of rubbish down the trenches beside a house. Dig the holes two feet deep and three long, as wide as the narrow bed allows, or fifteen inches for convenient digging. Fill them in the standard way for stone fruit suggested earlier in this chapter, and do not miss out the oyster shell because the soil is full of cement and plaster rubble. Modern cement is a double hydrated silicate of alumina, which makes far more lasting walls than the old lime mortar, but is no more a source of calcium than broken glass is of potash, and the calcium in modern plaster is just as well locked-up. There is no fear of the roots hungrily searching under the foundations for the missing plant foods, and though a poplar will go right under a house after water, wall fruit are as safe as century-old wistarias, with a good hole and plenty of food to take their roots well down at the start.

When the hole is filled in be sure that the soil surface is well below the damp course and the air bricks which are usually just above this.

Tree Fruit Without Troubles

If you bank a bed against the house up above the damp course you nullify the effect of this useful device for stopping the moisture from the soil creeping up inside your walls. A bed for wall fruit wants to be about two inches below damp course and path level so that a hose can be run into the bed to soak the soil which is often dry when the fruit is setting. The 'June drop' can take away the greater part of your cherries and your cherished peaches in a drought, without a timely soaking.

Tie the fan-trained branches to the wires with ordinary green waterproof garden string. During the summer tie in any side shoots to the wires and pinch back any that point outwards to two or three buds, whichever points *along* the wall. If one of the leaders intrudes on a window, or there are any that no longer fruit, cut these out before mid-July, because after this there is a risk of the spores of silverleaf disease (see under 'Plums', which get it most) and if any shoots are dead at the tips, snip these off till the wood shows clean and white.

Cherries fruit most on the one- and two-year wood, so they are never spur-pruned like apples. Watching for shoot tips that have died back and snipping them off in June is all the pruning they need.

No stone fruit should be pruned in winter when the spores of the fungi that get in through pruning cuts are most active. Standard and bush specimens need the same searching and snipping, but if there are no dead shoot ends there is no pruning to do, except for sawing out broken, dead or sickly branches, always in June, because then the trees are growing strongly and can take the shock, and will not weaken themselves by producing gum. The cut surfaces should always be painted or covered with Sellotape, if they are over an inch in diameter.

Wall cherries need their shoots tying in when they are thin and bendy, and it is important to see that they do not thrust up strong shoots known as 'water shoots' from near the bottom, as these take up the strength that should go to fruit. These should be pinched back while they are still soft, when you are looking over the tree for shoot tying.

The nylon net should be hooked to the back board as early as January if there are bullfinches about, because between then and March is the month when they destroy fruit buds. It can stay on too through the blossom period because the meshes tend to 'break the frosts' as they say in Kent, where coarse sacking netting called 'hoplewin' has been used to break up the currents of cold air that flow down hillsides, to save the blossom. It will not stop a bad one, but it makes a real difference and putting up the net earlier costs nothing when it can be hooked aside for tying in.

Cherries—Pests and Diseases

The dieback of cherries is easily pruned away, and it is caused by a fungus and several bacteria, but it can be controlled on wall fruit very much more easily than on tall and elderly trees. They are also attacked by the fungus *Gnomonia erythrostoma*, which causes infected leaves to hang withered on the tree through the winter, young leaves to have yellow patches on them and black spots to appear in the flesh of the fruit. The answer is to pick the leaves that stay on the trees after November ends and burn them.

Cherries have their own leafcurl, related to the one on peaches which is caused by the fungus *Taphrina minor*, and the best remedy is to spray with Burgundy Mixture before the leaves open in the early spring. Magnesium deficiency shows on the leaves as brown patches between the veins, and a watering with an ounce of Epsom salts in a two-gallon can the following spring should cure it, if the affected leaves are observed in the autumn. Iron shortage produces pale yellow leaves with the veins staying green, and here an ounce of iron sulphate (as used for moss in lawns) to the square yard, scattered on four square yards round the tree, should end the problem. Both deficiencies show before the leaves start changing colour in the autumn, and extra-early autumn tints of orange and yellow show nitrogen shortage, best cured by a two-inch-thick coat of manure on the bed beneath, which is the standard tonic for any ailing cherry.

The mottled umber, March and winter moths all attack cherries as well as apples, and if there is trouble from caterpillars, use a grease band round every tree. With cherries these are a wise precaution anyway, because they stop the ants that carry the cherry black fly (*Myzus cerasi*) from tree to tree. The young shoots of the cherry stay young for quite a while up their whole length and therefore it is not possible to control this pest by pruning as though it were an apple aphis. It is extremely common on the ornamental cherries such as the popular and upright 'Hisakura' (recently rechristened 'Kanzan' and now officially 'Sekiyama'. Fruit trees are less taxed by taxonomists, so 'Bigarreau Napoleon' has not become 'Bigarreau de Gaulle') and its winged stage can arrive on the wind from any neighbour.

Tree Fruit Without Troubles

The answer is to persuade local cherry owners to spray their trees with a winter tar oil wash to destroy the over-wintering eggs in January or February, and to spray your own, taking great care to squirt in behind the main stems and branches, poking the nozzle of the syringe sideways to get the spray in the corners. If the attack is only a small one, and a grease band has prevented the ants from spreading it, a quassia spraying will do least harm to the predators, but if other people's cherries are going to act as reservoirs of the pest, it will be hard to control without winter washes.

Winter washes are the last resort for dealing with the cherry fruit moth (*Argyresthia nitidella*) for they destroy its overwintering eggs and the cocoons which are inclined to hide behind the main branches and the wall. So if you have to spray for black fly, do it in January and catch the fruit moth too. As soon as the flower buds open the small green caterpillars bore into the sides and feed on the developing cherries, dropping to the ground in May and pupating in the soil. The only organic control method is to have a plentiful stock of predators of the ground beetle class in your soil to eat the pupae, or chickens between the trees which catch the crawling caterpillars before they can get under.

Poultry are also the best controllers of the pear and cherry slugworm (*Eriocampa limacina*) which is a sawfly larva that feeds from mid-June to September on the upper leaf surfaces, until the leaves become skeletonized. It is at first yellow but then becomes black, looking like a tiny slug, and when fully fed it drops to the ground and pupates in the soil, where it can be the prey of predators; but the chickens should get most of them. It might well pay to turn poultry into orchards between June and September when they can give most value as pest eaters, and confine them in a normal run during the spring. As the slugworm is a sawfly larva it can be killed with quassia with minimum harm to predators.

Damsons

Damsons will grow a fine tall hedge fast to hide a ruined view or temper the wind to a draughty garden, with a foam of white blossom in spring and fruit for jam, cheese and tarts through September. Damsons also bottle and will make a powerful wine that looks like a port, but with the sharp damson flavour.

The hedge and windbreak variety is Farleigh, bought as half

standards, branching about three feet from the ground, or as bushes, to plant three to four feet high. They crowd each other tall like trees in a wood and reach about fifteen feet more rapidly than costly conifers. Though they are not evergreen, they thicken up with thin and interlacing branches until they break up the gusts and have quite an effect on a view in winter.

Their fruit is on the small side and it is the one most commonly sold by greengrocers, because fruit growers pick it from their windbreaks, especially in the north. The damson to plant as a specimen standard is 'Merryweather', which is less upright and thickly branched, and has far larger fruit which are sweet enough for raw eating, that hang on the tree through September and October, and are just as good for cooking, rather better for bottling, and make an even stronger wine with the extra sugars. If a number are to be planted they should be twelve feet apart each way, but few people want more than a single tree, for this variety starts fruiting the second year after planting and can crop heavily for as long as forty years.

These two varieties are self-fertile and, like all damsons, need no pruning. Crowding branches can be sawn out of the middles, and dead wood can be removed between early May and mid-June, while the 'tree hedge' of 'Farleigh' can be clipped flat sides and top if desired then, though this is at the expense of fruit and blossom. Plant them like plums and insist that they should not be grafted on 'Mussel' stock. They must be either on their own roots or on one of the modern non-suckering stocks.

Damsons are almost pest- and disease-free. Those they do get are shared with plums, and their only drawback is their growth speed once they begin to move, so their best position is at the bottom of the garden. Putting the damson wine in the refrigerator, and picking out the lumps of ice from the water that freezes, leaves the alcohol behind and makes a kind of undistilled brandy very much like the Balkan plum brandies that produced such effects on British troops, brought up on beer, in World War II.

Greengages—see Plums

Peaches, Apricots and Nectarines—Varieties

The cultivation of all of these is so nearly the same that they are treated together, for they share diseases, and fortunately most are self-fertile so that there are no pollination problems, while all do well on 'Brompton' or 'St. Julien' used for plums. If possible, however, ask for them on 'seedling peach', for these are more vigorous and fruit well sooner. There is no harm in asking, for seedling peaches for stocks should be the wild species *Prunus persica*, not one that someone has raised from a stone.

Sowing peach stones is a gamble in which the gambler has at least a good chance of a show of blossom for his money, and with long-odds luck perhaps one year in eight his descendant of a variety bred for earlier springs will beat our frosts with its blossom. Then he wins peaches by the barrowload as his tree fruits with the stored vigour of seven cropless years. Like all gamblers, he does not count the loss of all the fruit that he might have grown in the space occupied by his thriving ugly duckling; such sowings have produced rather fewer swans than there have been large football pool winners.

To bring down the odds to nearer those on a 100–8 outsider, buy South African peaches in March or April which will have been picked in late autumn in the Southern Hemisphere and blossomed late in *their* spring. Even then one is gambling against Mendel's law, for a self-pollinated hybrid is going to produce variations on its ancestors.

Sow the stones in April or May, two inches deep in a sunny corner, and transplant to a permanent home when they are a foot high, remembering that with luck you will have something like a sizeable bush apple tree by the end of the six-to-eight years they take to reach fruiting size even with weather just right when they reach it. Losers who look gloomily at their spreading and fruitless monsters think of root pruning, ring barking or grafting. The first will make no difference, the second means a gummy death for the tree, and though apples can be 'top-worked' by grafting another kind on the sawn-off branch ends, no peach will stand this treatment. These failures are usually early variations on Italian peaches which are frosted before their blossom even opens, and the only answer is to saw them up for logs, which burn remarkably well.

No one with a small garden can waste time and space on raising peach stones, when there are hardy varieties bred for Britain which will grow even as bushes in the south, and on sunny walls in the north, and fruit as reliably as apples, though like these, they can catch an unlucky frost. Wherever they grow they need protection from cold winds because they are the earliest to flower of all tree fruit, starting in mid-March or early April.

Tree Fruit Without Troubles

The most popular and hardiest variety is 'Peregrine', which fruits about the middle of August, large, white-fleshed and crimson-cheeked, but as we saw in the table, the particular merit of the peach family is their high vitamin A, which has a wide variation. White-fleshed varieties range from 5 to 100 I.U.'s while yellows are from 880 to 2,000. Both kinds are delicious, but the yellow have more taste. The hardiest of the yellow free-stone peaches is 'Rochester', which is ready as August ends, and those who have room in a sheltered corner or on a wall can extend the season with 'Bellegarde', fruiting in September, yellow-fleshed, with a wonderful flavour and a striking dark crimson skin, and 'Duke of York' for July, again with a crimson skin and yellow flesh of glorious taste. These two are both nicer than 'Peregrine', which has toughness to recommend it, though if you have shelter or a south wall in Surrey, you might as well grow a set to eat over the longest period.

Peaches on a wall have the benefit of protection from the north, and the possibility of protection from frost with a nylon net, as well as some gain from the warming up and radiation from the wall. Bushes gain by needing much less pruning, from having a better root system (for wall fruit only roots outwards away from the wall) and from being sprayed all round, for the space between the wall and the back of the branches is where the pests and spores gather. Fan-trained peaches cost £3 to £4, bushes from about £2 each, and though most nurseries today stock only 'Peregrine', the others can be obtained from really good firms.

Plant wall peaches just like cherries, with a long, deep slot, and plenty of lasting food in the bottom, and a filling of topsoil and compost with some manure if available, and eight to ten feet apart on the wall if you have room for several. Bushes need the same deep square hole recommended for all stone fruit, and should go to twelve feet apart each way, with a strong stake to the first fork of the branches.

Newly planted bush peaches should have all their shoots shortened to half length in February, but in May they will need looking over to see if any of the already-shortened shoots has died at the tip. Snip it off and snip again and again until the wood shows white and clean with no brown stain in the middle. This early cut-back is very important because those shoots will blossom all the way up if left on, and this is a strain on newly planted peaches. After this first year the only pruning bush peaches need is removing any shoots pointing

236

towards the middle, and shoot shortening to remove dieback, always in May.

Cutting out the dead tips has the same tonic 'decayed tooth removal' effect on the trees as it has for all stone fruit, but pruning in winter, as with apples and pears, is equally dangerous to them all. 'Dieback' is not a single disease, it is the result of frost damage to young shoot tips, of bullfinches peeking out buds, or even of damage from pests; all of these let in spores from several fungi, including species of *Botrytis* and *Cytospora* which begin by attacking the dead tissue and then go on to the living. A common cause on commercial orchards and nurseries is damage by shotgun pellets used for firing at bullfinches, which can be worse for trained peaches than the birds, for a single pellet can graze as many as six branches. This also causes canker in apples.

If any fruitlets form the summer after planting, pick these off, but in the second season leave on up to a dozen, while in the third year it can bear as many as forty, if it is growing well. As the tree grows older more and more branches will grow into the middle and need cutting out, and also some of the lower branches will need sawing off in May, for they are inclined to weigh lower and lower with the fruit. They heal naturally at this time of year, with no need to paint the cut.

Thinning peaches is all-important because it is very easy to overstrain a tree that is going to crop every year, unlike a peach-stone seedling that may have eight years' rest between crops. They will be ready for their first thinning in May, when you should remove one from each where they are in pairs so that they are not less than four inches apart all over the tree. In June some will drop and towards the end of the month, when the drop is over and the young peaches are the size of thumbnails, thin to about eight inches apart. This is only approximate, for if you have a strong branch with only four or five on it near one end, leave them all even if they are only four inches apart. If you have a poor crop with all crowded on one part of the tree, thin to only three inches the first time and then only enough to stop them touching each other. The better the crop the more you thin, and the bigger and stronger the tree the more you can leave on. All the peaches grown for canning are bush specimens in the U.S.A. and Canada and Australia, and there is no reason why gardeners in Devon, Cornwall and Somerset should not take heavy crops of these hardy varieties.

Wall peaches must be pruned differently, and they should be first tied to their wires without any cutting back of the shoots, but in March the blossom should be snipped off when this is possible without damaging the leaves. If any shoots have died at the tips, cut them back in May as before, and this part of the pruning is standard.

Peaches can fruit on small spurs, but mostly on long shoots that grew the previous year. A new tree will produce some of these and they should be tied in to the wires and their older companions. When they have fruited, wait till May and snip them back to two or three buds, whichever points along the wall. Another kind of shoot rushes up thick and strong from the base; another 'water shoot', and these rarely blossom, so cut them right out to a sideways-pointing bud, which should be the policy for anything thrusting awkwardly out. If it is desirable to cover the wall, then let the fruited shoots grow again from the tips, which will mean fruit further and further out, but the extra pruning grows more shoots nearer the centre of the tree. Tie the new shoots in when they are young and bendy, and remember to watch for dieback each May.

Wall fruit get much drier than bush trees in the open, so in June and July run the hose in the border, but not later because of the risk of swelling the ripening fruit too fast and cracking the skins. If you have a July-fruiting variety, do not hose it after June. Thinning is the same as for bush, but the crops will not be so large, though in the north only the wall warms them enough to crop.

Peaches—Pests and Diseases

The only major pest is the peach aphis (*Myzus persicae*) which spends the winter and spring on peaches, which it leaves in May and June to spend the summer on cabbages, potatoes and a number of flowering plants. The creatures cause curling of the young leaves early in the year and it pays to attack them with derris during April to catch them before they leave for their holidays.

Peach leafcurl is the main disease problem, and is caused by the fungus *Taphrina deformans*, which curls the leaves that become reddish in colour and sometimes blistered. There is a theory that the fungus only attacks when there is a trace element shortage, and that spraying with a seaweed foliar feed will cure it, but though this is worth trying, the facts are not established. The best remedy is to spray with Burgundy Mixture in February or March, just as the buds start to swell, and this takes care of crown gall, bitter rot and a few other assorted problems that are more common in peaches under glass than those in the open. The main essential is to be sure to get the spray between the peach and the wall, for this is where the spores hide. Peaches have fewer diseases and pests than apples but their main stems should be grease-banded to prevent ants and earwigs which may damage the fruit.

Wasps, of course, are a problem in the fruiting season, and the traditional jam jar with jam or treacle and beer inside, with holes poked in a paper lid, can be hung to catch them. If the nest can be found mark the entrance and come back after dark when the wasps will be at home. Push as much as possible of a mixture of equal parts of flowers of sulphur and saltpetre (potassium nitrate) down the hole. A fuse should have been prepared separately by soaking string in a strong solution of saltpetre and water and letting it dry. Insert the string in this weak gunpowder and cover the entrance to the hole with soil. Light your string and await results. There should be a fizzing and a cloud of white smoke with a strong smell of sulphur, which is just as effective as cyanide and a great deal safer. There is no possibility of an explosion with this mixture. Real gunpowder, which cannot now be bought, was formerly used and burnt much faster, which gave some risk of burns but no explosion except in a confined space.

Apricots

The most common apricot is 'Moorpark' which ripens in late August, and is a well-flavoured kind, but subject to dieback. A better one is 'Hemskerke', less likely to get dieback, and hardier, with equally nice fruit ready in early August.

Both can be grown as bushes or on walls, but their problem is frosts, for as they blossom in February they need all the shelter they can get. An *apricot* from a stone has no chance at all of ever fruiting, and not even the most optimistic gardener has ever reported success. Plant exactly as for peaches, but the procedure for controlling dieback is more important.

Thin apricots like peaches, but because they are smaller begin at May pruning time when they are the size of hazelnuts, and finish when they are about an inch in diameter, thinning to five to six inches apart with a good crop, here again because they are smaller. Apricots start to go soft before they are ripe, so leave them on for some time while the flavour is improving, about a fortnight after they begin to soften. They can drop their fruit if there is a high wind when the fruit is soft but not ripe, and in Canada and the U.S.A. thick straw, say six-inch pads from a straw bale, is placed under the trees; you could place it along the wall bed as a precaution if you have some ready. Apricots bottle well and fresh apricot jam is delicious, though of course most gardeners prefer to gorge them raw while they last.

Apricots rarely get leafcurl, and dieback is their only disease problem. They can be attacked by winter moth, and grease-banding is the best precaution, but as these creatures can climb the wall, a long streak of grease band material painted on the brickwork and renewed each spring is better. It should be about six inches above ground level.

Nectarines

A nectarine is a smooth-skinned variety of peach, with the disadvantage of not doing well as a bush. The best-flavoured kind, which also blossoms latest with a better chance of missing March frosts, is 'Humboldt', which ripens in late August, while 'Lord Napier' is ready earlier in the month. Both are self-fertile but crop better with a peach near them. Treat them exactly the same as peaches for pruning and thinning, but give them more water. If 'Humboldt', which will grow as a bush, is raised in this way, give it a straw mulch, leaving a gap of about six inches round the trunk, in April and hose well in May and June.

The thin skins make them more attractive to wasps and other insects, so hanging butter muslin from the top of the wall while they are ripening is a good idea. Like apricots they get soft before they are ripe, and it is at this stage that they need protection. On the whole they are less satisfactory than 'Peregrine' or 'Rochester' peaches, which beat both apricots and nectarines in hardiness and chances of a really splendid crop of luxury fruit.

Pears

Pears are very much easier to keep under control when grafted on 'Quince A' dwarfing stocks and grown horizontally like apples, either on post and wire frames round kitchen garden beds as in the past, or on walls. They do well also as bush trees, cordons or dwarf pyramids but because they are nitrogen-greedy, they must not be grassed down. Standards take a long time to bear, and because pears by nature are tall and upright they soon get out of hand and become too big for pruning or the thinning they need to produce regular crops.

Their planting and distances apart are exactly the same as for apples, but they do appreciate a two-inch-thick coat of manure over the four-foot circle round the tree, applied in each of the first three springs after planting. The manure under these or any other fruit trees should not come closer than six inches from the trunks, and, particularly for pears, great care should also be taken to see that neither soil nor any manure or other mulch reaches to the above-graft bulge on the stem.

There are two reliable pears for one-tree gardens—'Fertility Improved', which is a larger and better-flavoured version of the old, almost round, russet-skinned cottage pear to eat in November, with a taste like sugared water, and 'Conference'. This is our most popular variety today, because it crops alone, is vigorous, and has fruit that remains eatable through October and November. It is the long thin pear that greengrocers sell, but not our finest for flavour.

The most famous we have is 'Doyenne du Comice' which is at its best in November, large, juicy, and delicious. It is moderately vigorous, excellent trained, and bears a heavy crop with the right pollinator. The two best are 'Beurre Hardy', which is also a first-class and strong grower and a heavy cropper, for eating in October, and 'Glou Morceau' for December and January, which crops well but needs a south wall because it wants some protection to finish ripening its late fruit. The first two will do as pyramids or bushes.

There is no pear that will keep like a Cox, so those who are fond of them must plant a number of trees for succession, but with shelter, especially in the north where wall-protection helps most. All blossom early so there is no chance of choosing really late varieties as with apples. 'Doyenne du Comice' and its companions are in the group that is latest to blossom.

An earlier set should include 'Joséphine de Malines', which keeps for December and January, and is a small pear of good flavour, going well with a 'William', which should be 'William's Bon Chrétien', and is called a 'Bartlett' in the U.S.A. where it is extensively grown for canning. This is the best early pear for September eating, with the nearest touch of a Cox flavour among pears, while 'Louise Bonne of Jersey', a December to January type, is almost as famous for flavour as 'Doyenne du Comice', and is a heavier cropper, and fits with a 'William'.

Tree Fruit Without Troubles

A new Australian variety is 'Packham's Triumph', which is reputed to be self-fertile, for November and December eating, a strong and good cropping pear with bright yellow, juicy and very sweet fruit, and the rare 'Fondante d'Automne' which is rather like it for flavour, but in September and October is also able to crop alone, though neither is as reliable as 'Conference', which will pollinate either if necessary.

Wild pears have thorns, and the cultivated ones use these as the basis of fruiting spurs, so it is possible for a pear to pile on the blossom for a crop that can exhaust it. The fruiting spurs will usually produce a whole bunch of fruitlets, and it is as well to wait till each is an inch long before the first thinning. Look then for any misshapen ones, and remove these for burning, because these will contain the larvae of the pear midge (*Contarinia pyrivora*) and this search in May is the best method of control, getting rid of hundreds of small white maggots in each fruit. Running chickens under the trees is also effective for they peck up the full-fed maggots that drop from the fruit, where trees have been allowed to grow too large for hand-thinning. Thin next in June, aiming at leaving one pear to every five inches roughly, which should prevent the branches breaking; make sure that every pear is a real beauty.

Pruning is the same as for apples, both winter and summer, for though leaving long leaders produces more blossom this strains the tree. 'Joséphine de Malines' is the pear equivalent of a 'Blenheim'—a tip bearer, and it should have its leaders left, and only inward-pointing or cankered or scabby spurs should be removed, and it needs no summer pruning. For this reason it should only be grown as a bush. Scab can show on the two- and three-year-old wood, but the same care in pruning will remove it. Where the trees are awkwardly placed for clearing out the dead leaves for scab control, the leaves can be dug into the bare ground.

Though most pears are 'sulphur-shy', spraying with Burgundy Mixture is effective against scab in all varieties and leaf blister, which is caused by *Taphrina bullata*, a relation of the one that attacks peaches. There is a new disease, phytophthora rot, caused by a fungus *Phytophthora cactorum* which produces brown patches on the fruit. This can be cured by collecting and burning rotten fruit and using a Burgundy spray as for scab. The spray should never be a 'routine' for it is not routine to have any disease in any fruit; this is a rare accident from something blowing on the wind.

Tree Fruit Without Troubles

The pear and cherry slugworm is treated as for cherries, and the leaf blister mite (*Eriophyes piri*) which produces greenish or reddish blisters on the leaves in spring, is cured by picking off and burning the attacked leaves. These tiny creatures have four or five generations a year, and spotting the blisters early, before they turn black, stops them from stripping the leaves off the tree. The mites themselves can be killed by spraying with lime-sulphur in February to catch them hibernating under the bud scale, but this will kill *Anthocoris*, and there is also a risk of damage to the young leaves if the job is left too late. As always, control is easy provided that the pear tree is a cordon or horizontal (espalier) or a bush or pyramid on a dwarfing stock. If you have a monster at the bottom of your garden, it can have trouble at the top that will stay hidden until too late.

There is a leaf curling midge (*Dasyneura pyri*) which attacks the young shoot tips, but this is cured by summer pruning as apple aphides are. The pear sucker (*Psylla pyricola*) is sometimes bad on wall trees because it is hard to get a tar oil wash behind the branches where it hibernates, and should be sprayed with pyrethrum. This is also the best answer for the pear thrips (*Taeniothrips inconsequens*) which attacks the blossom and young fruit, because it is possible to avoid harming bees by spraying in the evening, when the bees have gone home, with pyrethrum which will be spent by the morning when they are about again. A gardener with only a few trees can do this, and also gain the advantage that the pyrethrum is weak enough to do least harm to his *Anthocoris*.

There is, unfortunately, no remedy for fire blight, caused by the bacterium *Erwinia amylovora*, which is carried from blossom to blossom by pollinating insects, especially bees. It appeared first in the Southend area of Essex, in 'Laxton's Superb' pears, and spread rapidly. The infected blossom turns black, then as the bacteria spread the leaves blacken from the edges, the bark becomes grey-black and cankers form, consisting of wet-looking dark brown material directly beneath the bark. These cankers spread down the branches, becoming drier, and the leaves turn brown, so the tree looks as if it had been scorched by fire. It is quite distinct—first black then brown, entirely unlike any deficiency disease.

It has also attacked 'William's Bon Chrétien', 'Conference' and 'Doyenne du Comice', some apples, also pyracantha, cotoneaster, mountain ash trees and hawthorn hedges. Under the Fire Blight Order of 1958 all attacked trees or shrubs must be destroyed, and even

243

healthy 'Laxton's Superb' pear (*not apple*) trees should be grubbed, because this variety takes it first. In the U.S.A., where it began, it is nothing like as serious, for like many pests and diseases it has a clear field here. There the recommendations are to saw off the branch ahead of the cankers as we do for silverleaf or dieback, and to spray with white oils (the synthetic turpentine now widely sold) but this is illegal in Britain. While your tree is recovering it could be spreading the bacteria with every bee that visits it, and until more is known of it we cannot be sure that it is not spread also in other ways, perhaps blowing on the wind or being carried on the feet of birds.

'Laxton's Superb' pears have now been removed from all catalogues, and the question is whether the other varieties caught it because they are prone to the disease, or did they get it because they were the most common varieties?

Those who are planting pears could well take a chance on the two new nearly self-fertile varieties, or 'Fertility Improved' and in place of 'Doyenne du Comice' in the late-flowering threesome have 'Beurre Diel', also a pear of taste, but a triploid, like a 'Ribston Pippin', which needs *both* the pollinators, not just either like 'Doyenne du Comice', which was pollinated best by 'Laxton's Superb'. 'Durondeau' is another well-flavoured pear for October and November, a heavy cropper and compact growing, but its usual pollinator was 'Conference'. Alternatives would be 'Triomphe de Vienne', for September eating, or 'Bergamotte Espéren', the longest-keeping pear of all, lasting sometimes until March, and a good though scarce garden variety. This is a better keeper than 'Joséphine de Malines', though it has not such a fine flavour, but it does have the great advantage of not being a tip bearer.

Plums and Greengages—Varieties

The finest plum of all is a 'Victoria', for jam and bottling as well as eating, with a very heavy crop, so that it should always be grown as a bush or half-standard because these are easier to prop with wooden 'A's' made of 2-in. × 1-in. creosoted timber. It has a drooping habit, and the weight of the crop uses the long branches as levers to tear them off the tree, so propping and thinning are essential. 'Victoria' is ideal for small gardens because it is self-fertile and a good pollinator for other kinds.

The 'Old Greengage' is pollinated by 'Victoria', and anyone who has a greengage that never fruits should try planting a bush 'Victoria', which will not crop well for three years, but will have blossom to provide the pollen to start the old tree fruiting. If you are planting a greengage as well as a 'Victoria', have 'Transparent Gage', which follows 'Victoria' by fruiting in September, is strong and sturdy and has a really fine flavour that persists well after bottling. A second full-sized eating plum to follow 'Victoria' and enjoy its pollen is 'Anna Späth', starting in mid-September and hanging on the tree right into October. It crops well and is of a rich red-purple, firm, juicy and sweet, not so well flavoured as 'Victoria', but few other plums are.

The 'Cox' of plums is 'Kirke's Blue', for eating in mid-September, dark red-purple, good on a south wall if space can be spared, not a strong grower and incapable of bearing a crop with its own pollen. Plant it with 'Cambridge Gage', one of the best-flavoured and the most heavily cropping of the greengages, ready to pick in August. If you want to grow a greengage on its own, choose 'Oullins Golden Gage' which is self-fertile, not so tasty as the other gages but bearing a very large crop, and this is why it is the usual one on sale in greengrocers'.

Another good self-fertile plum is 'Czar', the purple cooking variety that bottles well and has the merit of thriving on a north wall like a Morello cherry, with the same treatment and pruning. 'Czar' is ready in early August, and it will pollinate 'Rivers' Early Prolific', a purple cooking plum of the same type to pick in July, on an otherwise wasted north wall, where 'Oullins Gage' will also thrive, taking the advantages of nylon net protection and the use of a narrow bed. 'Kirke's Blue' will take a west-facing wall as well as a south one, and here 'Oullins Golden Gage', or 'Belle de Louvain', a large late-August cooking plum, can be planted to pollinate it. On an east wall have 'Coe's Golden Drop', a good late-eating plum for September and October with a really good flavour, with 'Jefferson', a very delicious yellow plum to pick all through September. The two are very near each other, with the balance of flavour and crop on 'Jefferson', so 'Early Transparent Gage' as a good August greengage could replace 'Coe's'. The problem is that these blossom early and need the protection of both a wall and the frost-breaking effect of the nylon netting.

Though a 'Czar' is perhaps the toughest of plums, flowering late for cold gardens, there is an even later one, the 'Serbian Quetsche', which is upright, not drooping, and is entirely self-fertile. It has purple fruit the size of a damson, very sweet and with a distinctive flavour, in September and October. It makes an excellent jam and bottles well, but the powerful brandy it makes in Yugoslavia is not recommended for motorists.

Another hardy and unusual species is the 'Red Cherry Plum', with nutmeg-sized fruit in August every other year, for it is a confirmed biennial bearer. These are excellent bottled or in jam, but the value of the variety is as a hedge. Buy bush specimens and plant them three feet apart, with two stakes about three feet high between each. Snip off any dieback branches as with other plums, for the two years, but after this they run so little risk of it that Somerset hedgers chop branches half through when they are making the tall hedges that shelter cider apple orchards. After the first pruning, weave the shoots like a basket between the stakes, tying them firmly in place to begin with, and as they grow they can weave into a solid wall because their shoots are soft and bendy, unlike the brittle ones of a 'Victoria'. A hedge or 'plum wall' to divide one part of the garden from another is a sight in spring, with large white blossom in March an inch across, and the fruit is well worth its every-other-year habit.

Bush and standard plums need ordinary stone fruit pruning— snipping out of any dieback in early May, and sawing or snipping out of crowding branches or weak-looking wood only at this safe season. If a branch has broken half off in the autumn at picking time, do not tidy up the stump till May. It is possible, however, to shorten the main leaders to twelve inches in late June and the side shoots to six to eight as a kind of 'summer pruning' to slow down a 'Victoria' that is growing too much.

Plums produce their fruiting spurs on their one- and two-year-old wood, and therefore if you cut back their main shoots as though they were apples, you are cutting away the crop. Newly planted trees need no pruning, but any fruitlets that form the first year should be pinched off at hazelnut size because they will be a strain on the new tree.

Plums on walls should have their side shoots pinched back to three or four leaves, exactly as for cherries, but as they grow larger they will need root pruning. This is done by scraping away the soil round the stem until some of the roots are exposed, and cutting through the thick ones two feet away from the stem, leaving the newly formed fibrous ones. In another five years the job may need doing again, but as with peaches, wall plum roots will not go far under the house but all into the bed in front, so they can all be got at except any going straight down. Root pruning benefits plums that have fruited well in the past and are now growing more wood than fruit, but if they have *never* fruited, like some apples, they are probably waiting for a missing pollen partner.

The beds against walls are often dry, and plums need the hose just like cherries or peaches, after they have been thinned to their final spacing. It is possible, when there is a bumper crop, to thin so that the fruits are only three inches apart, and to hose well when the 'Victorias' are nutmeg size, but this risks a smaller crop next year. A bush tree well propped can take a hefty crop with ample water, and many commercial growers mulch under the trees with straw in April to retain more moisture and increase the humus to hold it in the soil. On a garden scale the straw system demands foot-high wire-netting round the outside, because birds will spread it everywhere, and it is costly when you are buying only a few bales. The mulch should be from three to four inches deep and is made by taking the bales apart in 'wads' after cutting the strings.

Plums are nitrogen-greedy as pears are, but they also need lime, and after they have been cropping for six years, scatter 1 lb. a square yard of slaked lime along the bed for wall fruit, and roughly this much on the square yard round each tree in the autumn. In the spring give them a coat of manure every other year, round the tree but not touching it, as with pears. If the fruit is small and the stone is larger in proportion than normal, the cause is nitrogen shortage and the answer is manure. Peat deep-litter poultry compost is excellent if it can be obtained, and so is straw-based deep-litter, but this is less tidy to put on.

Plums—Diseases and Pests

On chalky soils, plums can show symptoms of iron deficiency, which are yellowing leaves at the tips of the young shoots long before autumn; and magnesium shortage as yellowing *between* the veins on the lower leaves of the fruits. Gummosis, which is gum appearing on the fruits, is caused by bad drainage and shortage of lime.

The main plum disease is silverleaf, caused by the fungus *Stereum purpureum*, the spores of which blow round orchards just like those of the collection of fungi that cause dieback, but they are active over a longer period. The Silverleaf Order of 1923 demands that all fruit growers should saw out all dead wood from plum and apple trees each year, before 15th July, for the disease, which causes silvering of the foliage, can attack apples also. The spore-bearing fungus consists of flat or bracket plates of brown tissue which turns purple or lilac when wet, and is only found on dead wood. Though the Act does not specify the beginning of the sawing season, it is the first week in May.

If a shoot has silvered leaves, snip it off, and snip again until no more wood shows dark brown in the middle, then give the tree a mulch of manure on the surface as a tonic, at the end of May. Where there is more than a single shoot attacked, use the bark-slitting method developed by the late Mr. Justin Brooke and other commercial growers. Take a sharp knife and slit from where the dead or attacked branch was sawn off, down to the trunk and from there to soil level, cutting right through the bark to the living wood. This should be done between early May and mid-June, and it works like magic, though no one knows exactly why. It is an 'old husbands' tale' as distinct from an 'old wives' ' one, and has been known in Suffolk for centuries. Silverleaf also attacks poplars and elms, as well as laburnums and laurels, so saw out their dead wood within the safe period before they can spread a disease no fungicide will touch.

Powdery mildew, bacterial canker and a number of odd fungus infections are all curable by summer pruning for dieback, as for cherries, and spraying with Burgundy Mixture in January before the leaves stir. This is also effective against *Taphrina pruni*, a relation of peach leafcurl which affects the twigs, though it is advisable to prune away any attacked shoots. This disease can attack the young fruit, making them grow unnaturally long and have a white bloom, and these should be removed and burnt with the shoot that produced them. After sawing anything from a plum tree, coat the cut with a white-lead paint, for plums take infection through cuts more readily than any apple or pear.

However, plums have fewer pests, and if there is an attack of leaf-curling aphides between May and the key date of 15th July, snip off the shoot and spray with pyrethrum. It is far more important to get the spray in everywhere than to use anything extra strong. The red plum maggot (*Cydia funebrana*), a relation of the codling moth, can be killed when it is hibernating in cocoons by spraying with a winter tar oil wash in January, or by spraying with derris in July when the young caterpillars are about after hatching and not yet hidden in the plums.

Plum gall mites, of which there are two, make galls on the foliage, and overwinter in the bud scales. Birds, hunting for these sleeping mites, do far more damage by destroying fruit buds than the mites would do to the leaves, so the best answer is to put the nylon nets up early for wall fruit, and to keep a watch through the summer for leaves that have pouch-like blisters on them, which should be picked off and burnt. It is possible to kill the over-wintering mites by spraying with lime-sulphur in late February, but this risks killing *Anthocoris*, though these useful creatures will usually be still hibernating by then. March, as recommended in orthodox works, is on the late side. Picking off the first few leaves before the creatures spread is the best remedy, and taking a good look at your trees once a week, or even once a fortnight, is always the cheapest and safest pesticide and fungicide.

Quinces

The real quince is *Cydonia oblonga* and comes from Southern Europe, so though it will ripen its large yellow fruit like rather knobby apples in the south, it needs a wall for protection in the north and in Scotland. Its ideal position is by a pond, for it needs a moist position and here its two-inches-across white blossom in May reflected in the water is doubly beautiful. With time a bush or standard quince will grow twenty-five feet high, and they are reputed to live for a hundred years or more.

Perhaps the best varieties are 'Bereczki' and 'Vranja', both pear- rather than apple-shaped, but fruiting early in their lives and both named after towns in Yugoslavia, where they grew when this was Serbia, so they are hardier than the Portuguese or Italian quinces. They are self-fertile, so need no pollen partners, and are grown on their own roots from cuttings. The least successful quinces are those that have grown up from the stock of a pear that failed, which are bred to do a different job.

For southern gardens bushes are best and these should be pruned by shortening the leaders by half and the lesser shoots to a quarter, cutting always to outward-pointing buds, for the first three years after planting. From then onwards remove only dead or crowding branches. Wall trees are usually fan trained, but these are expensive, so a two-year-old bush can be planted against a wall and tied to the wires, with the outward-thrusting shoots taken off to sideways-pointing buds. On a wall quinces can be pruned like pears, and should they produce a sudden bumper crop, this should be thinned in the same way.

Quinces do well as standards planted in an apple orchard, and prefer to be grassed all round, so the one by the waterside can be clipped under as it thrives among the daffodils. Treating it as an apple rather than a pear has the advantage of preventing the quince leaf spot or leaf blight caused by the fungus *Fabraea maculata*, which has quite a search to find a home in modern gardens, though it can be awkward for nurseries raising quince stocks. The fungus overwinters on the fallen leaves and if these are collected or chewed up with those that may carry apple scab, there is no problem. The other pests and diseases are the same as those of apples, but rarely attack this odd man out among fruits.

Pick the quinces in November, but do not store them with pears, or these may be tainted with the spicy quince flavour. This is too strong for them to be suitable for eating raw, but they make jams and preserves as described in Chapter 9. If a quince tree is getting out of hand, or it has a bad aphis attack, it can be summer pruned like an apple, and a grease band prevents its main pest which is the winter moth.

The fruit of *Chaenomeles speciosa* can be used for all quince recipes, but they have nothing like the flavour. The best variety for both flowers and fruit is 'Boule de Feu' with scarlet flowers in clusters that start in February and finish in April, and fruit about three inches long and one and a half in diameter, rather like a rough-skinned pear. *Chaenomeles* must be trained against a wall, for though some species are shrubs they cannot support a good crop of fruit in the open. The real quince is a splendid tree, especially in blossom.

Walnuts

Very few people today have the courage to plant walnut trees, for the first few for eating will not arrive till three years after planting a four-year-old tree, and there are eight years to wait for a real crop. Yet another fifty years may see the last walnut trees of England dead as those the confident Victorians planted reach their allotted spans of 120–150 years.

Once there were many varieties, and the species *Juglans regia maxima*, called 'Northdown Clawnut', with nuts twice normal size that came true from seed, may well survive forgotten, but worth finding to pass on to the future (that may eat pep-pills rather than drinking port with its walnuts)—nuts that will still be far superior when fresh to the dried-up relics we import in polythene packets. Now we must buy what we can find if we are generous enough to plant for the future.

The usual variety now is 'Franquette', which has a good flavour and flowers late so that there is little risk of frost catching the catkins and ruining the crop. Luckily walnuts are self-fertile and are usually grown on their own roots, but cost between £3 and £4 for bushes or half-standards. If anyone wanted to plant a wood of walnuts they should go twenty-five feet apart each way, which would crowd them taller and taller after their sixtieth summer until in a hundred years they would be worth a fortune for furniture or gunstocks, though these may all be made in plastics by then. It is the demand for this beautiful wood that has swept away our walnuts when merely middle-aged in their eighties and nineties.

Plant them just like apples, in a grass orchard if you like, perhaps at the end of a row, remembering that if they are not crowded by neighbours they spread about thirty feet and grow fifty or sixty high. Take extra care with the planting and give them plenty of bone meal in the hole, to start that great root driving down into the subsoil for up to twenty feet. Stake them well, for any bend will last into the future, and perhaps put a 50p piece under the roots as a kind of time capsule.

They need little spraying for their diseases appear to have died out and their pests were few, but if any fungus appears, or if there are dark angular spots on the leaves, spray with Burgundy Mixture in January. Though they need no pruning, they can be brought into bearing quicker by pinching. In the third July after planting and for the next five, pinch out the tips of the strong shoots, not the thin ones that bear catkins after the fifth or sixth leaf. Never use secateurs or a knife, just pinch the young growing shoots, for walnuts bleed sap, and dead or broken boughs should be sawn out only in December or January, or the tree will waste its strength.

This pinching system brings a bush tree into fruit in eight years, or ten if it was merely a two-year-old, not the big four-year-olds that used to be planted. It also means that the fruit that will be first enjoyed will be low enough to pick easily. The nuts are covered with thick green coats like smooth-skinned chestnut burrs and they are ready to pick when they start to fall and these husks will split away from them. The most delicious are those eaten in the late autumn when the nuts have merely had this husk removed and been cracked, and then the yellow skin of the halves of the kernel peels easily away. Store them after shelling in a temperature of about 50° F for about a month to dry them and then store in a cool place, such as a dry cellar, when they keep easily round the year. Until you have eaten your own walnuts you never realize what tasteless imitations our imports are.

8

Tips and Tools

Garden tools began when steel made swords and craftsmen knew that good ideas need strength. The best tools for gardeners are not the gay gadgets that may hang unused but those that grow into old friends as they wear on through the years like good swords in a flimsy world.

A lady's fork is better for a child growing up to gardening than a brightly painted set stamped from sheet metal like seaside sand spades. Real gardeners of both sexes need full-sized spades and forks, of good-quality steel, not stainless, for this is brittle and will not hold an edge. Except for hand forks and trowels that do not lever heavy soil, the rust-resistance of stainless steel is an expensive white elephant of value only to those who put tools away dirty.

Never buy any tools of deliberately 'modern' design, for the traditional shapes of handle have been tested through several centuries, and a cheap hand fork with a turned handle, as an example, will not only be more comfortable to use than a square-tapered modern type, but a quarter the price. Two good forks, a spade, a rake and a swan-neck hoe, with a file to sharpen the blade of the last so that it will cut through weeds, are the essential tools, with a pair of secateurs for bush and tree fruit pruning. Buy them with a nylon garden line (which will not rot) on a metal winder, from a nurseryman's shop or a craftsman ironmonger, and pay for good steel. Never buy cheap secateurs. Pay extra for quality. Above all never buy cheap shears, for the cheaper qualities of these will not even last two days without needing sharpening to an edge they can never hold.

Before you buy a barrow, measure the width of any door or narrow gate it will have to go through and the width of the narrowest path on which it must stand. Then choose one with handles that spread

252

only wide enough to go through, allowing an inch clear of your knuckles on either side, and legs that fit the path with a minimum of four inches to spare. Otherwise the barrow will be a constant irritation when it topples over again and again because you have forgotten to stand it exactly right. Never buy one with legs bent from a metal strip like two 'V's'. The points of these will wear through and the strength of the barrow will be gone.

Beware of fibre glass, plastics, or basketwork for barrows, because these are made either with too small wheels, or with wheels at the back, which means that they tip over easily. A barrow will have to be tipped and shot sideways and this puts a great strain on it, and 'modern' designers think visually, in terms of colour photography and showing on TV rather than in terms of something strong that will go on doing its job for years. A barrow is an application of the principle of the lever and it is hard to improve on, though not impossible, but this needs understanding of all the jobs a garden barrow has to do. Most of the new materials like fibre glass and plastic are rotproof, waterproof and need no painting, but melt swiftly near a bonfire. A plastic hose is far superior to a rubber one, but if it ever rests on even the ashes of a fire, it is finished.

The 'Man' Tool Cleaner

Soil does not stain, it polishes, but mud rusts the metal it hardens on, so good tools need a 'man' to clean them. These can be made of hard wood, oak or beech, for pine frays and wears quickly. The drawing shows the design, which needs only a saw to shape it, a wood rasp to round the handle, sandpaper to smooth it, and a rub of linseed oil to keep out the wet and make the mud peel off easily. Use it on the flats and shoulders of spades, where mud collects on forks and on every other tool. Finish off with a wipe of oil on the metal, use your 'man' to clean the worst of the mud off your garden boots, and hang it, blade up, on two nails so it is always where you need it.

The name reaches back to Brindley and Brunel when the navigation canals were dug up by 'navvies' who wore this small wooden spade in the side of their trouser knee-straps, handy for cleaning the tools that were *their own*, unlike the grabs and bulldozers of today. They considered that clean tools made as much difference as an extra 'man' in a piecework gang of twenty men as they trenched their way across England with tools of blacksmith's steel, and with this strong

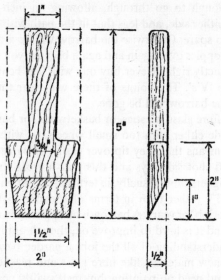

18. The 'Man' Tool Cleaner, as used by the 'navvies' who bought their own picks and shovels, unlike modern bulldozer drivers

and simple invention of an unknown navvy that has lasted longer than the canals.

Garden Machinery

The average small garden has no real need of machinery and though most people have motor mowers, few of these have work enough to justify their existence. There would be great scope for one whose manufacturer fitted it with a 'power take-off' like a tractor to run a hedge trimmer and above all a compost material chopper. These are sold extensively in the U.S.A. at about £80 each, but duty, freight and purchase tax make them impossible to import. Sheen Ltd., Greasley Street, Bulwell, Nottingham, make a good British one around this price.

Most compost material decays readily, but refractory stuff like hedge trimmings, rose prunings, cabbage stumps and paper and cardboard needs shredding before it will rot successfully. Municipal compost pulverizers make chewed paper heat like lawn mowings, but so far there is nothing that will enable the amateur to keep his rubbish at home, and leave only tins, bottles, metal and plastics for the dustcarts. Sink disposal units that grind up kitchen waste are not strong enough for anything heavy and solid like a serious Sunday paper with its business news, weekend review and colour supplements.

Because the vast majority of garden rubbish and kitchen refuse composts easily without chopping, any gadget would only be used occasionally, so as the motor is the major part of its cost, using the one on the motor mower to drive something like a tiny 'Robust' farm shredder, or a Royer 'Pneumalec' which nurseries use for soil shredding, would be the best way round.

The 'Rotoscythe'- and 'Fly-mo'-type mowers recommended for chewing up leaves in orchards will break up dead leaves spread in a six-inch-thick layer before stacking. This is useful where it is possible to get leaves of the London plane (*Platanus acerifolia*), with the mottled bark, by the lorry load, for these take two years to decay and shredding speeds them up. Chestnut leaves too are worth shredding, but with all others stacking and waiting takes least trouble. Any modern gardener, however, would rather use a machine than the leafmould that goes to waste piled in every large garden waiting to be wheeled and used, while the owner pays for baled peat.

Mowers of this kind, fitted with a grassbox, are excellent, but cannot work near the edges of beds and paths, though shears or a hand mower can bridge the gap. To the organic gardener, his lawn is a compost material mine and a source of weed-suppressing mulch, so he needs to feed his lawn to keep it in production. Between fruit, however, it is a source of humus. Therefore, use a grassbox except under fruit, and if there is a chance to acquire grass from council men mowing verges, a tennis club or sports ground, grab it.

There are many makes of garden tractor, and these are usually fitted with power take-offs, which will drive hedge trimmers, but no compost choppers are made for them. Small gardens have far too little work for these machines, of which the cheapest, and one of the best, is the 'Merrytiller', with a 2¼ h.p. four-stroke engine costing about £80, complete with what are called 'slasher rotors'. For a big garden they are ideal, and an allotment society or neighbours could club together for one.

There are two types of these mechanical diggers—those with power-driven wheels and the rotors at the back which go up in size to about 6 h.p., and the small kind like the 'Merrytiller' which are driven only on the rotors in front. These have handles that swing sideways so that there is no need to walk on the dug strip, and when you come to the end of the row there is nothing rapid to do with clutch and gears.

Pivot on the skid that controls the depth and it works round, digging as it goes. This skid should be extended most for deep digging with the handles held up, when the rotors will go down a foot, which is well below spade depth. Do not grip too hard and tire yourself—the engine does the work.

The 'Merrytiller' is driven by belt, and if the rotors hit something nasty in the subsoil, the belt just slips. There is no clutch, the drive is by tightening the belt with a jockey pulley, which makes it possible to give so much power for the price. The slasher rotors will clear the matted surface of a new or neglected garden two inches deep to begin with, to be followed by two more trips going deeper and deeper, which will take longer, but give a far better result than a hired tractor with ploughs and harrows.

One ploughing and harrowing spreads couch grass, convolvulus and the roots of any other perennial weed, and so will a single rotary cultivator. Four 'Merrytillings' in dry weather will chop these roots small and let in the air to dry them dead, which kills the couch grass completely, but not the convolvulus, oxalis or greater celandine, which must be killed with ammonium sulphamate.

In most districts there is a small contractor, usually advertising in the local paper, with one of the larger machines, like a 'Howard Rotavator 600', and it pays to hire one to cultivate a new garden while it is one clear strip, four or five times, going over again as soon as the weeds show through a summer. This will give the new garden an almost weedfree start and be far cheaper than employing any modern gardener who will simply dig the couch roots under, and cost far less sweat than digging the whole thing yourself and then wrestling with the weeds when you have laid out the garden.

Rotary cultivation leaves no trench, so manure, lime or sludge is spread on the top and distributed evenly through the top ten inches of soil. Its drawback is that it prepares a fine seed bed in one operation, which is splendid for all the buried weed seeds that are waiting in the soil. Taking what farmers used to call a 'bare fallow' before you start cultivating the garden will reduce these by killing the first germinations, and destroying the couch and the perennials, but leaves behind mostly the annuals that can be destroyed by hoeing. Gardeners with an affection for earthworms worry that these machines will be harmful, but they kill fewer than digging with a spade does because the vibration drives the worms deeper and deeper, and the rotors advance so slowly that they have time to crawl away. They do not leave a 'plough sole' by working always at the same depth, because with a 'Merry-tiller' it is easy to go a foot down and break it, and this is deep enough for anyone.

Anyone with a large garden, or who employs a gardener to produce vegetables, should buy a 'Merrytiller' and have the demonstrator show him how to drive it. He will learn more and more tricks and become a craftsman with it, digging beds as small as a six-foot square neatly and deeply. But the most important lesson to learn with any power-driven machine is that oil is more important than petrol. Without petrol the machine will not run until you fetch a tinful, without oil it will run, seize up and ruin the main bearings, which means £25 for a new engine. If only someone could invent a machine that would neigh and whinny when some fool was running it without oil!

The Flame Gun

Flame guns are giant blowlamps which do not 'kill all weeds instantly' as advertisements sometimes state, in defiance of the Trade Descriptions Act of 1969. They kill seedling weeds effectively, and a great many annual weeds, but are useless against perennials such as thistles, docks, dandelions, ragwort, nettles or any really serious pest that hoeing will not kill either.

They consist of a fat cylinder holding paraffin with a pump and pressure gauge connected by pipe and stopcock to a smaller cylinder holding the burner. It is held by the curved steel handle that balances as comfortably as a rifle. The instruction book should leave no excuse for a jet of frightening flame instead of a small hot blue one with an efficient roar.

Clearing weed seedlings from open ground is more efficient in terms of time than hoeing, but the paraffin consumed takes some of the difference if you are paying a gardener. Any saving vanishes between rows of vegetables because the rows must be handweeded afterwards, for it is not safe to bring the flame near seedlings. This applies between bush fruit and here a mowing mulch is far more effective. Paths can be cleared of annual weeds and grasses, but not plantains or dandelions, and care is needed on weeds in crazy paving for the flame can crack concrete.

The surface is left charred, and this produces partial sterilization by heat, which releases nitrogen from the bodies of slaughtered soil bacteria, and this gives a quick tonic to the perennial weeds with roots

R   257

safely below the surface. The greatest value of a flame gun is in a large garden where there are areas of weeds that have run to seed, for if they are cut these seeds will blow all over the place. First go over the spear thistles, groundsel or whatever you unfortunately have to wither them, and the next day burn them off, including all the blowing seeds on the surface.

The disadvantages are that all the weeds are burnt instead of being composted or used as green manure, and the surface looks quite unsightly, and though the job is slow and easy so that gardeners like it, hoeing is just as effective. This is why so many flame guns hang in sheds, having been used when they were new and never since come out except for a lick over a cresslike germination of seedling weeds, or to clean up paths before the gardens are open tomorrow, though their sooty look would shock the head gardener who once had six men doing the work that one scrambles through today.

Irrigators

The old-fashioned rotary lawn sprinkler was of little use to the vegetable gardener because its overlapping circles meant over- and under-watering as we tried to water oblong or square beds. There are now a number that sweep a fan of jets through a half-circle, and the larger models which cost about £5 (1972) will water a semi-detached garden completely in three positions of the irrigator. It should stand on a firm wooden box on the central path so that the jets are thrown high and clear of low foliage, but will need moving to either side if there is a cross wind.

The swaying action is driven by water pressure, and the nylon gears are rust proof of course, and the ingenuity and simplicity of the device make this one of the few completely new and worthwhile garden inventions of the past decade. Another of course is the 'Hoselock' hose connector for fitting together the lengths of half-inch plastic hose that every gardener should keep on a reel so that he can water any part of the garden.

This type of irrigator is extremely awkward if driven with a hose fitted on the kitchen tap, as well as the practice being illegal. Apply to your local Water Board for an outside tap, for which there is a rental of about £2 a year, and have the tap fitted by a plumber; it needs a screwthread on it, so a screwed connector can attach to a hose without squirting or dribbling to waste. In time of water shortage using these hoses and sprinklers is of course forbidden, but their value is greatest in the long rainless springs that so often replace February Filldykes and April Showers, before restrictions come into force.

One good soaking for an hour once a week is worth evening after evening spent walking up and down with cans, in terms of time and tiredness, with the disadvantage that it makes the weeds grow as fast as the vegetables. Hosing along the pea rows, where the soil will have sunk to take it, and in sunk beds and borders round stone fruit is better value for water, and the higher the humus level in the soil the less you need. An irrigator is well worth the £2 for the outside tap, and better value for early crops than cloches in most gardens as it gets seeds moving ahead early instead of waiting among the weeds for rain. The only crop that objects to cold water on the leaves straight from the mains is runner beans, and these can be hosed round the roots by hand.

Rainwater Storage

In summers when hoses are useless because of restrictions, we realize how fortunate are the few who have an antique pump sucking from a mysterious tank deep in the earth holding roof-caught rain. The past knew the value of independence and of a water supply in the middle of the kitchen garden to save steps on every canful. Today our excellent fibreglass waterbutts that never rot or need repainting have the great disadvantage of holding only 40 gallons, and the roof of an 8 ft. × 12 ft. greenhouse gathers 50 gallons for every inch of rain. So we can waste precious water even in summer thunderstorms, and our winters leave us no surplus.

Sunk concrete tanks are far less intrusive than a row of 40-gallon oil drums coated *inside* and out with bitumen paint, with screwed connectors leading from one to another so that they fill in succession. The cheapest way to make them is to gather the large cartons that hold detergent or other packets from your grocer's, to replace the wooden shuttering that needs some skill to make and costs a considerable sum for timber that will be encrusted with concrete afterwards and of little use for carpentry. One two feet wide and deep and twelve feet long holds 300 gallons, and needs covering with boards with a lidded opening for dipping cans, so that darkness inside prevents algae and mosquito breeding.

Dig the hole a foot larger in every dimension, then pack nine inches

259

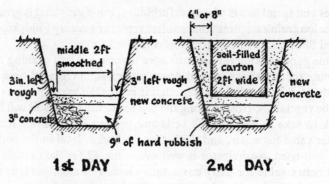

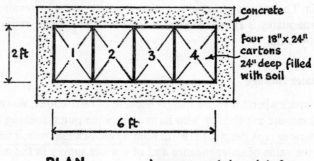

PLAN   leave a week to set before
digging out soil and cartons

19. A concrete rainwater tank can be cast with large cardboard cartons to save
buying expensive timber for shuttering

of hard rubble on the bottom, which is a useful way of getting rid of
builder's leavings in a new house, and accumulated broken glass and
bottles in an old one. Then spread a three-inch layer of concrete made
of three parts of gravel to one each of sand and cement mixed as
thick as porridge, and smooth it with the flat of the spade except for a
three-inch-wide margin round the sides and ends. Leave it overnight
to set, then stand the cartons together on the smoother portion, filling
each about a quarter full of soil. Damp the rough concrete round the
edges so that the new will stick to it, and shovel more concrete down
the sides, as well as more soil into the cartons, to hold them firm and
full against its weight. After finishing the concrete below ground level,
leave it a week to set, then dig out the soil, tear away the cartons and
wet the set concrete before smoothing on a surface coat of three parts
sand to one of cement.

260

Tips and Tools

Cover it with quarter-inch-thick sawn boards well creosoted, as in the diagram, and it will be as permanent as one of the catchment tanks of the past, but shallow enough for the boards to be removed so that it can be used as a small-scale splashing and boat-sailing pool for children (but not toddlers) which is also useful in drought. This size holds about a ton and a half of water, which is why it needs solid rubble under the concrete, and those who wish to make anything bigger should fetch in a builder unless they are young, strong and fond of hard shovelling.

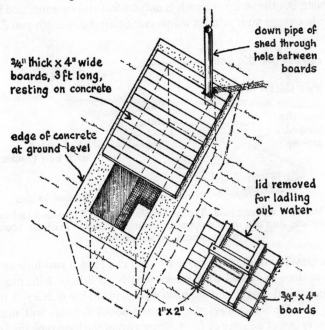

¾" thick x 4" wide boards, 3 ft long, resting on concrete

down pipe of shed through hole between boards

edge of concrete at ground level

lid removed for ladling out water

1" x 2"

¾" x 4" boards

SUNK CONCRETE TANK COMPLETED

20. The boards keep out the light and solve the mosquito problem as well as preventing evaporation and unauthorized paddling

Concrete Paths

The problem of all gravel or crazy-paving paths is weeding, and though it is possible now to buy mixtures of small stones and bitumen to roll flat and solid, these are quite remarkably expensive. Concrete paths are best for vegetable and fruit gardens where the barrow traffic will turn grass bare in summer and to mud in winter, apart from the time and trouble of mowing and edging.

When we make paths in a new garden, we can easily find that they are in the wrong place, and gardeners, unlike town planners, can undo their mistakes quite easily, by using the mixture employed by nurserymen for building back brickwork on greenhouse boilers which has to be chipped away each year when the flues are cleaned. This is five parts sand, one part of sifted fine ashes from a central heating boiler, and two of cement, mixed porridge thick. Leave out the ash for a strong cement, but the wear on a path is only by feet and barrows, and being able to change your mind is worth sacrificing the strength you do not need.

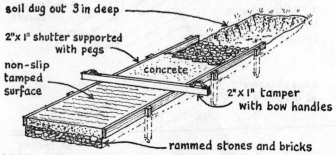

21. Making a concrete path. The tamper slides to and fro to level and smooth the surface, then lifts up and down to produce a non-skid finish for boots and barrow wheels in frost and wet

A gravel path that is a curse to weed can have a two-inch coat of the mixture shovelled on between lengths of 2-in. × 1-in. prepared timber set edgeways and supported by pegs on the outside as in the diagram. Do not trowel the surface smooth for this will make it slippery in wet weather or frost. Screw two of the loop type shed door handles to the upper edge of a short length of the wood to hold it by and pack the cement with the other side. This leaves a series of ridges as there are on a concrete road for a non-skid surface.

For a new path, dig out six inches of soil and stack it for other uses such as filling fruit tree holes. Then fill in with four inches of rammed stones, clinkers and broken glass or any hard rubbish, before adding the two-inch layer as before. If there is a shortage of rubbish, the layer need only be two inches thick, but the store of soil from taking up the turf and stacking it grass side down to decay, and digging out the top spit from under it, is a most useful starting stock.

Tips and Tools

Drainage

The only permanent cure for wet gardens and mossy lawns is drainage, and making a drain is very much easier than making a lily pond, if possible as a winter job when much of the garden is clear and you can see where the water lies.

The simplest drain of clay pipes alongside a middle path (out of the way of digging and on the wettest side) can clear unwanted water from beds ten to fifteen feet wide on each side. The pipes cost £4 per 100 for the three-inch, one-foot-long size: builders' merchants sell them, even in dozens.

Farmers have ditches, but gardeners have neighbours, so the only way out for water from flat gardens (which need drainage the most) is through a soakaway. A drain that starts fifteen inches deep near the house, with the 1–in–96 fall for good flowing, will be thirty inches down after a hundred and twenty feet, and the soakaway at the bottom of the garden should be at least a foot deeper. After filling it can be a bonfire or compost heap site, or a bed of primulas which delight in damp.

Begin by digging the trench a foot wide and deep, going deeper as you move along, roughly to the slope you finally need. The top soil should be put on one side of the trench and the poor subsoil on the other, to use for filling the finished drain. The bottom of the trench should slant a little towards the path.

Care is needed with the levels. Put a four foot length of straight, flat wood on a level surface and prop up one end half an inch. This gives a slope of 1–in–96. Set a spirit level on the wood and scratch the brass at each side of the bubble where it rests. Using the spirit level on the edge of a plank, test the fall of the pipes with the new bubble position, and scrape away or add packed soil to get a steady slope so that the drain trickles trouble-free for years.

The pipes need no cement, for water soaks in where they are set end to end, just touching, and through the sides. Cover them with four inches of cinders, clinkers or any hard rubbish (with a thicker layer at the soakaway end) and put folded newspapers or old polythene bags on top to keep the replaced soil from washing down and blocking the gaps between the rubbish.

Four feet square is a good soakaway size, but for wetter gardens it is easier to make it wider than to dig deeper. Fork the bottom loose and fill well above drain level with hard, awkward-shaped rubbish, and cover it with newspaper or polythene.

Tips and Tools

Lawns should have separate soakaways, with a drain straight across and one to each end so that no part of the lawn is more than ten feet from drainage. Always use topsoil for filling trenches under lawns.

Fruit and Vegetable Storage

It pays the gardener to buy two small sheds rather than one large one, for tools and bicycles run no risk of freezing, but can rust from the moisture breathed out by the stored vegetables, which need to be near the kitchen door for the shortest journey in rain or snow. The vegetable shed should be a lean-to type, which is cheaper than span roof, needs only a single length of guttering along the back to fill the waterbutt and keep the inside dry, and is easier to line.

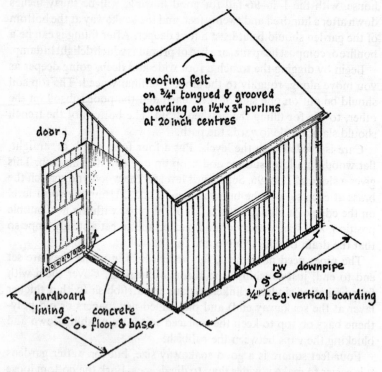

22. A lean-to fruit and vegetable store lined with hardboard is a good investment in pine or cedar, but asbestos smashes easily on moving day, for sheds that just sit on concrete bases are tenant's fixtures

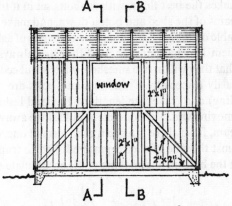

Inside elevation of front of shed.

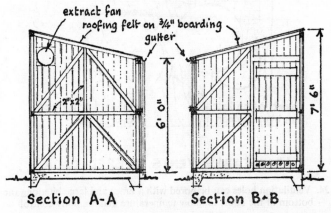

23. Sheds are best made in sections, and this one is designed by an architect to last a lifetime, so any good carpenter will see how to make it. Readymade ones are cheaper, but with less strength

The easiest and cheapest lining is tarred roofing felt, not polythene because this is inclined to condense moisture; it is nailed to the uprights, or to extra pieces of 2-in. × 1-in. timber, but the best is hardboard to confine the layer of air that keeps out both winter frosts and summer heat. Make a hardboard cover for the window to fix with turnbuttons and shut out the light, for this robs the vitamin C from bottled fruit (in Sweden milk is delivered in brown glass bottles to prevent vitamin losses) and turns potatoes green with a poisonous alkaloid, solanine.

265

Tips and Tools

Concrete makes the best floor, with ragbolts set in it to fit through the bottom beams of the shed and bolt it down, and make it a tenant's fixture removable on moving day. It is the brittleness of asbestos sheds that makes them bad bargains, though they are always cheap, for the odds are that they will arrive smashed, while stout cedarwood will come apart easily (especially if the nuts and bolts are well greased when assembling) and travel the length of England lashed safely on the back of a moving van. The concrete should slope away from under the bottom beam, for if there is a shelf, even a small one, enough rain will drive against the side of even a guttered shed to trap and trickle under, rotting the bottom and making pools accumulate on the floor.

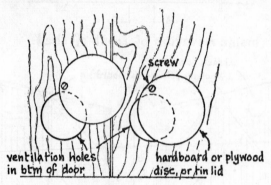

ADJUSTABLE VENTS IN SHED DOOR

24. Ventilation holes can be bored with a brace and large bit along the bottom of the door, to allow temperature and humidity control

Wooden 'sleepers' offered by the shed makers are not (as buyers imagine) *railway* sleepers, but pieces of 2-in. × 2-in. timber to rest on bricks and support the similar sized beams of a wooden floor, with the disadvantage that rats can make a home under the shed. Those who have a new house built can get the foundation of the shed concreted by the builders, who will build a shed themselves, twice as strong and four times the price of the mass-produced one made by any of the famous firms who advertise in the gardening weeklies.

Fit electric light inside. This is not only an advantage for vegetable-fetching on dark mornings, but a single 25-watt bulb left on all night inside a lined shed of the popular 6 ft. × 8 ft. size will keep out most frosts, while in really hard weather it can be exchanged for one of higher wattage. It is best to have the shed longer rather than wider or taller, because of more floor space and easier heating, and it is possible to fit an extractor fan at the highest part of the far end, and bore a row of inch-diameter holes six inches from the bottom of the door, each covered with a flap to twist aside and let in cool air at need. With a maximum and minimum thermometer inside and another outside, the gardener can work out the settings of the ventilation holes, light wattages and fan running times to hold the 33° F to 40° F which are the ideal fruit and vegetable storing temperatures.

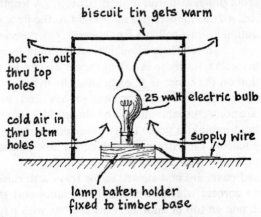

biscuit tin gets warm

hot air out thru top holes

cold air in thru btm holes

25 watt electric bulb

supply wire

lamp batten holder fixed to timber base

25. This simple heater is all that is needed to warm a small insulated fruit and vegetable store. The tin stands over the lamp which can be any wattage to fit the size of shed, 25 is usually ample

Potatoes are best stored in tea chests, standing on jam jars at the corners for air space underneath, and covered with something thick like a blanket if the shed has an electric light. The same tea chests serve for all root vegetables, but these are better in peat than in ashes, sand, or sawdust. Spread an inch-thick layer on the bottom, set out a layer of roots on it, not touching each other, cover with more peat, to leave an inch before adding another layer of roots until the box is full. Use baled peat, chopped fine but not damped, and this will take up moisture breathed out by the roots, but keep the local humidity so high that carrots, beet and parsnips have kept as long as ten months under these conditions.

A row of tea chests on jam jars along the low side of the shed hold the roots, for though potatoes can be stored in sacks, they are hard to get air space under, and real sacks are hard to find; for brown paper, and polythene still more, will condense moisture inside until the potatoes rot. If there has been any blight on the bed, even if it has only been necessary to cut the haulm down, sort through the spuds and remove any rotten ones. Their dampness will not spread infection, for this is merely from the many soft rots getting into lightly-attacked potatoes in which the spores are dormant.

Onions are the least fussy of vegetables and are often hung in laddered nylons under the eaves of a shed, so they can festoon the rafters in ropes; but bear in mind that a dozen 10-lb. strings are pulling the roof down with over a hundredweight. A lengthways roof beam of 2-in. × 2-in. timber with an upright to the floor to support it is a precaution against collapse from overweight, especially if there are pumpkins to store. These should never be hung by strings tied to their short stalks, for these shrink as they ripen and let them crash to destruction on the concrete floor below. The nylon nets in which greengrocers receive brussels sprouts, onions and many other vegetables are non-returnable and can be obtained free or cheaply, and these will hold pumpkins up to thirty-pounders, hanging safely and easily from nails in the extra beam, which can easily have a quarter ton hanging from it after a good pumpkin harvest.

Apples and pears are best stowed in the trays with raised wooden fillets in the corners which hold Dutch tomatoes and grapes, and which stack one on top of another. Line the box with paper and set out the apples stalk down and not touching each other, or pears lying on their sides, and pile the trays along the high side of the shed. Leave room to sort the stacks over, to remove any that have started to decay from chance damage, and watch for wrinkling.

A very useful gadget is a wet and dry bulb thermometer, to show the humidity, which should be 80 per cent for apples and pears, a level which the vegetables will tolerate. If the humidity is too low it is possible to increase it by watering the floor, and raising the temperature will reduce it, but rather than add water in winter it is best to run the fan, or leave the light off at night and cool the shed down. So long as the temperature is round 33–35° F everything will keep without shrivelling. The problem is to keep the storage shed cool, and yet to keep the frost out.

Many houses with central heating have fibreglass insulation between the rafters to prevent the heat escaping into the roof space. If the rafters are boarded over this makes a very useful storage area for trunks and the junk that is better in the loft than cluttering up the garden sheds. Before this area can be used for fruit and vegetables it must have skylights cut in the roof for ventilation, and the roof beams should have tarred felt stretched and nailed to them, for the felting that is just under the tiles is not enough for good insulation.

Use the maximum and minimum and wet and dry bulb thermometers to see if the roof space will hold 33–45° F and 80 per cent humidity, which is cool enough for apples, for though one is warned against the risk of the tank freezing, the main problem is to keep the space cool enough. If it cannot be cooled much, restrict storage to easy foods like onions and pumpkins hung from the beams, and bottled fruits in old bookcases or other forms of shelving, with curtains to keep the light away from them. The advantage of this kind of storage space is the ease of going up to bring down more fruit, with one of the many makes of loft ladder, ideally the metal type that shuts up like a trellis and sits on the trapdoor, so that there is no heavy wooden folding ladder to slide up and down and take up room above.

Older gardening books often recommend storing roots in a 'clamp', or long mound in the open covered with straw and soil as a miniature copy of the farmer's potato store, but this attracts mice and rats on a small scale. Enough rats to provide a morning's pleasure for a farmer's dog will eat too few potatoes to be noticed in a hundred tons, but the same number in a garden can ruin the winter stock for a family. Water voles are even worse, because they chew up carrots into small fragments to tuck in cheek pouches like certain squirrels and monkeys, and hoard these in tunnels that can contain several barrowloads.

The lofts above stables and cowsheds were ideal for fruit and vegetable stores, because the warmth of the beasts below kept the frost out, though care was needed not to hang bunches of drying gladioli bulbs or ropes of onions from rafters too low. It is surprising how high a cow can reach on its hind legs, and including tongue stretch, to bring down food it is not entitled to. A garage with a sump heater under the car is warm enough for most vegetables, and rigging wire-netting on a frame to hoist on pulleys to the roof will store onions and pumpkins safely, also dahlia tubers and gladioli bulbs, but the position will be too dry for roots which need tea chests and peat at ground level.

It is useless to take the trouble to grow the best fruit and vegetables and waste the crop when you need it most by bad storage. So many people today do not even know enough to pick their apples, merely gathering them as they fall to tip them tumbling and bumping into cardboard boxes, to spread their rottenness to each other before being dumped in the dustbin. Though thermometers, and even an extractor fan, have been suggested, these cost less than a set of plaster goblins, and the money they save and the quality they preserve through the years repays your outlay over and over again.

Gardening is the one art that everyone can use to express his or her personality, and the one science that anyone can master, if people will take the trouble and are willing to learn and go on learning what their land and the living things, visible and invisible, have to teach them. Every year is different, so is every garden, and every spring sees a new beginning, with a chance of using the knowledge that we gathered last year, and the interest of what we shall try this season. This is why old gardeners and their wives live so long and so happily, for they go on learning and enjoying until the day they die.

Recipes

Some of the following recipes have appeared earlier but they are repeated here for quick reference. So far as I know all the materials can be bought, but as freedom of choice narrows down from precedens to precedent, some ingredients may need a hunt through the more old-fashioned chemists' shops. Though they may sound a great deal of trouble to make up, it is quicker and better to spend an hour making something old-fashioned from home-made materials, and use it at once, than to buy something deadly on Monday and have no time to use it before the following weekend.

Today manufacturers are constantly taking the safe and simple off the market and replacing it with the new and dangerous which has higher profit on it. An example is the organo-phosphorus compounds which are deadly to users with certain liver and nerve conditions, and which even the orthodox acknowledge 'should not be used by those whose doctors have advised against them'. The recipes for pesticides and other garden needs that follow can all be used without medical advice, but organo-phosphorus compounds have been responsible for 6,000 deaths in ten years in Japan, and are deadly if drunk by mistake. This is a far higher death roll than came from nicotine in the days when every gardener used it.

Those who do not wish to use these do-it-yourself recipes should buy ready-made derris, pyrethrum and mixtures of the two, ready-made Bordeaux Mixture and lime-sulphur, while they can. They may be off the market tomorrow, so the alternatives are given in the section that follows. Allotment holders in particular will find it very much cheaper to buy the ingredients and make their own.

Fungicides—Bordeaux Mixture

This is much better bought because the ingredients are finely ground and dissolve better, but as Buisol, the colloidal copper compound which was much better, has been taken off the market by Messrs. Boots (recommended as suppliers of most of the chemicals described here) it is included.

Dissolve 3 oz. of copper sulphate in a gallon of hot water in a plastic bucket, leaving it overnight because copper sulphate dissolves slowly. Stir 4 oz. of slaked lime into a gallon of cold water and mix the two. Then spray, for this mixture is far more effective fresh, and rather better than the ready-made as a fungicide, because it only has to be stirred into cold water in a plastic bucket.

Burgundy Mixture

Dissolve 3 oz. of copper sulphate in a gallon of hot water as before and in the morning dissolve 4 oz. of washing soda (sodium carbonate) in a gallon of cold water, mix the two and spray. Use plastic containers for both these because the copper reacts with the zinc of galvanized iron buckets or cans. This one should also be used at once.

Carbolic Acid

Add one dessertspoonful of carbolic acid to a gallon of cold water and stir in 2 oz. of soapflakes (Lux or near, *not* detergent), then use for spraying against mildew on roses, peas or anything in the garden that has it. Dissolve 2 oz. of the carbolic soap used for washing dogs in a gallon of hot water and spray when cool, for a rather weaker mixture, which is, however, rather more effective against aphides on the roses, which is a secondary objective.

Washing Soda

Dissolve 3 oz. of washing soda and 1 oz. of soapflakes or soft soap in a gallon of hot water and allow to cool. Then spray on **American** gooseberry mildew, if this attacks in summer. It is safer than lime sulphur and harmless to *Anthocoris*.

Pesticides

The standard safe pesticides are derris and pyrethrum and mixtures of the two, but though they are safe for birds, pets and human beings, and break down rapidly in the soil, they destroy the predators with the pests. There is no point in reintroducing less effective pesticides in the same class, unless they have other useful qualities, and there is still less value in using pesticides just because they are old-fashioned. Paris Green was copper aceto-arsenite, replaced by lead arsenate and as deadly as paraquat or malathion to drink, while sodium fluoride was only rather less deadly than the fluoracetamide responsible for the Smarden disaster and now completely banned.

The pesticides that follow are for emergency use only, and it is always better to control by trapping, tricks of cultivation, using immune varieties, and enlisting the help of predators. It is also better to tolerate a moderate amount of insect damage to avoid losing the stock of predators that may have taken years to build up.

Borax for Ants

Mix equal parts of borax and icing sugar very thoroughly and sprinkle where the ants are observed. Though borax is now known to be a poison it was used for over fifty years in baby powders, and as a preservative in potted meats and sausages, with far fewer disasters than have resulted from using modern pesticides like the organo-phosphorus compounds. Too much in the soil is dangerous, but soils can suffer from boron lack. Because ants eat each other's droppings, sharing as it were a common digestive system, ants taking the boron home can destroy a nest completely and without risk to anything else. This borax bait, which should be kept in a tin labelled 'POISON', is very much safer than the persistent pesticides for use against ants in the house. It is desirable to kill ants in the garden when these are transporting aphides to roses and fruit trees, but as always when something is doing no active harm, it pays to leave it alone.

This borax bait is excellent for killing cockroaches and crickets indoors, but in the open it should be covered with a piece of glass or slate supported on stones to keep the wet off it.

Tips and Tools

Grease Band Material

So long as proprietary grease bands can be bought, ready-spread and needing only to have the protecting paper pulled off, these should be bought, but they are coming off the market, either because the public buy more advertised products, or because there is greater profit from pesticides.

Among the simpler of the mixtures used in the past are: (1) 8 parts powdered resin, 4 parts turpentine, 4 parts of linseed oil and half a part of honey. (2) 16 parts powdered resin, 3 parts treacle, 3 parts linseed oil. (3) Resin 3 parts, cottonseed oil 1 part. In each case the mixture was brought to the boiling point, while being stirred over slow heat, and then spread on greaseproof paper while still warm.

It is still possible, with some searching, to get fly papers of the old-fashioned type, and these can be spread round the trunks, but their purpose is to attract flies, while a grease band is intended to stop the traffic up and down the trunk, so they are less effective. These simple oil and resin mixtures can be smeared on the trunk itself when they are cold, but of course cannot be removed easily when they become congested.

Nicotine

This has served British gardeners well for the past century against caterpillars, and though it is a powerful poison, it is not a persistent one. D.D.T. was found in the fat of Antarctic penguins after only a bare twenty years of use, but Captain Scott's expeditions found none of the nicotine that had been in use all over the world for a hundred and fifty years. It is very much safer against caterpillars than lead arsenate, and breaks down in about four days. The safest way to keep nicotine in the modern garden is as cigarette ends.

Boil 4 oz. of cigarette ends (8 oz. if filter tips) in a gallon of water for half an hour. Strain the clear brown liquid through a nylon stocking and it can be used as one part in four with water for any pest that is hard to kill, or stronger as a winter wash against blackfly and small ermine moth caterpillars on Euonymus hedges. Add 1 oz. of soap-flakes to a quart of the mixture against cabbage caterpillars in the autumn. The mixture varies with the quality of the cigarettes, so if it is not effective at 1–in–4, try 1–to–3, or even 1–to–2.

Cigarettes themselves are of course more deadly than any pesticide or pollution, according to evidence that would be accepted in any other field, but while people do smoke, the gardener may as well get some value from the habit. By the time all Britain gives up smoking we can hope to have an improvement of the derris and pyrethrum mixtures which are at present our next strongest vegetable pesticides.

Potassium Permanganate

This has been used both as a fungicide and an aphis killer, with the advantages that it is very quickly spent, spares ladybirds, and may miss other predators, and leaves behind both potassium and manganese. It is one of the best ways of adding this trace element to the soil, apart from compost of course.

It was used against 'damping off' in seedlings with 1 oz. dissolved in two gallons of water, and used to water the soil before sowing. This treatment has been used against any fungus that is active in the soil, or where one has been, as an example on a raspberry bed that has had cane blight. This strength, however, is sufficiently powerful to kill small slugs, so in gardens where these are common, it is worth watering the potatoes at the rate of a gallon a square yard. Do not make it stronger, for 1 oz. to the gallon will kill earthworms.

An ounce to four gallons is the combined aphis and mildew spray for roses, as it misses ladybirds; also it can be used as a general insecticide for small creatures, and is worth trying against the plum and cherry slugworm. Because it is spent in about four hours it can be used in the evening on fruit in blossom, when it has a chance of catching small caterpillars, without doing harm to bees.

Quassia

This is made of chips of the wood of *Picrasma quassioides* from the West Indies, once used as a fever remedy and named after the negro slave who found it. Boil 4 oz. in a gallon of water for half an hour, pour off the yellow liquid and dilute with three parts of water as an all-round spray, with 2 oz. of soap flakes added to the gallon as a wetting agent for aphides that curl leaves and protect themselves with powder. This is also bee-safe and extremely selective in its action, hitting apple sawfly but not codling moth caterpillars, and rather more effective against pear and cherry slugworm than potassium permanganate. These two should be used when anything is attacking

274

the blossom, but unfortunately neither will kill beetles, which is how the ladybirds escape.

Rhubarb

Cut up 3 lb. of rhubarb leaves, boil for half an hour in three quarts of water and strain off the liquid. When cool dissolve 1 oz. of soap-flakes in a quart of water and mix the two. The active principle here is the oxalic acid that makes rhubarb leaves poisonous. It can also be made with elder leaves, using their hydrocyanic acid, by the same recipe. Both are aphis killers and capable of killing small caterpillars, so useful in an emergency.

General Recipes

These again are included because it is increasingly hard to be sure what is in the bought material, and too often the old is either adulterated with something new and dangerous, or taken off the market. These do-it-yourself methods are for the gardener who refuses to take what others have decided he must like, and prefers to spend trouble rather than money.

Lawn Sand

The organic gardener's lawn is his main source of good humus, and his best mulching material. If he buys a lawn sand today it will probably contain a selective weedkiller designed to kill everything but grass, and this will be far more effective against his peas, if he spreads the mowings between the rows, or even after composting, than against the weeds in his lawn. It therefore pays to make lawn sand, using builders' sand obtained locally, instead of paying the carriage on the sand from a distance; so home-made is vastly cheaper than bought.

The standard is 19 parts by weight of fine dry sand, 7 parts of sulphate of ammonia, and 3 parts of sulphate of iron. Spread this at the rate of 3–4 oz. a square yard on weedy lawns, or put a good pinch, about a teaspoonful of the mixture, on the crowns of daisies, plantains and dandelions. Broadcasting it is effective also against pearlwort and clover. This should be applied in March or April when the lawn starts to grow.

On some soils sand is 'coals to Newcastle' and here any 10–20 per cent moisture-dried sludge can be used instead, retaining the sulphate of ammonia because this is not being used as a fertilizer but a poison, especially effective against clover. Clover-root bacteria normally supply the nitrogen the plant needs by fixation from the air, receiving a living wage of carbohydrates in return. When ample nitrogen is supplied as sulphate of ammonia, the bacteria demand such high 'wages' for doing nothing that the plant dies. This is oversimplified but is roughly the effect.

Those who like their clover, which has the disadvantage of slipperiness on a tennis court, can cut the sulphate of ammonia and use 1 oz. of sulphate of iron to 15 oz. of sludge at the rate of 1 lb. a square yard, in April and again in July, but usually one dressing of sludge lasts the season. The dried sludges, of which there are many, are slow-acting and therefore keep up a steady yield of grass mowings through the summer, while sulphate of ammonia, nitro chalk or other chemical fertilizers bring a quick rush and then a tailing off.

Hungry lawns produce the most grass seeds in the sowings, and the least good mulching material, for one cannot expect to keep on taking a crop off the lawn without putting something back. Grass is nitrogen- and phosphorus-greedy, sludge is high-nitrogen and high-phosphorus, but very low potash which is not required, so 1 lb. a square yard twice a year of dried sludge will keep a lawn green and thriving, at about 50p a hundredweight for sludge against £3 for a lawn feed.

Moss in Lawns

The main cause of mossy lawns is poor drainage, but they can be short of lime, especially in towns where the sulphur in soot has locked up the lime, or sulphate of ammonia has produced the same effect. Scatter 8 oz. a square yard of slaked lime in the spring, which can go on at the same time as the sludge, and this will reduce the moss if the problem was lime shortage. It will also improve the clover, and regular liming in the autumn with sludge in the spring will help keep a lawn happy, for if you have *got* a motor mower it might as well take a decent cut of useful grass each time instead of scraping it down to brown roots in hot summers.

Where the moss is bad and includes the species known as 'liverwort', dissolve 1 oz. of sulphate of iron in 2 gallons of hot water, leave to cool and water on to the patches. Another recipe is 1 pint of Mortegg winter wash in eight gallons of water rosed on over 32 square yards.

Tips and Tools

Weedkillers

The problem of modern weedkillers is that gardeners expect them to kill everything, especially the one weed that is his special hate. There are many total weedkillers that are reputed to make further weeding unnecessary, but anything which can be used under shrubs and roses can only penetrate for a short distance. The many weeds that have roots deeper than that come up from below and thrive free from competition. View all of them with suspicion, and read the directions with care, especially the list of weeds they will kill, for this is usually much shorter than you imagine.

There is no value in killing chemically the weeds that hoeing will destroy, the easy annual kinds that fill our compost heaps every season, for the time taken and cost of the chemicals, apart from any other more serious objections, are prohibitive. The only weeds that merit chemical destruction are tough perennials, and path weeds, if we have gravel paths, which themselves are time and space wasters.

The total weedkiller that is both powerful and safe has been described earlier, ammonium sulphamate, to be used at the rate of 1 lb. in 1 gallon of cold water watered on over 100 square feet for the toughest perennial weeds such as spear thistle, convolvulus, celandine and oxalis. In three to four weeks it becomes sulphate of ammonia and is safe to sow after. It has been used by the Forestry Commission to kill under large trees rhododendrons which have their main roots well over a foot down, but it is not safe to use between bush fruits or rows of vegetables.

Ordinary sodium chlorate is also a total killer, used at 1 lb. to the gallon for destroying tough perennials, watered on over ten square yards or $\frac{1}{2}$ lb. for those nearer the surface such as couch grass. This is much cheaper but if it is used in the autumn it is safe to plant six months later after a winter's rain, while if used in the spring it should be safe by the following autumn. It differs from ammonium sulphamate in being a poison that stays in the ground. It can kill weeds when these are dormant, but ammonium sulphamate will not kill unless the weeds are growing, ideally in spring. Sodium chlorate is not poisonous to wild life, but it is explosive, and soaked boots or gardening aprons should never be placed near a fire. In a dry summer it can stay where it has washed off a path, then winter rains can wash it along to kill something suddenly in a bed yards away.

A safer killer for paths is 1 pint of Mortegg winter wash in $1\frac{1}{2}$ gallons of water watered on till the surface is thoroughly wet, but this will not kill deep dandelions. A cheaper one using the same effect is made by mixing a pint of creosote in a gallon of hot water, watered on thinly with a rosed can. This will kill some of the perennials and is far more effective than a flame gun on a large scale, where two waterings a year will keep the paths weedfree.

There is no weedkiller that you can water between vegetable rows, bush fruits and roses with safety, that will kill all weeds and leave all flowers and vegetables. Most gardeners do not want a weedkiller—they want a miracle, and though these may be advertised, they usually turn out to be like the gifts fairies bestow on greedy children—full of disadvantages.

Removing Moles

The mole, *Talpa europaea*, is one of our most interesting and least-known wild animals with many mysteries in his life beneath our fields, and unfortunately our gardens. Here he, she and the family must eat three and a half times their own weight of food a day, and this is usually worms, though they will eat cockchafer larvae and wireworms if they meet them underground. Organic gardeners value their worms, and because their gardens have more humus, they have many more than other people, especially if they use an irrigator which will draw worms from neighbours with less friendly soil in dry seasons.

Moles not only tumble seedlings about, they will also eat young beet and carrots, as well as consuming large quantities of the worms that are our friends, especially among fruit trees. Mole catchers will poison our moles with strychnine-treated worms and other worse substances, but few people wish to destroy our dwindling wild life and the best answer is to repel them, with a chance that they will travel for miles before they dig under again.

First find the main runway by looking for a large hill near the boundary of your garden through which the moles arrived. Dig down and clear it in both directions. It is quite distinct from the temporary feeding burrows just under the surface which are used once only, for it has been dug by the mole revolving on his axis with a screwing action that firms the sides. The old way was to buy calcium carbide, once used for cycle lamps and country house lighting, to thrust as much as possible in each direction, and to replace the soil, stamping it well down. The damp soil induced the carbide to produce acetylene gas

278

under considerable pressure which forced a lasting smell through every burrow, and as moles hunt by scent this made further hunting impossible, so the moles left. Unfortunately, carbide is almost impossible to buy, and though rags soaked in creosote provide a lasting stink in the tunnel system, modern moles may need stronger measures.

Borrow a moped, motor mower or any motorized gadget with the kind of two-stroke engine that has oil mixed with its petrol. Connect a hose to the exhaust pipe and lead the other end down the tunnel. Then start the engine and run it slowly, so that it goes 'pop-pop-pop-pop' instead of purring, which is known as 'four-stroking', and this will drive burnt oil fumes and poisonous carbon monoxide down the tunnels in both directions. Keep it running slowly for ten minutes to a quarter of an hour, ideally using an old radiator hose as an adapter on the exhaust pipe, for a plastic hose will melt and drop off as soon as this gets hot.

Wait till dusk to do the job, for your object is not to kill moles, which carbon monoxide can do, but to drive them away. Those whose pasts hold tunnels to freedom will sympathize with the moles breaking ground beyond the wire and escaping into the night, travelling fast on the surface until they find the safety of some far farmer's fields.

The Packet-life of Vegetable Seed

In 1557 Thomas Tusser (1524–80) wrote *A Hundred Good Pointes of Husbandrie*, the first book by a British farmer, and it has become a mine of history. It was then a best-selling 'chapbook' taken by the packhorse load by a 'Chapman' from fair to fair, a few folded pages printed on Caxton presses. Those who bought it for twopence could read it to others who would remember its verses as people nowadays learn our TV commercial jingles, and 'If Candlemas Day be fair and bright, winter will have another flight' is only one of the country sayings, from Tusser, that have lived on in every county of England.

Almost every year on the Sunday nearest New Year's Day, I used to write an article on the packet life of vegetable seeds. My first article in *Punch* was the following verse, in the style of Thomas Tusser, written in the hope that readers would remember it, even though it is nearer the verses used by medical students to fix our muscles in their memories, than the original which had the tripping feet of a folk dance from the clean green England of the past.

Here is a sample, with the spelling modernized:

Tips and Tools

> 'One acre composted is worth acres three,
> At harvest thy barns shall declare it to thee.'

Write the year of buying on the packets when you fold them over to
put them away in a dry drawer in a shed or not too warm room, and
remember the span of each, sowing your new lettuce seed in spring
for it gets away faster than old which serves for summer.

> You have in your drawer since Candlemas Day,
> All the seed packets you daren't throw away,
> Seed Catalogue cometh as year it doth end,
> But look in ye drawer before money you spend.
>
> Throw out ye Parsnip, 'tis no good next year,
> And Scorzonera if there's any there,
> For these have a life that is gone with ye wynde
> Unlike all ye seeds of ye cabbagy kinde.
>
> Broccoli, Cauliflower, Sprouts, Cabbage and Kale,
> Live long like a farmer who knoweth good ale:
> Three years for certain, maybe five or four,
> To sow in their seasons they stay in ye drawer.
>
> Kohl-Rabi lasts with them and so does Pei-Tsai,
> The winter 'cos-lettuce' to sow in July,
> But short is the life of ye Turnips and Swedes
> Sow next year only, enough for your needs.
>
> Mustard and Cress for when salads come round,
> Sows for three seasons so buy half a pound,
> Radish last four years, both round ones and long,
> Sown thinly and often they're never too strong.
>
> Last year's left Lettuce sows three summers more,
> And Beetroot and Spinach-beet easily four,
> But ordinary Spinach, both prickly and round,
> Hath one summer left before gaps waste ye ground.
>
> Leeks sow three Aprils and one hath gone past,
> And this is as long as ye Carrot will last,
> Onion seed keeps till four years have flown by,
> But sets are so easy and dodge onion-fly.

Tips and Tools

Store Marrows and Cucumbers, best when they're old,
Full seven summers' sowings a packet can hold.
Six hath ye Celery that needs a frost to taste,
So hath Celeriac before it goes to waste.

Broad Beans, French ones, Runners, sown in May,
Each hath a sowing left before you throw away,
And short Peas, tall Peas, fast ones and slow,
Parsley and Salsify have one more spring to sow.

Then fillen ye form that your seedsmen doth send,
For novelties plentie, there's money to spend,
Good seed and good horses are worth the expense,
So pay them your poundies as I paid my pence.

LAWRENCE D. HILLS,
1963

9

Vegetable and Fruit Cookery

Making the Best Use of Vegetables

Home cooks are not consciously cruel. We do not deliberately illtreat even a bought vegetable or fruit, much less one home-grown with loving care and attention. Nobody aims at being a killer in her kitchen, impartially murdering the minerals, enzymes and vitamins committed to her care and so depriving her household of these necessary nutrients. These are crimes of ignorance, not of intention, and are not only unconscious but largely unsuspected. They occur far too often, although they could and should be prevented.

Preparing Vegetables

The rules for preparing, cooking and serving vegetables to the best nutritional advantage are simple and few. Why are they so frequently not observed? Probably because the underlying reasons are not understood, and so their importance is overlooked. So here are the rules and the reasons together:

Rule for Preparation and Storage	*Reason for Rule*
(1) When gathering vegetables from the garden leave on the roots, tops and outer leaves. When buying, select those where this rule has been observed (except for potatoes, onions and sweet corn).	Vitamin values are increased until the onset of wilting, when vitamin values decline.
(2) Wash rapidly and thoroughly under the cold tap (except for above).	Soaking or the use of warm water causes the action of enzymes which destroy vitamins A, C and E.

Vegetable and Fruit Cookery

Rule for Preparation and Storage	*Reason for Rule*
(3) Drain, then pat dry smooth vegetables with a Turkish towel, and leafy ones by whirling in a bag made of this material, or an old pillow slip.	Prevents minerals, water-soluble vitamins B. Complex and C and flavours passing into the water in which they dissolve as readily as sugar and salt.
(4) Put into a plastic bag, screw-top jar, or other closed receptacle in the refrigerator until required for salad or cooking.	Prevents attack by oxygen and enzymes causing loss of vitamins A, C and E.
(5) All those requiring storage to be kept in cool dark place.	Light and warmth can steal much riboflavin, folic acid and vitamin C.
(6) Avoid peeling as much as possible.	Many valuable nutrients lie in and directly under the skin.
(7) Never discard liquids used in cooking.	These also contain extracted minerals and vitamins.

Cooking and Serving Vegetables

Vegetables have been called the glory of the cook. They can be. They seldom are, however, in this country. Our temperate climate, excellent plant breeders and good gardeners combine to produce probably the best and most varied range of vegetables in the world. Yet they reach our plates looking and tasting little better than badly made and soggy hay. The blame lies in our national passion for boiling.

To boil vegetables not only inflicts indignity on plants, but insult on palates. No one should ever be expected to eat, far less enjoy, such mutilations of the good things of the garden. So here we turn our backs on this method, and summarize the many far better methods of preserving value, flavour and appearance in cooking as follows:

(a) *Pressure-cooking by Steaming*

Providing it is done with split-second accuracy this method is excellent. The disadvantages are that overcooking occurs very quickly, breaking down the sulphurs which cause unpleasant odours, indigestion and flatulence; destroying many of the vitamin B Complex as well as

Vegetable and Fruit Cookery

vitamin C; harming the proteins and losing the flavour by expelling the aromatic oils (directions are supplied with equipment, so are not repeated here).

(b) *Waterless Cooking, so-called*

In fact a couple of tablespoons of water must first be heated to boiling point in order to replace the oxygen by steam in a utensil distributing the heat evenly to the sides and with a close-fitting lid. Thereafter the heat is kept so low, after the initial few minutes to heat the substance through, that no steam escapes and the 70–90 per cent of water in every fresh vegetable suffices for completing the cooking.

(c) *Steaming in a Steamer*

The vegetables should be left as unpeeled and uncut as possible, since moisture condenses on the available surfaces dissolving the natural sugars, minerals and water-soluble vitamins into the boiling water below. For this reason this water should always be saved and kept in the refrigerator for gravies, soups, etc.

(d) *Sautéeing in Covered Frying Pan*

Cooks vegetables largely in their own juices if about 2 tablespoons of oil are heated, the vegetables added and stirred well, to cover all cut surface and seal against oxygen, hold in the juices and prevent contact with moisture. Of course, the vegetable should be dried thoroughly first or else the fat will not stick to it. After replacing the tight-fitting lid, heat should be reduced as soon as heating through has occurred.

(e) *Simmering in Milk*

Milk acts in much the same way as oil to prevent the dissolution of nutrients, and should be stirred in thoroughly, while the temperature should not rise above simmering (about 200° F), taking about the same time as boiling in water, and not boiling over or scorching. Either half a cup of milk is used if the lid is a tight fit and prevents steam escaping, or enough milk is used to cover the vegetable. After use the milk not absorbed is saved to make a cream sauce or thickening or go into gravy or a creamed soup.

(f) *Grilling*

Tossing in oil or brushing with oil, heating rapidly at first and then keeping the heat low or moderate ensures a good appearance and crispness and prevents shrivelling.

(g) Frying

Vegetables must first be thoroughly chilled and dried. The advantages are that the cooking time is short, and only the oil and juices are used.

(h) Baking

The disadvantages are long cooking, slow initial heating and losses of vitamin C through exposure to oxygen if vegetables are peeled. This can be overcome to some extent if they are brushed with oil, or previously steamed and then transferred to a pre-heated oven. If casseroled the lid should be firmly in place to hold in the steam.

(i) For Young Children and those Unable to Chew Well

Taking unpeeled but cleaned vegetables straight out of the refrigerator then shredding and sautéeing or cooking them in a little milk, keeps the natural sweetness and little of value is lost since they cook so quickly.

Fats

All hardened (hydrogenated) fats are best avoided. Methods of heating liquid oils with hydrogen at high temperatures in production, can also produce abnormal and toxic fatty acids, and change the content of the essential unsaturated fatty acids required for many body processes. Nut butter, butter and lard unheated, are fair sources of essential fatty acids, but any vegetable oil from sunflower, peanut, maize and olive in descending order of merit, is far better and therefore to be preferred for salads and cooking. As noted by the South African poet and man of action, Roy Campbell, oil-eating Continentals do not suffer from constipation, and if Britons took to consuming vegetable oils in food instead of buying large quantities of liquid paraffin they would benefit greatly, since the paraffin literally removes from the body not only the essential fatty acids, but also the fat-soluble vitamins A, D, E and K. So buy oils untreated by heat (from health food shops) and keep them refrigerated to prevent unsuspected rancidity which can cause serious deficiencies.

N.B. Since anti-spatter agents are not present in natural oils, beware of spattering if you drop in any liquid.

Vegetable and Fruit Cookery

Seasonings and Garnishes

Salt

Sea salt is preferable to others since it contains trace elements and no additives. A sprinkle is about $\frac{1}{4}$ teaspoon, and a pinch about half that amount.

Pepper

Paprika is best: it cannot irritate a delicate digestion and is an excellent source of vitamin C. Black and white pepper are not recommended, but if used should come from freshly-ground peppercorns.

Herbs

Should be used with discretion. Better too little than too much, especially with garlic. Avoid submitting to high temperature in cooking for flavours are lost as aromas fill the air. Bay leaves and cloves may be put in at the start of cooking, but fresh or dried herbs should be chopped and added just before serving. Tastes differ so much where herbs are concerned that it is worth experimenting to find which are liked best individually.

Artichokes, Globe

Choose young green flower heads—purple ones are too old to be tender. Wash and turn upside down in a colander to drain, then whirl dry.

Cut off stems to base of stalk leaving the petals as a flower head, the edible parts being the fleshy portions at the root ends and the base from which they grow.

(1) *Whole Artichokes Steamed in Water* (*Allowing one for each person*)

Half cup of boiling water, or soup stock, in utensil with tight-fitting lid.

Place the stalk uppermost in the pan and replace lid. Steam for 20–30 minutes, depending on the age of the head. Drain well, saving the liquid for stock, sprinkle lightly with salt. Serve hot with melted butter into which the petals are dipped with the fingers or chill and substitute mayonnaise.

286

Vegetable and Fruit Cookery

(2) Simmered in Milk

Cut each head in half. Simmer in enough hot milk to cover, till tender. Drain, saving milk for cooking other vegetables. Serve as above.

(3) In a Steamer

Cook as in (1) or (2) in a rack above boiling water.

Artichokes, Jerusalem

N.B. Wash rapidly, scrubbing well with a nylon brush, or the sugars are not retained, and chill in covered container till required. Do not overcook or use too high a heat, which toughens them.

(1) Simmered in Milk

One pound of artichokes, diced or halved. Half cup hot milk.

Drop into the pan containing the milk and shake well to cover the pieces with the milk. Replace lid and simmer for 6–10 minutes. Sprinkle with salt and 1 tablespoon of chopped parsley, or chives, or the green tops of onions, or paprika if preferred.

(2) With Sauce

The milk may be thickened with wholemeal flour to make a sauce, adding a little dry grated cheese after removing from heat.

(3) Sauté

Heat 1 tablespoon of vegetable oil and one tablespoon of water in a pan. Drop in the sliced artichokes, raising the heat for a moment after replacing the lid, then lower and allow 8–10 minutes for cooking. Serve as it is.

(4) Grilled

Coat artichokes cut into fingers with 1 tablespoon of vegetable oil by tossing in a bowl with salad servers. Put them on a baking sheet under the grill keeping the heat high for about 2–3 minutes, when they should be brown. Turn with slicer to brown on the other side. Then lower heat and cook about 5 minutes longer.

(5) Roasted

Leave whole, selecting larger artichokes. Brush lightly with oil and cook like potatoes round a roast or pot roast.

Vegetable and Fruit Cookery

Asparagus

(1) Steamed

Break off the stalks where they snap easily and reserve tough ends for soup. Tie with tape into bundles of ¼ lb. per serving with heads all facing the same way and lay in a steamer above ¾ cup of boiling water or stand in a small amount of water in a kettle or the top of a double-boiler and steam for 8–10 minutes or till green part is tender. Lift out gently with a fish slice and remove tape. Drain. Serve on the strainer in a hot tureen or on a folded dinner napkin on a hot dish with a cover. Serve separately some melted butter. (N.B. Do not overcook or the tips will break.) Or chill when cooked and serve with mayonnaise.

Beans, French

(1) Steamed

Pick while still young and tender, as this stimulates more to come on. Drop 1 lb. of washed and whirled beans, whole or snapped in two, into ¼ cup of boiling water. Stir, cover with lid and cook over low heat for 10–15 minutes or till just tender. Add 2 tablespoons of oil, sprinkle with salt and chopped parsley, stir and serve. Or substitute 1 tablespoon of mayonnaise for the oil.

(2) Simmered in Milk

Drop 1 lb. washed and whirled beans, left whole or snapped in two, into ½ cup of hot milk and heat to simmering, stirring to coat surfaces. Simmer for 10–15 minutes. Sprinkle with salt and serve.

Beans, Runner

Use same recipes as for French beans but remove any strings and slice thinly before cooking.

Carrots sliced in fingers may be cooked with either recipe in place of half the quantity of beans.

Beetroot

This is a versatile vegetable, a fact seldom recognized.

288

Vegetable and Fruit Cookery

(1) Baked

Steam small beets for 10 minutes over boiling water on a rack in a pan or in a steamer. Then put them in a moderate oven about 350° F and cook for about 30 minutes, or till tender. Cut into petals like a radish and sprinkle with a little butter or cream cheese. Serve.

(2) Sauté

(a) Cut into slices $\frac{1}{4}$ inch thick and sprinkle with a little lemon juice. Drop into heated pan with 2 tablespoons of vegetable oil. Replace lid and cook for 10–15 minutes, turning occasionally.

(b) Instead, use $\frac{1}{2}$ tablespoon oil and 2 tablespoons water, cover with lid and steam.

(3) Shredded and Cooked

(a) Shred beetroot. Drop into a heated pan with 1 tablespoon water and lemon juice (or cider vinegar) and $\frac{1}{2}$ tablespoon vegetable oil. Cover with lid and shake, then cook over moderate heat for 5–6 minutes. Serve crisp and hot.

(b) Shred and place in a casserole brushed with oil. Cook in oven at 400° F for 7–8 minutes.

(c) First wash, dry by whirling and steam as above, in $\frac{1}{2}$ cup of boiling water, some of the tops of young beets. When wilted cut them into 1-inch pieces, and simmer for 9–10 minutes more. Meanwhile, shred the roots and add 5 minutes before serving. Season with a little lemon juice or cider vinegar to taste.

(4) Simmered in Milk

Dice beetroot in $\frac{1}{4}$-inch cubes or cut into fingers, and drop into pan with $\frac{1}{4}$ cup of hot milk, tossing the pan to coat the pieces with the milk, after replacing the lid. Simmer for 10–12 minutes. Sprinkle with chopped mint, chives or parsley before serving.

(5) Very Young Beets (Under thumb thickness—as thinnings)

These may be well cleaned and cooked with roots and tops together, either steamed with water or simmered in milk.

Broccoli

Broccoli has been called the poor man's asparagus and is perhaps most delicious cooked and eaten in the same way with each stalk dipped in hot butter with the fingers.

Vegetable and Fruit Cookery

(1) *Steamed*

Tie with tape in bunches for individual servings, leaving on stalks. Tie into one large bunch. Stand upright in tall pan or kettle in ½ cup of boiling water. Steam about 10–15 minutes according to age of buds. Lift out with fish slice, taking care not to break the heads. Cut tapes and lay all facing the same way on a strainer in a hot tureen or on a piece of toast or folded dinner napkin. Serve separately salted liquid butter. Or pour over buds some herb butter made by heating 1 tablespoon of oil and 1 tablespoon of butter and adding a squeeze of lemon and a pinch of fresh marjoram or basil or thyme. Do not overcook.

(2) *Simmered in Milk*

Lay whole stalks and buds in a large flat pan with enough hot milk to cover. Simmer till just tender, drain the milk and save. Sprinkle with salt and serve.

(3) *Sauté*

Sauté finely chopped shallot in 1 tablespoon of oil till transparent. Add broccoli buds cut into inches and some of the stalk cut into smaller pieces, drop into the pan, stir well, add 2 tablespoons water, raise heat, and cook for 8–10 minutes. Drain if water has not been absorbed, and serve with sprinkle of salt.

Broccoli Leaves

Do not discard these. Pick smaller ones, wash quickly, whirl quite dry, put in large bowl with 1 tablespoon oil and toss to coat well. Drop into hot pan with moderate heat. Turn with slice frequently till heated through. Replace lid, lower heat and steam for 10 minutes or till tender. They will cook in their own moisture. Do not sprinkle with salt till just before serving. Garnish with rings of raw onion cut very thin, if liked, or chopped chives.

N.B. This recipe can be used for leaves of young cauliflower, brussels sprouts, kale, radish, beet and turnip tops, Swiss chard, New Zealand spinach and spinach beet.

290

Vegetable and Fruit Cookery

Brussels Sprouts

(1) *Simmered in Milk*

Cut in halves or quarters if special tenderness is desired. Otherwise leave whole. Heat $\frac{1}{2}$ cup of milk to simmering. Add 1 lb. whole sprouts. Stir well to coat, replace lid, simmer till barely tender, 10–14 minutes. Drain and save milk for gravy or soup. Sprinkle with salt and chopped parsley or chives or paprika.

(2) *Sauté*

Brush frying pan with oil, cut sprouts in half, drop them in heated pan and stir. Add 1 tablespoon of hot water. Replace lid and cook at low heat for 5–7 minutes. Sprinkle with salt and paprika and serve.

(3) *Steamed*

Toss whole sprouts in a bowl with 1 tablespoon of oil and then steam. Save water for gravy or soup, add a walnut of butter or 2 teaspoons of oil, and serve.

Cabbage

Though green leafy vegetables are most valuable eaten raw, they should also be eaten cooked where there is less bulk and more is eaten to supply us with a sufficient quantity of their wide range of minerals and vitamins. However, not so young greens are often thoroughly disliked because of their bitterness as are sulphur-high vegetables such as onions, turnips, sprouts, cauliflower and cabbage because they cause odour, discomfort and indigestion. Fortunately the acidity can be neutralized by cooking with milk or some other protein, and the breakdown of sulphur compounds causing the generation of gas in the eater and the unpleasant smell in the kitchen can be avoided. This only occurs if these vegetables are left in water, cooked with too much water and left uncovered, cooked at too high a temperature, or overcooked. When carefully prepared and cooked not above boiling for short periods in closed pans, or cooked in milk, all vegetables become mild and sweet and cause no discomfort.

Cabbage, all green varieties, also kale, turnips and radish tops, leaves of broccoli, cauliflower, spinach, New Zealand spinach and Swiss chard:

Vegetable and Fruit Cookery

(1) Steamed

Have ready 2 tablespoons boiling water in a pan. Shred with a sharp knife half a washed, well-chilled cabbage. Drop gradually into the water or place on rack above it. Replace lid, raise temperature to heat through, then lower.

Simmer for 7–8 minutes. Sprinkle with salt and a pinch of brown sugar and if liked a walnut of butter or dessertspoon of oil may be added before serving.

(2) Simmered in Milk

Heat ½ cup of milk. Shred ½ head of cabbage, drop it in, replace lid, raise heat to heat through and simmer for about 8 minutes. Serve as it is or with golden sauce. (See p. 307.)

(3) Sauté

Heat 1 tablespoon of oil with 1 tablespoon of water in a pan.

Drop in shredded cabbage. Replace lid after stirring to coat well and simmer for about 8 minutes. Sprinkle with salt and serve.

(4) Creamed

Prepare a cup of cream sauce (see p. 307), add raw shredded cabbage, stir very well and simmer for 8 minutes. Sprinkle with a dash of paprika or grated cheese and serve.

Cabbage, Red

Vinegar, lemon juice, onion or some sharp apple must be used with red cabbage to supply the acid needed to preserve its colour, and it should be very thinly shredded to ensure quick cooking.

Sauté

(a) Shred finely ½ head of red cabbage and toss in a little lemon juice or cider vinegar until well coated. Drop into heated pan containing 2 tablespoons of oil and 2 of water. Replace lid, raise temperature to heat through, then lower and simmer for about 20 minutes. Increase heat at the end to evaporate off any moisture. Sprinkle with salt and brown sugar and serve.

(b) Chop an onion finely and sauté in 2 tablespoons oil till transparent, shred ½ head of red cabbage and stir into the pan till coated.

292

Add 1–2 tablespoons of boiling water, replace lid and simmer till tender, about 20 minutes. Sprinkle with salt and pinch of brown sugar and serve.

(c) Substitute for the onion a couple of small cooking apples diced and treat in the same way as above.

If liked, half the above dishes can consist of green cabbage shredded more coarsely, since it cooks more quickly. In any case the result should be juicy but not sloppy.

Carrots

N.B. Brush well but do not scrape as the red outer part is the most valuable.

(1) *Grilled*

Brush ½-inch fingers of carrot with oil, place under moderate heat and grill till they begin to brown. Turn with pancake turner and lower heat, cooking about 10 minutes. Season with salt and chopped parsley or mint.

(2) *Sauté*

Heat 1–2 tablespoons oil in frying pan, add about 7 carrots cut in rounds or fingers and stir well to coat with the oil. Add 1 tablespoon water. Replace lid, heat well then turn down heat. Cook 10–15 minutes, turning occasionally. Serve sprinkled with a little salt and dash of brown sugar if carrots are old.

Slices of apple or onion may be sautéd with the carrots.

(3) *Shredded*

Heat 2 tablespoons of milk, water or oil in frying pan. Shred carrots and drop them in. Cover and cook for 5 minutes. Sprinkle with grated cheese and serve.

(4) *Simmered in Milk*

Halve carrots, and lay in sufficient milk to cover them. Simmer for 10–15 minutes, with lid on. Drain (saving milk or use for cream sauce). Sprinkle carrots with a little salt and paprika before serving.

(5) *Steamed*

Drop about 6 whole carrots into a utensil containing 4 tablespoons of boiling water. Replace lid, raise heat quickly to heat through then simmer for 12–15 minutes. Cut in lengths and serve sprinkled with a little salt and 2 teaspoons of mayonnaise or butter. Chopped parsley or mint may be added.

Cauliflower

(1) Simmered in Milk

Break into sprigs and drop into ½ cup of hot milk. Stir to cover surfaces, replace lid and simmer till barely tender—about 10 minutes. Drain, saving milk for soup, etc. Sprinkle with salt, butter and paprika and serve. Or mix 1 tablespoon butter and 1 tablespoon oil, stir in a few minced almonds, heat, and pour over.

(2) Steamed

Break the chilled head into small sprigs, put in colander and pour through them a cup of water containing a tablespoon of vinegar to keep the whiteness. Steam for about 10 minutes with the least possible water. Serve still slightly crisp with sprinkle of salt and a little butter or oil and chopped parsley. No 'white blanket' sauce, please. Mayonnaise or French dressing or grated cheese are far better.

(3) With Tomatoes

Heat 1 tablespoon oil in pan, sauté in it 1 chopped onion till transparent. Add 3 tomatoes cut up or nearly a cup of bottled tomatoes. Raise heat and when boiling add raw cauliflower broken into sprigs. Stir, add ½ teaspoon salt, ½ teaspoon brown sugar and 1 teaspoon thyme or marjoram (fresh if possible, if not, a *pinch* only). Replace lid and cook for 10 minutes, then serve.

Celery

The white part is best eaten raw, but there is no need to discard the green outer stalks, which can be cooked as follows:

(1) Creamed

Simmer celery cut into dice in a very little milk for 10 minutes, stir celery into freshly-made cream sauce (p. 307) and serve, sprinkled with paprika.

Vegetable and Fruit Cookery

(2) Grilled

Cut into ½-inch chunks, and toss in 1 tablespoon oil. Place under grill at high. Leave for about 3 minutes, then turn with slicer, and cook the other side for another 2 minutes. Lower heat and leave for about 10 minutes or till tender. Season with salt and paprika or grated cheese.

(3) Simmered in Milk

Drop 2 cups of diced stalk into 2 cups of hot milk in a pan. Stir well to coat the dice. Replace lid, and heat quickly, then simmer for about 10 minutes. Drain and save milk. Season with a little salt and paprika and garnish with sprigs of celery leaves.

Courgette

(1) Fried whole

Picked small enough these miniature marrows can be fried in butter or oil as if they were sausages. When lightly brown, test for tenderness with a fork. Roll in chopped parsley and serve hot.

(2) Sliced and fried

When about 6 inches long they are better steamed above boiling water for about 5 minutes, wiped dry then cut in ½-inch slices and fried in butter or oil till browned on both sides. Sprinkle with salt and paprika and serve, if liked with grated cheese.

Kohlrabi

If eaten young and not allowed to grow old and stringy the taste resembles that of young sweet cabbage but the skin is too tough to be left on, so always peel.

(1) Simmered with Milk (the most attractive way, as they discolour quickly)

Peel and dice some young chilled bulbs of kohlrabi and drop into ½ cup of hot milk. Stir to coat with the milk, replace lid and simmer for 8–10 minutes, or till barely tender. Drain and save milk. Sprinkle with salt and hint of oil or butter and serve.

Vegetable and Fruit Cookery

(2) Steamed whole

Steam without peeling till tender on piercing. Peel with knife and fork while hot. Cut into petals, sprinkle with salt. Drop a knob of butter in each centre, cover with paprika or chopped parsley and serve.

(3) Sauté

Cut in thin slices and sauté in 1 tablespoon oil, turn with slicer and keep heat moderate till tender. Sprinkle with salt and chopped parsley and serve.

(4) With Tomatoes

In 1–2 tablespoons of oil sauté 1 chopped onion and a couple of kohlrabi slices, and a cupful of cut-up fresh or bottled tomatoes. Add a pinch of salt and ½ teaspoon brown sugar (or black treacle). Cover and simmer till slices are tender, about 10–14 minutes, and serve.

(5) Steamed

Cut chilled bulbs into fingers and drop into 2 tablespoons boiling water and a saltspoon of vinegar. Stir well to stop discoloration. Replace lid and steam for about 10 minutes. Serve sprinkled with salt and chopped parsley or paprika, or with a dressing of oil and vinegar or mayonnaise.

Leeks

See Onions (p. 297). Remember to wash extra carefully as soil tends to trickle down between the layers, and do not cut off all the green part, but use as much as 3 inches of this.

Marrows

Since these consist largely of water, they have little flavour or value, and cannot be compared with pumpkins. They should never, *never* be boiled.

(1) Steamed

Do not peel but cut into 1–1½-inch chunks. Drop into 2 tablespoons of boiling water or cook in steamer above the same amount. Heat quickly, then simmer for 10 minutes. A little diced onion or celery may be added to the water. Drain, sprinkle with a little salt and some paprika, or season with marjoram or mixed herbs.

(2) Sauté

Cut unpeeled marrow into slices. Drop into 1 tablespoon of hot oil with a pinch of thyme or celery salt, stir well, replace lid, heat through then simmer 8–10 minutes. Sprinkle with salt and serve.

(3) Sauté with other Vegetables

Use equal quantities (say a cupful) of chopped onions, or cut-up carrots or turnips with a cupful of sliced marrow.

(4) Simmered in Milk

Cut unpeeled marrow into 1-inch chunks, drop into $\frac{1}{2}$ cup of hot milk. Stir well, replace lid, lower heat when heated through and simmer for about 10 minutes. Sprinkle with salt and add a knob of butter or teaspoon of oil and serve.

(5) Grilled

Cut into $\frac{1}{4}$-inch slices, brush with oil, sprinkle with wholemeal bread-crumbs and arrange on oiled pan. Cook under moderate heat until brown. Turn with slicer and brown on the other side. Sprinkle with grated cheese, garnish with a small slice of tomato and continue under grill about 5 minutes. Serve very hot.

Onions

When there is a delicious smell of onion cooking, the air not the eater gets the best of the flavours, and the remaining sulphur compounds 'repeat' to cause digestive distress. The answer is *not* to overcook, but cook only till translucent or still slightly crisp, or to leave in their skins and peel just before serving.

(1) Baked in Jackets

Using large round onions bake them without skinning in a hot oven for about 20–30 minutes. Pierce to test for tenderness. Remove and skin carefully. Cut down towards the root end to make petals. Fill the centre with a knob of butter or teaspoon of oil, sprinkle with a little salt and paprika, sprigs of mint or parsley, and serve.

(2) Grilled in Jackets

Use flat but large onions, or if not available cut large round ones in halves horizontally. Do not remove skin. Set on oiled rack under grill about 2 inches from the heat, which should be as high as possible without scorching. After 10 minutes turn with slice, lower heat and continue grilling for another 10 minutes. Remove skin, holding with a knife and fork, sprinkle with salt, a dab of butter or a little oil and paprika or chopped parsley, and serve.

(3) Grilled in Slices

Cut large onions into ½-inch slices, brush on both sides with oil and lay on oiled pan about 2 inches from moderate heat. Grill for about 6 minutes, or when they begin to brown. Turn over and brown slightly on the other side and finish cooking on lowered heat. Sprinkle with salt and paprika, or garnish with a slice of raw tomato or strips of raw sweet pepper.

(4) Creamed

Peel some small white onions, steam till almost tender above 2 tablespoons of boiling water with a close-fitting lid on. Meanwhile prepare some wholemeal cream sauce (p. 307) and when this is ready add some chopped parsley and drop in the onions. Serve when well heated through.

(5) Creamed Green Onions

Cut the tops off a bunch of green onions leaving on 2 inches of the green part. Steam as above or simmer in 1 cup of milk, then use in same way as small white onions.

(6) Sauté

Cut large onions into ½-inch slices. Sauté in 2 tablespoons of oil for about 10 minutes, turning them once with a slicer. Serve sprinkled with salt and chopped parsley or paprika.

(7) Casseroled

Slice large onions and put in heated casserole with ½ cup of milk and 2 tablespoons of oil. Cook at moderate heat for about 15 minutes, or till transparent. Sprinkle with salt, and ½ cup of grated cheese. Turn off oven, leaving casserole till the cheese has melted, or brown under grill.

(8) *Stuffed*

Choose large round onions. Remove the central part and fill the gap with heated left-overs such as minced or diced meat, chopped ham, diced carrots, or chopped tomatoes. Sprinkle with salt and wholemeal breadcrumbs, and a knob of butter (or 1 teaspoon of oil), bake in a hot oven 15–20 minutes, and serve. If liked they can be covered with home-made tomato sauce just before serving.

Parsnips

Parsnips just cooked in water have earned many shudders, because they lose their sugar easily and go soggy. Untouched by water (after a good wash and dry) they can be delicious.

(1) *Baked*

Select short stout ones. Do not peel but brush with oil and bake in a moderate oven for about 30 minutes or till tender.

(2) *Pot Roasted*

Select short stout ones and do not peel. Put them in a hot pan, brushed with oil. Cover and cook at moderate heat for about 20–30 minutes. Or brush them with oil and set them round a pot roast of any kind, especially beef.

(3) *Grilled*

Cut into fingers, toss in oil and place on oiled baking sheet under moderate grill, turn when beginning to brown and brown other side a little. Lower heat to finish cooking. Beware of burning owing to high sugar content.

Peas

Best eaten young and raw.
N.B. *Never overcook*
  Pod as soon as picked, and if they are not cooked at once, refrigerate in closed container as room temperature causes loss of flavour.

(1) *Steamed*

Steam on rack above 1 tablespoon of boiling water with a sprig of mint in it, for about 7 minutes, but test earlier between thumb and finger for tenderness. Sprinkle with a little salt (and a pinch of brown sugar if not in their first youth), add a knob of butter, and serve.

(1) *Simmered in Milk*

Drop 2 cups of fresh peas into a pan containing $\frac{1}{2}$ cup of hot milk. Stir to coat surfaces, replace lid, bring to simmering point and continue for about 7 minutes or about 5 minutes if taken from deep-freeze. Season with finely-chopped mint (less than $\frac{1}{2}$ teaspoon) or 2 teaspoons of chopped parsley and salt and butter to taste.

Either steamed or simmered peas can be cooked with thinly-sliced carrots or celery.

Peas, Dried

Soaking the day before using is an advantage as it increases the vitamin B complex and vitamin C by starting sprouting. But it is important not to throw away the water which should be used for cooking them, since many of the minerals and vitamins have passed into it. However, if needed in a hurry they may be quickly cooked after rapid washing by dropping them into boiling water a few at a time so that boiling does not stop. This bursts the starch grains, breaking the outer skin, so that they now absorb water quite quickly and take less time to become tender. When they are all in, lower the heat and let them simmer only or they will toughen and take longer to cook. Do not add salt, or other seasoning until they are nearly tender, for the same reason. Dried peas are best used for soup but can be eaten as a vegetable.

Soaked Peas

Soak overnight in about 2 pints of water, 2 cups of dried peas. Next day bring them slowly to the boil in the same water. Simmer till they are almost tender on piercing, about $1\frac{1}{2}$–2 hours. Now add 1 teaspoon salt, a knob of butter or 1 tablespoon of oil, a sprig of fresh or $\frac{1}{2}$ teaspoon of dried mint, and 1 teaspoon of brown sugar. If needed more water should be added while cooking and the lid left off when finishing to allow unwanted moisture to evaporate. Alternatively they may be seasoned with chopped chives, onions or parsley. Or a ham bone may be added to the pan at the start.

Vegetable and Fruit Cookery

Potatoes

It is a great pity that the uninformed have classed potatoes as foods to be avoided, especially for the weight-conscious. They are nothing of the sort. Although mainly starch they do contain the vitamins necessary to break this down to the glucose needed for energy and to the water and carbon dioxide excreted by the body through the usual channels. This cannot be said of any white-flour product—white rice, sago, tapioca, refined cornflour, macaroni, or of sugar and the secret sugars in packaged cereals, ices, sweets, chocolates, jams, jellies and so on. It is these which menace the waistline and with it the general health. So let us cut out these denatured foods and reinstate with due credit as a valuable food the potato, as a cheap, easily-grown daily source of essential minerals and vitamins. A couple of medium-size potatoes can supply as much as 65 mg. of vitamin C (more than that in half a grapefruit and many times that in a lettuce) and the iron content equals that of two eggs. Yet the vitamin C and other water-soluble vitamins are too often destroyed and the iron and other minerals extracted and thrown away before they get to our plates. Potatoes must be prepared in the same way as other fresh vegetables in order to conserve their nutritional value. So refresh your memory with the rules and never *boil* them—all the vitamin C can be drawn into the water in about 20 minutes, and remember the shorter the cooking time, and the less they are cut up, the better.

(1) *Baked in a Pan*

Select long slim potatoes, scrub thoroughly and dry carefully. Brush all over with oil. Put them in a pre-heated pan with 1–2 tablespoons of oil, replace lid, and keep heat fairly high for 5 minutes to heat them through. Turn down and simmer for 20–30 minutes till tender when pierced, leaving off the lid for the last 5 minutes.

(2) *Baked under Grill*

Arrange unpeeled potatoes brushed with oil under the grill near moderate heat. Leave for about 15 minutes then turn with slicer to heat through. Then transfer to oven at 350 for another 15 minutes.

(3) *Baked in Oven*

Place unpeeled oiled potatoes in hot oven (450° F) and bake for about 45 minutes.

(4) *Steamed*

Drop required number of unpeeled small potatoes or large ones cut to equivalent size, into ¾ cup of boiling water or place on rack above boiling water. Replace lid and cook about 15–20 minutes or until tender. Peel, sprinkle with a little salt and chopped parsley, and serve.

(5) *Baked New Potatoes*

Scrub and dry small new potatoes, place them on oiled baking dish or pan and bake on the top of stove or in the oven for about 20 minutes, shaking a couple of times to turn them over. Sprinkle lightly with salt, butter and paprika.

(6) *Oven-Fried*

Wash, scrub and chill several potatoes. Do not peel but cut into thin sticks. Toss them in a bowl with 1–2 tablespoons oil. Put into hot oven (450° F) on a baking dish and leave for about 8 minutes. Lower heat and cook till tender. Sprinkle with salt and serve.

(7) *Grilled*

Select some medium to large potatoes. Wash and scrub well but do not peel. Chill. Cut into thin slices, brush both sides with oil, arrange an oiled baking sheet under hot grill. Cook for about 5 minutes, or until brown. Turn with slicer and cook for another 3–5 minutes till other side is brown. Sprinkle with salt and serve. If buttered when hot and spread lightly with Marmite or Yeastrel these can be eaten at tea time, in place of bread and butter.

(8) *Creamed*

Use either small new or old potatoes whole, or cut large ones previously chilled into similar size. Drop them, preferably unpeeled, into a pan containing 1 cup of milk. Replace lid and simmer for about 10 minutes or less if tender sooner. Make a smooth paste of 2 tablespoons of wholewheat pastry flour and ½ cup of milk. Stir into the simmering milk, sprinkle with salt and simmer for about 10 minutes. Serve sprinkled with chopped chives or parsley, or a grating of onion.

(9) *Emerald Potatoes*

Scrub, and chill, then cut in 1-inch chunks 4 large unpeeled potatoes (peeling only if pedantic). Simmer in ½ cup of hot milk in a closed

302

pan for 10 minutes or till tender. Heat ricer well over the pan, drain potatoes, press through ricer and return to pan adding 2 tablespoons of finely-chopped parsley just prepared, 2 tablespoons of top of the milk, beat with fork until well mixed, taste for seasoning with salt and serve at once.

Or steam above boiling water till tender then treat as above.

(10) *Potato Salad*

N.B. This is a misnomer, since a salad consists of raw ingredients. It is a pleasant way of serving them as a cooked vegetable but in no way a substitute for a true salad.

Steam above a small amount of water 4 large waxy unpeeled potatoes, cut in four, chill, peel and dice them. Mix in well ½ cup of home-made mayonnaise, sprinkle with chopped chives or parsley or mint and stand in refrigerator until needed. Serve on bed of watercress or ringed by mustard and cress or lettuce.

(11) *Quick-cooked Shredded Potatoes* (a special from Adelle Davis)

Hold a grater directly over a hot frying pan containing 4 tablespoons hot oil, and grate into it 4 thoroughly-chilled unpeeled potatoes. Keep the heat high, turn frequently, and cook for about 5–8 minutes or until golden brown. Sprinkle with 1 teaspoon of salt and a dash of paprika. A shredded onion may be cooked with the potato.

(12) *Left-over Steamed Potatoes*

Keep in refrigerator till needed. Slice and heat up in ¼ cup of hot milk or left-over gravy, sprinkle with chopped chives or a pinch of thyme, and serve.

Pumpkins

(1) *Breadcrumbed*

Dip pumpkin fingers in beaten egg then coat with wholemeal bread-crumbs instead of batter and proceed as for fritters (see 4).

(2) *Roasted*

Cut in wedges, after removing the seeds and soft central part. Brush with oil only and cook round a pot or oven roast for about 20–25 minutes only.

(3) *Steamed*

Remove seeds and cut in wedges, leaving on the skin. Steam over
½ cup of water for about 15 minutes or till tender. Serve sprinkled
with salt and dab of butter.

(4) *Fritters*

Make a batter with 1 cup of wholemeal flour, 1 egg, 1 cup of milk
and a pinch of salt. Sift the flour into a bowl and add the well-beaten
egg. Beat till smooth. Gradually add the milk beating all the time, till
quite smooth. Leave in a cool place for an hour or more. Remove
pumpkin seeds and cut into fingers, then remove peel. Dip in batter
and cook in hot oil till nicely brown, turn and brown other side.
Turn heat low to finish cooking. Serve with sprinkled chopped parsley.

(5) *Pumpkin Curd or Cheese*

Use 4 lb. pumpkin, ⅓ pint water, 4 lb. sugar (2 lb. white, 2 lb. brown),
½ lb. butter, 6 lemons.

Peel, dice and simmer pumpkin in the water for 15–20 minutes.
Drain and rub through a sieve. Add butter and sugar and mix
thoroughly. Grate rind off lemons, squeeze juice and pulp into mixture
discarding pips and pith. Boil 5 minutes. Let cool slightly and put
into jars, sealing as usual. Sets on cooling.

Tomatoes

Perhaps the chief value of tomatoes to a cook is that they contain
acid which tenderizes the connective tissues in meat which are found
in the cheaper cuts. Their high vitamin C content (a large tomato
nearly equals a small orange) also makes them valuable for eating
raw. But they can also be very good as a cooked vegetable.

(1) *Baked*

Put 2 large tomatoes cut in half, cut side uppermost, in a casserole;
leave off the lid. Stir together ¼ cup of wholemeal breadcrumbs,
¼ cup of finely-chopped onion or shallot and 1 tablespoon of parsley
into 2 tablespoons of mayonnaise, and spread this over the cut tops.
Sprinkle with a little salt, a pinch of brown sugar and a few more
breadcrumbs. Bake at moderate heat (350° F) about 10 minutes.

(2) *Grilled*

Hold 2 or 3 large firm tomatoes on a fork over some steaming water to loosen the skin, then peel them. Slice about $\frac{1}{2}$ inch thick, dip in oil and place on oiled sheet under moderate heat. Turn after about 5 minutes and cook other side for about 4 minutes. Sprinkle with a little salt, a pinch of brown sugar, and either grated cheese or a little parsley or chopped chives.

(3) *Bottled Tomatoes*

These are best used for soup or for tenderizing meat in cooking, but they can be used as a vegetable on their own.

(4) *Tomatoes on Toast*

Bring 1 lb. tomatoes to boiling in their bottling fluid, pour this off, and save for soup or gravy. Stir into hot tomatoes 1 tablespoon butter or oil, 1 teaspoon brown sugar and salt to taste, and pour over a piece of wholemeal toast in a hot vegetable dish and serve.

Turnips

(1) *Grilled*

Select small young ones, not thicker than an inch and a half. Scrub and dry well, leaving them whole and unpeeled. Brush with oil. Place on oiled baking sheet under grill at moderate heat. Turn after 7 minutes, grill other side for about 5 minutes and serve sprinkled lightly with salt and dabs of butter.

(2) *Baked*

Prepare in the same way then bake in moderate oven for about 12–15 minutes and serve, as above.

(3) *Simmered in Milk*

Quarter unpeeled turnips, simmer in $\frac{1}{2}$ cup of hot milk for about 15 minutes or till just tender. Sprinkle lightly with salt and a grating of nutmeg after pouring off any residue or milk which should be saved.

(4) *Shredded and Simmered in Milk*

Have ready $\frac{1}{2}$ cup of hot milk in a pan. Shred directly into it 5 unpeeled turnips and stir well. Replace lid and simmer for about 6 minutes.

Vegetable and Fruit Cookery

Sprinkle with salt and a grating of nutmeg or a dash of paprika or chopped chives or parsley. Serve when still quite crisp.

(5) *Shredded and Sauté*

Shred unpeeled chilled turnips into 1 tablespoon of hot oil in a pan. Stir well and replace lid. Cook for about 8 minutes, sprinkle with salt and paprika, and serve.

(6) *Steamed and Petalled*

Select round large turnips. Do not peel but give thorough washing. Steam above $\frac{1}{2}$ cup of water till tender, for about 18–20 minutes. Cut into petals and season with a little oil, salt, or mayonnaise, or finely grated cheese. Garnish with paprika and serve.

(7) *Scalloped*

Cut unpeeled turnips into paper-thin slices. Place in heat-resistant casserole in $\frac{1}{2}$ cup hot milk, with a few wholemeal breadcrumbs, some grated cheese and sprinkle of salt. Cook on top of the cooker or bake in pre-heated hot oven (400° F) for about 15 minutes. Sprinkle with paprika, chopped parsley or a grating of nutmeg, and serve.

(8) *Sauté in Fingers*

Cut unpeeled turnips in fingers, or slices, sauté in oil over low heat in covered utensil, turning at intervals, for about 10 minutes. Serve sprinkled with salt and paprika.

Sauces

N.B. Raw egg is not recommended, as it contains avidin, which steals biotin (part of vitamin B complex) but if well beaten and stirred into a hot liquid this cooks quickly, overcoming the difficulties caused by avidin.

Foam Sauce (for any vegetable but especially for cauliflower). It uses left-over egg whites.

> 2 egg whites beaten till quite stiff
> 3 tablespoons of hot milk with a pinch of sea
>   salt rubbed through a fine sieve
> 'Grating' of onion juice

Sprinkle the salt and onion juice into the beaten egg white and grate onion for juice over this. Gradually pour on the hot milk while beating well.

Cream Sauce

> 1 tablespoon butter
> 1 tablespoon oil
> 2 tablespoons wholemeal pastry flour
> 1 cup of cold top of the milk
> 1 teaspoon salt

Melt the fats in a pan using low heat. With wooden spoon stir in the flour to make a smooth paste. Pour milk in gradually, keeping heat low and stirring all the time. If lumps should appear, take off the heat and beat mixture with the spoon till it is quite smooth. Then go on adding the milk and stirring. When completely blended add the salt and simmer for 10 minutes.

Golden Sauce

> 1 egg yolk, well beaten
> ½ cup of hot milk
> Pinch of salt

Put the beaten egg in a bowl standing in a pan of boiling water. Pour on the hot milk and stir gently till the sauce thickens smoothly. Sprinkle in salt and serve over any green vegetable.

Fruit in the Kitchen

The basic problem 'to cook or not to cook' can be quickly resolved where fruit is concerned. Any fruit, but quince, is best eaten RAW. Next best method is lightly and quickly cooked without added sugar, NEVER stewed unripe and drowned in sugar. Worst of all treatments is entombment in a pie. There are few things more liable than pastry is to put paunches on husbands and inches on the waistline of the cook.

Clever cooks aim at keeping their households slimmer, feeling livelier and looking younger by using fruits as a sweet course for the sake of the fruit sugars they offer, and avoiding the usual oversweet concoctions of vitaminless starches which end too many meals, taking their toll in a lack of that radiant health we would wish for everyone.

Refer back to the general rules for preserving the nutritive value of vegetables (p. 282), for the same rules apply to fruits. Add one

Vegetable and Fruit Cookery

other rule. Avoid using unripe fruits (such as green bullet-like goose-berries) then swamping them with sugar to make them palatable, as the added sugar steals vitamin C and calcium; instead, gather all fruit as nearly ripe as possible to serve raw, or cook without sugar, and serve with yogurt, wheat germ lightly crisped under the grill, or top of the milk with a level tablespoon of non-instant (sprayed) powdered milk, well beaten into it. The additional lactose (milk sugar) not only sweetens but assists in the absorption of calcium, instead of decreasing it.

Apples

Apple Amber

Grate finely 2 large Bramleys. Stir in 1 tablespoon of honey and 2 well-beaten egg yolks. Beat till smooth then pour into oiled pie dish. Have ready the 2 egg whites beaten till quite stiff with 2 tablespoons of water, a tiny pinch of salt, a grating of lemon rind and 2 tablespoons of brown sugar. Spread over surface of pie dish and set this in a tin of water. Bake in slow oven (300° F) for 30 minutes. Serve as it is.

Baked with a Difference

Wash, dry, and remove core of large chilled apples. Peel only the upper quarter and place this side down in a heat-resistant casserole containing ½ cup of boiling water. Raise heat to heat them through, after replacing lid. Simmer for about 10 minutes or till nearly tender when tested with a fork. Turn with slicer, fill centres with some raisins previously soaked in a drop of milk, or some minced nuts and dates, and add a grating of nutmeg, or orange or lemon peel. Set under hot grill till lightly brown and serve with top of milk sweetened with non-instant powdered milk, yogurt or egg custard. Bramleys may be just heated through on the top of the cooker then transferred to the oven and cooked till almost tender, as before.

N.B. Shortening the cooking time prevents a good deal of nutritional loss and preserves more of the flavour.

Apple Crumble (not pastry)

Cut into flat slices about 4 apples after coring but not peeling. Lay them in a casserole dotted with ¼ cup of raisins. Pour on ¼ cup of water. Mix well ¼ cup of wholemeal flour, ¼ cup of brown sugar and ¼ cup of butter, and if liked ¼ teaspoon of cinnamon. Spread over the apple. Bake for 20 minutes, removing lid for last 5 minutes, or putting under the grill for 5 minutes after 15 minutes in the oven. Serve with top of milk or egg custard.

Apple Custard

Mix well 3 teaspoons brown sugar and 4 tablespoons powdered non-instant milk. Add 3 eggs, 1 cup of fresh milk and 1 cup of apple sauce, a pinch of salt and 1 clove or a grating of lemon peel. Beat till quite smooth. Pour into a shallow casserole and set in a tin of water. Bake in a hot oven for about 30 minutes, or for 40 minutes in a slow oven. Do not overcook as cooking continues while custard is cooling. Serve hot or cold.

Apple Pudding

> 4 medium apples
> ½ cup wholemeal breadcrumbs
> 2 tablespoons brown sugar
> 1 tablespoon of butter, 1 egg, 1 bay leaf or
>   2 cloves (to be removed)

Wash quickly and quarter the apples. Drop into a pan containing ¼ cup of boiling water and the cloves. Cover and steam till tender, for about 10 minutes. Remove cloves and press rest through sieve, and stir in the sugar and well-beaten egg. Put half the breadcrumbs at the bottom of an oiled pie dish, pour in the apple mixture and cover with rest of breadcrumbs. Add little bits of butter and bake for about 15 minutes in moderate oven. Serve with top of milk.

Apple Purée

Wash, core but do not peel required number of apples allowing 1 per person if large. Drop into ½ cup of boiling water and if very tart, add ¼ cup of chopped raisins or dates. Replace lid, raise temperature to heat through, then lower and steam for about 10 minutes. Remove and chill. Liquidize and strain to remove peel, etc., or pass through sieve. Serve with top of the milk, in individual glasses garnished with home-made pumpkin lemon curd or crab apple or quince jelly.

Apple Sauce

Wash and quarter without peeling or coring 4 tart cookers, drop into pan containing ½ cup of boiling water, and steam with lid on for about

15 minutes or until soft. Chill, then liquidize and strain or press through sieve.

Steamed

Wash, but do not peel. Remove carefully all sections of hard skin in the core (leaving any of this to be encountered as 'toe-nails' or 'fishbones' in eating puts many children off for good) cut into bite-size bits, drop into 2 tablespoons of boiling water with 1 clove to every 2 large apples and steam with lid on. Remove from heat while pieces are still firm. Chill and serve cold in individual glasses with top of milk or yogurt sweetened with non-instant powdered milk, and garnish with a half teaspoon of home-made crab apple or apple jelly on each serving.

Berries

Do not wash any berries (strawberries, raspberries, loganberries, blackberries, etc.) sooner than $\frac{1}{2}$ hour before serving. Use a large colander under running water and drain well. Serve with top of the milk, or cream as a treat. If cooking any berry (though they are all better raw), drop 2 cups of berries into $\frac{1}{4}$ cup of boiling water gradually. Cover and lower heat, steam for about 5–8 minutes. Chill and add a little brown sugar or honey before serving with top of the milk or egg custard.

Cherry Jelly

> 1 lb. of ripe Morello cherries
> 2 tablespoons of honey (or brown sugar)
> 1 dessertspoon of gelatine powder
> 1 gill of cream
> $\frac{1}{2}$ pint of water

Stone the cherries and drop them into a pan with half of the water, at boiling point. Add the sugar and stir well. Cover and simmer for 5 minutes. Meanwhile, dissolve the gelatine in the rest of the water which should be hot and add it to the cherries. Turn it all into a basin and when it begins to thicken, stir in the cream well whipped. Pile into glasses and chill before serving garnished with 1 teaspoon apple jelly.

Vegetable and Fruit Cookery

Currants, Black and Red

Best eaten raw with top of the milk. Second best in summer pudding.

Summer Pudding

Take 1 lb. of black or red currants washed under running water in a colander. Do not stem or top them but drop them into $\frac{1}{2}$ cup of boiling water. Cover, raise heat to heat through, then lower and steam for about 5 minutes. Press through sieve or liquidize and strain off stems and tops. Have ready some thin slices of stale wholemeal bread. Lay these in a bowl, pour on hot blackcurrants to cover, and continue with alternate layers till fruit is used up and bowl full. Put a saucer over it then a weight to press it well down and chill. Turn out on a dish and pour over it cold boiled custard or some whipped cream, or top of the milk, sweetened with 2 tablespoons of well-combined non-instant powdered milk. Serve cold.

Steamed Blackcurrants

Wash 1 lb. under running tap in a colander, after removing stems. Drop into $\frac{1}{4}$ cup of boiling water. Cover, raise heat to heat through, then lower and simmer for about 5 minutes. Serve with top of milk sweetened with 2 tablespoons of non-instant powdered milk well whisked together.

Blackcurrant Fool

Make a boiled custard, liquidize with an equal amount of stemmed currants, strain and serve in individual glasses garnished with 2 or 3 raw currants in the centre.

Plums

Wash but do not peel or remove stones. Drop required quantity, say 1 lb. for 4 persons, of plums into pan containing 2 tablespoons of boiling water, or just enough to prevent sticking to the bottom. Cover and steam for about 5–10 minutes. Add some honey or a little sugar sprinkled on. Chill and serve with top of milk sweetened with non-instant powdered milk or boiled custard.

Vegetable and Fruit Cookery

Quinces

As Cheese (Membrillo, pronounced membrilyo)

This Spanish and South American favourite as a dessert with milk or cream cheese of any kind is a thick paste which keeps like jam.

Wash 4 lb. quinces, cut in quarters and cook in ½ pint water till tender. Pass through a sieve, weigh and put in a pan with ¾ lb. of sugar to 1 lb. of fruit. Boil slowly, stirring to prevent burning till the paste leaves the sides of the pan. Have ready some flat shallow tins lined with greaseproof paper and pour in the hot paste. Place on rack above cooker or other warm place to dry for a few days. Either leave in same tins with lids on or cut in thick fingers, wrap in greaseproof paper, and store in air-tight tins.

Baked, with a Difference

Wash, after rubbing off the fine fluff, dry and remove core allowing 1 medium quince per person. Remove peel from upper quarter and place fruit with this side down in a heat-resistant casserole containing ½ cup of boiling water. Raise heat at first to heat through, then lower and simmer with lid on, for 15 minutes or till nearly tender on testing. Turn with slicer, stuff cavity with honey and a dab of butter. Set under grill at moderate heat and cook till lightly browned and quite tender on piercing near the centre. Serve not too hot with top of milk fortified with non-instant powdered milk.

Steamed

Cook as steamed apples, but expect them to take longer before they are tender.

APPENDIX

Where to Buy What

Once it would have been possible to buy almost everything mentioned in this book from a single good nursery with a sundries department, but today fewer and fewer firms stock a range of fruit trees, seeds or sundries. The firms mentioned here may well not be the only ones with the varieties mentioned, but all are firms from which I have bought for myself, and because they take the trouble to grow what is unusual and difficult they are likely to supply the ordinary in better quality. The grocer who bothers to get in nut-butter for a vegetarian is likely to supply the best bacon, because he cares more for his customers than the supermarket that stocks only the popular lines.

Seeds are the easiest to find, but we have only one at all 'organic' supplier in Britain, Messrs. Chase Compost Grown Seeds, Benhall, Saxmundham, Suffolk. They sell Japanese Pumpkins, 'Cook's Delight' beet, Russian Comfrey Bocking No. 14 plants, 'Kelvedon Wonder' peas, dressed with a mouse repellent, 'Harbinger' tomato seed, and a range of ordinary varieties. Then 'Monarch cabbages', 'Cherry Belle' radishes, 'Burpless' cucumbers and the Japanese outdoor varieties, together with almost anything you have difficulty in finding, are obtainable from Messrs. Thompson and Morgan, London Road, Ipswich, Suffolk. They have the largest range of vegetable and flower seeds in all Britain, if not the world. Messrs. Suttons stock pelleted seed of lettuce, carrots and leeks, which makes it possible to space these in the rows individually so that there is no thinning to do and less carrot fly risk. They also stock 'Nonesuch' and 'Winter Density' lettuces which they originated together with many other famous varieties.

'Giant Fen' onion sets are from Messrs. S. E. Marshall and Co., Wisbech, Cambridgeshire; 'Femina' cucumber seed from Dobies of

Where to Buy What

Chester; and 'Up-to-date' onions from Messrs. J. W. Boyce of Soham, Ely, Cambridgeshire. All these firms stock flower seeds as well and a set of catalogues from these and others should be on every gardener's desk for the annual seed order which should replace buying only when you see the picture packets and think of sowing time.

Few firms now supply seed potatoes. Messrs. S. E. Marshall & Co. stock 'Desirée', Messrs. Alexander & Brown, The Scottish Seed House, Perth, have 'Desirée', 'Maris Piper', 'Orion' and 'Record'; while Messrs. Brown & Sons, 50 Bedminster Parade, Bristol, sell 'Maris Peer', 'Maris Page' and 'Pentland Dell'. Suttons of Reading have 'Pentland Beauty'. This is only at the time of writing, and the best policy for gardeners is to start hunting in early autumn.

Green manure seeds such as Hungarian rye, annual lupins and buckwheat can be bought in garden quantities from The Henry Doubleday Research Association, Bocking, Braintree, Essex, who also sell quassia and compost activators and send a free booklet listing all the dried sludge on sale from Councils in Britain to those enclosing a stamped addressed envelope. This is not a commercial firm but an Association of amateur experimenters and organic gardeners, which anyone interested in gardening without chemicals can join, for £2 a year, which brings a quarterly Newsletter, many reports, and other advantages.

The largest sundriesman in Britain is Messrs. E. J. Woodman, High Street, Pinner, Middlesex; they supply gypsum, fruit tree grease, fishmeal and almost everything mentioned in this book, except chemicals such as copper sulphate obtainable from Boots or any good chemist. Marinure dried seaweed is made by Messrs. Wilfred Smith Horticulture, Gemini House, High Street, Edgware, Middlesex.

The largest collection of bush and tree fruit, including most of the apples mentioned in this book, on a range of stocks, and in cordons, pyramids and horizontal and fan-trained, is grown by Messrs. Hillier and Son, West Hill Nurseries, Winchester, Hampshire. Other good firms with large collections are Messrs. Blackmoor Nurseries, Blackmoor, Liss, Hampshire; Messrs. Jackman and Son, The Nurseries, Woking, Surrey (who grow the Quetsche plum) and John Scott, of Merriot, Somerset. As with seeds, it pays to gather in the catalogues and order from the best firms, for wherever you buy there will be carriage, and our island is too small for the climate to make all that difference if you buy your trees far or near. Even if you buy your apples from a Scottish firm, they will stand the wind no better in the

Where to Buy What

Orkneys than those you bought from Hampshire, though the carriage will be more. The lead labels for fruit trees, cast to order, are made by John Pinches Ltd. (Acme Labels), 3 Crown Buildings, Crown Street, London, S.E.5.

No beginner gardener can afford to hunt bargains in fruit trees in advertisements or markets. The saving in money is trifling compared with the time that a mis-named tree that fails to pollinate, or one on the wrong stock, can waste when you find yourself going back to the beginning with a fresh tree. Look for a craftsman, and pay for his knowledge and his skill.

Indexes

(a) Recipes for gardeners' items;
(b) Recipes, culinary, including cooking hints;

(c) General index.

(a) Recipes for gardeners' items

(b) Recipes, culinary, including cooking hints. As instructions are brief and simple, these entries are condensed in form

Index

Cabbage: cooked in milk or other protein, creamed, eaten raw, sauté, simmered in milk, steamed, 291–2

Cabbage, red: sauté (3 methods), 292–3; *see also* Chinese cabbage, 106

Carrots: grilled, sauté, shredded, simmered in milk, steamed, 293

Cauliflower: simmered in milk, steamed, with tomatoes, 294

Celery: creamed, eaten raw, grilled, simmered in milk, 294–5

Chard, to cook, 85

Cherry jelly, 310

Courgettes: fried (sliced or whole), 295

Fats, avoidance of hydrogenated, 285

Fruit, cooked and uncooked, 307–12

Herbs, including garlic, use of, 286

Kohlrabi: sauté, simmered in milk, steamed with tomatoes, 295–6; *see also*, 114

Leeks, 296; *see* Onions

Marrows: grilled, sauté (2 methods), simmered in milk, steamed, 296–7

Mint sauce, 110

Onions: baked in jackets, casseroled, creamed, creamed green, grilled in jackets, grilled in slices, sauté, stuffed, 297–8; over-cooking of, 297; to pickle, 124

Paprika, use of, 286

Parsnips: baked, grilled, pot-roasted, 299; water-cooking unsuitable for, 299

Peas: danger of over-cooking, 299;

dried, cooked with or without pre soaking, 300; eaten raw, 299; simmered in milk, 300; steamed, 299; to dry one's own, 130

Plums, steamed, 311

Potatoes: baked (new), baked in oven, baked in pan, baked under grill, creamed, emerald, grilled, oven-fried, potato salad, shredded quick-cooked, steamed, using left-over steamed, 301–3; unsuitability of boiling for, 301

Pumpkin: breadcrumbed, fritters, roasted, steamed, as sweet curd or cheese, 303–4

Quinces: baked, cheese, steamed, 312

Salsify, 148

Salt in cooking, 286

Sauces: cream, foam, golden, 306–7

Seakale, *see* Chard

Seasonings, garnishes, 286

Summer pudding, 311

Tomatoes: baked, grilled, on toast, 304–5; bottled, 158–9, 305

Turnips: baked, grilled, sauté fingers, sauté shredded, scalloped, simmered in milk (2 methods), steamed petalled, 305–6

Vegetable cookery generally: baking, 285; boiling as unsuitable, 283; conservative methods of preparing, 282–3; for young and those not chewing well, 285; frying, 285; grilling, 284; pressure-cooked, 283; sauté, 284; simmering in milk, 284; steaming, 284; waterless cooking of, 284

(c) General Index. Asterisk marks main reference

Acetylene guns, cherries protected by, 228

Actinomycetes (and other fungi) in compost heaps, 52

Adco M, for straw composting, 36

Alginure, as compost activator, 31

American blight (on apples), *see* Woolly aphis

American cress, *106–7

Ants, *see* White ants; borax-sugar bait for, 272

American gooseberry mildew, 184, 189, 271–2

Ammonium sulphamate, as weed-killer, 45–6, 277

Anthocoris, useful predator, principal

317

Index

references to, 163 *seqq.*, 179, 180, 186, 187, 223–8, 243

Apples, *201 *seqq.*; chickens ranging under trees, 207; choice of, 56, 210–14 (various qualities mentioned); choice of early, mid-season and late blossoming, 213–14; choice of, for Vitamin C content, 213–14; grass mowings under, 220; grass-surrounded (front-garden trees), 206, 214; harvesting of, 221–2, 269–70; pruning of, 214–19 (other aspects of management, 219–22); stocks, 201–2; storing in trays, 268; suckers, 163 (tree fruit generally, apples, plums, etc., discussed, 201 *seqq.*)

Apple blossom: weevil, 226; wilt, 223
Apple capsid, 225
Apple fruit weevil, 227
Apple powdery mildew, 222
Apple red spider, 225
Apple rot, *see* Brown storage rot
Apple sawfly, 72, 220, 221, 225, 274
Apple scab, 215, 222, 223
Apricots, *234–40; from stone, as unsuccessful, 239; leafcurl as rarity among, 240; stocks, 202 (tree fruit generally, 201 *seqq.*)
Arthritis, and vitamins, 19
Artichokes, globe, *76–7
Artichokes, Jerusalem, *77–8
Asbestos: as not ideal for sheds, 264, 266; used for protecting finally-earthed celery, 103–4
Asparagus, 56, *78–90
Asparagus beetle, 79
'Asparagus kale', 111
Aspidistras, flowering of, 51
Azotobacter, *see* Nitrogen-fixing bacteria

Baled peat, for roots storage, 87; *see also* Peat
Basic Food Guide to a Green Old Age (H.D.R.A.), 20.
Bastard trenching, 64
Battery hens, 26
Bean weevil, 73
Beans, *see* named Beans
Beer for slug traps, 74
Bees, and use of pyrethrum, 72, 81, 194
Beet blister beetle, 42
Beet fly, 87

Beet juice, betain of, in cancer treatments, 88
Beetroot, *86–8; Beets generally, 59–62
Beet (seakale or chard), *85–6
Big bud of blackcurrants, 163, 175, 178–9
Bindweed, *see* Convolvulus
Birds: attacking brussels sprouts, 92–3; pest control by, 64 (*and see* Tree fruit, items with asterisk); *see also* Fruit cage
Bitter rot of peaches, 239
Blackberries, *173–5
Blackberry mite, 175
Blackcurrants, *175–80; big bud of, 163, 175, 178–9; as nitrogen-greedy, 42; running chickens between bushes of, 207; vitamin content by variety (table), 176
Blackfly (blight) of broad beans, 73, 81; nicotine against, 273
Black-kneed capsid, as controller of apple red spider mite, 223–4
Black nightshade; and eelworms, 67; and potato blight, 139
Black Spanish radish, *145
Blackwater fever, and susceptibility to chemicals, 25
Blight: of broad beans, 73, 81, 273; of celery, 104; of tomatoes, 158; *see* Potato blight
Blossom wilt of apples, 223
'Bolting' of lettuces, 116
Bone meal: analysis, 41; some uses of, 42, 52; for blackberries, 174; carrot seed mixed with, 99; in fruit-tree planting, 208; for globe artichokes, 76; for gooseberries, 185; for loganberries, 190; for raspberry planting site, 192; for red and white currants, 181; for rhubarb, 146; for strawberries, 196, 199; for walnuts, 251
Bonfires, 27–8, 34
Bordeaux Mixture: for blackberries, 175; against potato blight, 136–7; for raspberry cane spot, 195; for tomatoes, 158; *see* Index (a)
Borecole, *88; borecole kales, *112
Boron deficiency, 161–2
Boysenberries, 191
Bracken: analysis of fresh and dry, 41; fresh, as compost material, 50; to kill, 71

318

Index

Index

Colhoun, J., *Clubroot Disease of Crucifers*, 96

Comfrey, principal references to, 36, 44–8, 50, 56, 59; Bocking 14, as potash source, 43; Bocking 14, some harvests of, 47; growing permanent bed of, 45; how to feed while growing, 46–7; for blackberries, 175; for gooseberries, 186; for raspberries, 193; for tomatoes, 48–9, 157–8; used as pig or poultry food, 48; wilted, 52; wilted, analysis of, 41

Common scab: of apples, pears, 215, 222, 223; of potatoes, 138

Compost, composting, 27, 28–33, 40, 59–62, 254–5; activators, 31–2, 314; compost box, to make, 28–30; domestic wastes, 32; holding in heat, 32; how to build heap, 28, 30–1; materials chopped mechanically, 254–5; materials to exclude, 33; mineral shortages and, 40; soil diet supplements from, and from manures, 51–2

Concrete: for paths, 261–2; for shed floors, 266; for sunk water-storage tanks, 259–61

Convolvulus (perennial weed), 46, 69, 184, 185, 256

Cooking methods, 282–5

Coral spot fungus of red and white currants, 183

Cordon apples, etc., 206–7

Corky scab of potatoes, 138

Couch grass, 46, 69, 184, 256

Courgettes, 118

Cow manure, 36, 37

Creeping buttercup, 185

Creosote: against moles, 279; against weeds, 278

Creosote stake soaker, made from old drainpipe, 168, 170–1

Cresses, *106–7

Crickets, borax and sugar bait for, 272

Crockett, S. R., 112–13

Crown gall of peaches, 239

Cucumbers, 56, *108

'Cumulative poisons' defined, 23

Currant, *see* Blackcurrant, Red and White currants

Currant aphis, and other aphides of blackcurrants, 179–80

Currant clearwing moth, 180

Currant gall mite, *see* Big bud

Currant moth of currants and gooseberries, 180

Currant shoot borer, 180

Cutworm caterpillars, 74

Daisies in lawn, 275

Damping-off fungus (lettuce seedlings), 117

Damsons, *233–4

Dandelions, 257, 275

D.D.T., build-up of, 23–4, 273

Deep-freezing of cabbage tribe, 92

Deep litter shavings, 36

Derris, 23, 38, 72, 75, 94, 117, 163, 270–2, 274; against red plum maggot, 248; on raspberries, 194; used with pyrethrum: against big bud, 179; against gooseberry sawfly, 186; against magpie moth, 180; against pea thrips, 129–30

Devils'-coach-horse beetle, as useful predator, 65, 97, 220

Dieback of: apricots, 239, 240; cherries, 232, 237; peaches, 237; plums, 246, 248; red and white currants, 183

Dock (weed), 257

'Domestic Preservation of Fruit and Vegetables' (H.M.S.O.), 203

Drainage (wet gardens, mossy lawns), 263–4

Dried blood, 22; analysis of, 41; as compost activator, 42; as nitrogenous tonic, 42; for: beets, 87; cabbages, 96–7; carrots, 99; cauliflowers, 101; celery, 104; spinach, 151; sweet corn, 155

Duddington, C. L., *The Friendly Fungi*, 67

Dwarfing stocks, 201–2; dwarf pyramid trees, 207

Earthing-up: of celery, 102–4; of potatoes, 135

Earthworms: as prey of moles, 278; *see* Worms

Eelworms, 55, 314; *see* Potatoes; and *Tagetes minuta*, 64, 67–9

Eggs, D.D.T. concentrated in fat of, 24

Eight-course rotations, 54–5

Elder leaf brew, against aphides, 74, 275

Index

Henry Doubleday Research Association, 20, 25, 31; comfrey, comfrey compost work of, 36, *and see* Comfrey; green manure seeds supplied by, 314; *Operation Tiggywinkle*, 74; potato trials by, 20–2, 44–5; 'Tagetes' work of, 68

Hepatitis (and other ills), and pesticides, 25, 270

Herbs, *109–10

Hoeing, preferred to chemical weedkillers, 277

Hondius, Pastor, in history of Jerusalem artichoke, 77

Hoof and horn meal, 41, 42, 52, 192; for blackberries, 174; for fruit-tree planting, 208; for globe artichokes, 76; for raspberries, 192

'Hoplewin' used with cherries, 231–2

Horse manure, 37; *see* Farmyard manure

Horseradish, to eradicate, 45

Hoverflies, as predator on woolly aphis, 228

Howard, Sir Albert, 36, 53

Humus, 27, 33, 34, 35, 69–70, 275

'Hungry gap' Kale, 111

'Hutchinson's spirochete', 36

Hydroponics, 53

Indore compost, 36, 44, 53

Iron deficiency: cherries showing symptoms of, 232; plums showing symptoms of, 247

Irrigators, 258–9

Jam, *see* 'Full fruit standard'

'Japanese All Seasons' radish, *145

'Japanese Climbing Cucumber', *108

'Japanese pumpkins', *141

Jeyes' Fluid, as soil sterilizer, 117

John Innes: Horticultural Institution: cherries, 230; tomato trials, 156; seed compost: for herbs, 110; for tomato seeds and seedlings, 156–7

'June drop': of apples, 222; of cherries, 231; of peaches, 237

'Kailyard School' of writers, 112–13

Kainite, 39

Kale, 88, *110–13

Karpin, Dr. S., report by, on melde poisoning, 154

Kew, first leafmould heap at, 34

Kirkman, Mr. Harold, comfrey harvests of, 47

Kohlrabi, *113–17

Labels, *see* Lead-cast labels

Lackey moth caterpillars of apples, 228

Ladybirds, 72, 163, 274, 275; nicotine and quassia harmless to, 72, 73

'Land cress', *106–7

Large, E. C., *The Advance of the Fungi*, 137

Lawns, 18–19; homemade sand for, 50, 275; curing moss in, 276; mowings, for mulching or using on compost heap, 32, 33, 49, 50, 51, 175, 183, 190, 193, 206, 255; used against carrot fly, 64, 100; using sludge to improve lawn grass, 275–6

Lead-cast labels for fruit trees, 210, 315

Leaf blister of pears, 242, 243

Leaf curl: of pears (leaf curling midge), 243; of plums, 248

Leaf mould, as food and humus, 33–5; of oak, 51; protection of, over earthed celery, 103

Leaf blight, 250

Leaf spot: of blackcurrants, 178; of celery, 104; of quinces, 250

Leather, as compost material, 33, 51

Leaves: over rhubarb crowns, 146, 148; over salsify, 148

Leek Clubs, 114, 188

Leek moth, 115

Leeks, 57, 59–62; *see* Onions

'Leg' of gooseberries, 184, 188, 189

Lemon balm, *109

Lettuce, 56, 57, 59–62, 63, 64, *115–17; pea-guards used for, 116

Lettuce root aphis, 117

Lima beans, 81

Lime, liming: and boron deficiency, 161; and clubroot risk, 38, 91, 94, 95; as essential, 38–9; excessive, 39; and scab risk, 55; times for, in rotation, 59–62; with plums, 247; with turnips, 161; with crop following potatoes, 58

Lime-sulphur wash, 179, 186, 223, 249, 271

Lind, Surgeon, and lime juice for sailors, 119

Lindane, 72

Index

Index

Index

Polythene bag 'cloches', 141, 142, 155, 157
'Pompost', 50
Poplar trees, as host of lettuce root aphis, 117
Poppies, annual, as possible clubroot carriers, 96
Potash: deficiency, seen in gooseberries, 186; essential to beans, 38, 80, 81, 82; and onions, 119
Potassium permanganate, for soil sterilizing, 117
Potassium shortage in orchards, 221
Potato blight, 38, 40, 67, 132-8
Potato chitting trays, 134
Potato scab, and use of lime, 39
'Potato onions', *124
'Potato sickness', 67
Potatoes, 20, 55, 57, 59-62, *131-41; as easy crop, 65; as key item in rotation, 66; analysed (table), 139-40; eelworm-resistant, where to buy, 314; green colour in, 137, 265; seed, 314 (chitting trays, 134); storing, 267; trials: for taste, 20-2; with comfrey, compost and manure, 44-5; vitamins of, 19, 57, 140; waxy and floury, 131; wilted comfrey in growing of, 47-8; wireworm attacking, 75
Poultry manure, 36-7, 221; poultry under trees, in pest control, 207, 233, 242
Powdery mildew of plums, 248
Pratylenchus, and other non-cyst-forming eelworms, 68
Prickly spinach, *151
Primroses, double, 26
Pruning, see named bushes and trees
Pumpkins, 59-62, *141-3; analysis of (and of marrows), 143; storage of, 268, 269
Pybus, Professor F. C., 'Cancer and Atmospheric Pollution', 28
Pyke, Dr. Magnus, on an alkaloid of onions, 123
Pyrethrum (see also Derris) as safe to use, 72, 75, 194, 243, 248, 270-1, 272, 274

Q.R. compost activators, 31
Quassia, 72-3; against: apple sawfly, 225; gooseberry sawfly, 187; on

cherries, 233; where to buy, 314; see Index (a)
Quetsche plums, 314
Quinces, *249-50; ideal position for tree, 249; on own roots, 249; stocks, 250-1

Rabbits, and green manure crop, 71
Radishes, 59-62, *143-5; among gooseberry bushes, 185; as catch crops, 96, 125, 126
Ragwort, 257
Rainwater, storage of, 259-61
Rape, sold as 'mustard and cress', 107
Rape kales, *111
Raspberries, *191-5
Raspberry beetle, 72, 193-4
Raspberry moth, 194
Red currants, *181-3
Red plum maggot, 248
Red spider: on apples, 223, 228; on gooseberries, 187
Remontants (strawberries), 197
Reversion virus, affecting blackcurrants, 175, 178
Rhubarb, 56, *146-7; analysis of, 165-6; as nitrogen-greedy, 42; using leaves, stems, as anti-clubroot and pesticide, 73, 95, 96, 161
Rhubarb beet, *86
Ridge cucumbers, *108
'Rollerberry' strawberries, 197-9
Roof space of house, storage in, 268-9
Root aphis of Jerusalem artichokes, 78
Root crops generally, 63, 87, 126; see named items
Root-selection of molecules, 27
Root vegetables, minerals in (table), 126
Rotations explained (organic gardeners'), 54 seqq.
Rothamsted, 55, 68, 136
Rove beetles, 220
'Royal jelly', 89
Ruby chard, *85-6; see Beet (seakale or chard)
Runner beans, 56, 59-61, *84-5
Running couch (weed), 185
Rye (grazing rye) as green manure crop, 55-7, 59-62, 64, 70; where to buy seeds, 314

Sacking, grease bands, uses of, 225-7

325

Index

Index